Will Kingdom is a journalist who has specialized in
the paranormal. He is married and lives at the foot
of the Black Mountains.

www.**booksattransworld**.co.uk

Also by Will Kingdom

THE COLD CALLING

and published by Corgi Books

MEAN SPIRIT

Will Kingdom

CORGI BOOKS

MEAN SPIRIT
A CORGI BOOK : 0 552 14585 8

Originally published in Great Britain by Bantam Press,
a division of Transworld Publishers

PRINTING HISTORY
Bantam Press edition published 2001
Corgi edition published 2002

1 3 5 7 9 10 8 6 4 2

Set in 10.5/12pt Sabon by
Phoenix Typesetting, Ilkley, West Yorkshire.

Corgi Books are published by Transworld Publishers,
61–63 Uxbridge Road, London W5 5SA,
a division of The Random House Group Ltd,
in Australia by Random House Australia (Pty) Ltd,
20 Alfred Street, Milsons Point, Sydney, NSW 2061, Australia,
in New Zealand by Random House New Zealand Ltd,
18 Poland Road, Glenfield, Auckland 10, New Zealand
and in South Africa by Random House (Pty) Ltd,
Endulini, 5a Jubilee Road, Parktown 2193, South Africa.

Printed and bound in Germany by
GGP Media GmbH, Pößneck

Thanks – for crucial technical assistance – to Richard Morris (hypnosis), Ken Ratcliffe and Mike Kreciala (ballistics).

And thanks especially – for the core plot and a brilliant edit – to my wife Deborah.

Prologue:
The Lines are Open

Trust no-one, Seffi's telling herself, as she does so often lately. Trust none of them. This has been a mistake, this is very wrong . . . even by *my* strangled standards.

Despite all the people, a party going on, she feels something hollow in the room. Sometimes, in her head, there's the sensation of a bright white, penetrating light, turning to grey, turning to black.

And then, suddenly, Kieran's here. A boy of eighteen or nineteen. Instantly she trusts Kieran, he's so messed up and full of shame. He's sending her a faintly fogged picture of himself: bare feet no more than three inches above the . . . hay?

No . . . rushes. Rush matting. On the floor of – *light through slats, no glass . . . greenery . . . bars of sunlight* – a kind of rough, rustic summerhouse. A gazebo.

Kieran's hanging there. Seffi, sitting very still on her straight chair, in her claret-coloured velvet gown, hands enfolded on her lap, is aware of Kieran hanging.

How does she know his name? She just does. Reticence is rare unless you're dealing with a personality for whom formality's an obsession or a way of life – say a former army officer, or a butler.

9

'OK, Kieran, hold on,' Seffi murmurs, nodding. He's pressing her, innocent as a big puppy. 'Just . . . wait . . . We'll get to it, yah?'

'Miss Callard?'

Sir Richard Barber's buffed face is tilted to hers. Behind him all those half-pissed, crass, glassy smiles. When the drawing-room lamps were first dimmed, it was like facing the rows of skulls in those catacombs under Rome or Paris or somewhere: nothing behind the smiles but dust – no grief, no sorrow, none of that hopeless yearning which one often perceives as a kind of sepia mist.

Also, no discernible respect. She's . . . the entertainment. Half of them think I'm a phoney, she realizes, with a bright flaring of rage. And the other half want excitement, spectacle. They're here to have fun.

One particular man seems to be laughing all the time now, in an irritating, rhythmic way, atonal and repetitive like a tape-loop. Seffi's seething. She might as well be a hired pianist or a stand-up comic. That *fucking* Nancy.

'Give me a minute,' she tells Barber. 'All right, Kieran, I do know you're there. Who is this for? Who do you want to reach?'

A hush is spreading in the room now like steam. They didn't know it had begun. Christ, she didn't realize at first – usually, there's a thickening of the atmosphere, a sense of the essences gathering around her like a cloud of summer midges. Kieran, in his fuddled desperation, that awful dismay at what he's done, has fallen through. Like a small, thrashing fish through a net.

Glasses are accumulating now on side tables, cigarettes being crushed into ashtrays. Seffi finds herself under the gaze of one of the obvious un-believers, a woman. She's sitting in a wing chair about seven feet away; she has short hair dyed dark red, vulgar trophy earrings, a wide, carnivorous mouth.

And she's saying sharply, 'Did you say *Kieran*?'

Seffi doesn't blink.

A big, broad-faced man in a white tuxedo turns at once from a conversation with a younger woman, hissing, 'Don't be stupid, it's just a name.'

OK. So it's the red-haired woman. She's the one. She isn't going to like this.

'If this means anything to you,' Seffi says coolly, 'Kieran tells me he killed himself.'

Dead silence in the room.

And then the poor bloody woman's rising up as though electrically jolted, her big mouth falling open.

'*God!*'

Seffi finds herself smiling slightly. Yes, obviously, it's wrong to enjoy the shattering of disbelief in such circumstances, but she's only human.

The man in the white tuxedo's staring hard at her, several expressions chasing across his face. One of them: *hunted*? He converts it quickly into anger, soften-ing this to exasperation. Speaks through tightened lips.

'Don't make a fool of yourself, Coral.'

In Seffi's head, Kieran's pulsing hard. *OK, calm down, there's a good boy. We're getting there, yah?*

Nobody's talking now; she can hear the music playing softly out of hidden speakers: Debussy, *Nocturnes*. She brought the CD with her – more for them than for her; music's no longer essential. All right, let him come. *Talk to Seffi, Kieran.*

11

'Ah.' She nods, very slightly. Just a boy who's done something impossibly stupid. He was twenty years old – it was the day after his birthday. His mother persuaded his father to buy him the sports car, the black . . . Mazda? Finding out about . . . *Kelly – is that the name?* on his birthday compounded the sense of injury and blinding humiliation.

Finding out what, Kieran? Come on, what did she do? What did Kelly do to you?

Kieran is hanging from a thin, plastic-covered washing line. It's bright red; from a few feet away it looks like a wound around his neck, as though he's slashed his throat.

In a garden summerhouse, a gazebo-thing. Kieran's body half-revolving then swinging back. His tongue out.

Revolting.

This is what Kieran's thinking now. The manner of his dying disgusts him.

So what exactly did you find out, Kieran? What did you find out to make you do this?

'Please . . .' The red-haired woman's half-out of her chair; she'll be on her knees soon, poor bitch. 'For Christ's sake, *tell me* . . .'

'*No!* I don't *do* this sort of thing. I'm not a bloody nightclub act.'

Ten days ago. An outraged Seffi snarling at Nancy.

Who simply put on her glasses, reread the letter – on notepaper as crisp and creamy as her own – and then nodded, all mild and motherly. Well, of course, Nancy knew exactly what Seffi was. Nancy, the agent-manager, wise and discreet, sculptor of one's brilliant career.

'And this guy, Barber . . . he's not even an MP any more, is he?'

Nancy raised her eyes for a moment over the half-glasses. 'On the other hand, he is *Sir* Richard now.'

'Well, big fucking deal,' said Seffi Callard, whose father had been Sir Stephen for most of her life. She walked around the room a couple of times, biting her lower lip, getting ready to despise herself.

'How . . . how much was it again?'

Nancy silently pushed the letter across the desk towards Seffi, flattening it out. The long figure now ovalled in green ink.

'Nancy, for *one session*?'

'Rather vulgar, in one sense, but . . .' Nancy shrugged '. . . he wants the best.'

'I don't even like to think what he wants for that much.'

'Well, there'll be a personal reason. There always is. Perhaps he's lost someone. Perhaps he would be too embarrassed to approach you on an individual basis.'

'You mean he'd hate anyone to know he was consulting someone like me, so he's setting me up ostensibly to amuse his friends, like you'd hire a bloody soprano?'

'Say a string quartet,' Nancy said soothingly.

Seffi froze. Was Nancy in on this? Was it the start of a subtle reshaping of her career, taking in discreet cocktail parties and country-house weekends? Seffi knew too many who'd gone down that road – sincere enough at first and then, inevitably, it had become an act, a routine, and on those occasions when it failed to happen they'd fill the void with imaginary voices.

'Up to you.' Nancy picked up the letter between thumb and forefinger, swinging her arm, cranelike, to a position over the wastebin. 'Do you want me to . . . ?'

Seffi snatched the letter.

Barber, with his politician's false deference, is gliding like a game-show host between Seffi and the red-haired woman addressed by the tuxedo'd man as Coral. But when Barber turns to Seffi, it's with un-certainty. No mistaking that fractional hesitation; he isn't quite sure what's supposed to happen. This makes absolutely no sense, not with the money he's spending.

'Miss Callard, are you . . . ? Have you . . . ?'

'Started? No. This is a . . . wild card.' Seffi smiles thinly. 'Sometimes they just can't wait.'

She has everyone's attention now. Some of them standing, some sitting in chairs pushed together, all in a bunch. Cocktails clinking, teeth and jewellery twinkling in the half-light. She notices Barber's sweating. Pretty bloody obvious he doesn't want to be doing any of this. He's actually paid over twenty grand for something he doesn't want to be happening.

So who does? Some woman? Barber's long divorced; is there a new woman, out there among the teeth, whom he's trying to impress?

And yet he was making no pretence of friendship nor even of knowing Seffi before tonight. All this *Miss Callard*ing. Shaking hands in a distant sort of way when she arrived, the merest meeting of eyes. Curious, because she has actually met him before, during that tedious period of attending receptions on her father's arm.

Something very wrong about this. But then she's always known, hasn't she, that there would be?

14

The woman whispers, 'Is it Kieran Hole?'

'*Fucksake*,' the man rasping out, 'get a grip.' He looks powerful, this guy, big shoulders. Seffi feels Kieran's hatred for him. She puts a steady hand on the red-haired woman's bony wrist, stares candidly into her contact lenses.

'Your son didn't leave a note, did he?'

'No.' A whisper. Hand full of rings tightening around the stem of her glass.

'He thought you'd know, you see.'

'Know?'

'What a load of old shit!' The man's local accent rolling through. People frowning at him, wanting him out of the way because this is getting interesting.

'*Shut up! Leave us alone!*' The woman turning her stiffening back on him, spilling her drink. 'Go on,' she pleads to Seffi. 'Go *on*.'

And oh, there's a belief now, all right. And hunger in the wetness and the slackness of the lips.

'Hold on . . .' Seffi lifts a finger. 'He's asking my advice, I think. At first he dearly wanted you to know, but now he's not sure it would do any good. He's angry and upset, and confused above all. We tend to imagine death confers wisdom, but that's not how it goes.'

'. . . cking *shit*.' The man spinning away, fists clenched.

'He *can* move on. That's my feeling. He isn't earthbound, just weighed down, like a hiker with an overstuffed rucksack, yah? He needs to shed some of it before he can go on. It's a question of whether you're prepared to take it on. Take the weight. It won't be comfortable. Are you going to be OK with that? You have to be sure.'

The woman nodding, but looking bewildered, lowering her glass to the carpet.

'All right,' Seffi says. 'Kelly. Was there a Kelly?'

'I'm going.' The man pushes through the faces and the drinks. 'Get yourself a cab.'

Seffi shaking her head. 'Sorry, *Kirsty*. It was Kirsty, yah? I'm sorry.'

The man stops at the door, reeling sharply, as though he's been hit by a sledgehammer in the small of the back.

'His girlfriend!' The woman gripping Seffi's hand. 'Kieran and Kirsty. They were getting engaged. She was his girlfriend . . .'

'So she's done her research.' He's got the door half-open. 'She's had some of us checked out, hasn't she? That's how the black bitch does it, you stupid woman, can't you—?'

'*Bloody get out!*' Coral screeches.

A man murmurs, 'Easy, now, Les,' two other guys on their feet, guys the size of bouncers, guiding the tuxedo'd man from the room.

'There'd been a row, OK?' Seffi says. 'It was about nothing in particular. It was after . . . a party?'

'Yes. His birthday party. We hired—'

'They were both pretty drunk. He'd been mouthing off and she told him . . . Kieran says he must've blanked out what she told him. It didn't really hit home until . . .'

Tangible suspense. The only lights are from the muslin-shaded porcelain lamp on the Chinese table to her left and the white tongue of the ball-candle which is supposed to dispel cigarette smoke.

'. . . until he awoke the following morning. Terrible hangover. Sickness. The usual.'

16

'Yes. Yes, he did! He looked awful! How could you have known that? No-one could've known that!'

'And it's swirling round and round him, what she said, right? What Kirsty said. Round and round in his head. All that day. He can't go out. Can't face anybody. Walking. A sunny day. Late afternoon, long shadows. Big garden. Red brick.'

'We were, oh God, living in a farmhouse. Eighteenth century . . .'

'A gazebo at the bottom of the garden. He's walking round and round it.'

Coral's lips are spreading into a silent wail.

'Round and round the gazebo.' Seffi's breath coming hard and fast, like gas. 'He doesn't want to see anybody. All the time hearing what she said, what Kirsty said.'

Coral waits for it, her face lined and bloodless. Coral knows. Coral knows already what this is going to be.

'About how his father's a better fuck,' Seffi says.

Eventually a woman takes Coral out of the room, supporting her as though she's been found in the street, knocked down by a car, and there could be something broken.

The lights are on, the atmosphere in Sir Richard Barber's drawing room raw with excitement, spattered with emotional shrapnel.

Seffi sitting in the aftermath, surrounded by nervous laughter, unwilling awe, shrivelling scepticism.

'I'm sorry,' she tells no-one in particular. 'He wanted to come. Sometimes they just . . . do.'

Look, it needed to be done, she used to tell herself. All those comfy old mediums who sanitize everything,

17

only pass on the innocuous stuff, the trite crap. Times change. Honesty is what is needed now.

Yet it horrifies her: twenty thousand pounds for exploding a bomb under a marriage?

Seffi Callard is suddenly personally afraid. All eyes on her. And these are . . . these are *nightclub* people. About twenty of them, all expensively dressed, but perhaps too expensively. More than a hint of the garish. Money, certainly, but not old money. And the sense that Barber doesn't know any of them very well. A room full of comparative strangers. Extras in a movie.

Of which Sir Richard Barber is not the director.

'Miss Callard . . . is there anything I can get you?'

'Sir Richard,' she says quietly, 'I think it's time I left, don't you? Could someone call me a taxi? This was a mistake.'

His unhappy eyes agree with her; his mouth says, 'No. Emphatically *not*.'

'We'll return your cheque in the morning.'

There, in the background, goes that tape-loop laugh again.

'Miss Callard—'

'Sir Richard, people think it's going to be a game. It never is. I was never a cabaret act.'

'We know it isn't a game.' She can sense a desperation in him, fear – but not of the supernatural, this is fear of the *known*. 'We want you to stay. We want you to carry on.'

'Who does?'

'. . . I do. Miss Callard . . . please.' Barber signalled to a young guy in a maritime white jacket, and the lights begin to go again, one by one. 'I . . . we . . . need you to stay.'

Well, of course she should get out of there right now if she's got any sense. But what if poor bloody Coral's husband is outside? What if he's out there waiting for the *black bitch*?

Quite often you get a rush of them coming at you like primary school kids when the doors are opened to the playground. Most mediums are happy to employ an outside filter, known as a spirit guide, but Seffi's been through all that and finds it unsatisfactory: hand-holding, patronizing. She doesn't need any of those old cliché props. Nor even a feed-line – although this is expected and everyone has a variation on the traditional *Is there anybody there?* Like, *Do we have company?* Or the cringe-making *Are there spirit friends amongst us?*

She lowers her eyelids, focuses on a point three feet in front of her, so that the opulent room becomes a soft blur and none of the guests exists as individuals.

Letting the music flow into her, slowing her breathing. Hands on knees, long neck extended, she yawns luxuriously and gathers herself into trance.

There's quite a space around her, like the space left by spectators standing back from a road accident or a street fight. As though the earlier exchange has caused a shock on *that* side too. Only Kieran remaining for a moment, a more nebulous presence than before – confused, unsure how to proceed. There should be someone there for him; he needs only to become aware of this.

Look around, she says to him, gently. *See who's there.*

Waiting now for him to react, for the confusion to evaporate. It's at moments like this when you realize you almost always are stronger than they are.

19

And then Kieran is gone. On the edge of her vision, the candle flame becomes a tiny planet of light.

'The lines', she announces softly, 'are open.'

Later –

when it's cold . . . when the music, with a busying of woodwind, gains power and the voices come in, the first swelling cry of Debussy's night nymphs . . . when women are pulling cardigans and evening shawls around their shoulders, expressions of vague distaste puckering several faces . . . when Coral's chair is no longer empty . . . when exploratory hands are dry and fibrous on Seffi's skin.

– how she wishes she could claw back those words.

Part One

From *Bang to Wrongs: A Bad Boy's Book*,
by GARY SEWARD

*Listen, you have a kid hits you with a stick, you hit him back
and you do it good and hard and you do it fast. And, most
important, you do it with the jagged side of half a brick.*

*As a country boy in the East End, I had to learn this
quickly. I was six years old when my old man done a runner
and me and my mum come to live with my Aunt Min in
Saxton Gate. I was the only one in our street ever seen a cow
and I had this funny hayseed accent and so the other boys
naturally took the piss, and you cannot tolerate this, can
you?*

*The first one I done, his name was Clarence Judge and
when I done him with the brick I didn't realize he was the
hardest kid in the street. This was a piece of real good
fortune because me and Clarence, when his scars healed,
we become the best of mates and we still are.*

1

The truth of it was, Grayle didn't much like spiritualist mediums any more – was now prepared to admit never having encountered one who seemed wholly genuine. All this, *I have a tall, grey-haired gentleman here, he says to tell Martha hello and he wants her to know he doesn't get the migraines now.*

Hey, screw the migraines, you wanted to scream . . . what's it like over there? What does *God* look like?

Plus, they were usually creepy people. They had soft voices and wise little smiles. You looked at them and you thought of funeral flowers and the pink satin lining of grandma's casket.

Of course, as an accredited New Age writer, Grayle was supposed to relish creepy, was supposed to *embrace* creepy.

Uh-huh. Shaking her head, driving nervously towards the next traffic island. Couldn't handle that stuff the same any more, since Ersula. If this woman started giving her little personal messages from across the great divide, she was out of there.

Pink satin lining. No-one would ever know what kind of lining was in the special casket she had to obtain to take home what remained of Ersula. Closed for ever. Vacuum sealed.

Grayle shuddered at the wheel. She wished it was a brighter day, but this was mid-March – March still at its most unspringlike, blustering over Gloucester, a grey place every time she'd been here, which was maybe twice. Stay out of the city, that was the rule. Each time you meet with a junction, aim for the hills.

She swung hard right in front of a truck, which was not enormous by US standards but big enough to crush the Mini like a little red bug. The driver was leaning on the horn from way up there, glaring down at Grayle, who was gripping the wheel with both hands, cowering. *OK, I blew it again, I switched lanes without a signal. But you're a big rig in a tiny country. You should make allowances. Asshole.*

In England even rural roads were now so crowded that driving had become small-scale and intricate, like macramé. OK, no comparison with New York, but in New York Grayle took cabs.

Places like Oxford were on the signs now. But what about Stroud? Was this OK for Stroud? There were hills ahead, at least. Not big hills, but in England the further east you went, the more they lowered the minimum height for hill status.

From behind, another horn was blasting her out. In her driver's mirror she saw a guy in a dark blue van gesturing, moving his hand up and down like a conductor telling an orchestra to soften it up. *OK, what did I do now?*

It was three miles further on – Gloucester safely behind her, the blue van gone – when Grayle found out. This was when the clanking began, like she'd just

26

gotten married and someone had attached a string of tin cans to the fender.

All too soon after this delightful image came to her the noise became more ominous, this awful grinding and then the car was sounding like a very ancient mowing machine.

Grayle pulled over, climbed out.

There was a dead metal python in the road with an extended lump in the middle, like it just dined on a dachshund. She realized what the van driver's up-and-down hand movements had been about.

This was wonderful. This was just terrific.

She looked around. Suddenly the British countryside seemed an awful lot bigger.

The garage guy stood over the mangled exhaust system, doing all those garage-guy things – the head-shaking, the grimaces. Showing her how the pipe had apparently been attached to the underside of the car at one end by a length of fence wire. *Fence wire?*

Grayle said, 'Couldn't you just like patch it up and kind of . . . shove it back on?'

The garage guy found this richly amusing. Wasn't that odd: the world over, garage guys having the same sense of humour?

It began to rain. Because her mobile was out of signal, she'd walked over a mile to a callbox, where she'd found the number of the local car repairer on a card taped to the backboard. Then walked all the way back to the Mini and waited another half-hour for this guy to arrive like some kind of knight in greasy armour.

'Problem is . . .' he kicked the pipe '. . . it's not gonner be too easy finding one like this.'

'You're kidding, right?'

She stared at him. Was this not the most famous British car there ever was? A *classic* car? This was what the second-hand dealer had told her when she bought it – quiet-voiced middle-aged guy in a dark suit, not slick, not pushy. Marcus had been furious when he heard how much she had paid, but the car had run fine, until now.

'As you say – *was*. Not any more, my sweet.' The garage guy took off his baseball cap, scratched his head, replaced the cap, all the time grinning through his moustache at the dumb American broad. 'How long you been over here?'

'Oh . . . quite a while.'

'This car of yours . . .' The guy gesturing with a contemptuous foot. 'Got to be well over twenty years old. Maybe twenty-five.'

He went silent, looked her all over, with that fixed grin. Over his shoulder she could see a copse of leafless trees and some serious clouds: the English countryside in March.

'OK,' she sighed. 'What do you have in mind?'

Anything. She was at his mercy. She should have been there by now. No matter how you felt about the practice of mediumship, you did not turn up hours late for an interview with somebody as notoriously prickly as Persephone Callard.

The garage guy leaned on his white truck, pursed his mouth, sniffed meditatively. 'Tow it in. I reckon. I could ring round a few of my mates in the trade. See what I can come up with.'

'Right.' She nodded. 'OK.' He had her. He was going to take several hours and then come up with something which, due to being a rare antique component, was going to cost—

'Where you got to be, my sweet?'

'Huh?'

'Where you heading?'

'Oh. Uh . . . it's a place . . . couple miles out of Stroud. Mysleton?'

He considered this. 'Ain't much at Mysleton. 'Cept for Mysleton House.'

'Yeah,' she said. 'That's the place.'

'Sir Stephen Callard?'

'You know him?'

'I know his place.' He wiped his hands on his over-alled thighs. 'I could take you there, if you like.'

'Is it far from your workshop?'

'Few miles. I could take you over there, then pick you up afterwards when we find an exhaust system.'

At some kind of price, she supposed. Or maybe he truly was a helpful person.

Whatever, was she going to get a better offer?

'That would be most kind,' Grayle said, collecting her purse from the passenger seat, tucking hair behind an ear, figuring to come over a little more English and refined.

They went first of all to the garage, which was not at all what she was expecting.

It was on the edge of this very cute Cotswold village: dreamy church, old cottages built from stone like mellow cheese-crust. Then you came to a newish housing estate created out of fake Cotswold stone, designed to maintain the golden glow all the way to the boundary.

But the garage made no compromise. It was hidden behind a bunch of fast-growing conifers close to the housing estate. It was not golden, never had been.

She saw a grey concrete forecourt, decorated with a couple of wrecked cars and two old gas pumps which had clocks with hands to measure the fuel throughput. The black rubber hoses were so withered it must have been years since any fuel passed their way.

The place was deserted and looked long dead. Either the other mechanics were out to lunch or this was a one-man outfit.

The guy – his name was Justin – unhooked the tow rope and left the Mini standing on the spider-cracked forecourt. Grayle surreptitiously gave the car a reassuring pat, making it clear she planned to return – if she was a car brought here she would figure it to be some kind of sad ante-room to the breaker's yard.

Maybe it was the dereliction of the garage behind the beautiful façade of the village, but as they drove away in the pick-up she felt suddenly desolate.

It should be possible – like with the cottages – for age to confer beauty, for people to become golden with kindness and wisdom. How come they always ended up cold and grey and drab and flaking, like this garage?

Grayle had been in Britain over a year in total. Twenty-nine when she first arrived, now she was thirty-one, a mature woman who'd seen some death.

'You a friend of Sir Stephen's then?' Justin asked. Curious, as well he might be – how many friends of Sir Stephen Callard, retired diplomat, would be driving around in a 25-year-old Austin Mini, the exhaust held in place by fence wire?

'Uh . . . his daughter,' she said.

Regretting it immediately. This was not for broadcast, Marcus had warned; the woman didn't want it known she was down here.

'You what?'

Justin had turned his head and was staring at her. Without the baseball cap, he didn't look as old as she'd first figured. Maybe forty-five. His hair was still mostly black and curly, quite long. He had a gold earring, bigger than it needed to be.

'No, uh . . . *I'm* not his daughter, I'm just here to see his daughter, but I would be grateful if . . . Jesus, look where you're—!'

Justin glanced at the road as a big hedge came up fast in the windshield, dead ahead. The road was about as wide as a garden path. Driving with two fingers crooked around the wheel, Justin spun around the bend, then turned back on Grayle.

'Seffi Callard, eh?'

Grayle sat up hard, pulling her flimsy black raincoat together across her thighs, dragging her purse on to her lap.

'Relax, my sweet. I've travelled this ole road about a million times.' Justin swivelled his gaze lazily back to the windshield. 'I know every little bend, every pothole.' He smiled, his big moustache spreading. 'Every little hump.'

Hump? She closed her eyes briefly. Another goddamned ladies' man. Kind of guy who'd just realized he wasn't going to have too many more years of scoring chicks below a certain age threshold, not even puny, nervous, 31-year-old blondes. Grayle coughed, tucking flyaway hair into her coat collar.

'So she's staying with her old man.' Justin was now using one crooked forefinger to control the throbbing wheel. 'Paper said she'd gone abroad.'

'Well, just don't spread it around.' Grayle was annoyed with herself for saying too much.

'Who would *I* tell?'

'She'll like, uh, probably be going abroad tomorrow.'

'Close friend of yours, then, Miz Callard?'

'Not awful close.'

'Quite a girl in her time.' He glanced at Grayle again and winked. She noticed his overall had become unbuttoned to just below the waist. He smelled of engine oil. *Were those overalls next to the skin?*

'Really,' she said.

'That's what they say,' Justin said airily. Grayle supposed that if she'd been a guy, this was where they'd be starting up with all the ribald, sexist stuff, Justin outlining all the things he wouldn't mind doing with Persephone Callard.

'Who?' she said.

'What?'

'What *who* say?'

'Oh,' he said, 'the papers. You know.' Maybe a touch wary now, in case she really happened to be a close friend of the Callard family, fallen on hard times.

'Right,' Grayle said. 'The papers.'

'They're saying she's cracked up. Lost her marbles. You believe that?'

'Well, I wouldn't know, Justin.'

'So she's not a *close* friend of yours, then.'

'No.'

'Ah.' Justin slowed up. 'You're a reporter, right?'

Grayle sighed. 'Kind of.'

His smile was now too smirklike for comfort. She knew what he was thinking now: what kind of reporter drives a 25-year-old heap with etcetera, etcetera?

'I work for a small, specialist magazine,' she said

32

quickly. 'You wouldn't have heard of it.'

'I see.' Justin the ladies' man leaned back, relaxed again, as the rain came down harder on the ochre ploughed fields to either side. She could guess *his* idea of a small, specialist magazine. 'So, er . . . does she *know* you're coming to interview her?'

'Well, of course she does. You don't drive all this way if you don't expect someone to talk to you. Least, *I* don't.'

'So she's expecting you.'

'Sure. She's expecting me in like . . . like a couple hours ago.'

'She is, is she?'

'Most certainly.' This shameless probing was making her decidedly uneasy. 'We talked on the phone just this morning. She's probably calling around by now to find out why I didn't show up.'

Complete lie about the phone; according to Marcus, Persephone Callard was not taking any calls right now.

'What's your name, my sweet?'

'I—'

'To put on the bill?'

'Oh. Right. Underhill. Grayle Underhill.'

'Grayle.' Rolling it around his mouth like candy.

'As in holy.'

'And are you?' His hand moved up and down the gearstick suggestively.

'Devout,' Grayle snapped. Jesus, however creepy Persephone Callard turned out to be, she was unlikely to be in the same league as this guy with his big moustache and his overalls open to the groin.

'You believe in that stuff? Her stuff?'

'Uh . . . some.'

33

'You ask me,' Justin said, 'she's a total bloody fraud, your Miz Callard. All that mumbo-jumbo and communicating with the departed spirits. Load of ole bloody twaddle.'

'That's what they say around here, is it?'

'It's what I say, Grayle. Way I see it, look, the stuff she does, if she was some old lady with a crystal ball she'd be lucky to get fifty pence for it in a bloody tent at the village fête.'

'Well,' Grayle said carefully, 'that's, uh . . . that's one argument.'

''Stead of which, Grayle, she's mugging the aristocracy for five K a time, and they all thinks she's somethin' special on account of her ole man's loaded and got a title and a big bloody house. You wanner see her strutting round Stroud in her fancy clothes, nose in the bloody air. Nothin' snottier on this earth than a coloured girl that reckons she's a cut above. You know what her mother was, don't you?'

'A nurse,' Grayle said tightly, 'as I understand it.'

'Oh, that's what they calls 'em now, is it? You're a reporter, why'n't you expose her for a cheat and a phoney?'

'Well, I, uh . . . my job is . . . Are you sure this is the right road to Mysleton?'

'It's the picturesque route.' Justin laughed, like his display of self-righteous, racist rage had blown down a barrier between them. He looked more relaxed. Not a good development, in Grayle's view.

'Um, Justin, in light of the time I already lost, I think I would prefer to take a chance on the shabby route .... like through the factory estates and stuff?'

'There aren't any fac—' He turned to her. 'You're bloody having me on, Grayle!'

34

And what he did next . . . she could not *believe* this . . . he reached over and rubbed her goddamned thigh, pushing up the hem of her skirt, like they were long-time lovers sharing an intimate joke.

'Jes—'

By the time she unfroze enough to grab his hand, he'd already pulled it casually back. The truck speeded up, going insanely fast for a road this narrow and twisting.

'This is my famous Cotswold Tour, Grayle. You want the commentary?'

'Look—'

If anything came around the bend now they'd be dogmeat.

'Relax, my sweet. Listen, if we don't get that ole exhaust sorted, you'll be looking for a hotel, right? I can probably help you there.'

'But it's gonna be . . .' Grayle bounced off of the door as the truck took a tight bend on two wheels '. . . fixed, isn't it?'

'Friend of mine does accommodation.'

'Huh?'

The bastard actually thought he was going to fix her up with a room in some sleazy flophouse? She had to get out of here. She pushed herself up against the door, as more hedgerow reared up in the windshield.

Her mobile bleeped in the purse on the seat, between her and Justin.

'Excuse me . . .' Diving into the purse, scrabbling for the phone, fumbling for the green button. 'Hello?'

'. . . erhill?' Marcus? His voice was breaking up badly. 'Underhill, I've . . .'

'It's my . . .'

My boss, she was about to say. She bit that off and

35

jammed the phone hard to her left ear so that Justin couldn't hear the voice the other end. He'd slowed down and was watching her intently.

'Oh!' she cried. 'Ms Callard! Yeah, I'm just on my way. I had a problem. My *car* broke down. No . . . really . . . nothing too serious, and I got lucky – I've been given a ride by a very . . . a very kind gentleman called . . . called Justin. Runs a small garage? In a village about three miles out of Stroud? Justin. Yeah. You know him? Gave me a ride in his . . . his . . . white . . . Toyota . . . truck.'

Justin slowed to a crawl, and she thought for a moment he was going to snatch the phone.

'. . . UCKING SCOTCH!' Marcus roared.

'So I should see you in about . . . Oh, I should guess ten minutes? That would be terrific. Bye . . . bye, Ms Callard.'

Marcus had broken up into unintelligible crackle. Grayle pressed the *end* button. Trying hard to keep her breathing steady as she dropped the phone in her purse.

Justin's eyes were back on the road.

'Ten minutes, would that be about right, Justin?'

''Bout that,' Justin said sullenly.

'Good,' Grayle said, breathless. 'Terrific.'

Justin's face looked dark with suppressed rage.

2

Psychic Seffi Gives up the Ghosts

by Stuart Burn

Super-psychic Persephone Callard has turned her back on the Other Side.

The £5000-a-session medium is being treated for clinical depression, it was revealed last night.

And Seffi, 35, whose clients have included TV soapstars and the late Princess Diana, has told friends her career has reached a dead end.

Seffi's manager, Nancy Rich, said, 'She's been overworking – that's all.

'She's not had a holiday in about three years and she's desperately tired.'

But a friend said the high-society psychic had been having trouble sleeping and had lost two stones in weight.

'She went to see her doctor and was referred to a consultant psychiatrist. She just

wants to be left alone and won't be taking on
any more clients for a while – if ever.'

Last night, Seffi's whereabouts were a
mystery. It was believed she could be on her
way to the villa in Tuscany owned by her
father, ex-diplomat Sir Stephen Callard.

Seffi Callard has been a controversial figure
since she was a teenager.

Twenty years ago she was expelled from a
top public school after the havoc caused by a
sudden wave of poltergeist phenomena.

Witch doctor, they'd said behind their hands, the
night the dormitory window blew out. JUJU WOMAN
GO HOME, Marcus Bacton had found the next day,
daubed in lipstick on the girl's locker. Even the other
staff were wary. Eventually the head had brought in a
psychologist.

Bastards. Marcus had read the bloody tabloid
cutting too many times. He balled it, tossed it into the
opened stove, piling twigs on top to rekindle the fire,
and then an oak log. Slammed the stove door, pulled
off his glasses, snatched a handful of Kleenex to mop
his sore, pouring eyes.

The race factor had figured strongly, if obliquely, in
the psychologist's report. The bottom line had been
that the subject – 'rather immature for her age, lonely
and alienated from her peers' – had attempted to
create a mystique around herself by fabricating a
fantasy history of her late mother's West Indian
family, involving ethnic magic and occult practices.
Producing what the psychologist had called 'evidence
of her own assumed powers'. The fantasy enveloped
her to the extent that 'a certain self-deception was
evident'.

38

Blinkered wanker. Marcus recalled storming into the headmaster's office. Bloody hell, was the head *mad*? Didn't he understand the overwhelming significance of this? Didn't he realize that this overpriced, underachieving internment camp was about to go down in parapsychological history?

Bacton, the head had said aridly, *'did it ever occur to you that what you choose to call parapsychological history is merely a tawdry chronicle of fraud, lies and mental illness?'*

Marcus wiped sweat from his glasses.

It had been one of those archaic boarding schools which, after about four centuries, had been induced to admit girls. There were probably a whole bunch of black girls there now, but Persephone – Afro-Caribbean/Home Counties English – had been the first.

'And took shit from kids of both sexes, I guess,' Grayle Underhill had said, when he'd given her the history, working on her to meet Persephone on his behalf.

'Especially when things started disappearing,' he'd recalled.

Small things at first, like pens, then there was a watch – from classrooms and dormitories where Persephone had been, and then fingers had been pointed. Made no difference when some of the items had turned up again, sometimes in the same place, sometimes not. Kleptomania, they sneered. *Always go for glittery things and coloured beads, don't they?*

Underhill had looked sceptical. 'So you're saying this was . . . what's the word?'

'Teleportation. I was convinced of it. Many of the

disappearing items were things no-one would ever want to steal. And they would vanish so swiftly and completely that unless she'd been a master of sleight-of-hand . . .'

He saw her grimace, heard the whispered *Beam me up, Scotty*.

Yes, all right. Where Persephone was concerned, all Marcus's own cynicism went out of the window.

'By now, some of the girls had switched from patronizing her to basically shunning her. While from some of the boys she had what today would be described as plain sexual harassment.'

All of which had made her withdrawn. But she wasn't inarticulate and maladjusted like the psycho-kinetic kids in all those overblown films. Persephone was highly intelligent and aware of the unearthly beauty of it all.

'Confused, obviously. A little scared – who wouldn't be? But there was also this tremulous excitement. She resented being treated like some sort of pariah, but equally she was glad not to be . . . normal.'

'So what *was* this, Marcus? Just straight up poltergeist activity, or what?'

'Energies channelled through her, I suppose. It happens. I wondered if, like many people with this kind of ability, she'd had some sort of electric shock as a young child. But if she had, she didn't remember it.'

'Or chose not to. I guess Ms Callard would hate to think all this was down to some unfortunate accident during infancy.'

'But she never once ran away from it, Underhill. What she resented was the randomness of it – didn't like to be out of control, like a psychic puppet. Hated being used. Wanted to know how to use it. And after a while she *did*. It was how she first came to my attention, actually. All those essays in a variety of handwriting styles.'

'Oh, *right* . . . She was getting the spirits to do her . . .'

'Her prep. Something like that. I never actually taught her in class, you understand. I was the A-level Eng. Lit. man, and she was only fourteen then. But one day her English mistress brought me a piece of apparent verse Persephone had handed in. I couldn't make head or bloody tail of it at first, and then I realized . . . it was Chaucerian English. And more than that . . .'

Marcus staring into the stove, the embers reflected in his glasses. Reliving the sheer excitement of it.

'It was Sir Topaz,' he said.

'Who?'

'There's this spoof bit in *The Canterbury Tales*. Where Chaucer himself is invited by the Host at the inn to tell a tale. He begins to relate the story of Sir Topaz – doesn't matter who *he* is. Point is that after a few minutes, the Host interrupts Chaucer and informs him, in no uncertain fashion, that his tale is bollocks.'

'Which is a joke, right?' Underhill said. 'We all know Chaucer's written all the rest of the stuff, so he must be pretty smart, therefore—'

'Exactly. Persephone's verse seemed to be *continuing* the tale of Sir Topaz, where Chaucer left off.'

'Good stuff?'

'The whole point', Marcus said irritably, 'is that the Host is critical of Chaucer's literary skills. The notable line being, as I recall, "your dreary rhyming isn't worth a turd".'

'So like if Seffi's poetry was not of sufficient literary

merit to be recognizable as vintage Chaucer coming through Callard, it could still be genuine, because this is Chaucer deliberately writing bad poetry. That's smart.'

'Too bloody smart for a fourteen-year-old girl who'd never been exposed to Chaucer.'

Soon after the night of the exploding window, Marcus had resigned, cleared off to the other side of the country and back into state education, in which he'd remained until the opportunity had arisen to purchase *The Vision*, or *The Phenomenologist*, as the magazine had been known then – memories of the Callard affair fuelling his resolve to take the gamble.

Because he knew the girl was *absolutely bloody genuine*! Adolescents, particularly at boarding school, relied on friends, peer support. No fourteen-year-old girl would choose to condemn herself to life as a social outcast.

And he'd seen the incomprehension in her eyes.

His head full of fever, Marcus glared out of the window at the farmyard and the castle ruins. Feeling like a bloody prisoner. Dripping a little single malt into his glass. Which left just under an inch in the bottom of the bottle. How the hell was he supposed to survive flu on *an inch of whisky*?

'*BOTTLE OF SCOTCH!*' he'd bawled at the static surrounding Underhill's bastard mobile phone. '*BRING BACK A BOTTLE OF FUCKING SCOTCH!*'

All right: if he was honest, the whisky had also been an excuse. He'd assumed Underhill had reached Persephone Callard by now. Had hoped she'd be able to pass the phone over to Persephone, so that he might explain why he was not there in person. And make sure that Persephone understood that, contrary to her appearance and general attitude, Underhill was, in fact, relatively trustworthy.

Another week – another three days, even – and he might have been fit enough to drive over there. Right now, he was too fucking ill to walk to the pub in St Mary's for a bottle of Scotch. He couldn't think straight and Persephone's letter was burning up his brain.

> . . . know we haven't spoken since my departure many years ago from A Certain School. Perhaps you feel disappointed or offended by my subsequent commercial exploitation of my God-given Abilities.
> . . . surrounded by leeches, parasites, false lovers. You remain the only person who has ever been there when I needed understanding, tolerance and common sense . . .

The letter pleaded for Marcus to come and see her at the lodge at her father's house. Not to write or phone – she was afraid her calls were being monitored.

'Crazy,' Underhill had said. 'She's blown it, you only need to read the papers. You don't need this shit. Call her up when you're on your feet, but play it cool. Don't get involved.'

> . . . I still recall our talks with the deepest gratitude. If you only knew how often I've wished that there was someone like you with whom I could discuss my grimmest fears . . .

'*Oh Marcus, you were like a father to me.*' Underhill raising her eyes to the oak beams. '*Like the father I*

43

never had on account of he was always across the sea in some God-forsaken consulate . . .'

'She's never—'

'Subtext, Marcus.'

'Underhill, I was simply a teacher at her boarding school. A teacher who listened. She thought she was going mad, with all the things that were happening to her, and I was the only teacher who was prepared to consider the alternatives.'

'Twenty years!' Underhill yelled. 'You haven't seen her for *twenty years*! Like, did she come for your advice when they were touring her all over Europe and the States? When Diana was calling her up in the middle of the night, did she ask you how to handle it?'

'She's in trouble. I know this girl.'

'Well, pre*cisely*. You knew a *girl*. This is a grown woman now and by all accounts she's manipulative and paranoid in equal measure.'

'You don't know her.'

'I know a lot of people like her.'

'Believe me, you don't.'

Underhill had looked stubborn.

'She's in trouble,' Marcus insisted. 'We can't let this hang fire. I need you to go and talk to her.'

'Like, she's gonna talk to *me*? She's in hiding from the media, she won't take phone calls, and you think—?'

'What else can we do?' Marcus had started coughing, and the coughing had gone on for a long time and Underhill had sighed and given in.

Marcus pulled off his glasses, clutched the Kleenex to his streaming eyes. Never seemed to get colds or flu when Mrs Willis was alive and keeping house for him

44

– first sniffle and the dear old soul had always been there with some mysterious, brown, stoppered bottle. Now he'd been forced back on the inhalers, expectorants and headache pills produced by fiendish pharmaceutical multinationals which, he was convinced, directed a meaningful element of their astronomical profits into the development of new and virulent strains of influenza.

Bastards.

He sagged back into his old chair, and the castle disappeared from the window, displaced by the last weak sun seeping into the Black Mountains. The study door edged open and Malcolm, the bull terrier, ambled in.

'What are *you* grinning at?' Marcus dragged the phone from the desk. A recorded message told him it was not at present possible to reach the mobile phone he was calling and he should try again later.

Waste of bastard time, mobile phones.

3

What she'd hoped for was that the community of Mysleton would be another pleasant, cheerful, big village with yellow-stone cottages and a pretty pub with tables outside and a scattering of early tourists trailing kids and dogs.

Oh, *sure*.

Clouds like industrial smoke banked over clay-coloured ploughed fields. The rain came in tough spatters, like abuse.

'This . . . this is the place?'

Justin didn't reply. Justin had become real silent; his lips had vanished into his moustache. He looked bigger, somehow.

Mysleton was not any kind of village. It was just like . . . a name. On a map, presumably; there wasn't even a sign. You could see a few farms, well back from the road, but no two dwellings appeared to be within about three hundred yards of one another.

They came to this gap in the roadside hedge and, about ten yards in, two broken-down gateposts, no gate.

'Mysleton House,' Justin said.

But like suppose this wasn't Mysleton House at all?

Suppose that at the end of the track there was just some place which Justin knew was derelict, where no-one could hear you scream?

In what already seemed like standard Mysleton policy, there was no sign on the gateposts. Justin drove between them, into an avenue of bare poplar trees. Though it was only about four-thirty, the day was darkening rapidly on account of the rain, and the rain was coming harder – one of the truck's wipers squeaking to this awful, chugging rhythm, like it was trying for an orgasm.

Grayle clenching her fists. Come *on* . . . even if he'd worked out that the call had not been from Persephone Callard, nothing was going to happen. This was Gloucestershire, England.

Jesus, what is that supposed to mean? Frederick West, the leering, sex-driven builder and repeat killer of women and girls, operated out of freaking Gloucester . . .

Always the same: when you saw olde-English-quaint, you saw harmless. A mistake.

And what you did *not* do, when your car broke down, was call up the number on the scuffed card that was always stuck up in the lonesome callbox. Because the guy on the other end of the phone *knew* that callbox, and if it was a woman's voice he could guess she was alone. Maybe Frederick West had his card in lonely callboxes: *F. West, general builder; cellar conversions a specialty.*

'OK, stop!'

They'd reached a low, smallish house, enclosed by trees and bushes and well covered with ivy creeper. Dirty stone in between the creeper, no Cotswold glow. Didn't look so very old by English standards, maybe Victorian. Could this be it? The lodge?

Justin braked, but didn't switch off his engine.

'This ain't the house. This is only the lodge, Grayle. You can tell it's empty. Look – no lights. Tiny little windows like that, this time of day there'd be lights.'

Marcus had said, *There'll be no lights, no sign of life, no car visible. She doesn't want the press to think there's anyone at home because, if anyone sees her, the word'll spread like wildfire and there'll be a dozen bloody photographers peering through the windows.*

Justin was waiting, revving the engine in short, kind of masturbatory bursts.

Grayle plucked at the passenger-door handle.

'Maybe I'll walk from here.'

'In this? Don't be daft, girl.' Justin accelerated through the trees, past the lodge, along a level black-top track. 'House is round this bend, 'bout a hundred yards.'

'Thanks, but there was no . . .'

Aw, leave it; she'd just have to get out at the house, thank him graciously and smile. Walk right back to the lodge, just as soon as he'd driven away.

Mysleton House sat firmly at the end of the track, open fields behind it. It was no stately home, but no chalet either: one of those substantial stone-built rural dwellings that didn't answer to any particular style and tended to escape the attentions of those English Heritage guys Marcus Bacton hated worse than tax inspectors.

And, of course, no smoke issued from its tall chimneys and there were no cars parked outside. Justin stopped the truck in front of a five-barred gate dividing the track from a garden with trees and stuff.

48

He was looking so damned smug.

'Ain't nobody here, my sweet.'

'They'll be around back,' Grayle said confidently. 'Look, I'll call you about the car. What time do you close?'

'Seven . . . eight. Sometimes later. Countryside hours. I'm a hard-working man.' Justin didn't smile.

'I'm sure you are. Look, I really would be grateful if you *could* get it fixed tonight. Could I give you a . . . a deposit?'

'I got the car, Grayle. And I trust you.'

'Right. Well, thank you for, uh, for all you did.'

She backed out of the truck, shouldering her bag. Walked through the rain to the five-barred gate, which – thank Christ – did not have a padlock, only a latch. She glanced back at Justin as she lifted the latch. He was just sitting there, watching through the snapping wipers. Seeing her safely to a front door which he knew was not going to be opened.

The door had a bellpull. Grayle looked up at it and turned away. Raised a hand back at Justin – *no problem, everything's just fine* – and walked right past the door, following a concrete path around the side of the lightless house.

Flattening herself against a wall below a bright yellow burglar alarm, sheltered from the rain by the eaves, she pulled out her phone.

There was a signal. Just.

Call the cops?

Well, no officer, he didn't exactly do *anything; he was just conveying an unmistakable menace. The way he talked . . . the kind of questions he asked. And – oh yeah – he grabbed my leg. My thigh . . . Well, sure, we were going around a tight bend at the time; it's*

49

*possible his hand kind of slipped, but I sure don't
think so. Press charges? Uh . . .*

She dumped the phone back in her bag then took it
out again, brought up 999 on the little screen, did not
press *send*. Shoved the phone, primed for fast action,
into a pocket of her raincoat and moved on around the
house.

It might be the biggest dwelling in Mysleton, but it
wasn't so big, maybe six bedrooms. It was clear there
was nobody living here right now, but if she stayed
this side for a while, out of sight, Justin surely would
have to accept she'd gotten in.

She came to a glass-walled conservatory. Cane
chairs and a sofa inside. Also plants – so somebody
must come in to water them.

'*Grayle?*'

Shit. She clamped a hand around the phone in her
pocket and ran away from the conservatory, across a
lawn and into some trees, as Justin appeared around
the side of the house, his overalls flapping.

'You all right, Grayle?'

He couldn't see her, she was sure, but she moved
further into the dripping trees, which were soon
assembling themselves into a small wood, dark and
boggy, Grayle sinking up to an ankle in brown water.

Nightmare, or what? All she could hear now was
her own panting breath and the grey noise of the rain
which muffled other noises like, say, footsteps coming
up behind you and the furtive glide of a zipper.

Gulping back a sob, dragging the sodden foot out of
the hole, she stumbled on through all kinds of dank
shit, until she came out on to an overgrown footpath
running roughly parallel to the black-top track.

There was a wall ahead. She almost ran flat into it –

a stone wall with a wrought-iron gate in it. The path stopped here. There was no place to go but through the iron gate and into what looked like a long-untended walled garden, a messy nest of brown bushes. A short gravel path led up to a wooden porch open to a solid back door painted dark green, with no obvious bell, no knocker.

The lodge, right?

Sure. But this was still all wrong. There was going to be nobody here. Like Persephone Callard – superior, graceful, elegant, supermodel-slim – was going to be holed up in a dump like this?

In fact, the whole set-up . . . this rich and famous woman issuing a cry for help to an old guy she'd last encountered when he was a world-weary teacher and she was a very weird schoolgirl . . . what kind of sense did that make? Pushing into the porch, Grayle had a flash picture of Marcus Bacton, hunched over his woodstove, nursing his flu and his fantasies. Asshole.

She stood in the porch, furious and scared, hair hanging like seaweed. She banged and banged on the door, with both fists, until it hurt and then some. No answering footsteps in the hallway, kitchen, whatever; no lights coming on.

But lights were appearing behind her. Headlights. Good old Justin easing his pick-up back down the track, lighting up the trees, scanning the ground for his prey like a poacher lamping a hare. Grayle tried to push open a narrow letterbox, but it was rusted tight.

'Ms Callard . . .' Hissing it, scared to shout.

A rattle and a creak of brakes, a shaft of white at the end of the garden: the pick-up stopping outside the lodge. Justin was bold. Justin had done this stuff before and gotten away with it. Grayle's knuckles felt frayed and sore. She went down on her knees in the porch, her mouth to the only opening, an enlarged keyhole.

'Ms Callard, listen, Marcus Bacton sent me. You get that? *Marcus Bacton*. If you're there, just . . . please just let me in.'

Justin would go first to the front door, but he'd soon come around back. Grayle got ready to escape down the garden, out the iron gate. Saw herself running through acres of filthy fields to some stark farmhouse, the door answered by this grinning, naked guy who would turn out to be Justin's insane brother.

She collapsed onto her hands when the back door of the lodge opened unexpectedly into darkness.

4

What she saw first was the blade. It sliced clean through the moment of relief at finally gaining access to the lodge.

The blade was wide – wide like a machete – and it had a reddened edge, and there was a figure in shadow behind it that didn't move.

Grayle came unsteadily to her feet, backing up against the wooden door – a heavy *thack* from the latch as she closed it with her ass.

'*Who are you?*'

This harsh, low voice. Grayle blinking in the gloom of a low room with small, square, leaded windows.

A woman. With blades.

She was not holding the big blade, but she was standing next to where it hung from this like torture-chamber wall. It was on the end of a thick wooden handle bound with cord, the whole item like a butcher's weighty, stubby chopping knife for splintering bone. Next to this knife was a rusty sickle with no handle. Above them, a razor-edged hook on a five-foot wooden pole.

Some kind of rustic armoury. Grayle saw, with faint relief, that the red on the butcher's blade had been a reflection from a low-burning fire – little coals glowering sullenly out of a black, sunken grate.

'Uh . . .' Trying to make out the face as the woman moved out from the wall. 'You're Pers . . . Persephone?'

Not a stupid question because this did not look too much like a cool, silky fox with skin like Galaxy chocolate and calm, penetrating eyes. Maybe her older, embittered sister.

'I *said* . . . who are *you*?' Arms hanging loose, sleeves pushed up, like she was still ready to pull down a lethal weapon from the wall. 'Your *name*.'

'I . . . Grayle Underhill. I told you, I work for . . . with . . . Marcus Bacton.'

'As what?'

'As a writer.'

'So where is he?'

'Sick. The flu. He's existing on whisky and paracetamol. You wouldn't want to catch it.'

But when the woman stepped out, she looked like she already had: in the grey light from the window, she seemed fleshless, a scarecrow in a powder-blue cashmere cardigan, half-buttoned over probably nothing. Hair like a coil of oily rope. Eyes burning far back, like the coals in the black grate.

'Who's that in the truck?'

'That's, uh . . . the garage guy.' Grayle was picking up a tired and sickly smell of booze. 'My car broke down a few miles back. The guy drove me here.'

'And naturally you're terrified of the man who's repairing your car.'

'Well, not *terrified* exactly, I—'

'Look at you!'

54

'OK, yeah, he was . . . he was kind of forward. On the way here.'

Grayle fumbling out an explanation about the exhaust system. The card in the phone box. Fred West. All of that. Sounding completely half-assed, like she was just now making it all up. Often the way of it with the truth.

'He doesn't know I'm in here. He thinks the lodge is empty.'

'That case, you'd better keep your voice down and stay away from the window. Sit in that chair, if you like, next to the fire. Dry off.'

Dry *orf* was how she said it. She looked wrecked, but she talked like out of the royal family. Grayle sat. The chair had a high back and faced away from the window. The fire was probably kept low so there'd be no glow on the room. Siege procedure. The woman was living here in darkness, like a ghost. It could only be Persephone Callard.

'All right, be quiet, he's coming.'

She slipped back into the shadows beyond the armoury – actually, Grayle realized, a collection of rustic, rusted hedging implements. There was an old bowsaw beneath the butcher's-type hacking tool and then the wall ended in a wooden stairway.

'Don't speak until I tell you. Don't move.'

The greasy squeak of Justin's fingertips on the window made Grayle stop breathing. A coal fell out of the grate.

'Stupid, huh?' Outside, the truck's engine was starting up. 'He's probably a nice man.'

'No, you're probably right,' Callard said. 'He

55

imagined he was on to a shag. How will you get your car back?'

'Call him in an hour or two, I guess. I don't know. He works till seven or eight, he says. What else can I do?'

'You had him drop you at the house.' Pronouncing it *hice*, like Prince Charles. 'So he knows you were coming here? He knows why? That man knows I'm here?'

'I'm afraid he does,' Grayle admitted. 'I let it out I was coming to meet with you. That was indiscreet. I'm sorry. I have no excuse. Marcus fully apprised me of the situation.'

Persephone Callard found a small smile. Then a clutch of bottles on a table. 'Vodka, gin, Scotch?'

'Well, maybe a Scotch . . . Plenty of water? Thank you. You don't have a car here?'

'It's in one of the garages up at the house.'

Grayle peered out at the walled wilderness. 'How long you been here?'

'Just over a week. I don't want to open up the house.'

'Too big, I guess.'

'Too obvious. This is more discreet. Have to be out of here in a couple of weeks, however. From Easter, we let it out as holiday accommodation. Have to be out even sooner now, if your friend Justin shoots his mouth off.'

'I'm sorry. You're here all alone?'

'As I'm sure Marcus Bacton's told you . . .' Persephone Callard's voice put on a weight of irony '. . . people like me are never *entirely* alone.'

One time, Grayle had done a piece for the *Courier* on how many mediums were practising in New York

City. She'd established two hundred and thirty-five, which was just over twice as many as there'd apparently been in 1850, when the first boom had been on.

Even in those early days, most of the mediums had been exposed as fakes . . . inventors of table-rapping devices, experts at pulling strings of muslin 'ectoplasm' out their nostrils.

Sure, Justin had been largely right. It was exploitation of the bereaved. About taking the sting out of death, like your loved ones were just a phone call away. Always a ready audience for that.

Some of the working mediums Grayle had talked to were kind of genuine – even though a lot of the information they relayed was inaccurate, they seemed to have contact with *something*. Just that they usually came over just as gullible as their sad clients, needing to believe they were bonding with the departed. Plus they did tend to be so pious and all knowing, putting on the air of church ministers.

And sure, in those years as a New Age columnist, Grayle had never encountered anyone she could honestly believe was in contact with the dead.

Callard had come to sit on a Victorian sofa on the other side of the fireplace from Grayle's chair, facing the window. She had a tumbler half-filled with some kind of immoderate Martini mixture.

'You know why I drink too much?'

Grayle said nothing. It was so dark in here, now, that you didn't like to move in case you knocked something over. She began to feel cold, edged her chair closer to the underfed fire.

'Because when I'm pissed I don't receive.'

'Right,' Grayle said uncertainly.

'Nothing significant gets through alcohol.'

'That's interesting.'

'Don't feel . . .' Callard leaned back, with her head against the wall, maybe observing Grayle for the first time '. . . that you have to fucking patronize me. What did you say your name was?'

'Grayle Underhill.'

'Grayle?'

'Underhill.' She sipped weak whisky from a glass that felt greasy.

'Oh my God.' Callard did this short snort of a laugh. 'Not that dreadful . . . You don't have a column in one of those ghastly American tabloids. Under the name . . .'

Grayle sighed. 'Holy Grayle. But not any more.'

'Holy *Grayle*.' Callard threw an arm behind her head and peered at Grayle across the murk. 'Oh my *God*. I was in New York doing some television and my agent brought me some copies. You really wrote that drivel?'

'Don't feel you have to patronize me,' Grayle said.

Callard snorted, took a graceless slurp from her glass. She sat up, grabbed a poker, stabbed at the coals until a feeble white flame spurted.

Outside it was getting too close to dark. Time, Grayle figured, to cut to the chase.

'Ms Callard, why did you write to Marcus?'

'Did I?'

'Marcus Bacton.'

In the wan firelight, you could see her navel between the bottom of the cardigan and the top of her dark jeans, then a fold of skin creased over it. She was anorectically thin.

'Marcus Bacton', she said, 'was the only person in

my entire fucking life who ever pitied me.'

She dug a bare hand into a bucket and came up with a clutch of small lumps of coal, scattering them over the fire, wiping her hand on her jeans.

'People are suspicious of me. Or afraid. Or they want a piece of me. But I mean, *pity* . . . that was something new, even at the time. I was profoundly offended at first.'

'Best of all,' Grayle said, 'Marcus likes to offend.'

'When I think about him . . . I picture him striding up and down the corridors, with his wide shoulders and his little pot belly. Glaring through his glasses and roaring at pupils. Teachers too, sometimes.'

'Uh huh.' Grayle finished her whisky, gratefully put down the glass in the hearth. She noticed that Callard's tumbler remained half-full. She'd drunk hardly any.

'One night – this is on record . . . in the books – a big window just exploded in the dormitory. Glass everywhere. I was at the other end of the room, but they knew . . . the staff knew things happened around me. They actually put me into a room no bigger than a cupboard. Locked the door, as you would with a dangerous mental patient. This was the headmaster and the matron. Didn't know how else to handle it. Mr Bacton was furious. Came out in his dressing gown, and when they wouldn't give him the key he kicked the door in and brought me out and we went for a long walk in the grounds. Talking. For hours, it seemed like. He resigned soon after that, and I was taken away from the school. I haven't seen him since.'

'What did you talk about?'

Callard didn't reply. Whatever they'd discussed, that must have been the night Marcus connected, showed her he understood what it was like having psychic ability – although he had none himself. The bond between them had been formed that night, and Grayle was no kind of substitute.

Callard poked at the fire again. 'Flu, you said.'

'Marcus has this theory that men get it worse than women. He's real low. But he was flattered, I guess, when you wrote to the magazine, trying to reach him. He's been feeling a touch insecure.'

'Marcus Bacton *insecure*?'

'In his way,' Grayle said. 'Feels he wasted too much of his life not doing what he wanted to do . . . investigating the Big Mysteries, showing people that the world was so much wilder than the scientists and the politicians wanted them to think. And now he's past sixty, running this small-time magazine that the right people don't read, and he doesn't think he's ever gonna get where he wants to be.'

Callard rose unsteadily. It didn't show in her voice, but she must already have drunk plenty today. Reaching that stage where it no longer made you happier, just kept the fires of hell tamped down. But now she'd stopped drinking and the alcohol in the glass didn't seem to be tempting her.

'And what do you do exactly, Grayle?'

'Oh, I . . . came over from the States for . . . personal reasons, and I met Marcus and I started helping him with the magazine. Which was seriously rundown. And like now we've changed the name and it's starting to make this very small profit, which I thought would make him happy. But perhaps he feels it's being taken out of his hands. Or losing its peculiar integrity. I don't know. He's a complex individual.'

'And where is this?' Callard moved to the window,

pulled thick, dark curtains across. 'Apart from on the Welsh border?'

'He has this farmhouse inside the ruins of a medieval castle. Which sounds grander than it is. But it's Marcus's fortress against the cold, rational world.'

'Nothing's changed then.'

'I guess.'

'He was a hero to me at the time.' Callard sat down again. 'When they threw me out of the school and my father was advised to hire a private tutor, I wanted it to be Mr Bacton. I've never been entirely sure whether he turned down the job or my father lied about offering it to him. My father was . . . diffident . . . about the psychic world. He'd worked in the Diplomatic Service in too many strange places to dismiss it entirely, but he didn't want anything to do with it.'

'Your father was still working abroad?'

'No, Foreign Office. When he married my mother he came back, bought Mysleton.'

'Your mother died, right?'

'My mother died when I was four. I don't think she could stand the cold and the drabness and stiffness. A black woman in the Cotswolds, even then . . .' A match flared. Callard applied it to a candle on the mantelpiece. 'They said she died of cancer, but I think she withered.'

'Withered?'

'Like an exotic flower,' Callard said heavily.

'You remember her?'

'I remember her essence.'

'Right.'

Callard slumped back into the sofa, said snappishly, 'When people keep saying "right", it usually means

61

they haven't understood anything and don't propose to.'

The candle sat crookedly in a pewter tray. It looked warmer than the fire.

'I don't think you want to tell me what this is about, do you?' Grayle said.

'I don't know you. I don't trust journalists. I might be reading about it in the *New York Courier* next week.'

'You might be reading about it in *The Vision*.'

Callard smiled. '*That* I could cope with.'

Grayle thought, *Me too. I could just about cope with this if it was gonna make a feature for* The Vision. She'd never even dared suggest that to Marcus, but yeah, it had been at the back of her mind.

'Listen,' she said, 'I didn't *want* to come here. You contact a guy after twenty years, no way are you gonna want to talk to the help. I came because Marcus was too sick to come, and Marcus felt you were in some kind of trouble, and he didn't want it to be . . . too late. Or something.'

'Do I look like I'm in trouble?'

'You don't look too good, if I can say that. You look like the papers had it right.'

'The papers are suggesting I'm mentally ill.'

'Not necessarily that.'

'Of *course*, that. No journalist who wants to stay on the national press can be seen to accept the spiritual.'

'I did.'

'Quite,' Callard said. She laughed.

Grayle stood up. 'Maybe I'll call Justin, find out if he tracked down an exhaust for my car.'

In the candlelight, she saw Callard shrug. She reached for her bag and dug out Justin's card.

'That was rude of me,' Callard said wearily. 'Don't go.'

Grayle didn't look at her. Held the phone up to the candle, punched out the number, which she now realized was a mobile. Clearly, the rundown garage was no longer on the phone.

Callard said, 'Why don't you stay the night?'

'That's not possible.' She heard the phone ringing at the other end.

'Look,' Callard said, 'as soon as the oaf picks up your scent again, he'll start reviewing his options. First, he'll lie about your car . . .'

'Mayfield Garage,' Justin said.

'Uh . . . it's Grayle Underhill.'

'*Hello*, Grayle!' Real jovial. 'You find Miss Seffi Callard then, did you?'

'Yes. Listen, I wondered if you managed to hunt down any kind of exhaust.'

A pause. A chuckle. 'Ah dear,' Justin said. 'I rang round six mates between here and Swindon. No can do tonight, but one of them reckons he might put his hands on something tomorrow.'

'Oh.' *Not on me he won't.*

'You'll have to spend a night in the glorious Cotswolds, my sweet. Look, there's a good country-house hotel not far from where you are. I could pick you up, take you there . . .'

'That's kind of you,' Grayle said quickly, 'but I already made a provisional reservation. In . . . in Stroud, I . . . Ms Call . . . Seffi's gonna take me there.'

'Fair enough,' Justin said neutrally. 'Fair enough.'

'So I'll call you from there tomorrow.'

'Whatever you like.'

'Well, uh . . . do your best with the exhaust.' Grayle

pressed *end*. 'He can't fix it tonight. I need to find a hotel.'

'I told you,' Callard said. 'There's a spare room here. Terribly twee and rustic.'

Grayle shook her head. 'I'll call a cab. You have a phone book. Yellow Pages?'

Persephone Callard didn't move. Except to close her eyes.

'Forget it.' Grayle took the phone to the candle. 'I'll call Inquiries.'

No reaction from Callard. She was kind of breathing heavily. Jesus, she fell asleep? She fell asleep from all the booze?

Callard's glass, still untouched, stood on the mantelpiece. Grayle punched out 192. 'Directory Inquiries,' a woman's voice said brightly. 'What name, please?'

Persephone Callard sat up on the couch and her breath came out in a long, hollow *whooooosh*. Grayle jumped. Somehow, it was like a corpse rising.

'Directory *Inquiries*.'

The candle went out. Just went out. On its own.

Grayle said, too loudly, 'Uh, could you give me the number of a hotel in Stroud, please? A big hotel.'

'Tell me, Grayle,' Persephone Callard said softly, 'what was the awful thing that happened to a young woman very close to you?'

5

The room which had been, until her death, the bedsit occupied by Mrs Willis, Marcus's housekeeper and resident healer, was now the editorial suite of *The Vision*. Marcus stumbled in with a glass and his dying bottle of Glenmorangie, brushing a hand down the light switches, gazing around in bleary despair.

The shelves which had held the herbal potions were dense with box files – Underhill having bought them as a job lot from a local farming accountant who was switching to computers.

The boxes contained – for the first time alphabetically sorted and categorized – the many years of handwritten case histories sent in by an ageing army of correspondents the length and breadth of Britain.

Loonies to a man, Marcus thought morosely. Although, in truth, most of them seemed to be women. Many of whom had, over the years, made vague proposals of marriage to the editor, whom they'd never even seen. And who were now expressing dismay at the large number of young women who appeared to be working with him.

Meryl Taylor-Whitney, Alice D. Thornborough and the rest.

All the pseudonyms of Grayle Underhill, who was changing everything.

For most of its life the flimsy pages of *The Phenomenologist*, as it was then known, had been grey with dense and smudgy type, its headlines not much larger. A typical one might read,

Report of Presumed Fairy Ring Received from Central Cornwall

'And what the hell's so wrong with that?' Marcus had demanded of Underhill during their first, tempestuous editorial conference last year. 'It's straightforward, accurate and a direct statement of fact. The magazine has received, from an old biddy in Truro, a garbled letter relating to what is probably a mildly anomalous circle of mushrooms on her front lawn, but which she, in her precarious mental state, presumes to be a nocturnal meeting place for tiny men with bells in their little bloody hats.'

Underhill had let her unkempt, blonde head fall forward into her hands and had groaned. He'd stared at her, baffled and resentful.

'Marcus,' he'd heard from under the hair, 'it just isn't . . . it isn't *sexy*, is it? And what are we doing with a magazine title that most people connect with a bunch of crazy German philosophers pre-World War Two?'

And so, just over six months ago, to surprisingly few complaints from the residual readership, *The Phenomenologist* had been relaunched as *The Vision*.

Marcus poured himself a quarter-inch of Scotch, held the whisky in his mouth as long as he could taste it. Sitting in the high-backed chair behind the bastard computer he refused to use, he leaned his head – thick grey hair lank with sweat – into its soulless foam-rubber padding.

Underhill had energy, enthusiasm and – though he was never going to admit this to her face – a certain dexterity with the written word. A touch flip, a trifle coarse – but what could one expect from a New York tabloid hack?

Hey, you know, this is fun, Marcus. We're gonna make it happen, I can feel it. Like, if we start by bringing it out like bi-monthly . . . like six times a year? Then we go to monthly . . . Oh, sure you have the material . . . You just got to stop cramming it all together . . . have bigger type, photographs. And bigger headlines which are more, uh . . . evocative. Plus, you need to attract advertising. And also, of course, you have to start trying to sell it to people other than the correspondents themselves. Hold on to the subscribers, sure, but get it into the newsagents. You appreciate what I'm saying?

Well, of course he did. Known all this for years. If it had happened with *Fortean Times*, it could, presumably, happen to *The Vision*. As she told him, there was a market for 'this sort of thing'.

But *should* it?

Look here, he'd told her. You know I can't possibly pay you a decent wage.

She'd shrugged. Then she'd have to make it so that he *could* start to pay her. *It's gonna happen, Marcus. It was* meant *to happen.*

Because Underhill, in her ingenuous American way, believed in destiny: coming to Britain, initially, in search of her sister, an archaeologist, who had gone missing; who, it later emerged, had been an early

67

victim of an obscene ritual murderer residing perilously close to Castle Farm itself; Underhill accompanying the decayed remains of her sister home to the United States, where their father was a prominent academic . . . and then making an unexpected return within three months, arriving on Marcus's doorstep with two large suitcases and a pale, shy, unsure smile.

Destiny.

And now *The Vision* was bi-monthly and designed on a computer, and each issue carried several stories investigated and written by Meryl Taylor-Whitney and Alice D. Thornborough. Underhill was volatile and frantic, and there were times when Marcus suspected she was no more balanced than the crazed biddies who wrote to him about their haunted coalsheds and their stigmata.

Yet the journal's circulation had already increased by forty per cent and, even after the expense of the computer and sundry publishing software, there was a small but appreciable profit.

But was the magazine's destiny compatible with Underhill's? Was *The Vision*, any more than its editor, ever meant to be commercially successful?

The phone rang. Marcus fumbled it wearily to his ear.

'Bacton.'

'Marcus, it's me.'

He stiffened. 'Where are you? Have you seen her?' His head burned, his eyes and nose filling up.

'I'd have called earlier,' Underhill said, 'only the car broke down.'

'Piece of bloody tin.' Mopping his eyes with a

handful of tissue. 'Are you telling me you haven't even *got* there?'

'Oh, I got here all right.' She sounded unhappy. 'Looks like I'll be spending the night here.'

'With Persephone?'

'Yeah. I feel so privileged I could weep.'

'How—?'

'She's OK. Kind of. I don't know too much yet, and I don't think I want to. You wanna speak to her?'

'What?'

'You want me to bring her to the phone when she—?'

'I . . . is she there now? Is she with you?'

'She went to the john, so I took the opportunity to call you. She'll be back in a couple minutes, if you—'

'*No*,' Marcus said, panicked. 'I don't want to speak to her like this. Tell her you couldn't get through. Tell her the line cut out. Tell her—'

'Marcus, you're really in some kind of awe of this woman, aren't you?'

'Don't be stupid.'

'Listen, I can see the dangers. I'm trying to resist is all. I'll call you tomorrow when I leave. Uh, tape Cindy for me, would you?'

'Oh, for God's sake—'

'You don't have to *watch* it, just press the damn button. Eight p.m.'

Marcus snorted and got off the phone, fearful of Persephone returning.

What was the matter with him? Why was he glad that it was Underhill, rather than himself, who was spending the night under the same roof as Persephone? Was it just the flu or was he losing his bottle?

Marcus sat down behind the blank computer. He didn't even know how to turn the thing on.

Malcolm, the bull terrier, waddled over and stood looking up at him, a possible glimmer of pity in his psychotic eyes. How long before it was just the two of them again? Underhill was thirty-one years old and not unattractive. And an American. Had she got a proper work permit or whatever was needed? How long could she be expected to stay in a remote elbow of the Welsh border, where the idea of an eligible batchelor was a man with two tractors?

And when she left – within the year, if he was any judge – how could Marcus possibly fake the racy prose of Alice and bloody Meryl? How could the magazine ever again revert to Question of Telepathy between Budgerigars Posed in Lanarkshire?

'IT'S THE NATIONAL LOTTERY . . . *LIVE!*'

Marcus winced, reached for the remote control.

'AND COULD THOSE BIG-MONEY BALLS BE IN SAFER HANDS . . . THAN THE BEJEWELLED FINGERS OF THE GLAMOROUS, THE SENSATIONAL . . .'

Marcus stabbed in panic at the sound button, which failed to respond.

'. . . CINDY . . . MARS . . .'

Why was it now impossible to buy a bloody television set with a row of bloody *knobs* on the front?

'. . . LEWIS?'

Marcus recoiled. The entity wore a tight black, ankle-length dress glittering with a thousand sequins. Earrings dripping almost to its shoulders. Bangles the size of manacles hanging five to each skeletal wrist.

The studio audience – tickets presumably handed out free to anyone who could provide the correct answer to the question: *Are you a greedy, moronic prick?* – responded to this vision with whoops and whistles and crazed shrieks, and Marcus sank back in his chair, feeling – if that were possible – slightly more ill.

Half the nation, it seemed, now lived in a drugged dream, from Lottery night to Lottery night, convinced that they deserved to be millionaires.

'How're *you*, my lovelies?' Mars-Lewis's arms flung wide, bangles jangling. 'All right, is it?'

Marcus growled. The numbers on the video recorder appeared to be turning satisfactorily. He could switch off the television, couldn't he?

'And before we go any further . . . no . . . stop that now, come on . . . just listen, lovelies, let me just tell you that tonight's jackpot winners will share . . . are you ready now . . . ? A grand total of . . . SEVEN AND A HALF *MILLION* POUNDS!'

The audience keeled over with what sounded to Marcus like narcotically enhanced rapture. He shook his head slowly. How the hell could bloody Lewis have let himself become associated with this nauseous exhibition of mob avarice?

Money, of course. Tonight's fee was probably ten times what the man – Marcus was *almost* certain Lewis was a man – had earned in an entire summer season of bottom-of-the-bill cabaret on Bournemouth Pier. And about ten thousand times what Marcus had ever paid him for an article in *The Vision*.

'Now, I must show you this, see . . .' The creature looked furtive, producing a fold of paper. The syrupy Welsh Valleys accent became more pronounced as it acquired a confidential wheedle.

'Came today, it did. Signed jointly by the Director General of the BBC and the Managing Director of

Camelot, organizers of the Lottery. Just listen to this. *Dear Ms Mars-Lewis . . . Ms! There's* progressive.'

The response to this, accompanied by the creature's arched eyebrow, suggested that several hundred people had spontaneously soiled themselves.

'*Dear Ms Mars-Lewis. Moderately accepting though we are of your personal manner and general deportment . . .*' Lewis sniffed and smoothed his dress '*. . . we are bound to express dismay at the attitude of your avian associate . . .*'

Uncertain laughter, as the cretins pondered possible meanings of the word *avian*.

'*We feel the continued and unwarranted cynicism exhibited by the bird is not in the spirit or indeed the best interests of the National Lottery as we see it, and unless there is a radical change we intend to take a hard look at the terms of your contract.*'

Lewis lowered the paper and looked glum.

'Oh dear. Well, now, despite what you see, I'm not as young as I was . . . And I'm not a *rich* person.'

This was true enough; the creature apparently wintered in a rusting caravan in Tenby.

'The DG now, he has a *terrible* long memory. And I have to think of my future, isn't it? Which is why I've come to a decision. I've decided, I have, that from now on I shall have to work . . . alone.' Lewis straightened up, nose mock-heroically in the air. 'I shall be . . . *a solo artiste.*'

To which the audience produced a passable simulation of a tragic Greek chorus.

'What else can I do?' Lewis shrieked in torment. 'What can I *do*?'

The camera backed up to reveal a large, pink suitcase

splattered with airline stickers. A muffled squawk seemed to emanate from within.

'*You can start by getting me out of this bloody scented boudoir, you old tart!*' screeched Kelvyn Kite.

'Definitely not. Your services are no longer required. You can sign on in the morning.'

'*You'll regret this, Lewis!*'

Marcus sat up. What? 'Hmmph.' He shook his head and poured the last centimetre of Scotch into his glass.

'*Je ne regrette rien!*' Mars-Lewis defiantly throwing out his arms. 'My loyalties are to Camelot and to the BBC!'

The audience booed. Marcus sank the whisky and switched off the set.

6

Live television.

The danger. The living in the moment. The *being here*ness of the whole exercise.

Possibly the ultimate non-shamanic high, and Cindy Mars-Lewis in his element. As though he is two feet above the set and the studio audience and the millions watching at home. His responses co-ordinated to the second, his movements choreographed from within.

And all the time the buzz growing. The lights flashing out the brash magic of money. The air thickening with the coarse energy of lust and longing. *Let it be me, let it be me.* The build up to the tight, breathless moment when lives are changed dramatically for ever but – as Kelvyn knows – rarely for the better.

The future in the balls.

'*OK, Cindy. To Camera One.*' Jo, the producer, in his ear. But he doesn't need the producer any more; his senses are attuned to the pitch of the moment.

He steps out.

'Right, then, lovelies. Now there's still a few individuals . . .' meaningful glance at the case containing the bird '. . . who think the National Lottery's a bit of a swizz. But I can assure you that *nobody* can control

74

those magic balls . . . not even my next guest, who is . . .'

Pause. Widening of eyes. A contriving of awe.

'. . . the Miracle Mesmerist from Malvern . . . the incredible Mr . . . KURT CAMPBELL!'

Cindy steps back two paces, watching Camera Three track Kurt down the glass stairs which lead nowhere. Kurt with his strawberry blond lion's mane, freshly washed and bouncing. Tall, dishy Kurt with his grand-piano smile and his tight trousers.

Oh, the arrogance of youth. Not yet thirty and believes himself the most powerful person in light entertainment. A stage hypnotist with pretensions.

What is hypnotism, though, but another spiritual cul-de-sac? Why, Cindy himself could have been a Kurt Campbell, if he'd wanted to. Well . . . perhaps not at twenty-nine. Nobody was anybody at twenty-nine, back when Cindy was twenty-nine.

'Now then, Kurt . . .' Cindy wading into the receding tide of applause, 'I said the Miracle Mesmerist from Malvern, not because you were born up there in Worcestershire, 'cause you're a London boy, as we know, but Malvern . . . well, that's where you've just bought yourself . . . your very own *castle*!'

Pause for *oooooooooooooh* from the audience.

'That's quite true, Cindy,' Kurt says smoothly, in his soft baritone. 'I've wanted to own a castle all my life. This one cost me . . . well, an arm and a leg, but . . .'

'And didn't even get a Lottery grant, poor dab . . .'

'. . . but it's worth it, because, as you know, I've had a lifelong interest in psychic matters and paranormal phenomena, and this castle . . . Well, to be honest, it's not really a very ancient castle, not much more than a hundred years old actually . . .'

'Oh, thought it was a *proper* one, I did!'

'. . . but what's fascinating about it, Cindy, is that this is actually Britain's only *purpose-built haunted house*.'

'Away with you, Kurt! You can't have a purpose-*built* haunted house. Got to collect whole centuries of gruesome deaths, you have, and even then you have to take what manifests, isn't it?'

'Well . . .' Kurt throws a confidential arm around Cindy's shoulders. 'I'll tell you – very briefly, Cindy – how this came about. Overcross Castle was built in the nineteenth century by a millionaire industrialist who, like me, had a fascination with spooky things. And that was when spiritualism was becoming very fashionable, and so he invited all the star mediums of the day to come and hold seances in his castle . . . and actually attract a few ghosts.'

'And did he succeed, then?'

'That . . . is what I'll be finding out. And, hey, everyone else can find out too. Because, you see, Cindy, we're going to turn Overcross Castle – *without* a Lottery grant – into a huge exhibition centre for psychic studies and we're going to have all kinds of exciting events . . . psychic fairs, the lot. And if this sounds like an advert, it is . . . because the proceeds from our opening event are all going to various charities . . . including the BBC's very own Comic Relief fund!'

Burst of applause. Cindy nodding emphatically.

'Terrific! Can't miss that, can I? Now, Kurt, I know you're going to start tonight's balls rolling in a few minutes' time, so . . .'

Music starts to swell. Kurt steps out and raises a hand. 'Whoah, whoah, whoah,' he cries, as arranged.

'Cindy, hey, I thought I was going to hypnotize you. It's how they persuaded me to *come* tonight.'

Cindy backs away. A squawk from Kelvyn in his case.

'Not on your life, boy!' Cindy shrieks.

'Aw, go on, Cindy . . .' Kurt appeals to the audience. 'Submit to my magical, mental powers. It'll be a hoot.'

'No way!' Cindy flaps his bangles in terror. 'What if I do something . . . indiscreet?'

'*Coward! Coward!*' shrieks Kelvyn in his case.

'GO OOOOOON, CINDY,' the audience roars, as instructed.

'*Ten seconds, Cindy,*' Jo says in his ear.

'I'm a terrible subject, anyway,' Cindy protests, arms folded over his foam breasts.

'GO OOOOOON!'

'Oh, all right, but I bet it doesn't work.'

And it doesn't. Of course it doesn't. Because Cindy studied hypnotism many, many years ago, and he knows what Kurt is looking for, and he knows how to fake it.

But does Kurt know? Is Kurt smart enough?

Cindy's pretty sure that, at rehearsal, Kurt was fully convinced he had Cindy where he wanted him. Kurt's a smart boy, see, well read, plenty of contacts, and he knows about Cindy's shamanic training: the years of weekending at the farmhouse of the Fychans, fourth- and fifth-generation wise men of Dolgellau. Once, ambitious Kurt even tried to contact the *dyn hysbys*, Emrys Fychan himself, claiming that as a Campbell he was qualified to learn the inner secrets of Celtic shamanism. Canny Emrys saw him off by refusing to speak to him except in Welsh. Well, Cindy can't speak

Welsh either, mind, no more than *tipyn bach*, but he admits the old language has its uses.

At the rehearsal the mischievous Kurt, having established that Cindy was a good subject and truly tranced, made him put on the inevitable strip show.

A nice idea, in this particular case, given that millions of people would dearly love to know exactly what Cindy keeps under there, at both ends.

And it was well done. Kurt is a smooth and practised mesmerist. Indeed, on almost anyone else in show business – and therefore not seriously inhibited – it would have worked.

Cindy went along with it, naturally, letting his eyes drop into neutral before sliding off his paste and plastic bangles one by one and sending them spinning into the audience of grinning technicians. Then lifting up his frock, as commanded, to reveal the bottom of his suspender belt and removing his stockings with a flourish, tossing one neatly over the camera shooting him.

It was stopped, obviously, the moment the shoulder straps came down. Kurt having to pretend to glance at his watch, realizing there'd be insufficient time for the Lottery draw. Oh, what a shame, perhaps another time. All right, when I snap my fingers, Cindy, you will . . . awake.

Click-click. Cindy blinking and, spotting the stocking on the camera, shrieking, 'Oh you bastard!' Technicians laughing their cans off. A triumph. Go down a bomb on the night.

'Now, Cindy,' Kurt says – they are sitting on two adjacent cane chairs and the lights are lowered – 'I want you to relax.'

Cindy's on his own. Out of contact with his producer, but Jo trusts him.

'Relax? Me? Nervous wreck, Kurt. Oh, all right then.' Straightening his dress over his knees and laying his hands demurely in his lap. 'In your hands, I am. Big Boy.'

And, to a low *whoooh* from the audience, Kurt takes Cindy's hand and holds it up. Remarks on the bangles, how heavy they must be – taking his own hand away, leaving Cindy's hanging there. How very, very heavy. As heavy as his eyelids.

Cindy smiles, letting his body relax but carefully detaching his consciousness, watching Kurt as from a couple of yards away. Studying Kurt's performance – that low, midnight voice, a seasoned seducer's voice. Ostensibly having a chat, but the words coming very slightly slower than normal, the tone a little thicker, textured, conveying a conviction – the sense of certainty which must swiftly be impressed upon the subject.

This is the art of *informal* hypnosis. People think you need a swinging watch or a deep, fluid gaze. Not true.

Cindy's arm falls slowly to his lap. Kurt is telling him he's simply resting, allowing his mind to relax. Telling him he can hear everything Kurt is saying to him but he really doesn't have to think about it because he's so pleasssssantly drowwwwwsy. Talking evenly, to deepen the trance, and after little more than half a minute, Kurt's voice is pouring into his head like warm olive oil.

'You hearing me OK, Cindy?'

'Yes.' A whisper. Cindy's whole attention is fixed on Kurt, as though the set and the lights and camera and the studio audience no longer exist. He produces a couple of butterfly blinks.

'It's very comfortable here in this chair, isn't it?'

'Yes.' Deepening his breathing.

'Warm.'

'Yes.'

'And getting warmer.'

'Yessss.' Should he attempt to sweat?

'Getting warmer and warmer still under these very strong lights. You're beginning to perspire and your clothes are feeling tighter. Very *much* tighter.'

'Oh, yes.' Cindy squirms a little, gives an apparently involuntary swallow.

'You've simply *got* to take something off.'

A little smile on Kurt's leonine face. He's quite a big-boned man, probably has to watch his weight. By middle age, he will be a formidable presence. But already, at twenty-nine, Kurt has an undeniable strength and his influence is growing. His television work is now merely the icing on a very rich cake, filled with the lucrative cream of consultancies – Kurt has his own company, operating in industry, where he motivates sales forces, perhaps even passing on (highly improper, in Cindy's view) some tricks of the trade which will enable salespersons to apply gentle hypnotic pressure to recalcitrant customers.

'Your wrists have expanded in the heat, so that the bangles are tight. Take one off.'

Cindy shrugs off a bangle, which clatters to the studio floor. He's thinking that when it comes to buying himself a castle, Kurt Campbell is a man who certainly has no need of a Lottery grant. Or a Lottery win. Or the Lottery show itself . . . but perhaps it's to serve his ego. Or perhaps Kurt also gets that live-television buzz which, coupled with the hypnotist's power buzz, must make for a *very* intoxicating surge.

'Hey, Cindy . . . You're a star. A performer.'

Cindy smiles, giggles faintly.

'If you're going to take off your bangles, you want to make a performance of it. Stand up.'

Cindy comes gracefully to his feet.

'You . . . are a *stripper*.'

Squeals from the audience, to which Cindy doesn't react.

'You know how a stripper performs. You've done it soooo many times you could do it in your sleep.'

'Yes.'

'So when your music starts up, you're going to begin by taking off your bangles . . . like a stripper.'

And so it begins. Apparently oblivious of the audience laughter, Cindy tosses his bangles one by one into the crowd, where they're scrabbled for as trophies.

Kurt Campbell smiles, but he's always watchful. A professional.

The taped music – no originality required *here* – bumps and grinds along its languorous, familiar catwalk.

Up comes the skirt, to howls and wolf whistles. Cindy feels a real sweat breaking out. How easy and pleasant it must be to surrender to hypnosis . . . but what a careful combination of attention and detachment is required to carry out the commands to the letter while remaining *un*hypnotized.

The pop of the suspender, a glimpse of knicker – from the rear, naturally – and off comes the first stocking, landing at the feet of a young man who hesitates, unable to decide whether retrieving it will be his

81

moment of celebrity or mark him out as gay, poor dab.

Off comes the second stocking, and Cindy aims for the camera he isn't supposed to be aware of, knowing what a nice shot this will make, but the stocking falls short.

One minute, Cindy estimates, before the rather risqué hypnotism sketch must be wound up and the famous National Lottery machine activated.

He drops a black shoulder strap, provocatively flexing the arm muscles to an intake of breath from the audience – most of them at last having come to believe that this is the real thing; you can tell by the sudden hush.

While young Kurt Campbell, of course, *knows* that it's real. And that he must presently bring Cindy out of his trance.

Cindy does an exotic twirl, turning his other shoulder to the audience and to Camera One. On the way round he comes face to face with Kurt, and Kurt's face is impassive; he's leaning back in his cane chair, legs stretched out, relaxed, enjoying the show. The music swells to its final climax. After the second strap is lowered, the music will fade and Kurt will look at his watch in apparent alarm, come to his feet, wander casually over and stop the performance, bringing Cindy safely out of trance . . . bemused and appealing to the audience to tell him what appalling atrocities he's committed.

Down comes the strap. Cindy feels his bodice start to slide. Take it carefully now, or two foam-rubber tits will drop out and go rolling into the audience. Trophies indeed!

The music fades.

Nothing happens. Cindy does another twirl.

Which shows him that Kurt, smiling complacently, has remained seated.

The music continues at background level.

Christ.

Cindy continues his voluptuous weaving, the bodice continues to slip – thank the Lord he doesn't have a hairy chest – and still Kurt Campbell doesn't move . . . Kurt Campbell who firmly believes, because he's done this thousands of times before and is absolutely sure of his power, that he has Cindy in deep trance and about to disclose his small, male nipples.

And this is not merely mischief, because Kurt knows that Cindy's act depends on that continued ambivalence . . . *is he or isn't he?* – with so many levels to that question – and that the revelation of his padding will literally be the end of him . . . the end of his credibility, the end of his career even on Bournemouth Pier.

Why does Campbell want to do this to him? What has he ever done to the boy to inspire such cruelly reckless disdain?

And what is Cindy to do now?

Up in the gallery, Jo, the producer, will be in a panic, on her feet, probably unsure – because she's quite young for this job – how to stop it.

Now some members of the audience have started a rhythmic slow handclap. This is definitely not in the running order. Cindy does a last, desperate twirl. Kurt is smiling. The *shit*.

Cindy pauses. Pushes out his chest.

The spotlight encircles him. Cindy backs up and it follows him. He's standing now in front of his chair.

The crowd whoops. Kurt no longer smiles, no longer has that certainty.

The moment has come. No avoiding it.

The pink suitcase still standing, half in spot, next to Cindy's empty chair, emits a raucous squawk.

'*Get 'em off, you old tart!*' shrieks Kelvyn Kite.

When Kurt Campbell started the machine for the draw, a number of people, Cindy among them, noticed that his smile was tainted by a pure, black fury.

The winning numbers were six, fifteen, thirty-six, forty-two, forty-three and forty-six.

Kurt did not look at Cindy again, but Cindy could almost see the rage shooting out of him like thick, black arrows.

When the team gathered in the green room for a drink afterwards, Kurt had gone. Jo Shepherd dragged Cindy into a corner. She was white.

'*Christ . . . !*'

'I'm sorry, Jo.'

'What the hell *happened*?' There were great sweat stains under the arms of Jo's blouse.

Cindy was calm, but no longer high, no longer living in the moment.

'I think', he said, 'that young Kurt forgot his cue.'

'He bloody didn't. He wanted you . . .' Jo was near to tears '. . . all fucked up in front of twenty million viewers. I knew it was the wrong thing, I bloody *knew* it.'

Cindy blinked. 'I'm sorry, lovely?'

Jo shook her curls. 'Never mind, you got out of it. You turned the tables. You're a brilliant man, Cindy, we all thought you were completely under. How did you do that?'

'Wasn't me, lovely. Kelvyn, it was.'

Jo was smiling and shuddering at the same time.

'I'll tell you what, Cindy – public humiliation on the

84

National Lottery . . . that guy is never going to forget this. I think you've probably made yourself an enemy for life.'

'Yes.' Cindy bent down and flipped open the case. 'I suppose I have.' He extracted Kelvyn Kite, all beak and feathers and big rolling eyes. 'There's unfortunate, isn't it?'

7

Most of the night, Grayle had avoided it.

Ersula. The matter of Spirit.

She'd taken down the numbers of two hotels in Stroud, but it was clear Persephone Callard was in no fit state to drive her there and she wouldn't have a cab calling here for Grayle – there were already too many people who knew the house wasn't empty.

No way out of this.

Past midnight: she lay on her back, in her sweater, under an eiderdown on the iron-framed, brass-headed bed, in the plain, square Victorian bedroom with its small iron fireplace and a view into the dark woods.

From the next room she heard Persephone Callard snort and then moan in her sleep.

They'd eaten microwaved Marks & Spencer's Chinese food – Callard leaving most of hers – and then drank and talked for over four hours, with a lot of stuff coming out.

But none of it explaining what Callard was hiding from. Either she was playing with Grayle or whatever it was really could only be said to Marcus Bacton.

*　　*　　*

Fathers. They talked about fathers.

They'd discussed Dr Erlend Underhill, eminent Harvard Professor of American and European History, who had two daughters: Ersula who, in her father's image, was studious, serious, humourless and an archaeologist, and Grayle, of whose writings Lyndon McAffrey, Deputy City Editor of the *New York Courier*, had once said, *This may be journalism, but not as we know it.*

They'd spoken of Stephen Callard, the knighted career diplomat, who had become besotted with a lovely black nurse in Kingston, Jamaica, brought her home to be his wife, have his child and die.

'So what does your father think about what you do?' Grayle had asked.

'What I *did*.' Persephone Callard's eyes were hot but hard in the candlelight.

Grayle had accepted a second weak Scotch, but Callard's tumbler remained on the mantelpiece, and Grayle kept thinking of what she'd said earlier: *When I'm pissed I don't receive.*

'So how does he feel about it, your father?'

Callard shrugged. 'I don't know how he feels now. I haven't seen him in two years. He's over seventy, spends most of the time in Italy, studiously avoiding the kind of English newspaper that might contain items about me and . . . what I did.'

'He's embarrassed?'

'He's glad I'm rich and going my own way. I don't think he's really wanted to have anything to do with me since I turned twelve. I was the only woman who reminded him of my mother at her ripest and also the one woman he couldn't fuck. Hardly remind him of her now, would I? Look at me!'

87

'Why are you doing this to yourself?'

'Maybe I want to die,' Callard snapped. 'Maybe I want to die and find out if there's any truth at all in the kind of shit I've been feeding people for the past fifteen years.'

As always when she lay alone in strange beds, sleep receded like the tide on a long beach, leaving Grayle cold and tense and thinking, *Why am I here?* On every level of the question.

She knew – because he'd said so several times – that Marcus firmly expected her, at some stage, to leave her rented cottage in the village of St Mary's, on the border of Herefordshire and Monmouthshire, to take up a *real* career.

She kept telling herself she wasn't going to do this, at least until *The Vision* was making enough money for Marcus to hire another writer and maybe a sub-editor too.

So perhaps she was destined to be there all her life.

There should, of course, be a man. There always used to be a man. And yet she'd been faintly horrified when her old boyfriend, Lucas, the Greenwich Village art-dealer, had written to her saying he'd be over on a buying trip in the spring and maybe they could like *get together*. Cool, refined, Ferrari-driving Lucas, who talked all night about the need for an inner life and would just hate ever to have time for one.

Lucas, Grayle decided, had his place in history and that era had been covered.

It was hard to find a man with an inner life. Maybe this was what drew her back to Marcus. Not in *that* way, of course, but Marcus, even though he raged and threw things, was certainly the father she kind of wished she'd had.

Grayle also thought sometimes about Bobby Maiden, the English cop. Who'd died in the hospital after a hit-and-run incident – and then been resuscitated and come out of it different. Events had tied them together. Losing loved ones to the same killer.

It was Bobby – mercifully, not Grayle – who had been there when Ersula's decaying body came to light.

'Why do you say it's shit?' Grayle had asked eventually, when the candle was burning low in the pewter dish. 'Why do you think you were feeding people shit?'

And the woman had bowed her head, her tobacco hair falling forward.

'It's a gift. It *is* a gift. You can't believe it yourself at first. Dead people out there, just queuing up to talk to you. So many of them that you have to appoint an agent over there to filter them.'

'Agent?'

'Spirit guide. I've had several. Even a Red Indian. A *Native* fucking *American*. I said, "Piss off, Mr Running Bear, whatever you call yourself, you want to completely ruin my credibility?" But he stuck around, the poor old sod. He was very friendly in his gruff way, I quite took to him. All the clichés – you get *all* the bloody clichés. Table-rapping – that works as well. I'm not saying scores of people didn't fake it, but . . . it happens.'

'Ectoplasm?'

'Why not? Not in my experience, but there's evidence for it. And it's a word that sounds good, isn't it? Sounds scientific. That was the big thing when all

89

this started in the mid-nineteenth century. It had to be seen as another great scientific leap forward, like electricity and photography. All these huge developments were linked into spiritualism – it wasn't religion, it was human scientific knowledge crossing the final frontier. Man was becoming so clever so fast that it was obvious we were going to solve the mystery of death, sooner rather than later.'

'I did a piece on all that once,' Grayle said, 'but the evidence was that it was nearly all one big scam.'

'No.' Callard blinked balefully. 'That's not the scam. Or rather, much of it was, but it's not the one I'm talking about. I haven't produced ectoplasm, but I've had materialization. Visuals. Energy forms.'

'Ghosts?'

'You believe in ghosts, perhaps?' Callard eyeing her thoughtfully.

'I . . . think so.'

'You've seen?'

'I don't know.'

'You do know, Grayle. No-one who's seen has any real doubts.'

'So why is it shit?'

Callard stretched her long neck. She was looking firmer now, less sick. OK, beautiful; no getting around that.

'For a number of years, I'd go into trance and receive these clear, comprehensible messages from what I had every reason to believe were departed spirits. The fact that the messages were mainly banal in the extreme was neither here nor there. One day Einstein might come through and it would be different. Meanwhile, I relayed the trivial messages to my well-heeled clients – sort of people who would *never* consult Mrs Higgins in her council flat – and everyone was happy.'

Grayle on the edge of her chair by this time, never having heard a medium putting down the profession. Callard was something else.

'And then Einstein *did* come through,' Callard said.

'Oh boy.'

'Albert Einstein. *The* Albert Einstein. Saying just what you'd expect from him. How disappointed he was that modern physicists had failed to develop his ideas. How he was full of regrets at the way he'd treated his first wife, but they were blissfully reunited now. He also said that, from his present position, he was able to see where some of his theories fell down.'

'How was that?'

'You have scientific knowledge?'

'Not to speak of.'

'Me neither. I offered him automatic writing to explain, and the results looked like the authentic minute calculations of a mathematical genius. Lots of little brackets and bubbles and algebraic symbols. My agent, Nancy, got frightfully excited and had them photocopied and dispatched discreetly to a certain professor in Munich or somewhere. Who said, of course . . .'

'That it was complete horseshit?'

Callard sighed.

'Why does that always happen?' Grayle wondered sadly. 'The psychic artists produce Van Gogh plastic sunflowers, and the psychic composers . . . you'd think Mozart would reach sublime new heights, being dead and gone to heaven and all, instead of . . . some pale, music-school imitation. Why?'

'I don't know why. Or, rather, I think I do now. It's

91

because mediumship, as it's usually practised, is a low-level art . . . mundane and mediocre. It attracts low-level, inconsequential dross. Psychically speaking, the pits. Spirit shit.'

'But still from like . . . out there?'

'Who knows whether out there is really *in* there? In the end, I can't tell you where the messages come from – perhaps some area of the brain we don't yet understand. I just don't believe they come from where we think they do when we first start to receive them. One comes to realize that the challenge is to separate the truth from the random disinformation.'

Grayle had drunk some more whisky from the greasy glass, journalistically excited, spiritually disappointed.

'But it's all soooo plausible when you need it, Grayle. When you've lost someone.'

'I guess.'

'So.' Persephone Callard leaning on an elbow, hunched up in a corner of the Victorian sofa in that state of drab sobriety that comes after long days of serious drinking. 'Would you like to speak to your dead sister, tonight?'

Grayle's mouth was suddenly parched in spite of the Scotch. She shook her head, alarmed.

The woman grinned at her discomfort, displaying white, perfect teeth in the candlelight.

'What have you got to lose, Grayle? You might get some special insight. You might achieve peace of mind.'

Grayle shaking her head.

'Perhaps there's something you'd like to have told her before she died.'

Grayle staring into the crimson cinders.

'. . . something you wish you'd shared.'

'We didn't have too much in common outside of parents,' Grayle said tightly. She looked up. 'And anyway . . . you don't think it really would be my sister.'

'Who am I to say? Only you would know that.'

Grayle said nothing, feeling trapped. God damn it, why couldn't Marcus just have written, told Callard he'd come see her when he was over the flu.

'You're afraid, aren't you, Holy Grayle?'

'Maybe I just don't want to learn something which may, if what you say is correct, have no basis in truth.'

'Too close, eh?'

'Huh?'

'I mean, it's OK when it's somebody else. When it's journalism.'

'You are very astute,' Grayle said hoarsely.

'Family connections, where there's been a difficult death, are usually the strongest. Things which need to be explained. I can feel she's near you. Some of the time. Now. She wants to come, I think.'

'No.'

'You know, when I said there'd been manifestations . . . the strongest one, the one which everyone in the room saw, was a mother of twins who died in childbirth. Both sisters were there, grown up now. And we had the seance in the room – I didn't know this at the time – where she'd actually died. She had the babies at home – she'd had two already – and she was . . . Anyway, this was a bungalow, and it was the living room now, not a bedroom any more. And there were photos of the mother all around the walls, and her favourite things scattered about . . . clothes, handbags. And all the family – the husband, the twins, another sister – all of them there. And the room was dense with her before we started . . .'

'I don't think I want to know about this,' Grayle said.

Well, of *course* there were things she wanted to say to Ersula. Things she wanted to ask.

Grayle stared at the ceiling. There were times when the dead, unhappy Ersula had appeared to her in dreams. Or what had seemed, with hindsight, to be dreams.

How very close we all were to madness.

And yes, she'd been afraid.

From the next room Persephone Callard, sorceress, con-woman, cried out crossly in her sleep. Maybe turning over, in her subconscious mind, all those things she wouldn't tell Grayle but might just tell Marcus.

Dark stuff. Grayle wasn't sure she wanted to know about it.

Like, what had really happened to make her conclude that the Spirit World was not to be trusted? It surely went beyond the Einstein incident; there were so many well-documented cases of earthly genius failing to survive death, great talent coming back half-assed.

'So *this just came over you, this fit of conscience about misleading people – it just hit you, and you couldn't do it any more?*'

'*Something like that.*'

No way. It was more than some kind of crisis of faith. Something more personally traumatic.

Grayle went to sleep thinking about it and dreamed of a cavernous, candlelit ballroom, empty but full of noise . . . a clamour of voices, a hubbub of the unseen.

Occasionally she would catch a phrase which seemed to make thrilling sense, then it was gone and unremembered. And then the mush of voices was pierced by the purity of a thin scream, and Grayle was awake in a much smaller room with no candles.

And no voices, only another scream.

What?

8

She was still lying on top of the bed, and the heating had gone off and she was freezing, hands and legs numb, and all she could think about was the dormitory in the private school somewhere in the south Midlands, the night the big window exploded, all the girls screaming. Paranormal things happened around Persephone Callard, Queen of the Unseen.

But this was just one scream. It came from downstairs. It was a real scream. Grayle went into foetal position for warmth, rubbing her shins, and the next thought she had was:

Scam. Persephone Callard faking some psychic-shock drama.

Don't respond. Don't do the obvious.

What time was it? She couldn't see her watch, only the pinprick red light of the mobile phone charging up at a power point in a corner. It didn't matter what time it was; this had to be a scam, aimed at Grayle to scare her. Why else had Callard wanted her to stay the night? She was a manipulator, a conjurer, a stager of effects.

Grayle lay there for maybe half a minute, trying to rationalize it, to will away the fear. But fear was what screaming was all about and when it started again it was instantly contagious.

She heard, 'Get the *fuck*—'

Callard.

Those were the only intelligible words – Callard's voice, rising, then cut off, muffled into a squeal of outrage. Oh Jesus. Grayle was rolling off the bed, pulling on her skirt, feeling for her shoes, seeing a beam of light bounce from the window frame.

She stumbled over there, barefoot on pine boards, recalling that the bedroom overlooked the rear of the lodge and the woodland. A light from the woods? A poacher, a lamper of hares?

The bedroom seemed to be directly above the kitchen, this window right over the back door. Through which she saw someone entering Mysleton Lodge, following a flashlight, its beam like pale grey tubing in the night mist.

Someone coming into the lodge. Someone big. A man.

Grayle reeled from the window, hand at her mouth.

JUSTIN, JUSTIN, JUSTIN.

The name going on and off like a neon sign in her head. Hadn't she picked up all along that he was a bad guy, a small-time psycho on the prowl? If he was back, she was scared, sure, but – damn it – angry, too. That *bastard*.

She located her shoes, squirmed into them, moved quietly in the darkness to the bedroom door, turning the handle slowly, holding her breath. Because Justin would have no idea that she was still here. Justin would think she was in a hotel in Stroud.

Justin would think that Persephone Callard was here alone.

He'd come after *her*?

Struts around Stroud in her fancy clothes and her nose in the air . . . nothing worse than coloured girls when they reckon they're a cut above . . . You know what her mother was, don't you?

He'd broken in. Callard had heard him and gone downstairs and—

Grayle stood at the top of the narrow stairs, discovering she was panting. Discovering that she did not want to go down. Flattening herself against the wall, beside a small landing window, through which she could see nothing but dark mist.

And so cold. *Jesus, help me.*

Calm down. Go back upstairs, find the cellphone and call the cops. Right. That makes sense. That makes *sense*.

Unless, of course, there is a reasonable explanation for all this and you just had a bad dream after an uncomfortable night following a stressful day.

Fuck it. Check it out.

Vague scufflings from downstairs, but no more screams. Grayle went down one step.

Clack.

No carpet; she'd forgotten that. She sat down on the topmost stair, pulled off her shoes. From below, she heard, *mmmm, mmmm, mmmm,* and what sounded like the skidding of a chair across a hard floor. Grayle stood up slowly and began to edge down the stairs, her back to the wall. Wishing there was some kind of weapon to hand, but all she had was her shoes with two-inch wooden heels. She gripped one by its toe, raising it over her shoulder like an axe.

The stairs came out directly into the parlour with its low ceiling, its blue window – curtains pulled back now – and its sour aroma of old alcohol.

There was no movement in here. No glimmer from the remains of the fire. What she ought to have done was bring the phone with her – damn all use plugged into the wall up in the bedroom.

Grayle stepped into the room.

Noises to the right. A closed door. The kitchen. A line of yellow light appeared underneath the door. Behind it, a man said, 'I don't *want* to hurt you. Can you hear me? Are you listening to me, you slag?'

Grayle froze up. Oh . . . my . . . *God*!

It was not Justin's voice.

Which drained away the anger, leaving the fear. Grayle felt a trembling in her bowels. Justin was scary and repulsive, but at least he was a known danger. She sucked in a lot of air, went back hard against the wall . . .

. . . the one with all the rustic implements on it, and her shoulder hit the bowsaw, pushing it into the wall with – oh no, oh *no* . . . this loud shivering *twang*.

And another of the tools was dislodged and it fell against the bowsaw and she tried to catch it and failed, and then there was, in the silence of the lodge, this huge, strident clash of collapsing metal.

No place to go. Grayle just shrank into the wall.

In dreams, in nightmares, there was usually an inevitability about a situation. It would descend into ultimate blackness and then you would wake up. Some part of your subconscious knew there was a fail-safe, a trip mechanism, and so you'd find yourself kind of beckoning the blackness: *come on, come on, let's get this over*.

In reality, you knew there would be no awakening,

so you always held out that hope, right up to the end, that it was going to be all right. That there was something you didn't know – like, in this case, that Callard had an ex-husband or an estranged partner, and what was happening here was some overblown domestic incident, loud and emotional but just between the two of them, and that when they saw you standing there they'd just be embarrassed as hell.

The kitchen door was opened. Not flung open; it was done without hurry, real casual.

Two men came in with the yellow light.

For a moment, they were standing together in the doorway, looking at her in silence. And these two men, they were wearing kind of army camouflage trousers and dark green army jerseys and their hands were in these tight, black leather gloves and their heads in these dark woollen hoods with eyeholes.

Grayle was frozen to the wall, the final hope shrivelling like a burst balloon in her stomach. She couldn't speak.

When one of the men moved into the parlour, she could see Persephone Callard on her knees, on the kitchen floor, and she was bleeding, great gouts of bright red blood splashed all over her long white nightdress.

'*Oh* God,' Grayle finally said, the words gulped out, up and down on the breath, like vomit.

Callard's hands were taped up behind her back. A strip of black, shiny tape across her mouth reminded Grayle of Justin's big black moustache.

'What . . .' Grayle's jaw trembling. 'What have you . . . ?'

And stopped. The big red blotches were not blood, just the pattern on the nightdress.

100

But the tape was still tape, Callard still trussed and gagged.

'Jus . . . Justin?'

Because, one of these guys, she hadn't heard him talk, and so – the final, *final* hope – it might still be him. Might be Justin. That is, one of them might be basically human.

Neither of them spoke. Callard stared up at Grayle, her eyes hot and wild.

Why?

Why were they here? There was nothing of value to take, anybody could see that. Maybe in the big house there was plenty, but they hadn't broken into the big house. These were not small-time local felons come to steal your TV and your VCR for drug money. These were men with no faces. Men with no fingerprints. Fit-looking men in army clothes. Serious men.

They didn't even ask who she was.

Because it didn't matter. She was here and she'd walked into what they were doing, and that was enough.

'OK,' Grayle said, 'you get out of here. You get . . .' her voice rising higher and higher '. . . the fuck out of here. You hear me?'

They glanced at one another just once and then they both looked back at Grayle and began to move slowly towards her, their arms hanging away from their bodies. One of them . . . his fingers in the black, tight gloves . . . his fingers were beginning to flex.

The thing was, she had no recollection of taking it down, only finding it was there in her right hand: the hedging tool that was like a butcher's knife. The hacker.

101

It was even heavier than it looked. Finally she had to lift it with both hands, stepping away from the rural museum wall, the rustic armoury wall, and swinging it hard back.

And it must still have been real sharp because when it went into the guy's face it was like slicing a green pepper. Until it made it through to the bone.

Part Two

From *Bang to Wrongs: A Bad Boy's Book,*
by GARY SEWARD

The night my mum died I went out and trashed a church.

Some schoolmates and I, we done a newsagent's that day and had to hurt the geezer when he was stupid enough to 'have a go'.

But my mum, she was a Christian her whole life and never really hurt nobody, and He let this happen. It even happened almost in front of a church, St Mark's. The driver was pissed and so it was his fault, obviously, and I heard he himself had an unfortunate accident some years later, but that was nothing to do with me as I was fifty miles away at the time, which I was able to prove to the police. But it was the Big Geezer I was after that night because He had let it happen and that was inexcusable, so I took a Stanley knife to His altar cloth and then I carved some choice words on the side of His pulpit and smashed some other stuff; I was in a real bitter frenzy.

I realize now that what happened to my mum was a profound lesson for me, in relation to the meek inheriting the earth and all that old toffee, but I was too young for philosophy then. I just did not want to believe my old mum was truly gone, and that was when I started to see spiritualists and mediums and such. I did not see why God should be able to get away with taking people out so that you lose contact for good. It was a liberty I could not tolerate.

9

He was driving down through darkened Cheshire in a state verging on real fear. *The genetic code*, Bobby Maiden thought. *What if there's no breaking the genetic code?*

He drove along the old A49, over the river – or was it the canal? – with all those iron bridges, towards the southern suburbs of Warrington, which went on for ever.

It was as if the old man was still in the car. Sitting up in the passenger seat, straight as a lamp post, glaring out suspiciously at the desultory night traffic. Noting the speeders and the ones with a brake light not working. Eyeing sullen youths outside an off-licence. *Little toerags. Anybody under sixteen out past nine p.m. should be pulled in and banged up for the night. See that woman under the streetlamp, end of that wall? With the red hair? On her own? Bloody brass, tell 'em a mile off. Warn her off now, I would. Respectable people live in them houses.*

Yes, Dad.

In the mornings Maiden had taken to looking carefully in the bathroom mirror for signs of his eyes hardening and growing closer together, his lips tightening between deep, disciplinary radials.

Couldn't see it. Could he?

Every six weeks or so, usually on a Wednesday night if he wasn't working, Maiden would drive north and take his dad for a meal. Tonight they'd been to this new Beefeater, out towards Irlam.

'I like a good steak, me,' Norman Plod had declared, as he always did. 'Nowt beats a good steak, done rare, for keeping your eyes sharp and your gut tight.'

Then he was staring at his son's plate with a look of blatant dismay not dissimilar to the one which had bloomed on his hard face that night, many years ago, when Bobby had expressed a wish to go to some nancyfied art college.

'What the bloody hell's *that*? Turning into a bloody rabbit are we, lad?'

'I had a big lunch, Dad.'

'Watching our weight, are we? By Christ, policemen eating *rabbit food*. No wonder it's not safe to walk the bloody streets.'

'Stomach's a bit off, actually,' Maiden had murmured.

Ashamed at the deceit, but this was not a good time to explain to Norman Plod about becoming a vegetarian.

In fact, there never was going to be a good time, was there?

'Too much ale, eh?' Norman looked up, lips wet with bloodied gravy. He winked. 'I know what it's like when the lads get together after a fine result, a grand collar.'

Maiden had been telling Norman about the neat

108

smack circuit which Elham CID had broken after two weeks of freezing nights with a video camera on a church tower overlooking the Redbarn estate.

'Excellent stuff. It's just a bloody shame Mr Riggs weren't there to see it,' Norman said.

Meaning Superintendent Martin Riggs, now early retired.

'Mmm,' Maiden said, non-committally.

Norman had met Riggs just once, while visiting his son in hospital. But he'd followed the newspaper reports, read between the lines, knew Riggs was Old Force and his lad'd had the best boss he could wish for in these slack times.

'Because', Norman said, stoking his mouth with steak, the Brylcreem shining on his fuse-wire hair, 'whichever way you look at it, busting them bastards – that were a direct result of the Riggs regime. Tight as a drum. Zero bloody tolerance. No little toerag shifted a bag of pills without Mr Riggs knew about it.'

'Mmm,' Bobby Maiden said.

How very true that was.

He's gone. All right? He got out. You dropped him off at his bungalow half an hour ago.

But the smell of Brylcreem remained, half-manifesting the ghost of Norman Plod. Once a copper, always a copper. *I'll be seeing you, lad* – Norman's familiar finger-wagging warning to the toerags. Maiden almost snatched a glance in the driving mirror just to make sure that it wasn't Norman's eyes glaring back.

Norman Maiden: still very much alive, but his glowering ghost was following Bobby Maiden around. And getting closer? Bobby was thirty-eight years old; at what age did you start turning into your father?

While they were parked in front of the bungalow, Norman had asked his son, 'They told you who's replacing him yet? Mr Riggs? Likely one of them shiny-arsed, university fast-trackers, am I right?'

Maiden had told him how, in the light of Riggs's sudden retirement, there'd been some reorganization in Elham Division. From now on, there wouldn't be a Superintendent based at Elham; there'd be a Chief Inspector over the uniforms and for the first time – an experiment – an acting DCI in charge of CID.

On the way up here, he'd thought he might discuss this in greater depth with his dad. In the end he couldn't face it.

It took him just over an hour to drive back to Elham. A diversion, due to the laying of new water pipes under the ring road, brought him into town past the General Hospital.

He found himself turning in between the two white lamps.

Just like . . .

. . . the old days.

The sprog coppers hanging round, drinking Sister Anderson's strong coffee – these wee cops often smelling of vomit, arising from that first severed head on the hard shoulder or the fried child on the burnt-out back seat.

Casualty: where young coppers and young nurses met at moments of high stress, a great aphrodisiac. Casualty was a government-funded dating agency.

Wasn't quite the same these days, mind, now that man-hours were rationed and the police had their own counselling service – which, of course, took a whole lot more out of the police budget than Sister Andy's coffee cost the Health Service.

She closed the door against the warm blast of Accident and Emergency, sat down at her desk and motioned Bobby Maiden to the spare plastic-backed chair. Looked him over for signs of damage.

'And there was me thinking it was all coming together for you, Bobby.'

'And me thinking you were leaving to become an alternative practitioner down at St Mary's,' Bobby Maiden said.

He sipped at the coffee and winced. Andy smiled. Still killer stuff, eh?

'It'll happen,' she said. 'One day soon, I'll be just a memory here. A grating Glaswegian growl in the night. A stale smell of high-tar smoke in the lavvy.'

Bobby shook his head. 'You hate this place far too much ever to leave.'

'Jesus God,' Andy said. 'This is what the psychological profiler course did for you, is it?'

He smiled ruefully. 'What the psychological profiler course did is *far* worse than that.'

'Oh?' Andy peered into his eyes. The boy had been looking so much better lately, too, the brain-stem problem maybe causing less numbness. She could tell he still had some pain over the eye, though.

'It put me in direct line for promotion.'

'Oh aye?'

'So they've offered me acting DCI.'

'Acting?'

'Eventual permanence implied.'

Andy thought about this. 'That would be more of a desk job, right?'

Bobby nodded grimly.

'Well,' she said, 'for a start, you should try and have your desk facing east and make sure you've no' got a door at your back.'

'*Feng shui*?'

'Welsh style. Cindy Mars-Lewis dropped in while you were away and rearranged ma furniture. I'm a much calmer person now, is that no' apparent?'

'He's been *here*?'

'Just passing through. He was sorry tae miss you, Bobby.'

So they talked for a while about Cindy's new fame on the Lottery Show. Bobby had only seen him the once. Andy said she was amazed how the guy kept getting away with it.

'Stands up there and attacks everything the Lottery stands for. Rails at the audience for their greed. Warns them it'll all end in tears. No' him, of course, it's the bird. *How dare you say that, Kelvyn? Back in the case for you!*' Andy chuckled. 'Audience loves him. I reckon even the boss guys at the BBC believe, in some weird, subliminal way, that they are two separate personalities, him and that bird.'

'Shamanism,' Bobby said thoughtfully. 'I wonder if they know.'

'Ach, it wouldnae matter a damn – he's got the charm tae carry it off. Just like nobody ever asks about his sexuality and gets a satisfactory answer. So . . . does acting DCI give you a key to the executive washroom or are you still standing side by side with the guys figuring tae shaft you?'

Oh aye, Andy remembered Riggs. And all the things you couldn't say about him, not out loud.

The one time Andy had actually met the Superintendent, he was urgently looking for Bobby. Because Riggs knew that Bobby knew. About Riggs.

And about Tony Parker, the 'businessman'. Friend of Riggs from London, invited to Elham to 'regularize' a rather 'chaotic' drugs scene. Tony's new system offering small dealers two simple options: either shelter under the Parker umbrella or get yourself very swiftly shopped to the police – thus providing the new chief with a terrific clean-up rate and a wonderful reputation in no time at all.

That broad, beaming face in the local paper week after week. Guest speaker at the Rotary Club. Guest of honour at the Magistrates' Association dinner. And a copper's copper, too, always popular with the troops. Excepting Bobby Maiden. Bobby had known Riggs from when he was with the Met. Known what he was.

Now Tony Parker was dead – natural causes – and Riggs had taken early retirement and calmly walked away before any of the shit could reach the Vent-Axia.

'Where is he now, Bobby?' Andy poured herself a killer coffee. 'Tax exile on the Costa del Crime?'

'Oh, no. Worcester. You heard of Forcefield Security?'

Andy shook her head. 'They on the level?'

'Far as I know, absolutely reputable.' Bobby sighed. 'Riggs is executive director. Nothing like a distinguished retired senior police officer to bestow that aura of tough respectability.'

'Is there no bloody justice, Bobby? That scumbag tried tae have you killed. What about the guys close to him? Beattie?'

'Still in there. And a few others. You can tell who they are. They're the ones keep a formal space between

113

you and them. They call you "sir" instead of "boss".'

No doubt blaming Bobby for having to live off their pay packets again. So now he was going to have to organize guys who saw him as having profited from Riggs's downfall while their own personal finances had taken a tumble. Who needed that?

'Can you no' apply for a transfer?'

Shook his head. 'Not so soon after being virtually offered promotion. Obviously, I'd like to get out altogether, but what would I do?' Still shaking his head, the old injury affected by the hard fluorescent light. 'Sorry, Andy, I didn't intend to burden you with this. I was just . . . passing. Just had supper with the old man. Who thinks Riggs was God.'

'You never told him the truth?'

'Like he'd believe me?'

'These other guys know you've been offered the job? Beattie?'

'I don't know.'

Sister Andy sighed. It was a terrible indictment of how isolated Bobby was in this scrappy, bent little Midlands town. In his personal life too. Mother dead in a road accident when he was a kiddie. Some years divorced now from Lizzie Turner, the avaricious wee nurse he'd met as a sprog cop, on this very ward. And then there was Em, who was funny and smart and would have been so very right for him, had she not become the penultimate victim of the psycho-killer calling himself the Green Man. That whole episode, coming so soon after the personal death experience, throwing Bobby clean off his axis.

It was flattering to think he came back here because of Andy, as some kind of tough mother-figure. More likely he kept returning because this was where his

114

heart stopped and was restarted. Where he'd died and where his second life began.

'So, how long before you officially start as DCI?'

'Acting.'

'Yeah, yeah.'

'About three weeks,' Bobby said. He had some leave owing. Was thinking he might go away for a few days.

'On your own?'

He shrugged. Said he could do some painting. Find a lonely shore. Solway Firth or somewhere. Get really cold and wet and miserable.

Andy had one of Bobby's paintings in her house. Sea and sky merging in shades of flat grey. The work of a guy who was always looking for the vanishing point. Most people, they had a near-death experience, they became born-again Christians or just wandered around in the warm glow of knowing there was *something else*. Bobby Maiden had to be difficult.

'Just a thought,' she said. 'Would you no' like to go spend a few days at Marcus Bacton's place?'

Andy's office door opened, Nurse Kirsty Brady's big face in the gap. 'Mr Trilling . . . ?' Brady made a face. The wee nurses were all a little scared of Mr Trilling.

'Aye, I'm coming,' Andy said. 'Hey, give it a thought, Bobby. I believe, ah . . . I gather the wee American girl's back.'

'Grayle?'

'Trying to put *The Vision* to rights.'

Bobby Maiden rolled his eyes. 'Then she's got enough problems.'

Because he never thought he'd stay long in Elham, he was still living in the same apartment in this grimy Victorian heap in Old Church Street. One day they'd extend the bypass and the Victorian block would vanish.

The flat wasn't much more than a studio now. He liked it smelling of paints. He liked having the work in progress, a triptych of big canvases, covering a whole wall. Another life in progress.

The sequence was coming together from drawings he'd done, photos he'd taken, the last time he was down at St Mary's – the three canvases joining up to show the line of the Black Mountains at dawn under mist. The point being that, viewed from St Mary's, the Black Mountains were featureless, a long bank. But the whole of Wales lay behind them.

He remembered what it was like going up there with Cindy Mars-Lewis. Cindy with his Celtic shaman's drum and his shaman's cloak of feathers – ridiculous and yet unexpectedly dramatic, a big bird against the skyline. Cindy starting to chant, and it was like he'd thrown his voice into the mountains.

Meeting place (THUMP)
Meeting place (THUMP)
Here the Sky
Here the Earth
HEAR the Earth
Meeting place (THUMP, THUMP)

A weird bloke in a bird suit stirring up primeval forces. Now also the man with the big-money balls. Bizarre.

Maiden unlocked the communal front door, entering the hallway. Keeping the keys in hand as he strolled across to the door of his ground-floor flat. And found he didn't need any keys for this one.

*   *   *

OK, he wasn't expecting it – was anybody, ever? – but it was no big, devastating shock to find the door of his flat splintered again, all around the lock.

The first time this happened to you, even as a copper, you felt sick, invaded. You were never going to settle until you'd seen the bastards in court. The second time, it was a profound inconvenience but it didn't keep you awake.

This was the fourth time. Maiden felt weary. There was nothing worth stealing in there, except the portable TV and the CD-player. Three hundred quid the lot.

Still, he went carefully. One time, they'd still been inside. A steel toecap had messed up his left eye.

He kicked open the door and stepped back into the hallway.

Nothing. Maiden was sure he could somehow tell these days if a place was empty, that he could sense a presence. He walked in and switched on the lights. Stood in the doorway and looked around.

Nothing. Everything as it was. The CD-player on its shelf, the TV on its stand over by the bricked-up fireplace.

He went back to look at the door. Unsubtle. A crowbar job. There would have been some noise involved, unavoidable, but it didn't look as though they'd cared. Five flats in the building, but two of them empty. Students in the others, out most nights.

But why? What was the point? They hadn't even turned the place over. He went back in, kicking something which skittered across the boards and finished up on the rug.

Stanley knife with the blade out. He didn't touch it.

He looked across at the wall with the three canvases hanging on it.

Stood gazing at the joined-up picture for nearly a minute.

They must have spent quite some time on it, because the lettering was quite regular, spread over all three canvases, each letter about three inches high, carved out of the misty flank of the Black Mountains.

It looked like the Hollywood sign.

It said

CONGRATULATIONS SIR

10

Having been stormed in the fifteenth century by the Welsh pretender, Owain Glyndwr, and later plundered for stone by generations of local builders, the castle's surviving tower was probably only half its original height.

But still the best place from which to observe invaders.

Yes, yes, this was a little early in the year for invasion. Nearly a month before Easter and the first carloads of cretins. *Can I buy a guidebook? Where are the toilets? Do you sell ice-cream?*

Read the bloody signs! Marcus would roar. *Piss off!*

Continuing problem when your house was inside the remains of a medieval castle. It seemed entirely beyond the comprehension of the average bloody tourist that not all historic masonry was there to trample over, picnic on, have sex under or turn into a bastard adventure playground.

. . . and if that child jumps twenty feet to his death, under the impression that all castles are bloody bouncy castles, I don't want to hear you whining to me, madam!

But all this was weeks away. At six-fifteen on a brisk

March morning the highest part of the castle was a place where a sick, congested man could go to breathe.

After – at best – a fitful night's sleep, Marcus had woken at five, his nasal tubes like concrete and his temper in rags. He'd gone stumping across the farm-yard to the sawn-off tower, stumbling up the remaining spiralled stone steps to emerge into the grey-pink dawn sky and the high, fresh air.

Recipe for surviving influenza: start with fresh air, progress to single malt . . . if you could get it.

In his ancient naval officer's duffel coat, he and Malcolm were slumped over a stone slab smoothed by the centuries, waiting for the red sun to flare over the Malvern Hills and suspecting it wasn't going to happen . . .

. . . when the car appeared.

Marcus sat up. It was unusual for any vehicles, even Land-Rovers and tractors, to use the narrow, mountain road this early in the day, especially this early in the year. Marcus recalled, with an unpleasant tingle, the time he'd been occupying this very spot, with only a damaged pitchfork to use against two armed, homicidal thugs who'd arrived in a featureless white van.

This vehicle was dark, possibly green, and as big as the van had been. Seemed to be one of those posh Jeeps beloved of obnoxious city dwellers with weekend cottages. Marcus didn't know anyone in this area who owned one. When the Jeep slowed at the final bend, he tensed. Couldn't possibly be coming *here*.

But it bloody well could . . . curving into the damned entrance and out of his line of sight. Marcus

120

moved to the edge of the tower, leaned over, heard someone get out and open the gate, then watched the big green vehicle cross the yard twenty-five feet below.

Malcolm quivered, and Marcus clamped a hand over the dog's muzzle as the car stopped and the person who had opened the gate came into view.

Marcus sprang up.

'*Underhill!* What the bloody hell—?'

And, oh Lord, who was that with her?

Several times on the journey, the horrific green-pepper moment had sprung up at her and she'd shaken her head and said despairingly, '*We have to call the cops.*'

'No way.' Persephone Callard steering the Grand Cherokee with one hand low on the wheel, eyes fixed on the road and maybe some other place that Grayle couldn't even imagine. 'Out of the question.'

'But what if he—?'

'So?'

'Well, OK, *you* can say that. You didn't do anything. You were just a victim and you stayed a victim the whole time. Me . . .'

Callard had packed a case and then they'd cleared up the lodge and hung dust covers so it looked like no-one had been living there. Callard had an apartment in London but could not go back, she said, because of the media.

But it wasn't just the media now, was it? The media were the goddamn least of it.

Grayle had thought at once of the dairy at Castle Farm, where visitors stayed, where – fate, destiny? – Persephone Callard could become reacquainted with *the only person in my entire fucking life who ever*

121

pitied me. And where Grayle might just find out what all this was really about before the cops took her away.

How could she hang it on Marcus, a sick man?

On the other hand, it was Marcus got her into this.

'Grayle, for Christ's sake, what else could you have done?' Callard had demanded, as they came down from Gloucester towards the M50, with the first amber lines of morning in the southern sky. 'What else could you have done sufficiently drastic to get us out of there?'

'Maybe I could've explained that to the cops . . . ?'

'You do not deserve', Callard said firmly, 'to spend hours in some smelly police interview room for *that* . . .'

'The interview room I could take. If it ended there.'

'Yes, well I'm afraid one can't necessarily trust the police any more. Or, indeed, believe in British justice.'

The famous Seffi Callard driving coolly on, her hands unshaking on the wheel. Her upper lip was swollen where one of them had hit her and then squeezed her face before applying the masking tape. But she seemed already separated from the terror. She actually looked less gaunt than last night, less hollowed. Driving efficiently, with purpose. Maybe she also had that sense of fate and destiny, was thinking that Marcus Bacton would know what to do, make things all right.

'I just want to believe the two halves of that guy's face are still joined together, is all,' Grayle had said miserably.

She stepped down from the big, plushy, air-conditioned Jeep.

The air was hard and made everything real again. Her legs felt like saplings.

She watched Marcus and Persephone Callard approaching each other slowly across the yard, which was still half-shadowed from the night.

Marcus's eyes were wet. Just the flu, Grayle hoped.

'She was right.' Callard had stopped a few feet from Marcus. 'You're not well, are you?'

Like they hadn't seen each other for . . . maybe several weeks.

Callard had on this long, baggy, cream jumper with a leather belt and a heavy cowl neck. Kind of medieval and suited to the location, except she was part of Marcus's history, not the castle's. Grayle pictured her as she'd been not five hours ago, all taped up like a sado-masochist's Christmas present.

At the thought, she started to shake again, breathed out hard and leaned over the hood of the Jeep. So deeply relieved to be back that she wanted to kiss the castle stones.

Marcus stood there in his overlong duffel coat, blinking behind his glasses.

Marcus astonished. *Marcus Bacton lost for words.* Jesus *Christ.*

The dog, Malcolm, growled.

'Look . . .' Marcus backed away. 'I . . . don't come too close, Persephone. I've got this . . . virus. Germs everywhere.'

'I don't catch things from other people.' Seffi Callard smiling her crooked, damaged, loose-lipped smile across the yard at Marcus. 'Never have.'

Damn germs wouldn't have the nerve, Grayle thought. She was a little freaked at Marcus – the guy was behaving like this was some kind of royal visit.

Anybody else, he'd be asking what the fuck they were playing at turning up unannounced at goddamned cock-crow.

'Marcus,' Grayle said, 'just, like . . . quit gawking and make us some coffee, huh? We . . . we're in some kind of shit.'

11

Grayle shivered deeply – like to the bone – and hunkered over the opened stove in Marcus's study, close to hugging the blazing logs. Maybe she'd finally picked up his flu.

'Had a sleep?' Marcus appeared in the doorway.

'Oh sure, what do *you* think?' Folding her arms for warmth, noting that he'd been upstairs, changed into the retired-colonel-style tweed suit. And the bow tie. Still haggard with the flu but making a bid for the old dapper Bacton.

All for *Persephone*.

Who, after a haphazard meal prepared by Grayle and involving mainly toast and Marcus's disgusting instant coffee, had been shown to the Castle Farm guest apartment, the small, whitewashed building which used to be a dairy.

Persephone. Finally, a person Marcus didn't address by her surname. Grayle didn't like this one bit.

On the lumpy sofa, she'd had four hours of anxiety dreams involving Justin with a red opening where his moustache had been and Ersula, liquefying in the red soil.

Woke up shivering and Callard had not reappeared.

'You'd better tell me,' Marcus said. 'Don't you think?'

She could see it all again, like a slow-motion sequence. Because that was how it had seemed to happen, real slow. No big explosion, just a dampening, the blood soaking through the guerrilla-mask.

'But . . . like *massively*. All of it soaked. And he . . . he's just standing there . . . like he can't believe it.'

The glass chinking against her teeth. Water. Just when you needed whisky, Marcus had no whisky left.

'And I'm there with this . . . big, heavy blade hanging from my hand, like . . . like an executioner, you know?'

Marcus just nodded. Well, *thanks*, Marcus.

'And then he like . . . he raises one hand to his face and when his hand touches where the wound is he just *screams*. This one long, awful scream. And he's wheeling round now and trying to tear off the hood, and there's blood all over his hands, and he can't do it, it's too painful and . . . and when his head turns there's this like *mist* of blood spraying off of it. And he starts to *sob*, he lets out this long, shuddering kind of sob, and he suddenly rushes out the room and through the kitchen and out the house.'

She took a drink and coughed.

'Leaving the other guy, right? The other guy's standing very still and like just staring at me through his eye holes, like he's taking in every detail of my face, and I want to drop the big knife but I can't, and I . . . this single drop of blood falls from the blade to the floor. Like *plop*. His friend's blood. And this guy, he's just looking at me and it's real still, you know, the atmosphere is soooo *still*, and the guy goes, he looks straight at me through the holes and he goes – and this is just like a whisper, I wouldn't even know that voice again, and he goes . . . *You . . . are dead.*'

Grayle stood up, walked across to the window and looked out towards the castle walls for signs of life, imagining the second guy clambering through the ruins with a twelve-gauge shotgun. She turned back to Marcus.

'And then he goes after his friend and like . . . Well, he turns just once in the doorway and he points at me . . . his finger real stiff and steady . . . Then he walks out, and after a while there's the sound of a car starting up. And it's like whole hours have passed, but just a couple seconds I guess, and I see Callard all trussed up, edging herself upright in the corner, and I . . . drop the knife. And I just like burst into tears.'

'He didn't touch you?'

'I figure only because I was still holding the big knife.'

'And Persephone? What had they done to her?'

'Bust her lip was all. I think to shock her, stop her screaming. We were both pretty . . . fraught. I wanted to call the cops, but Callard's like, "Don't be stupid, you hurt that guy bad, they'll haul you in, you'll be all night making statements, they'll have you saying stuff that isn't true." She just wanted out of there.'

They'd spent about an hour cleaning themselves and the house up. Following the trail of blood to the back door. They'd nailed some hardboard over the window in the door which the men had broken getting in.

'All the time I'm thinking, *What if they come back?* but I guess that was pretty unlikely. The guy would've needed hospital treatment. Marcus . . .' Grayle felt herself begin to come apart again '. . . suppose he's *dead*? I mean, suppose I put the knife into his brain? Suppose, when they cut off the hood, half his damned face came away like . . . like a piecrust?'

'These things are never as bad as you imagine,' Marcus said inadequately. 'You can get an enormous amount of blood from a common nosebleed.'

'You don't *know*. Do you?'

'Well, no. I suppose not. Did Persephone say what happened before you came downstairs?'

'She said she woke up and heard noises downstairs, and she thought it must be me, and she listens out for me coming back upstairs, and I don't and she goes down and into the kitchen where there's a light on, and one of them grabs her, the other hits her. They don't speak, they don't . . . touch her sexually or stuff like that. They're businesslike. They tape her mouth and then they tape her hands.'

'Look, I . . .' Marcus was groping for a tissue and his senses. 'I don't understand. Who were these men?'

She told him about Justin, who'd come to attend to her car, had made sexual overtures and expressed a possibly prurient interest in Persephone Callard. But she knew it didn't fit, somehow.

'And you're saying this man could have been one of them? You recognized his voice?'

'No, I . . . the one guy, I heard him talking to Callard, saying he didn't wanna hurt her, calling her a slag. I didn't recognize his voice, it wasn't Justin. The other one, I only heard him scream, and that didn't even sound human.'

But if it wasn't Justin and some sicko friend of his, then who were they? Burglars? Not much worth stealing in the lodge, but maybe they were figuring

Callard had keys to Mysleton House. Tie her up and strip the big house?

'You should've gone to the police.'

'What I feel, Marcus, is Callard will do anything to avoid publicity. They'd gone, they weren't gonna come back with the cops and, *Yeah, that's the broad carved up my friend after we broke in and blah, blah, blah . . .*'

'What did you do with this hedge hacker?'

'Dropped it in the River Wye at Ross.'

Marcus closed his eyes.

'So there's no way we can go to the cops now. We left the scene, we destroyed evidence.'

'Well,' Marcus said, 'I suppose you can explain all that, if necessary. You were in shock. Let me think about this . . . That's Persephone's vehicle outside, is it? In which case, where's—?'

'Still at the damn garage,' Grayle said miserably. 'Still at Justin's place.'

Marcus sighed. 'So if this man's found . . .'

'Dead.'

'. . . badly injured and they find your car at his garage . . .'

'What do you suggest? Like I go back, and the guy who told me I'm dead, *he's* there? You gonna come with me, Marcus, threaten him with your nasal spray? Listen, I'm gonna go home for a while, think this over.'

The little terraced cottage in St Mary's had never seemed more appealing. Bar the door, light a fire, banish all thoughts of last night.

Marcus looked alarmed. 'You can't do that. You can't leave me alone with . . .' He glanced behind him.

'What? In case she seduces you for old time's sake? What's the matter with you, Marcus?'

129

'This man . . . this Justin . . . have you tried to ring him?'

'OK, I'll do it now.'

She found Justin's card in her bag, picked up the phone, punched out the anonymity code then the number.

A computer told her the mobile phone she was calling had been switched off. Well, sure, he might be out someplace, helping extricate cars from a smash up; didn't *have* to be getting his head sewn together under major anaesthetic – cops waiting outside for news of his death, other cops tracing the number of the antique Mini in the garage. After which . . . the banging on the cottage door. *Grayle Underhill? Would you come with us, please, Ms Underhill?* The statements, the hearing, the whatever passed these days for deportation.

Grayle cut the line.

'Bit of a bloody nightmare really,' Marcus conceded.

'Can I borrow your car to get home?'

'Can't you just stay here tonight?'

'On this sofa? No way. Keys, Marcus?'

'Underhill—'

She peered hard at him. 'Why don't you want to be alone with her?'

'That's nonsense.' Marcus's use of the word displayed his lack of conviction. If he'd meant it, he'd have said *balls* or *bullshit*.

'Maybe she isn't quite the person you remember?'

'People change. Obviously. She was a child.'

'Naw,' Grayle said. 'She's spooky in ways you didn't expect.'

Silence. The study was lined by about four thousand books on aspects of the paranormal. The unexplained:

always safer sandwiched between hard covers.

Marcus looked old and stressed.

'What does she *want*, Underhill? You haven't even mentioned that. What does she think I can do for her? What did she tell you?'

Nothing, she told him. Nothing that accounts for anything.

She stayed. The police never came. The day grew gloomy, the fire in the stove grew brighter. The two of them had a small lunch – can of soup.

Marcus kept glancing up at the door, blinking and blowing his nose, maybe wondering if Callard had been some fever dream, the screwed-up schoolgirl metamorphosed into this strange, austere, beautiful woman.

'You want me to go knock on the dairy door, Marcus? See she's OK?'

'*No. Don't* . . . don't disturb her.'

Like he was scared that if Grayle knocked on the door the windows would blow out. He grunted, pulled off his glasses and began to wipe the lenses. Stared into the fire, which must, without his glasses, look like some misty sunset. Persephone Callard had been his inspiration. His first signpost to the Black Mountains and Castle Farm, *The Phenomenologist* and the miracle healing of Mrs Willis. Callard was the shining saucer in the sunset sky. The Holy Mother on the bleak mountain.

Grayle recalled Marcus's story of Callard and Chaucer and Sir Topaz. She sniffed.

'Callard told me last night she had Einstein through one time and it turned out to be total horseshit.'

Marcus hissed through clenched teeth. 'Look.

131

Whether it comes from the Undersigned or not is essentially a side issue. The fact is, it was coming from somewhere . . . some *exterior* source. Just because the – for want of a less contentious term – spirits may not invariably be who they say they are doesn't necessarily reduce her status as a *medium*.'

'So she stops herself being a patsy for poltergeists, having windows explode on her, all this, by letting the . . . entities communicate with her. By acting as a mouthpiece for the dead. And, incidentally, making a lot of money out of it.'

'You make it sound sordid,' Marcus said.

'Well, some people would say that. Like, how long has she *known* that half the stuff she's passing on to the bereaved might be horseshit? From the picture you're giving me of her, I think she has a lot of explaining to do, Marcus.'

And then they both saw the shadow in the study doorway.

'Whenever you want,' Persephone Callard said.

12

Vic Clutton wanted to meet in the Crown because it was his local now, how about *that*? The most expensive hotel in Elham. No villains, right?

Or none that Vic knew. Diving into the genial after-work crowd in the mellow oak bar, Bobby Maiden spotted an iffy estate agent drinking with a solicitor named in four too many wills and a county councillor believed to have imported kiddie porn and plastic sex aids from Amsterdam.

But, OK, not Vic Clutton's kind of villain. This man was Old Crime, and Maiden was almost sentimental about him. He bought a large malt whisky for Vic and a Malvern water for himself.

'How long you been back, Victor?'

'Never been away, Mr Maiden.'

Victor/Mr Maiden: quaint Old Crime courtesy.

'Just hanging out below eye-level, sorter thing,' Vic said. 'Wallpapering. Carpet-fitting. Old girlfriend of mine, her bloke died, left her a house. Danks Street, just round the corner almost. Nice area. Upmarket.'

Maiden nodded. 'You're looking well on it, anyway.'

'Feeling better, Mr Maiden.' Vic looked plumper and untypically ungrizzled. New suit, light blue. 'Feeling very much better, thank you.'

Couple of years now since Vic's son, Dean, the lowest kind of freelance doorway dealer, was grassed up by Tony Parker's establishment and formally nicked by Riggs's man, Beattie. Occupational hazard. But while on remand – here was the catch – Dean hanged himself in his cell.

At least, the coroner saw no reason to doubt that Dean had done it himself. But Maiden knew an example had been made of Dean to underline the downside of freelancing on Parker's ground. A slice of bitter irony for Vic, who, as Parker's man, had in fact planted the smack on his son – for his own long-term good, Vic had thought, the boy being a user, too.

Very bitter irony, and for a while Maiden had thought there was a real chance of Vic giving evidence that would send Riggs down.

'I'd've done it, Mr Maiden,' he said now, apologetic. 'I *would* have, you know that. But where was the point, with Parker dead, Riggs gone? Where was the point in me getting meself a reputation?'

Maiden nodded. Understandable. And after all, if it hadn't been for Vic on the night he nearly lost his eye, it could have been significantly worse. Like death, for the second time.

Equally, if it hadn't been for Vic – in a way – there wouldn't have been a first time. Still . . .

'Reason I called you, Mr Maiden.' Vic sipped delicately at his whisky. 'The word is, your personal premises was penetrated last night, yeah?'

Maiden drank some Malvern, said nothing.

'I hope this isn't a nasty surprise. I mean, I presume

134

you've been back there since last night. Knowing how wedded to the job you lads is.'

'Can't have been obvious,' Maiden said. 'Or I'd have reported it to the police.'

'That is true,' Vic said. 'Oh well. Perhaps it didn't happen after all.'

'Who told you it did?'

'Possibly the lad who didn't do it,' Vic said.

Maiden leaned back in his chintzy chair, had to smile.

Vic looked pained. 'Mr Maiden, I'm trying to help you here.'

'All right,' Maiden said. 'Say it happened. In fact, to go further, say your friend was indirectly commissioned by one of my fun-loving workmates.'

'Yes.' Vic nodded sagely. 'I would say you're on target there, Mr Maiden. Making it difficult to be too hard on the boy, as I see it.'

Maiden flipped over a diffident palm. 'Almost impossible.'

'Good enough. All right, say this lad was a mate of Dean's and therefore sees me as an uncle, sorter thing. Confides. Not happy at all about the associations he's been forced to make, when all he was trying to do was pay his way through college. Art student, yeah?'

'Art critic, too,' Maiden said.

'Well, he probably found the work in question a bit . . . what's the word?'

'Passé?'

'You know what these youngsters are like, Mr Maiden. If you can tell what it is, it's not art. Getting to the point, though, what happened, there was a raid on this flat. Up the Hillholm? A student party?'

'Right.' About three weeks ago. Tip-off. Beattie had

gone in with DC Darren Guttridge. Very disappointing, Beattie said next morning.

Vic Clutton smiled. 'That's what they said, is it? Likely what happened, there may have been a preliminary visit. Substances removed to a place of safety, sorter thing, while new friendships is forged.'

So an art student found in possession of serious substances had been spared prosecution in return for carrying out minor favours for Beattie and Guttridge. Maiden shook his head sadly.

No wonder the lettering was neat.

Maiden wondered if his impending promotion was general knowledge, but Vic didn't appear to know about it.

'Congratulations. That would make you the governor, sorter thing. Be in a position to change things, put certain careers on hold? Like you make recommendations to on high, and they'd have to listen to you, am I right?'

'Mmm . . . to a point.'

'Be your responsibility to clean out your own kitchen is what I'm saying.'

'That *is* the point.'

Vic nibbled his glass. 'All right. Listen. This is no more than hearsay, so don't go taking it down on no tablets of stone, yeah?'

Maiden spread his hands. No notebook, no wires.

Vic Clutton brought his head and his voice right down.

'Who's your favourite ex-policeman?'

'Go on.'

'Word is he's never got over it,' Vic said, addressing the table. 'You probably understand the psychology of this better than me, being filth, but first and foremost he saw hisself as a copper. Officer of the law, sorter thing. No matter he made the odd half million greasing Parker's wheels, it was all in a good cause. Keep the streets clean and tidy for the ladies of decent Rotarians and such.'

'Mmm.'

'Law and order, Mr Maiden. Mr Riggs still believes he was the best thing ever happened for law and order in this town.'

Maiden bent to try and catch Vic's expression. Vic still didn't look at him, talking to his drinks mat.

'All right, you'll say, but he's down in Birmingham or somewhere now and in the private sector, probably making so much straight money he has no need to grease anybody's wheels no more.'

'Well, not the same wheels.'

'But the point is, Mr Maiden, he's still smarting. If he hadn't gone – and he's said this . . . very, very bitterly, I'm told – if he'd been still around, he was in direct line, within eighteen months at the most, for the great and exalted post of Assistant Chief Constable of West Mercia. A position very much suited to his lifestyle and social skills, Mr Maiden.'

'I'm sure he looks really smooth at the Private Security Companies' Ball.'

Vic said, 'There could be a danger, Mr Maiden, in taking this too lightly, sorter thing.'

'You're saying he's still got an interest up here?'

'Got a very deep personal interest in you,' Vic said. 'Almost obsessional is what I hear.'

'From whom?'

'Drink up, Mr Maiden,' Vic said. 'My lady'll have my dinner on the table.'

*   *   *

These days Elham got unplugged at five-thirty. Now, close to seven, it was dark and damp and already empty. In the hotel car park, the symbols of small-town wealth were awaiting removal to the outlying villages: a Series Seven BMW, a Mercedes next to a Lexus next to the space where Maiden had parked. Now a space again.

It was close to the road, not far from a streetlamp.

'Bugger,' Maiden said. 'This hasn't happened to me in quite a while.'

'It don't take them five minutes these days, Mr Maiden. Even the kids. You have an alarm? Mind you, nobody takes any notice of an alarm these days. Specially if it only lasts a few seconds, which is all they need.' Vic glanced around. 'Sod's Law. All these Mercs and Jags and they go for your . . . what was it?'

'Golf. Four years old.'

'Not your week, Mr Maiden. Sorry I can't give you a lift, but I'm on foot. Being a local now.'

Maiden said it was OK. Not that far for him to walk either. He might call in at the station and report it. If he could face the humour.

'Car thieves. Joy riders. I despise those bleeders.' Under the sterile sodium streetlight, Vic frowned briefly. 'You take care, Mr Maiden. If you're walking, stick to the main roads, sorter thing.'

No stars in the sky, only a chemical haze. Elham by night: like being inside a giant warehouse storing nothing much at all.

Maiden walked past the shut-down Carlton cinema. Past the bus station, where late buses and a tea-bar were social history. Past the late Tony Parker's Biarritz

138

Club in its cage of scaffolding – about to become possibly the only building that ever went upmarket by being turned into a McDonald's.

He didn't call in at the police station. He would phone.

He'd changed the lock on the flat himself. Not a brilliant job, but it would hold. If they really wanted to get in, they'd get in.

They. Someone working for someone working for someone working for Martin Riggs. He saw Riggs's face – the broad forehead, the long, narrow chin, the almost translucent skin. Head like a lightbulb. Was it really possible that Riggs was still, in some undetectable way, employing Beattie, maybe a couple more policemen . . . and monitoring Maiden's movements?

And wanting Maiden to *know*?

He changed into jeans and a sweatshirt, called the station and reported the theft – WPC Lisa Starling tutting sympathetically. 'The Crown, eh? They've been advised to install CCTV that many times!'

Maiden was aware of his hand shaking when he put down the phone, aware of how hard and fast he was breathing.

Riggs would have been gratified to see this.

OK. Lose it. He made himself a cup of tea then went into the bedroom, closed the door and sat on the side of his bed. Put on the blue-shaded table lamp. Quiet light.

He sat for several minutes, at first conjuring the image of Riggs in the air three feet from his head. Holding it there, summoning all his negative emotions about Riggs. And then letting go of them. Watching the lightbulb head go dimmer, fade, disappear.

139

And then straightened his back, systematically relaxing his body, starting with the toes, working upwards, tightening muscles and then letting them go. Finally, inhaling slowly, aware of the air entering his nose and throat and expanding his lungs. Fixing his attention on a point in his throat, he held the breath for ten heartbeats, then exhaled through his nose.

The throat being the first chakra.

He let his attention shift to the second, which was in the middle of the chest: the emotional centre. Inhaled again. Ten heartbeats. On about the seventh, he became aware of a gentle warmth in his chest but didn't allow himself to dwell on it.

Next chakra: the solar plexus. Maiden inhaled again as, on the bedside table, the phone rang.

'Bobby.'

He rolled off the bed. 'Andy?'

'You all right, son? You sound a wee bit strange.'

Maiden wanted to tell her about the books he'd been reading on spiritual development but felt embarrassed.

'I fell asleep,' he said.

'Well, have a biscuit and a glass of water, then get yourself over here.'

He ran all the way. By the time he reached the General Hospital, his body felt half-numbed down the left side, lingering side-effect of the brain-stem injury. He was sweating in the cold and the damp. Just outside, under the Accident and Emergency sign, stood plump, trilby-wearing George Barrett, the Division's longest-serving Detective Constable, lighting one of his small cigars.

'Thought you was on leave, boss.'

'Tomorrow.'

'Another day, boss. Another day.'

'Who's in there with him, George?'

George fitted a rough grin around his cigar. 'DS Beattie. And one of the traffics.'

'Here quickly, was he? Beattie?'

'Probably here before it fucking happened.' George blew out a contemptuous ball of smoke. He had less than a year to serve, didn't give a shit any more.

'What do we know?'

'No eye-witnesses. Bloke out dog-walking reckons he saw a car coming out of Danks Street with a bit of tyre-squealing. Didn't get the number. Poor bugger. You always knew where you were with Vic.'

Maiden's head was spinning. It was unreal.

He went into Casualty, wondering how he was going to manage to look into Beattie's face without smashing it with whatever piece of heavy resuscitatory equipment was closest to hand.

13

Grayle sat at the end of the sofa, outside of the lamp-light, watching Marcus Bacton doing this courtly minuet stuff around Persephone Callard. So annoyed at the way he was behaving – this complete reversal of the one-time teacher–pupil relationship, so that now Callard was the big guru and Marcus the humble acolyte.

Which was just *so* much bullshit because she was merely someone that weird things happened to. Not a spiritual person, not an exalted human being, not even an authority. Whereas Marcus's knowledge of the unexplained, in all its aspects, was possibly unrivalled anywhere.

But maybe this was it: Marcus knew everything about paranormal phenomena except how to make them happen. He was perhaps convinced that, between them, he and this haughty broad could evolve some of the answers he'd spent most of his life groping towards. Answers he was perhaps half afraid of.

And if Grayle was less convinced, was she not just envious of Callard's beauty and her fame and her power over the legendary curmudgeon?

Marcus was saying, 'Persephone, you had scientists studying you at one point, didn't you?'

He hadn't blown his nose or wiped his eyes in a full half-hour. He was hunched at the edge of his chair, from which stuffing was leaking like the so-called ectoplasm in those phoney Victorian spiritualist photos.

'Oh *Lord*.' Callard relaxed into the full Prince Charles drawl. 'That was *frightfully* tedious. They'd have one sitting in some little glass room concentrating on an object in a sealed, transparent container and trying to move it with one's mind. Or there'd be someone in the next room concentrating on a particular image and you'd have to draw it. I mean, what's the point? What *is* the point? If you succeed, someone's always going to say it was a fix.'

'And did you succeed?'

'Sometimes. Sometimes I was *told* what the object was. And sometimes I was lied to.'

'By the spirits?'

Callard shrugged. 'I submitted to this nonsense for about four months, in New York and Boston, throwing various professors into paroxysms of joy and then troughs of despair.'

She was leaning against the desk, long legs stretched out in front of her, half out of a long, split skirt, bare feet in scuffed sandals. She'd changed into the skirt and a white silk blouse, for dinner – more soup and tuna sandwiches and a dusty bottle of Cabernet Sauvignon Grayle found behind the fridge.

'Then one day I said, "That's it, no more laboratory monkey," and caught a plane home.'

'Figuring it was time to start making some money out of it,' Grayle said cynically.

143

Persephone Callard turned on her those deep, lazy, amber cat's eyes. Her lip was still swollen, but otherwise she was casual and sleek and sexy. Her hair, freshly washed, was spread over her shoulders, dense and lustrous. There was a leather thong around her neck, supporting an amulet or something hidden down her blouse.

She looked rested. Cleaned up, softened, detoxified. She would accept only one glass of the wine, signalling that she did not have a drink problem.

'You think I'm just prostituting myself, don't you, Grayle?'

'You made a lotta dough out of this,' Grayle said flatly.

'True,' Callard said, gaze unwavering. 'The public sittings. The television. The books. Sure. A lot of . . . dough.'

'But now you're gonna give all of that up, right?'

'I'm apparently supposed to make one more appearance. Kurt Campbell's international psychic festival in the Malverns around the end of the month.'

'And after that?'

'There isn't an after that. I don't think I'm going to do it.'

'What, because you don't feel the messages you're relaying are genuine? Or because you've made enough money and now it's becoming, like, tedious?'

'Uncalled for, Underhill,' Marcus said.

'I used to be a journalist,' Grayle snapped. 'It's what we do. Are you scared of what you're doing to people, Persephone? Is that what you're saying? All the lives you f—'

'Look!' Callard arched forward into the lamplight. 'If I received a message I thought was going to

144

seriously disturb someone without especially benefiting anyone, I kept it to myself.'

Untrue. If you read the press cuttings you were soon aware that she'd quite often had people leaving her seances in tears. It was why she was considered more convincing than the rest. Also, Grayle recalled the almost sadistic excitement Callard had given off when she was offering to contact Ersula . . . when she thought she had Grayle halfway to cowering in a corner.

She turned her head away from the amber eyes, tired of firing all the shots. Gave Marcus a glance. Marcus nodded.

'Persephone . . .' taking his glasses off to clean them and maybe so he wouldn't have to face the gaze 'has something else happened to you?'

There was silence. Callard came and sat down at the opposite end of the sofa to Grayle.

'How did you think I could help you?' Marcus said gently.

Grayle shuffled a cushion. She noticed that Malcolm, who would habitually curl up by Marcus's feet or on the sofa, was not around.

'Would you find it easier to talk to Marcus if I wasn't here?'

'Harder, probably.' Callard smiled. Grimly, Grayle thought.

'Does it have anything to do with those guys last night?'

'I don't know.'

Grayle said softly, letting the thought out as it formed, 'They didn't come to rob the place, did they? They came for you. They were gonna take you away.'

'I don't know.'

'Kidnap her?' Marcus ramming his glasses back on.

'I guess. They had her taped up like a parcel. What did you feel about that, Seffi?'

Because Callard had never spoken about what was going through her mind when it was happening. Only describing the assault in purely technical terms.

'I don't know.'

'A ransom thing?' Marcus said. 'To get money out of your father?'

'I don't *know*, I . . .' Callard shook her head violently. 'No, that's ridiculous, this isn't bloody Sicily.'

'Maybe they just needed a medium,' Grayle said. 'Like they wanted you to contact Blackbeard the Pirate. Find out where he stashed his doubloons.'

Marcus frowned.

'Or something like that,' Grayle said.

They both looked at Callard, waiting. She was half in shadow. She sat straight-backed, hands on her knees. This would be how it began at a sitting, Grayle thought, sure she could feel a change in the atmosphere like an electric current. She felt a touch nervous and was annoyed with herself.

'I'm trying to think of the words you say.'

Callard looked up slowly, eerily showing the whites of her eyes. 'Words?'

There was a stillness around her. Marcus, oblivious of it, finally blew his nose.

'Like "Is there anybody there?" Only you don't say that, do you? You have your own phrase. Like a radio phone-in host. Something like—'

'*No!*'

Callard leapt up, rigid.

'Those are not words I utter lightly.'

146

A hand sliding instinctively down her blouse, bringing out what was on the end of the leather thong.

Grayle, expecting an ankh or some astrological talisman, was shocked to see the dark gold cross glowing sombrely on the edge of the circle of lamplight.

Callard said, 'I wanted to . . . talk. I just wanted to talk. To someone who believed in what I used to be. Who wouldn't judge me. Who understood where I was coming from. Didn't *despise* me . . . wasn't *jealous* of me . . . didn't want to get into my *knickers* . . . didn't have a *piece* of me.'

She looked down at her sandals. Yup, Grayle thought, that's Marcus Bacton.

'I do need help.' Fingering the cross – so alien on her. 'Only, the people who might be able to help me are not people I'd feel comfortable going to. Old-fashioned mediums, spiritual healers I've slagged off, in my arrogance, over the years. Cosy old psychics bringing it down to the level of afternoon tea, I always despised that – the way sittings would begin with these ragged Salvation Army hymns, some old dear on the harmonium.'

'Grandma's leisure hour,' Grayle said. 'When the bingo hall's closed. Uncool.'

'I've cut myself off, that's the problem. Sometimes I'd get word that they wanted to meet me – the late Doris Stokes, people like that. Well, Christ, one had one's image to consider . . .' Ruefully shaking her head. 'I fucking wish I could talk to Doris Stokes now.'

'Well, shit, if you really—' Grayle bit her tongue.

Marcus leaned forward. 'What would you ask her?'

It got weird then. Grayle found that the palms of her hands, where they were gripping her knees, had become damp.

She looked at Seffi's cross and imagined hundreds of little crosses on the walls, formed out of the gold leaf and silver glittering from the shadowed spines of the books about poltergeists and leylines and ritual magic.

Talking in this oddly subdued tone, lightly supporting her cross in the palm of her right hand, Persephone Callard said she would ask Doris this:

What do you do, how are you supposed to react, when you achieve the strongest, most defined manifestation of your career . . . when the closeness and the intensity of it makes you almost cry out, at first, with wonder?

If you were becoming blasé, cynical to the point of contempt for your trade, how would you handle what appeared to be clear and unambiguous proof of the reality of the spirit?

And how would you deal with it when the dead thing facing you, across a room full of living people, is also hideously and unambiguously evil?

14

'Clean filth.' Her voice was husky with tears and smoke and gin. 'That's what he used to say about you. Maiden's clean filth. He liked that.'

The Edwardian sitting room was lit by one small Tiffany lamp, and the long velvet curtains were open to the period glow of Danks Street with its imitation gaslights.

Her name was Shelagh Beckett; she sounded like a Londoner. Maiden recognized the voice, thought he'd seen her before, but not for a good while.

'I can see why he said that, Maiden. You don't look like a copper. It's them big, dark eyes. Coppers develop little squidgy eyes, you ever notice that?'

And she laughed. She was saving the real crying, she said. She'd make a night of it, serious grief, then pick herself up at five in the morning, take herself to bed with the gin.

'How long had it been?' he asked her. 'You and Vic.'

'Well, I'll tell you, Maiden . . . me and Victor, it was convenience more than anything, and he'd have told you that himself. What he loved most of all was this address, this big brick townhouse with the high ceilings and the plaster coving. And the mahogany four-poster, Victor loved that four-poster.'

He thought for a second she was going to break her vow on the crying, but she laughed again, and this time he realized: it was the name which had misled him, Shelagh Beckett.

'Connie?'

'Blimey,' she said, 'you must be older than you look.'

Used to mind the lower bar at the Biarritz. Before that, a regular on the Feeny Park beat, when Maiden was a young copper. Consuela, she'd called herself, accentuating the Latin look: big earrings and black frocks with mega-cleavage.

She peered at him. '*You* never nicked me, did you, Maiden?'

'Never did,' he said. And was glad. The hair was shorter and near-white now and she'd put on a couple of stone since Feeny Park. She was spread over the peacock-blue sofa, in her lime-green frilly dressing gown. On the carpet was the jersey dress she'd worn earlier, with Vic's blood all over it from when she'd cradled his pumping head.

'Listen,' she said. 'I can't keep calling you Maiden. What's your name?'

'Bobby.'

'Sweet. We had a cat called Bobby. Listen, Bobby, I know how it is – somebody like Vic goes the way he did, somebody who's done bird, and the police look into it without much interest for a couple of weeks, and then it's like: Oh, it don't involve the general public, it's an underworld thing, it ain't worth the candle. If it don't look like escalating into gang warfare, they just let it go. That's what happens, isn't it?'

'I won't let it go, Connie,' he said.

'I know you wouldn't, darling, not left to yourself.'

'It's why I'm here again.'

'Again?'

'I was here earlier. With George Barrett?'

'So you was.' She shook her head as if to clear it. 'Georgie Barrett. *He* nicked me once. Never again, though – I done him a quickie in his Panda, and I said if he bothered me again I'd tell 'em down the station. Give a description and everything, you know what I mean? I would have too. See, there I go . . . I'm telling you that 'cause you don't look like a copper.'

'Can you tell me who did it, Connie?'

'Victor?'

'Who was driving the car?'

'I never seen it and that's God's honest truth. If I'd seen it, I'd tell you. I didn't know nothing till the neighbours come banging on the door. They seen more than me . . . Mr . . . what's his name . . . Parsons. He seen the back end of the car.'

'George talked to Mr Parsons. What I'm thinking of, Connie, is not so much what you saw as what might've occurred to you. Having had a couple of hours to think about it.'

She gave him a shrewd look over the cigarette she was lighting. 'You're on your own, ain'tcha? You got history too, you and Vic, I'd say. Things he never told me. Well, Bobby, I wish I could help you. Don't you go thinking I wouldn't love to grass up the cowardly vermin, after I've been down there in the road with Victor, thinking, if he's got to die, please God let him die in my arms. But he'd already gone, hadn't he? I reckon he'd gone. I hope he'd gone. State of him.'

She curled her legs underneath her on the sofa.

'I knew who did it, Bobby, I'd be telling you and if you couldn't make it stick I'd be waiting for him in a dark alley some night, with a ballpin hammer . . . There I go again. But I would. I'd do it. What's to lose?'

'More than there used to be, maybe?' Maiden looked around the room.

'Yeah. Nice, innit?' She smiled. 'It's an *address*. A real address. Victor thought he'd died and gone to . . . Oh Gawd, now he has, poor love. Listen, you wait till you see the funeral I'll give him. Nothing naff, none of your Victor spelled out in white carnations kind of crap. Class. Real oak coffin. Marble headstone, proper verse. I knew him twenty years, on and off.'

Maiden said, 'But only on again quite recently?'

'Like I said, convenience. When you get to our age, comfort and convenience is important.'

'Vic implied an old boyfriend died and left you the house.'

'He *implied* that, did he?' Connie shook her head, chuckling. 'You know who give me this place? Dorothy Parker.'

'What?'

'Tony's wife. Widow. The one he kept in style, down the swish end of Essex, away from all this murky stuff and who never come up here, not once, not till he snuffed it. Well, of course, shocked when she seen it all – the scale of it, for a start. All the property. Forgetting you can buy a palace up here for the price of a bungalow down there. But she didn't want it, any of it. Didn't like the town, didn't like the atmosphere, didn't like the picture she was getting of Tony as Little Caesar. So she hires a fresh solicitor to organize flogging the clubs. And the odd properties, she just . . . give away.'

152

'This house was Tony Parker's?'

'He bought it about three months before he passed on. Repossession job put his way by Laurie Argyle, the estate agent. Tony was going to divide it into bedsits. Asked me was I interested in looking after a couple of good-class girls here. Small, respectable set-up, nothing sordid, no drugs. Well, see, I was the one went around with Mrs Parker, giving her the grand tour, so I told her all about it. What was to hide any more?'

Maiden had heard about Dorothy Parker's grand tour. He'd been away at the time, compiling the file on the Green Man.

'Took a shine to me, I think,' Connie said. 'Must've been the accent. Plus I told her nothing but the truth, and all the bits of it she didn't know. Next thing she's bunging me the house.'

'Just like that?'

'*Just* like that. Start a guesthouse, she says, make an honest living. Worth over a hundred grand now, apparently. Deeds made over in my name, Shelagh Beckett. Blimey, I thought Tony's ashes'd come spurting out the casket.'

Maiden smiled.

'Course, there was a good bit of fuming among certain people about the things she done, disposal-wise,' Connie said, 'but she didn't want none of it. Wanted it off her hands for good and all, and the quicker the better. So Victor and me, we moves in, figure we'll live in style for a while before doing the guesthouse bit. Victor done most of the decorating. What do you think?'

'It's very tasteful, Connie.'

Maiden felt a lump in his throat, knew he wasn't ever going to let this one go.

'Victor wouldn't have nothing for nothing, Bobby, not ever. I says here, take my credit card, go out and buy yourself a new suit. He comes back with this bright blue number, fifteen quid from the Oxfam shop. That's the kind of bloke he was.'

'Yes. Connie, when you said *certain people* were put out by what Dorothy was doing . . .'

'People with investments in the businesses.'

'The businesses.'

'The businesses she couldn't sell on account of there being no books, no spreadsheets. *Them* businesses. You know?'

'Got you.' Maiden nodded.

'See, she'd made them businesses unmanageable by destroying the infra . . . what's the word?'

'Infrastructure.'

'Right. Now, one person in particular was thinking to take over the Biarritz, through a third party. Because, without the Biarritz . . . But you probably know this.'

'No,' he said honestly.

'Bet you know the person we're talking about, though.'

'Maybe.'

'Victor learned about it. What this person was after. Victor told me, I told Dorothy. See, Tony I could work for. Tony, I knew where he was coming from. But you have a geezer you know you're *never* gonna know where he's coming from . . .'

'Vic knew exactly where he was coming from.'

Vic's switch of allegiance, following the death of his son, had been slow and careful and linked to his esteem for Parker's daughter, Emma. His removal of a killer – probably hired by Riggs through an inter-

154

mediary to deal with Maiden – had been, fortunately, unprovable.

'Connie, did this person know the extent to which Vic messed up his long-term plans?'

Connie pushed herself back into the cushions of the peacock-blue sofa. She still had style. He wondered who Vic's successor would be.

'This is what you really come about, innit, Bobby?'

'I think so.'

'This is the geezer I should be after with the ballpin hammer. Martin Riggs, yeah?' Connie said. 'Just to confirm it?'

'Shhhhh,' Maiden said softly.

In the CID room, when he walked in, coming up to nine p.m., DS Beattie was on the phone.

'Rear offside tyre,' Beattie said. 'Right, OK. And it's not hedgehog blood, is it?' He laughed. 'Yeah. Absolutely.'

George Barrett beckoned Maiden into the passage and told him the worst.

Traffic had found Maiden's car tucked into a layby two miles down the bypass. A meaningfully dented wing, a significantly smashed offside tail lamp.

The vehicle which had mounted the pavement and broken both Vic Clutton's legs, before being fast reversed over Vic Clutton's top half, had then clipped a brick gatepost on the corner of Danks Street and Ironbridge Road. Shards of tail-lamp cover had been hoovered up by SOCO within a few yards of the post and Vic's squashed and leaking head.

15

Grayle could hear Malcolm outside the study door. He was padding up and down the hallway. She got up to let him in, but Malcolm backed away and sank down, panting, in the doorway of the editorial room, where Mrs Willis had done her healing.

Grayle came back.

'Happens all the time,' Callard was saying. 'Last year, a Sunday paper offered me a quarter of a million to contact Diana.'

'Tempting?' Grayle wondered, sitting down.

'Don't be ridiculous.'

'Which paper was that?' Marcus asked.

'I've no idea. The offer was made through . . . well, a PR man you'll have heard of. The deal was I wouldn't find out who it was until I'd signed a secrecy agreement. They were obviously afraid I'd tell a rival tabloid I'd been approached and *they'd* do a story about what a shoddy outfit the first paper was. I say no to everything like that.'

Diana. Out of pure curiosity, Grayle had combed Marcus's Callard file for anything relating to her sessions with the Princess of Wales. No mention. Even after Diana's death, Callard had revealed nothing.

'But you accepted twenty-five grand from this MP, right?'

'*Ex*-MP. That's the point I'm making. At least he wasn't trying to conceal his identity.'

'Who *is* this guy, Marcus?'

'Richard Barber? Time-serving back-bencher. Low-profile. Rural constituency. Lost to the Lib-Dems, I think. Where exactly did this happen, Persephone?'

'A party. Sort of. In Cheltenham. An expensive flat, newly refurbished, in one of those discreet blocks near the Rotunda. I was told Barber had sold his constituency house, bought something in France, plus this *pied à terre* in Cheltenham, because his daughter lives there, apparently.'

Marcus sniffed. 'More like dubious business dealings in the area. Never met an MP of any political persuasion who wasn't a greedy little shit.'

'Normally, Nancy, my agent, has instructions to bin invitations like this on sight. But the crazy money Barber was offering for a single sitting . . . plus the fact that this was the eminently respectable former honourable member for somewhere green and quiet. I mean, it was all terribly civilized – a suite booked for me at a hotel in the town centre, Barber sends his . . . driver to fetch me.'

'How long ago was this?'

'A month? Five weeks?'

Grayle said, 'The guy lives most of the time in France, but he keeps a driver over here?'

'The man certainly wore a chauffeur's hat. He was very amiable, very chatty. He said his esteemed employer had a great and abiding interest in spiritualism and couldn't wait to meet me. Which, in hindsight, seemed rather odd because the welcome I

157

got from Barber was lukewarm, to say the least, and the event turned out to be some sort of extremely bland cocktail party – the kind someone like him might host on behalf of a charity. He didn't appear to know the guests particularly well, he was quite distant – didn't really know what I did. Just seemed to want to . . . get it over.'

'After paying twenty-five grand?' There were people in the States who'd toss this kind of money about; in England, unlikely, in Grayle's view.

'I suppose, by the time I began the sitting, I was feeling rather resentful. There was this dreadful cabaret atmosphere – people drinking rather a lot and some of the men were ogling me as though I was a stripper. So when I had a message through from a boy who'd killed himself, I made no real attempt to filter the information. To the . . . dismay . . . of a particular middle-aged couple.'

'Message?' Grayle was still finding it hard to get her head around this stuff being entirely routine for Callard.

'It's irrelevant really. The boy got in a state and killed himself more in anger after he found out his girl-friend was sleeping with his father.'

Grayle was appalled. 'The mother didn't know about this and you told her?'

Persephone Callard scowled. 'I was in a bad mood.'

'What if it was bullshit?' Grayle threw up her arms. 'Jesus, so much for if you receive a disturbing message you keep it under your ass!'

'Look,' Callard snarled, leaning forward, 'I never claimed to be Mother Teresa. Don't be so fucking holier than thou, Grayle. Go back and read some of your more lurid columns.'

'Can we scratch each other's eyes out later?' Marcus levered himself up in his armchair. 'What happened then?'

Callard leaned back. 'What happened was that the father walked out. Then a couple of the women took the mother upstairs or somewhere. And I was feeling rather sick and disgusted with myself and disgusted with Barber for setting it up. So I decided to leave, too. Told him he could keep his money.'

'What did he say?'

'He grovelled.'

'How do you mean?'

'Kept saying, *We want you to carry on. We want you to stay. Please don't go.* That sort of thing.'

'*We*?' Grayle said.

'That's what he said. I think he was frightened.'

'Of what?'

'I don't know. I was a bit scared myself by then – had a feeling the father was going to be out there waiting for me. I don't think he believed it was a message from his son; he thought I'd been given information about the suicide in advance. That he'd been set up. I really didn't want to run into him in the dark while trying to attract a taxi. So I stayed. I did the sitting, proper. I had them play my music, my spooky Debussy, and I . . . said the words.'

Grayle remembered. '*The lines are open.*'

'Yes. It's become fairly well known now, more of a catchphrase than an invocation. But it's useful because it acts on the . . . audience. Shuts them up. I mean on both sides of the curtain.'

'Shuts up the spirits?'

'What usually happens then is that I'm aware of almost a *throng*. Like when you're tuning a radio –

159

fragments of voices, questions, pleas, and static. Only worse because it's like half a dozen stations coming at you at once. At this point one can either request a guide or guidance or suggest that they form, I suppose, an orderly queue.'

The lamplight showing up a sheen on her face that hadn't been there before. She was being deliberately prosaic – all this about radio stations and orderly queues – maybe to keep from spooking herself. It wasn't working. Grayle became watchful. *We're coming to something.*

'This time, the voices were far back.' Callard moistened her lips with her tongue. 'And about as comprehensible as a football crowd when you're driving past the stadium. I couldn't bring them *up* because of *him* . . .'

Callard closed her eyes, and Grayle saw her fists tighten on her knees. Outside of her blouse now, the dark gold cross was in shadow.

Marcus said, 'You mean Barber?'

She blinked. 'Barber?'

'You said because of *him*.'

She sat up. 'I don't know who he is. He doesn't talk.' The sheen of sweat on her face was dense as tanning oil. 'Sometimes I think he's the devil. Satan. Sometimes I think I've brought down Satan.'

There was silence.

Outside the door they could hear Malcolm padding up and down the hallway.

'I don't understand,' Marcus said eventually.

'He was just there,' Callard said. '*It* was there.'

Grayle and Marcus both stayed silent, Grayle thinking it was maybe only the tea-party approach and the Salvation Army hymns that prevented spiritualism

160

from mutating into some kind of dark necromancy. *It was there?* Jesus.

'I smelled it first. This happens sometimes.'

'A scent of violets.' Grayle remembering some old country-house ghost story.

'No. It was rather acrid and oily and spiced with that . . . that smell one tends to associate with violent, male lust.'

Grayle said, 'Huh?'

Marcus looked uncomfortable.

Grayle was thinking, *Justin. Motor oil. The bitch is making this up.*

She said, 'Maybe, when you're feeling resentful, you don't get violets.'

Persephone Callard, not even looking at Grayle, said mildly, 'The bitch is *not* making it up.'

Grayle froze. A log shifted inside the stove.

Outside the study door Malcolm howled once – sharply – and then Grayle heard the patter of his heavy paws, receding.

16

The word went up to headquarters and, around ten p.m., Bradbury himself arrived in Elham, brought in from home.

Bobby Maiden was kept waiting nearly an hour. Sitting alone in the CID room, drinking tea from the machine, while the Superintendent talked first to Steve Rea from Traffic and then to Barrett and then Beattie, God forbid.

Eventually, Beattie came back, expressionless. 'Mr Bradbury'd like a word. Sir.'

No look of triumph, at least. The clock over the door said 23.54. In the passage, Maiden heard a drunk en route to the cells, screaming, 'Tried to touch me up, that fucker. You see that? Bleeding police bum-bandits . . .'

The door to the DCI's office was ajar. Maiden tapped.

'Come in, Bobby.'

The man strongly fancied as the next ACC (crime) was draped tiredly behind the desk that was supposed, in a couple of weeks' time, to be Maiden's.

Generally loose kind of bloke, Bernard Bradbury. Big, clean, pink hands, but otherwise insubstantial, somehow, a blur materializing in bigger and bigger chairs. Maiden's dad had known Bradbury when the boss had been a young PC up in Wilmslow, where Norman Plod was an old PC. Norman sneering when Bradbury got his stripes at twenty-six, *Shiny-arsed clerk. He'll go far, you watch.*

'Sit down, Bobby. With you in a second.' Bradbury was reading statements, looking unimpressed. Maiden's own statement would be somewhere in the pile.

He sat quietly. He was not quiet inside. Inside, he was like a burning building, everything collapsing inwards. Almost expecting Bernard Bradbury to be feeling it, pushing back his chair from the heat.

But Bradbury, this mild, schoolteacherish presence, was immune to heat. And straight, Maiden thought. This was the man who, two weeks ago, had strongly suggested Maiden apply for the proposed DCI's job.

He shuffled his reports into shape, packed away his reading glasses, faced Maiden at last.

'Thought you might like an unofficial chat at this stage, Bobby. Or shall we pull in a third party? Up to you.'

'Expect I'd say the same things either way, sir.'

'*Would* you?'

'Yes.'

'I see.' Bradbury hit the reports with the heel of his hand. 'So this is a pile of manure, is it, Bobby?'

'I think I can smell it from here, sir,' Maiden said.

'Let's not call him Vic,' Bradbury said. 'Let's call him Clutton, shall we?'

'He's the victim, sir.'

'Not necessarily, from where I'm sitting,' Bradbury said.

163

He talked about Maiden's car. 'Not hedgehog blood,' he said, echoing Beattie.

Maiden said nothing.

'We've got another witness now, Bobby. Girl of twelve doing her homework in her bedroom. Heard the car hit the gate and rushed over to the window. This is the house next door but one to Clutton's girlfriend's house.'

'This girl see the driver, sir?'

'What if I said she did?'

Maiden shrugged.

'Well, she didn't. Not from that angle.'

'Pity.'

'Yes,' Bradbury said. 'All right, let's go back over the sequence. According to your statement, you met Clutton in the Crown just before six. We also have statements from three, ah, respectable local businessmen who were occupying a nearby table. All of whom confirm that the discussion between you and Clutton was, at times . . . heated.'

'Not from where I was sitting, sir.'

'A solicitor. An estate agent. And a county councillor.'

'Sorry, sir, I thought you said respectable.'

'Let's not get clever, Maiden. Right – Clutton was your long-time informant, correct?'

'Yes.'

'Or your friend, perhaps?'

'There are levels of friendship.'

'You're agreeing that there *was* a more personal connection between you and Victor Clutton then?'

'We had some history.'

Bradbury hissed softly through his teeth. 'This is really not what I want to be hearing from you, Bobby.

164

What were you and Clutton talking about?'

'He'd asked to meet me. He had some information.'

'About what?'

Maiden sighed.

'Don't piss me about, lad.'

'My flat was broken into. I, er . . . didn't report it.'

'You didn't report it?'

'There was nothing stolen. And not much damage.'

'You *didn't report it*?'

'It would have reopened a can of worms I wasn't quite ready to reopen.'

Bradbury drew a long, long breath.

'As you can imagine, I'm already under pressure to fling open the doors to the jackboots from CIB.'

'Mmm.'

'I don't want those buggers clumping round the place if it can be avoided. You're not helping me avoid it.'

'With respect, boss,' Maiden said, 'CIB should have been in here en masse two year ago.'

'*Don't.*'

'Sorry?'

'I can see your little bloody can of worms rolling towards me, Maiden. I would like you to pick it up very carefully and place it neatly back on the shelf behind you.'

'You're saying you don't want to know what we were discussing in the Crown?'

'I said place it *on the shelf*. I didn't say throw it in the bin.'

'Just that some things have a limited shelf-life,' Maiden said.

Bradbury began to hiss through his teeth again, tapping his knee as though he was trying to keep something off the boil.

165

'All right,' he said eventually, 'off the record, I think we both know that quite a few people were very glad when that business appeared to have sorted itself out. An inquiry would've cost silly money with no appreciable change in the situation.'

'Except that a senior officer of this division might have been doing serious time by now.'

'And this force would be under the wrong spotlight again.'

'But the bastard's still—'

'*Maiden*.'

Maiden shut up.

'I'm trying to help you, lad,' Bradbury said.

Come on, Mr Maiden, I'm trying to help you . . .
No-one had seen Vic die. No-one had heard him scream, probably because he hadn't screamed. The killer must have been parked, in Maiden's car, out of sight but close enough to watch him and Clutton emerge and go their separate ways on foot.

Maiden said quietly, 'I really, really want the bastard who nicked my car and drove it over Vic Clutton. Whoever he is. Whoever he's . . . linked to.'

Bradbury hit the reports again. 'Lad, there are some people, not ten yards from this office, who think we've already got him in the building. *No*. I mean *you*, you daft bastard! You say in your statement that you and Clutton came out of the Crown and there was your car . . . gone. Anybody else in the car park at the time to back this up? Apparently not. So, you've got only one witness to the apparent theft and he's dead. Right. You could've gone back in the pub and used the phone there to report the car stolen. You didn't. You could've called in here – not much of a detour, if my geography's reliable. You didn't. You went home. Mr Cool.'

166

'Did they find any prints on the car?'

'Apart from yours?'

'Oh, come on, boss,' Maiden said. 'Whoever did this didn't even *attempt* to make it look like a hit and run.'

'Ah yes.' Bradbury leaned back. 'Hit and run. You know a bit about hit and run, don't you, Bobby?'

'This and that,' Maiden said tonelessly.

'Never caught whoever ran you over, did we? Night you snuffed it.'

Maiden said nothing.

'You see, if we open up your famous can of worms, we also find the old rumour that your accident co-incided with your ultimately fruitless investigation of the late Tony Parker . . .'

'Only fruitless because he died, sir.'

'. . . whose payroll, at that time, as is fairly well known, included one Victor Clutton.'

'But—'

'Working, I believe, as a driver. And minder to Mr Parker's daughter, Emma, who—'

Maiden stood up. 'That was nothing to do with this, and you bloody well—'

'Sit down, Bobby. I'm merely pointing out what's going to be said if we open the can of worms. Sit the fuck *down*.'

Maiden sat.

'Now,' Bradbury said, 'while nobody is suggesting you deliberately planned this man's death, being stupid enough to knock him over with your own car, there *has* been the more likely suggestion that you and Clutton fell out in the pub and he walked out and you followed him in your motor, in a bit of a rage, and . . .'

'Whose theory is that?'

167

'. . . quickly abandoning the car and later reporting it stolen.'

'In which case, how did I get back from that layby up the bypass in time to report the theft to Lisa Starling? No buses. Could have hitched a lift, I suppose, but that would've been a risk.'

'Perhaps you're very fit, Bobby.'

'Not any more.'

'You still made it to the hospital on foot. Who told you about it, by the way?'

'Mutual friend. A nurse. Why don't you just caution me, boss?'

'This is the unofficial chat, Bobby. You see, while I'm a man best noted for not costing the Service any money when it can be avoided, you, on the other hand, are that rarity – a copper who's managed to progress through actual thief-catching talent. Which, admittedly, means fuck all these days – it's people like *me* who are valued by our masters, Home Secretary downwards. However, in these very particular circumstances, it seemed clear to me that you should be the man to take charge of Elham CID and I still believe that, all right?'

Maiden couldn't form a reply; he was losing touch with Bradbury's reality.

'But if that can gets opened now, Inspector Maiden, there's no way you'll get that job. Your career goes on ice until it's sorted. Which may be a while.'

'I don't really know what you mean.'

'You bloody do, Bobby. Now . . .' Bradbury slid the thin sheaf of statements into a cardboard file '. . . I understand you're on leave. Two weeks. Beginning tomorrow morning.'

'Boss?'

'So, off you go. Much as we would value your input on this vexed issue, I'm afraid we can't afford to pay you, Bobby.'

'Pay's not a problem,' Maiden said.

'Go *home*, lad. *I* don't believe you murdered bloody Clutton, but I'm not having you anywhere near the investigation. Until we pull somebody, we'll tell the media it was a hit and run and the car was nicked, which is why the driver pissed off. We won't tell them who it was nicked *from*.'

'Somebody will,' Maiden said.

'And I shall make it known', Bernard Bradbury half-rose, 'that if anybody leaks this, I will have his balls on a saucer, next to his warrant card. And *you* – I don't want you muddying waters. I don't want any freelance stuff, any private sniffing around. If you go away – which I strongly recommend – leave me a note with address and phone number. In fact, take your mobile and keep it charged.'

'What if I disappear?'

'You won't. Will you?'

'No,' Maiden said.

'Right,' Bradbury said. 'Have a nice time.'

'Guy's right,' Sister Anderson said over after-midnight fish and chips in the hospital grounds. 'How's he gonnae get to the bottom of it with you trampling the evidence?'

It was Andy's breaktime. Maiden had bought the chips from a van outside Feeny Park.

'It's a question of what they wanted the most, Bobby – you set up or Vic out the way. No' for you to speculate. Get out the place, let the boss guys take care of the cleaning.'

169

'Except they won't. In the end, they'll just recarpet,' Maiden said gloomily. 'They don't want the scandal and they don't want to spend the money. Nothing changes.'

'In which case, you're no' gonnae change it on your own, are you, son?' Andy stabbed at her chips with a wooden fork. 'Jesus God, Bobby, for a guy working tae expand his inner consciousness and find enlightenment, you can be a real dense bastard sometimes. I was doing Saturday night patch-up jobs on Victor Clutton when you were still writing to Santa Claus, and I can tell you, this is no' what the guy wid want. And don't you go canonizing him. He'd only pawn his halo.'

Maiden smiled. Andy looked up as an ambulance came in – no flashing lights, so that was OK.

'Mind, y'ought to tell Marcus Bacton Vic's gone. If the auld thug hadnae been around that day at the castle, Marcus's guts'd be spread over his own doorstep.'

'I'll ring him tomorrow.'

'Why don't you just go call on him. Stay awhile in his wee dairy, borrow some of his weirdy books and contemplate your immortal soul.'

'What, like you contemplated yours?' Maiden said. '*Aw, ah'm gettin' oot o' this, Bobby. Ah'm awa tae the sticks tae be a healer*. See, when it comes down to it, you're still here and I'm still here because we're half-afraid it's where we're meant to be.'

'No' a problem. I'll jump when I'm ready, but I may have to push you out the hatch. Meanwhile, you go off on your own to some sodden shore you'll just think about it the whole time. Go listen to Bacton rant. Consider the Big Mysteries. Take a stroll in the hills with wee Grayle Underhill.'

170

'I'll think about it.'

'No, you won't. You'll think about bloody Riggs and bloody Beattie. I'll tell y'another thing – *you*', Andy pointed the fork, 'need a woman. You cannae fret over Em till you're too old tae get it up.'

'Who brought that up?'

'Go home, Bobby. You want a herbal sleeping pill?'

'No thanks.'

When he'd gone, Andy went back to Accident and Emergency and smoked a cigarette, hanging out of the sluiceroom window.

Remembering the night, not so long ago, when Bobby Maiden lay on his back, the crash team backing off, despondent – *three minutes gone, three and a half.* Andy refusing to call off the defib, hands on the top of his head, his hair all stiff with blood. Feeling, inside her own head, the sun rising beyond St Mary's, through the gap in the stones of the High Knoll burial chamber, the heat travelling down to her fingers.

A healing place.

Despite the best efforts of the Health Service bureaucrats, Elham General was a healing place, too – though this was sometimes harder to credit than the legend of the Holy Virgin's appearance at High Knoll.

Andy dropped back into the room, looked down at the watch on her breast pocket: 2.25 a.m. She'd call Marcus when she came off shift, before Bobby could get around to it.

She dunked her ciggy in the sink, went to take a look at Mr Trilling on the ward.

17

'So now we know,' Grayle said.

Laying on the cynicism like mayonnaise because she really didn't want Marcus to think she believed any of this stuff.

The study looked tired and bleary. The fire in the stove was down to a bed of ash. Marcus put on a small log from the depleted basket and hauled his chair closer.

'Great story, though,' Grayle said, not allowing herself to think about it. She yawned and lay full length on the sofa, kicking off her shoes.

Around half-past midnight Callard had elected to return to the dairy, maybe realizing that Marcus and Grayle would have a lot to discuss. Standing by the bulkhead light, Marcus had watched her cross the yard under the shadows of the ruins. He'd looked tired, weak, hopeless.

'It's late, Marcus, and you're sick.' Grayle pulled a cushion under her head. 'Go get some sleep.'

'Not tired. Or rather, I am, but . . .'

'You want some cocoa?'

'No, thank you.'

'What *do* you want?'

172

'I want to know what you really think about this.'

'Me? You're asking the help?'

'Don't piss about, Underhill.'

'Let's talk about this tomorrow.'

'I want to bloody talk about it *now*,' Marcus thundered, snatching off his glasses, mopping his eyes and nose, thrusting the glasses back on.

'You really don't.'

'You mean *you* don't.'

'OK.' Grayle sighed. 'Whatever.' Swung her feet to the floor and sat up, hands clasping on her knees like in prayer. 'Let's lay this thing out.'

'Go ahead.'

'Me?'

'I want your opinion, dammit!'

Grayle shrugged. 'OK. Well . . . essence of it is, after like fifteen years as this cool, fashionable, high-society psychic, Ms Persephone Callard can't cut it any more on account of, whenever she tries to do a seance, only one spirit comes through and this is a bad spirit and it's real close, closer than anything she ever experienced before and she's like . . . soiled and full of fear, and the next day she's debilitated, feels like shit. How'm I doing?'

'Go on.' Marcus opened the stove, put on a second log to produce flames.

'What do you want me to add? All of this goes back to a particular night at the home of this former MP, Sir Barber, who's paid out big money for no good reason.'

'So you didn't find it convincing.'

Grayle didn't reply. Callard's evocation of the scene had thrown her a full and clear picture of this Barber's sumptuous drawing room on an extraordinary night. A movie, with sounds: voices and a music track.

173

And a smell. Callard describing how several people in the room had picked it up simultaneously – distaste on women's faces. Then the drop in temperature, as though the heating had cut out, the same women reaching for jackets, cardigans, evening shawls.

Persephone had looked up and seen a man sitting there, at the back of the room, clear as Marcus was now, she said.

The man gazing impassively into her eyes.

And *his* eyes were cold and cloudy and almost white, and seemed to lead nowhere. And while Callard had been describing it, Grayle was seeing it and feeling it. Deeply, deeply chilled, a cold worm in the spine, but doing her damnedest not to let it show.

As she looked into the empty space suggested by the near-white eyes, she realized she was seeing into a space where the man had been. And then Callard had felt his freaking hands on her freaking face – moist, precise, surgical hands.

Her voice cool, precise and clinical as she described it, but Grayle knew that same worm was also deep into Seffi's spine.

So. Why couldn't she just have lost the trance-state, dropped out of it? A medium does not become possessed; the medium remains in control. The essence, the spirit, is dependent upon the medium for energy. Whereas this . . .

This was so close and clear and impressively defined that even Callard had been in thrall to it. Although she knew it was entirely negative, it had an incredible . . . a compelling physicality, and some sick, greedy part of her didn't want to let it go.

Grayle shuddered now and tried to smother it by

174

leaning forward and hugging Malcolm, who, now they were alone, had sidled into the room. 'You didn't like her, did you, honey? Freaked you out, right?' Dogs almost invariably picked up disturbance, whether psychic or psychological.

'OK, what spooked me', she said to Marcus, 'was the way she was able to describe the face. But then I'm thinking, if you were trying to dream up a really evil face it would look something like that.'

A dark face. Thin-featured. Callard shaking her head in a swirl of lamp-lustred hair. *Hooked nose. Hair flat, slicked back. When he first appeared, he was looking away from me, looking to the side, and I thought he was wearing glasses, and then he turned slowly, to face me. And then he smiled . . . he smiled at me. And when his face crinkled, I saw that it wasn't glasses, it was a scar. Almost encircling one eye and running all the way back to his ear.*

Marcus asking, *How far away was he from you?*

I should think, ten, fifteen feet . . .

Yet he was able to . . . you thought he was somehow touching you with his hands.

How fast does a thought travel?

Hmm. What was he wearing?

A grey suit. Three button, all the buttons fastened. Neat.

'I mean, a scar?' Grayle said to Marcus. 'A goddamn scar?'

'Be interesting to talk to someone who was at the party,' Marcus said. 'Someone else who saw . . . saw it.'

Someone who saw what happened when Callard twisted out of her chair. Someone who heard the loud crack in the air, like a gunshot. Who witnessed the

175

dislodging of a large Chinese vase from a niche in a corner of the room where nobody was sitting – shards of it everywhere, panic, people leaping up and running for cover, as though they imagined everything in the room was going to start exploding.

For Callard, it must, at first, have been a merciful release of energy.

. . . and then, being thrown, jerked, out of trance like that, I immediately experienced a wave of self-disgust. It was as though I'd been a willing participant in some ghastly sexual violence, some perverse crime. I felt like . . . I don't know . . . Myra Hindley or somebody.

Grayle recalled how she'd lost her lustre as she talked, had been hunched up into a corner of the sofa, her arms around her knees. Hell of an actress, if she was making this up.

What did you do? What did you do then?

I got out of there, Marcus. In the middle of the chaos, I slipped away and into the lift. I caught a taxi in Cheltenham and had him take me directly home . . . not to the hotel, all the way back to Mysleton.

'And also, how come Sir Barber didn't follow this up?' Grayle demanded now. 'Apart from to send the cheque . . . like, he actually *sent the cheque*.'

'Perhaps they'd had what they wanted out of her,' Marcus said. 'A few moments of paranormal excitement. Something for them to gossip about for weeks.'

Grayle wrinkled her nose in disbelief.

'And anyway', Marcus said, 'she sent it back. Tainted money.'

'Tainted career. Let me get this right – in the following ten days or so, she tries two other sittings, one for this regular circle she holds in London – rich matrons and like that – and no sooner does she hit trance than . . .'

'The inference being that whatever came to her in Cheltenham, she took it away with her. Like a disease. A virus.'

'Yeah, yeah, yeah, but . . . and you know this is unlike me, Marcus, to go looking for the psychological answer . . . but could we not be getting a mental projection of this woman's own increasing negativity? She admitted that when she came out of it she felt a wave of self-disgust, right?'

'Yes, but, Underhill—'

'Marcus, you have a good hard think about this before you blow me out the sky. Could not that scarred, evil face be an image of her own soiled inner being? A realization of herself as a psychic trickster preying on the sick and the lonely and the frightened and the bereaved?'

'Good God, Underhill!'

She spread her hands. 'I just throw this in, Marcus, for the sake of argument.' *And for the sake of a night's sleep.* 'Curious that it all comes to a head the night she takes a pile of money – against even her own better judgement – for putting on a psychic sideshow.'

'And the smell?'

'Like a dirty dick? Interesting to think what *that* might be saying, hmmm?'

'And the cold? And the Chinese vase?'

'Look, I'm not gonna deny she may have psychokinetic powers. Sure, it could be coincidence, but let's not argue about that. Think about the central issue – what do we have? We have a big karma crisis. Nervous exhaustion resulting from a major guilt trip. Of *course* it went with her when she left the party. It's

177

a part of her – an ugly reflection of her dark side. And every time she sits down to contact her friends, the dead folks, out it comes again. *Wooh, gross!'*

Marcus started to say something and dried up. She heard him breathing like an old steam train in an echoey station yard. Then he came heavily to his feet.

'She really has nobody to turn to, you know, Underhill. Her father's abroad. She has no siblings. She isn't in a relationship. No friends she can count on. She doesn't even trust her own agent. And now this physical assault . . .'

'She still puts on an act. Like when I first found her, you'd've thought she was an alcoholic, the way the place stank of booze. But is she drinking that way now? Uh-huh. See, I guess that was because she thought you were gonna come in person, and you'd be like, *Oh my God, Persephone, how did it come to this? How can I help? What can I do to save you from this degradation?* You want my opinion, Marcus, I think there's still major stuff she isn't telling us. Too many things that just don't meet in the middle. But right now I'm not thinking too hard about the big mysteries. All I want is my car back out of Justin's garage and for Justin, whatever kind of bastard he is, to still have a face, you know?'

'Yes.' Marcus bent and shut the woodstove. 'Think I'll go to bed.'

'Good.'

Grayle awoke under a woollen rug on the sofa, listening to the wind in the eaves and Malcolm snoring.

A cold, silky moonbeam filigreed the books on the high shelves.

178

She turned her head and saw by the darkness that the stove was out. She felt the weight of all the books on the walls. All that knowledge. All that speculation. You couldn't trust anything in a book. You couldn't trust your own memory, your own eyes, your own ears.

She'd woken up thinking, *Maybe I said it out loud. Maybe I actually spoke the words.*

THE BITCH IS MAKING THIS UP.

Maybe she'd said it under her breath and Callard's hearing was incredibly acute. Whatever, twice now, the first time at Mysleton Lodge, the woman had seemed to repeat to her her own thoughts.

God-damn.

Grayle thought, *We need you out of here, Ms Callard. You're an unhappy presence. A poltergeist. Marcus can't help you with your problems. And me – I need my car back and you out of here.*

Throw that one back at me.

18

Under an oyster-shell sky, Grayle approached the stones through stiff, yellow grass.

A big vista from up here. Over to the east you could see the Malvern Hills, a line of small bumps. But there was no sunrise. No big, red, rolling ball today.

'So, OK, what happened . . . one morning – it was midsummer – a young girl called Annie Davies came up here from Castle Farm. This was about 1920 and I think it was her birthday. She would be thirteen, and I guess all her hormones were churning up like the inside of a washing machine, so maybe she was ready for anything.'

Grayle laid a hand on the collapsed capstone.

'This monument is about four thousand years old and was oriented, we think, to the midsummer sunrise. A shaft of first light would pass through a slit in the stones and into the chamber. Though with the capstone collapsed, it's hard to see precisely how that worked now, but you get the idea.'

Persephone Callard nodded. Perhaps faintly bemused about why Grayle had insisted on bringing her up here, banging on the dairy door in the morning mist.

Bemused – that was no bad thing.

'So Annie Davies is up here – we don't know whether she was standing on top of the capstone, which was already partly collapsed by then, or if she was inside. It's still possible to get inside, if you're small.'

'Like you,' Callard said.

'Yeah, I did it, once. It was . . . strange. A strange experience. Anyhow, this is where she had the vision. On midsummer morning the sun came down in a giant red ball and settled on the ground and it rolls towards her along the hills, and out of the sun strolls this . . . lady. It's hard to get a picture of it on a dull day in the wrong season, but—'

'It isn't hard at all.' Callard wore jeans and a black, hooded sweatshirt. No time for make-up and her hair was still loose. 'These places were very carefully sited according to the landscape and the heavens and the effects they have on you. Can we see Castle Farm from here?'

'Down behind those trees. You can see the village over there, St Mary's . . . the church . . . Uh, the legend of High Knoll is not too well known on account of the villagers, for all kinds of reasons, covered it up about Annie Davies. The Border temperament: play it down, don't draw attention. No way did they want another Bernadette. Plus, the Anglican Church was apparently suggesting the kid was either lying or evil.'

'Typical.'

'Yeah. And when Marcus heard about it, he was . . . well . . . You know Marcus.'

'Furious.' Callard looking amused now. The wind blew her tobacco hair across her face.

'See, for Marcus, this story . . . these stones, symbolized a whole lot of things about how it all went wrong. About people closing their eyes to the miraculous – turning a blind eye to the Big Mysteries. The establishment clamping down on whatever it can't fit between its own cramped parameters.'

''Twas ever thus, Grayle.'

'He hasn't had a lot of luck, Persephone. His wife and his little daughter both died; there was some talk of medical negligence, which is how come he hates doctors. Doctors and lawyers and politicians and scientists and . . . teachers.'

'Yes. A teacher who hated teachers. I remember.'

'So when *The Phenomenologist* came up for sale . . . and also Castle Farm, which at the time was even more rundown . . . Marcus grabbed the chance to get out of formal education and into . . . into finding *out* stuff, undermining received wisdom, spreading a sense of wonder. He *likes* to be called a crank, an anarchist, an old curmudgeon. And maybe . . . maybe a crank is a fine thing to be, you know?'

Persephone Callard pulled the hair out of her face. Her amber eyes glittered. 'Let me try and analyse what you're saying, Grayle. Why you brought me here.'

'Well, I've come to realize what part you played in all this, is all.' Grayle turned away, watching a buzzard wheel and mew. 'You were his first big breakthrough. Incontrovertible evidence of the world being a bigger place. Marcus's Philosopher's Stone. If Annie Davies was the legend and the inspiration, you were the proof. And maybe, all the time he was scraping together the money, he was holding you in front of him, just as much as Annie.'

'Whereas *you* know I'm just spoiled and neurotic.'

'Aw, look, I never . . .' Grayle tugged her hair into bunches. 'I'm not a sceptical person. I'm a *gullible* person. Holy Grayle, remember? Mind so wide open you could store a Freightliner in there. Underneath, I wanna believe what you're saying, what you represent, just as much as he does.'

'Oh, sure.' Callard walked around the burial chamber until she was facing Grayle across the capstone. 'But you also want to protect him. Because suppose Callard's lying. Or fooling herself. Or become a psychiatric case? Or always was? Suppose she's not a Big Mystery at all, just a medical anomaly? What's that going to do to poor old Marcus – finding out that everything he cares about is founded on angel dust?'

Grayle bent and rested her cheek on the cold stone. She felt suddenly near to tears. It sometimes happened at High Knoll.

Callard said, more softly, 'There's something else about this place, isn't there? It means something to you.'

'It . . .' Grayle sighed. 'This was also the place Ersula – my sister – came. When she was a research archaeologist at Cefn-y-bedd. The University of the Earth?'

She straightened up, folded her arms on top of the stone.

'They had a research programme into the effects of ancient monuments on human consciousness, which involved sleeping out at places like this and recording your dreams. It was how she got killed.'

Callard stepped back from the stones. 'Here?'

'I don't think she was killed here. They found her body in a shallow grave, a co-worker at the centre and

183

a police detective, Bobby Maiden . . . But that's all over, the killer dealt with and all. You read about it. Everybody read about it.'

'But this is why you came back here, to work? To be near . . . ?'

'Or in spite of being near. I'd got to know Marcus, I liked what he believed in . . .'

'Until now?'

'I don't know.'

Callard said, 'You want me to leave.'

'I don't know. I don't know that he can help you. He has a lot of books and a lot of contacts. He'll find out if any other mediums ever got stuck with a . . . presence . . . they couldn't lose. He'll find out how they handled it. But in the end, I—. Look, you don't need to involve Marcus. He's sick. Why can't I help you?'

Callard blinked. 'How?'

'Practical stuff. Seems to me if there's an immediate problem it relates to you and me and what happened the other night. Like, personally, I'm not gonna be able to rest until I find out what that was all about and what I did to that guy . . . who he was, all of that.'

'Don't go thinking that's *your* problem. It isn't.'

'It is now,' Grayle insisted. 'Also, on the most basic level, I need to get my car back. So . . . what I figured . . . maybe you could take me over there this morning, while Marcus is poring over his files and phoning his mediums. And then when we get the car or . . . or we deal with that in some way . . . we could go over to Cheltenham, see this Barber . . .'

'He's in France.'

'Oh.'

'And I wouldn't want to go back there.'

'Isn't that just the place you *oughta* go? He has to know stuff that could help you. Like suppose his apartment was like haunted – infested with this . . . this presence? How do you know he didn't *plan* to unload the shit on you? Seffi, however you look at it, that bastard was holding out.'

'And what do I do? Offer to give it back to him? No. It was a bad place. I couldn't go back.'

'Bad place? What's that mean?'

'Oppressive. I don't know.' Across the big, flat stone, Callard looked vague. 'I'm just a receiver, a monitor. I'm not the whole computer.'

She turned her back on the stones, walked away to the new stile and the pathway down the hill.

Grayle followed, pausing to pat the capstone. 'Wait there, OK?'

It was Marcus's long-term plan, if *The Vision* ever made real money, to try and buy this scrubby field and this monument and then erect a pedestal with a glass case on top to relate the story of Annie Davies and the day the sun rolled across the hill.

The former dairy had four small rooms, including a kitchen with a hotplate and grill and a refrigerator. The living area was basic, with a pine-framed sofa like a child's cot with the side down, a chair and a low table. Apparently, Marcus's friend Andy Anderson, the nurse, had fixed this place up for him as a source of extra income. It was done out in her favourite colour: hospital white, bright and sterile, halogen wall lights reflecting the dazzling whitewashed stones back at each other.

185

The door to the bedroom was ajar. From the chair, Grayle could see Callard's suitcase open on the floor; she hadn't even properly unpacked.

'I do expect a bill for the use of this place', Callard said from the kitchen, 'before I leave. You have sugar in your tea?'

'Two. I don't put on weight, I use nervous energy.'

She was, as yet, unsure about how successful the expedition to High Knoll had been. On the one hand, she was on the way to getting this basket case off Marcus's back. On the other – disturbingly – she was less sure that Callard was a basket case.

Grayle said, 'Uh, this may be simplistic, but did you ever think maybe a priest—'

'*God*, no!' Callard flung back from the kitchen. 'Not having anybody gleefully wheeling out the bloody bell, book and candle trolley for *me*.'

'But you wear the cross.'

'It's different,' she said quickly.

'I guess so.' Marcus would understand that: the radiant symbol transcending all the dogma and the liturgy and the politics. 'But there are other kinds of priests is what I was thinking. Guy we know . . . he has abilities in this general area. He's helped people. I guess.'

'What does that mean?'

'Hard to know how to describe it. But he's had results.'

'This is someone Marcus trusts?'

'Uh . . .' *bloody prancing pervert, deranged deviant* '. . . trust may not be the appropriate word in this instance. I'll need to think about this. Look, should I tell Marcus we're driving over to Stroud, or what?'

Callard came in with two mugs of tea. 'I'm not

186

entirely happy about it, but I can't see an alternative. We'd have to go carefully.'

'Naturally.'

'I . . .' Callard hesitated. 'I've been thinking about Barber. And that party. There is another possibility. I'd forgotten about this, but we had a letter from the woman whose son committed suicide. Coral . . . Coral Hole. Asking if she could see me again. A private consultation.'

'You didn't follow up on it?'

'Nancy sent the usual reply – I'm committed for the foreseeable future, but if she'd care to write again in six months' time. They never do.'

'So,' Grayle drank some sugary tea, 'if you were to get her address from your agent, maybe we could get some information out of this woman. How this party came to be organized, what was behind it, who was invited and why.'

Callard nodded.

'So what was the tone of the letter?' Grayle asked. 'She mention her husband? I mean . . . nothing to suggest they might no longer be . . . together?'

'She just asked for an appointment. What are you getting at?'

'Just I was thinking, if my marriage had been broken up by a passing remark from a spiritualist medium . . . if she'd destroyed my life, set me up for a costly divorce, well, maybe I wouldn't feel too well disposed towards her.'

'What are you—?' Callard's hand shook slightly, had to put down her mug. 'You think the husband might be behind the *attack*?'

'You said he stormed out of the apartment. You said he was an aggressive kind of guy and you were afraid

187

to leave in case he was waiting for you. Could he have been one of them? One of them spoke. Called you a slag?'

'That wasn't him. The accent wasn't the same.'

'What about the other one?'

'I don't know.'

'In light of that possibility, would you still be prepared to go see that woman?'

'I don't know. I'd need to think.'

'Let's put it to Marcus. He should be up and about.'

'All right. I'll ring Nancy and get the woman's address.'

'Good.' Grayle stood up. This was practical. This was movement. This was getting Callard and her ghost out of Marcus's space. Although hard into Grayle's – and this particular relationship still had some way to go before mutual trust was in sight.

'Persephone, would you tell me one thing? When we were at the lodge, you seemed to get a . . . a sense of Ersula.'

Callard sipped her tea, eyes watchful over the mug. 'Perhaps I was getting a sense of *you*.'

'Please don't try and deflect this. You were ready to let Ersula come through, right? Why would you do that, knowing that if you went into trance, the bad thing would come up like shit out of a drain? Why would you take that chance?'

'Because it wasn't a sitting. It wasn't formal.'

'I don't understand. What's the difference?'

'I wouldn't *expect* you to understand, Grayle. There's no logic to any of this or, if there is, I can't see it. I'm a sensitive, yah? Things come. I may wake in the night and something's there, on the periphery. Or, meeting someone for the first time, I'm aware of

188

another someone. But never – thank *Christ* – him. That would be possession, and that's not what this is. If it was, I'd probably kill myself.'

'You're saying it only happens . . .' tamping down the incredulity in her voice '. . . when you sit down formally. Play the music, say the words?'

Callard said nothing, didn't blink.

Always, with this woman, just when you thought you were halfway to connecting, the walls of the old credibility canyon got pushed back again, leaving you with one foot hanging stupidly in space.

But Marcus looked a little better. Not much colour in his face beyond the raw redness of his nose; his body still sagging, rather than plump. But the will to eat and a little mild walking on the hills would maybe deal with both problems.

'You sleep OK, Marcus?'

'Some of the time.' He was sitting at his desk. He had books out. He looked up beyond Grayle at Callard and then beyond her to the door, like she might have brought someone unpleasant in with her.

'Coffee?' Grayle said. 'Breakfast, even?'

'Give it a try, I suppose.'

'Try hard, Marcus. Listen, I've been giving some thought to the problem of the car.'

'Sorted,' Marcus said, eyes directed back to the page.

'Persephone's gonna drive me over there and we're gonna check out the situation. OK?'

Marcus looked up. 'Don't you ever listen to me, Underhill? I said it's sorted. Arranged. Your vehicle will be picked up by lunchtime.'

'What?'

189

'And brought here by tonight.'

'Marcus . . .'

'Yes?'

Grayle facing him, hands on hips. 'By whom, for Chrissakes?'

'By the police,' Marcus said.

19

A month short of the tourist season, only one of the three village shops seemed to be open: a newsagent's and general self-service store. When an elderly man in a pale blue bobble hat came out, Bobby Maiden walked over the cobbled street to intercept him.

'Garage? Lord, no.' The old man gathered up his bicycle from the shop wall, stowed a box of eggs in its saddlebag. 'You want a garage, Stroud's about your nearest.'

'Bloke called Justin runs this place.'

The old man laughed, began to push his bike up the street. 'Sorry, I thought you said a garage.'

Maiden walked alongside, half-smiling.

Peaceful, golden village. Stone footbridge over the little rippling river. A platoon of ducks waddling up the bank. Maiden had come by taxi from Gloucester station. He felt the cool air all around him, a sense of detachment, a strange freedom. With a car, you were always somehow umbilically connected to the place where you'd parked it.

'Justin Sharpe you're after, is it?' The old man swirled his lips, looked like he wanted to spit.

*　　*　　*

A set-up.

Maiden shouldered his canvas overnight bag. He'd been set up.

Putting it all together, it seemed that Andy Anderson had phoned her old friend Marcus Bacton early this morning. By eight-thirty, Marcus had phoned Maiden. They hadn't spoken for six months, but Marcus came on like they'd been cut off thirty seconds earlier. *Look, word has it, Maiden, that you're without a car at the present time. As it happens, Underhill needs a vehicle, ah, retrieving . . . silly cow lost her exhaust in the middle of the Cotswolds. Course, I'd see to this myself if I wasn't at death's bloody door . . .*

Well, OK, Maiden accepted that Andy had his best interests at heart, was unhappy at the thought of him being solitary on the Solway Firth.

Marcus, however . . .

He found the screen of fast-growing conifers on the edge of the village, and what they were concealing: derelict petrol pumps, cracked concrete forecourt, a crumbling grey utility building with big double doors.

Nobody around. He strolled across the forecourt. Saw what the old guy had meant about the definition of the word *garage*. No way were these working business premises. But when he reached the grey building and peered through a window thick with sagging cobwebs, he thought he saw a small red vehicle in there.

Grayle's Mini?

Just pay for the car and then get a receipt, would

you, Maiden? If the chap's reluctant to hand it over to
you, give me a call and I'll let Underhill talk to him.
Absolutely straightforward.

'You're some piece of work, Marcus. How could you
do this?'

Marcus put on an innocent, wounded expression.
Grayle had seen it too many times.

'Are you insane? Are you one hundred per cent
freaking *insane*? Bobby's a *cop*. Cops operate
according to some cop version of the Hippocratic
Oath. They learn about a crime, they are obliged to file
a report.'

'Of course he won't file a bloody report!' Marcus
fished out a bunch of tissues. 'Man's on our side now.
Stared into the abyss. Eyes opened to the larger truths.
Anyway . . .' shuffling a stack of notes '. . . if there's a
problem, he could find out for us, couldn't he?
Through the police computer. If there's anything
known on this Justin fellow. If anyone's been taken
into hospital with severe facial injuries and no
adequate explanation.'

'Aw, yeah, *great*.'

'And if there isn't a problem, then . . . no problem.'
Marcus blew his nose.

'How much did you tell him?'

'Told him the address.'

'You mean you didn't even suggest that Justin might
be a vaguely dubious character?'

'Should I have?'

'Bobby's walking into this blind?'

'Well . . .' Marcus grunted. 'I mean, how much does
he need to know? Picks up the car, brings it over here,

193

you take him out to dinner at the pub or something and . . .'

'You shit.'

Back on the road, he found the old man leaning on his bike under the conifers.

'Not there?'

'Not there,' Maiden confirmed.

'It's a bit early for Justin, mind.'

'It's lunchtime.'

'Aye. Try his house, I would. Even his wife knows where he is, sometimes. Well, I *say* wife . . . But if she doesn't know where he is, if you go in the Lion around half-one and you ask for young Scott Ferris, he knocks around with Justin, at nights. Scott Ferris. Big lad, ginger hair. Now then, mine of information, aren't I? Eyes and ears. What would your business be with Justin, you don't mind me asking?'

'He's repairing a car for this friend of mine, broke down a few miles from here. She found his card in a phone box.'

'She?'

'Mmm.'

''Bout your age?'

'Few years younger.'

'Oh, dear me,' the old man said. 'Oh, bloody hell.'

On the western rim of the village was an estate of former council houses, mostly sold to tenants now – you could tell by all the porches, cladding and extensions. There were more signs of life here: washing lines, toys and bikes in the gardens. Maiden guessed many of the old cottages in the village centre were holiday and weekend homes.

Set back from the main road, just before you reached the estate, was a plain, modern, detached house in the same reconstituted Cotswold stone. There was a swing in the garden and a slide. A half-sized motorbike, for kiddy scrambling, was leaning against the side door, which opened before Maiden reached it.

'Don't ask me, cause I don't friggin' know,' a woman snarled.

Razored blonde hair. Fierce.

'You must be Sandra,' Maiden said.

'And who are you, her husband? Well, don't come whingeing to me, mate, I've had this situation more times than you.'

'Where do you reckon they are?'

'Fuck knows.'

'When did you last see him?'

'Not long ago enough.' Sandra half shut the door. 'Why don't you try the pub? That's his second home. This is his third home. Maybe.'

Sandra shut the door all the way.

Maiden stood by the slide.

Marcus Bacton. Wouldn't you know it would be like this?

Problem with pubs, they had too many eyes, especially for a stranger outside the tourist season. It was nearly an hour before Scott came out of the White Lion. Maiden had watched him through the window, idly tossing darts. One of only four customers, so no mistaking him: big lad, well built, straight ginger hair combed forward, old-fashioned pudding basin.

He stumbled slightly on the steps; he'd had a few pints.

'A word, Scott,' Maiden said.

195

'Who're you?' He wore no earrings or anything of that nature.

'Army?' Maiden wondered.

'What of it?' Scott looked ready to smash his face in and throw him in the river.

Ah, well. Maiden displayed his warrant card.

'I'm not driving, squire,' Scott said.

'I'm not Traffic. Just want a word, that's all.'

'What's this about?' Scott looked worried, but not worried enough for it to be significant. Maiden led him to a bench above the riverbank.

'Justin Sharpe. Mate of yours?'

'Not specially. I know him.'

Maiden shook his head.

'What's he done?' Scott said.

'What do you think he *might* have done?'

'How would I know?'

'You don't work with him, then?'

'Nobody works with him.'

'Why's that?'

''Cause he . . . cause he don't employ anybody no more. Look—'

'The word is you go out at night with him, on the piss.'

Scott closed his eyes briefly. 'Look,' he said, 'just spell it out. What's he done?'

Maiden waited. Scott breathed in, bit down on his bottom lip. A duck came over to check if they were eating sandwiches. Maiden leaned back on the bench, clasped his hands behind his head. What the hell was he getting into here?

It was about Vic Clutton, he concluded. He had this pent-up rage inside him. He was looking for a target. Any target.

Scott said, 'If he's in trouble, it's nothing to do with me. I don't need any trouble. Coming out the army in a few weeks.'

'What will you do?'

'I'm looking around.' The lad smiled faintly, embarrassed. 'Been thinking about the police, actually.'

'Really.' Maiden kept his face expressionless.

'So you see the problem,' Scott said.

'Of having a mate like Justin?'

'He's not a mate really. He just latches on to you. Wants to go clubbing with you at weekends, down Gloucester, Cheltenham. You know?'

'Wife and kids, though, hasn't he?'

'Sort of. Some of the time. What's he done?'

'What about women? Likes to put it about?'

'You need me to tell you that? Mind, he talks a lot of bullshit – this totty, that totty. You don't believe half of it. Like the other day, he reckoned he picked up this American tart, like a hippy type, and she's all over him, and so he give her one in the grass round the back of the garage. That's Justin.'

'I see.'

'Man, you must know what he's like or you wouldn't be asking. Old feller died, left him these garages and he flogged the other for a building site, but the council wouldn't give him planning permission for this one so he's letting it go to rack and ruin, deliberate eyesore. While he spends the money he got from the other place.'

Maiden nodded. It was what the old man with the bicycle had told him.

'Now he thinks he's this big man. Likes to hang out. In Gloucester and places. Gives you all these stories. How he used to go round Cromwell Street and shag

Rose West when Fred was out fitting somebody's bathroom. All this shit you know he's made up. And how he's got all these hard friends.'

'How hard?'

'Got to be harder than Justin. Comes over tough, but you lean on him, he'll fall over.' Scott stood up. 'Look, I said enough, all right? He ain't a mate, but I ain't a copper yet, neither.'

Maiden stood up. 'Good luck then, Scott,' he said. 'Might see you around.'

Again, behind the screen of conifers it was a different world, a different season – the old petrol pumps sad sentries under the white sky. The only colours were the oily rainbows in the old puddles which defined the forecourt's cracks and hollows. There was no car outside, no truck, only the sombre remains of a disembowelled van at the side of the garage.

Behind the grey building, a fence of corrugated metal sheets divided the garage from a field. *Picked up this American tart and she was all over him, and so he give her one in the grass round the back of the garage.*

Lying bastard. Hopefully.

Maiden shouted, 'Justin!'

A crow flew up, protesting, from behind the building. He tried the doors.

One opened a few inches. A padlock fell from a hasp. Maiden widened the gap enough to squeeze through.

Inside, the garage was cobwebbed and derelict, the concrete floor slippery with old grease. Rags of grey light trailed from slimed-up, cobwebbed skylights.

'Oh hell,' Maiden said.

198

He'd smelled the smell.

There were two vehicles in here, an ancient VW Beetle and a red Mini. Maiden walked around the Mini.

It had an exhaust pipe but not a new one. Maiden bent down and saw that the silencer was held in place by a length of wire, wound round twice. Justin had failed to obtain a new system – or hadn't even tried – and had simply tied the old pipe back the way it had been before it fell off.

His shoes sliding on a grease slick, Maiden walked over to some workbenches. Under dusty grey drapes of light dangling from the roof-panes, he saw the tools on the workbench gleaming blue. Very few of them, spanners and stuff, nothing as sophisticated as welding equipment.

Justin must have sold most of the gear. There was about enough here to change a wheel and that was it. Yet he was still leaving cards in phone boxes in rural areas. A way of picking up women?

Maiden went back to the car, tried the door. It opened. The key was in the ignition. He looked over into the back and on the floor. He took out the key and opened the boot. Spare tyre, tools, three copies of *The Vision*. He closed it quietly, got into the car, pulled out the choke, turned the key. The engine fired first time. Good. Because he'd need to get Grayle's car the hell out of here.

He switched off. Went over and put his shoulder against the garage door and opened it wide. No need for both doors to get a Mini out of here.

He took some breaths of fresh air, then he went back into the garage.

With the door open, white light fanned through

cobwebs dotted with mummified flies. It lit up the old Volkswagen and the splayed fingers in the grease.

'Maiden? Is that you? Where are you?'

'I'm in the car park of a roadside diner. Marcus, is Grayle there?'

'Did you get the car?'

'Yes, I'm in the car now. If you could just put Grayle on.'

'Excellent. *Underhill!* No problems, I assume, Maiden?'

'Well, we can talk about that.'

'What's that supposed to . . . ? Yes, it's Maiden . . . hold on a second.'

'Bobby?'

'Hello, Grayle.'

'You got the car?'

'Yes, I—'

'You saw him? You saw Justin?'

'Grayle, what does Justin look like, exactly?'

'He's, uh . . . quite a solid-looking guy. Dark, crinkly hair?'

'Moustache?'

'Yeah, yeah, big black moustache.'

'Earring?'

'One earring, quite large. Kind of showy. Bobby, didn't you talk to him?'

'Look, I'm bringing the car over now, Grayle, so don't go anywhere, will you?'

'Bobby?'

'Should be there in about . . .'

'Oh, Jesus.'

'. . . an hour? Just over?'

'Oh Jesus freaking Christ.'

'Don't say any more, OK?'

'He's dead, isn't he? He's fucking *dead*. Bobby you have to . . . Oh God, no. Bobby, lis—'

Maiden cut the line, put the Mini awkwardly into gear. Over the city of Gloucester the clouds were closing in for rain.

Part Three

From *Bang to Wrongs: A Bad Boy's Book*,
by GARY SEWARD

*I suppose I better watch what I'm saying, 'cause the fact is –
and any professional will tell you this – that you only go
down for a small fraction of what you actually done.*

*Course some people is not so fortunate as others – like my
old mate Clarence. Clarence has done over twenty-five years
all told, I reckon. But I have always been 'lucky', and there
are still some senior policemen grinding their teeth every time
they think of me, but that's the way it goes. Bar a couple of
messy bits, I have had what you might call a charmed life, and
now I have returned to my roots and live among the rural nobs
in one of the 'big yellow houses' that I remembered from my
childhood. One of my neighbours is Prince Charles and,
although I have not yet received an invitation to dine with him
and his lady at Highgrove, I am sure it will happen one day.*

*Yes, my life is pretty good and I live it the way I have always
done, taking great big bites out of the pie but always aware of
the signs and omens. Signs and omens are very important and
why I have been lucky. This is not superstition, far from it. It
is recognizing that there are times to move and big pickings if
you get it right. You see the signs and you have to react; you
got to have the nerve to go for it, no matter what other people
say. The older I get the more I am aware of signs and omens,
but if you call me a mystic I'll still break your bleedin' arm.*

20

Rain and a phone call drove the inhabitant of the pink caravan indoors.

The phone call was from London. 'It's me,' Jo said. 'I've found out why he did it.'

The rain was from Ireland. Normally it would not have bothered him, for there was something energizing about rain billowing in over the sea. But it might not be terribly good for the little mobile phone and so he carried it back into the caravan, sitting on the edge of his bed-settee.

'So', he said, 'there *was* a reason. Other than the humiliation of a creepy old man.'

He was looking down the field to the other caravans. Four there were, in all, in the field above St Bride's Bay.

What have I told you about going near that creepy old man?

The three green ones would be uninhabited until Easter, when the owner of the pink one would be obliged to wear ladies' clothing nearly all day for the benefit of small children who had no reason to suspect he was not of the female gender.

The false eyelashes could be a *soupçon* problematical, but generally one didn't mind. Who could resist such warm acceptance? It was, after all, no more than a year since he'd heard, through the caravan window, a mother dragging a child away – *What have I told you about going near that creepy . . . ?* Etcetera.

Last autumn, however, the very same woman: *Now, I'm sure if you go and ask Cindy very nicely, you can be introduced to Kelvyn Kite.*

Creepy old man to cosy celeb in a matter of months, through the magical power of television. Soon it would be the impromptu weekend matinées again, Cindy and Kelvyn at the top of the field recycling the old Bournemouth Pier routines for a handful of holidaymakers and Ifan Williams's brood from the farm. A little tiring, but it had its compensations. And – who could say? – such was the transience of television that this time next year it could all be over. And the following year, back to . . .

'Creepy!' Jo said. '*You're* not creepy, for heaven's sake. Certainly not compared with him.'

'Kurt?'

'Well . . . his obsession with this haunted castle, all that cheesy crap. It's not *healthy*, is it? Anyway, that's beside the point – well, not entirely, it partly explains why he wanted the money.'

'Money?'

'From the Lottery.'

'He especially wanted to win the Lottery?'

'He wanted to present the bloody *show*, Cindy! Kurt Campbell wanted your job. In fact, he virtually *had* the job. Look, after they dumped Alison, you – me too, come to that – we were supposed to be strictly temporary, right? Fill in for a few weeks until they appointed a new presenter and an innovative new producer.'

'Yes, yes, girl, I know all that.' Sad, it was. Even at twenty-eight, little Jo had no illusions about the expendability of her production talents in the eyes of the BBC hierarchy. *I'm only here as long as you are, Cindy; we were a lucky fluke.* Well, yes. Who wanted liver-spotted hands on their big-money balls?

'But listen to this, Cindy . . . What you *didn't* know and *I* didn't know was that they'd been talking to Kurt Campbell for several weeks – *very* keen to get him for the show, and Kurt knew it, and he was just holding out for more money . . . I mean *much* more money – three, four times what they're giving you. And with the ratings down and the whole deal looking iffy, they were scared enough to hand it over. Signatures were about to go on contracts. Like within the week.'

'When was all this?'

'Like I said, just about the time you came in as a temp. And the rest is history – you turn out to be this enormous and entirely unexpected hit, up go the ratings . . . and suddenly they realize that they no longer need to spend megabucks on greedy Mr Campbell. Suddenly, everybody's happy. Especially the accountants.'

'Except', Cindy said, 'for Mr Campbell.'

The rain came down on the caravan roof like the drums of war.

'I'm told that Kurt Campbell', Jo said, 'was absolutely livid *beyond* livid. The job had been *his*. In the can. For an unbelievable fee. A couple of years and he could have bought a proper castle. *Two* castles . . .'

'Who told you all this, Jo?'

'Let's just say someone in the know. Someone who saw Wednesday's show and how close Kurt came to . . .'

'What did he hope to get out of it? Kurt, I mean.'

'I think he just wanted to shaft you, Cindy. Revenge, frustration. Mind you, he has got friends on the inside – maybe he thought there was still a chance, if you were out of the picture. And that if the stunt had worked, he'd have been a folk hero, like Jarvis Cocker the night he took the piss out of Michael Jackson. I don't know . . . he's obviously just extremely vindictive.'

'Well,' Cindy said, 'it was good of you to tell me, but I think we should try and forget about Mr Campbell. More to the point, how is poor Mr Purviss?'

'Oh,' Jo said. 'Yeah. That's something I should have told you. We'll have to mention it on the show. Be in all the papers, I suppose.'

Last month the podgy, fun-loving Mr Gerry Purviss, aged sixty-one, had won just over three million pounds on the Lottery and within a week had married a Miss Michele Murray, aged twenty-three. Mr Purviss was one of those Lottery winners who just *asked* for the Cindy treatment, indeed revelled in it. *It'll all end in the cardiac unit!* Kelvyn had shrieked joyfully, to huge audience merriment, when Mr P and his large fiancée had appeared on the show.

Well, how was Kelvyn to know that Mr Purviss did indeed have what was considered at the time to be a relatively mild heart condition.

He had been in hospital for nearly a week.

'Apparently', Jo said, 'he had another one in hospital. Died early this morning.'

'Oh dear, dear, such an amiable man.'

'That's one very rich big blonde.'

'So how am I supposed to react on the show?'

'There's going to be a meeting about it.'

Of course. This was the BBC. There would have to be a meeting.

'I'd guess you should say nothing,' Jo said. 'It wasn't a sick joke at the time, Mr Purviss himself had a good laugh, so . . .'

'Poor man.'

'Let's face it, Cindy, bloody *stupid* man.'

'Then again,' Cindy said, 'that was probably the very best week of his life. Not many of us get to go out on a *real* high.'

When young Jo was gone, he went to the window and watched the mist making white whorls over St Bride's Bay, wishing Mr Purviss's jovial soul the smoothest of passages.

There would be no comeback. They were flying high, Cindy and Kelvyn both. And higher still after the Kurt Campbell incident.

A true professional, they were saying Upstairs. It took an unflappable, seasoned operator to turn the tables so neatly on Campbell. Such an immaculate piece of double-bluff!

And didn't those tabloids love him to death? Yesterday, on his return from London, Ifan Williams had come out to open the gate for him, brandishing the *Mirror*.

CINDY'S TRANCE OF THE SEVEN VEILS

But flash Kurt can't con the Kite!

211

And the mobile phone had started to trill its little tune, the offers tinkling in:

An invitation to exercise his wit on the tricky Clive Anderson's TV talkshow. (Easy.)

To chronicle his lifestyle in the *Sunday Times Magazine*'s 'Life in the Day of . . .' feature. (If I must.)

To be a subject for the radio programme *In the Psychiatrist's Chair*. (Well, why not?)

And an inquiry from a company interested in marketing cute little Kelvyn Kites to hang in car windows. (No, no, no, a million times no . . . surely there's quite enough carnage on the roads.)

Meanwhile questions were being asked in the serious papers about Kurt Campbell's previous shows: how genuine were they? How many hypnotic subjects 'randomly selected' from the audience were, in fact, plants?

This disturbed Cindy a little. He didn't want to ruin anybody's image – and Kurt Campbell, in his brash way, had done a great deal to awaken public interest in serious paranormal research. Perhaps, instead of avoiding the press, as he had been on this issue, he should make a meaningful statement to the effect that he believed entirely in the power of hypnosis and in the extraordinary abilities of Mr Kurt Campbell.

As for Kurt, his only public comment had been to the effect that it was impossible to make people do, under hypnosis, something very much against their will.

Cindy knew this popular claim to be less than true.

It all needed some pondering. He left the mobile phone in the caravan and wandered out in the rain until he could see the sea sloshing the rocks forty feet below. Another hour and he would have to be off to

London again, for the rehearsal and the Saturday evening Lottery Show. A tiring schedule – the driving part, at least. But the spirit of Pembrokeshire always restored him and, when he was back here on Sunday, perhaps he would stagger up to Carn Ingli, the holy peak of the Preseli Mountains, where compass needles changed direction and unexpected insights were gained.

At that moment, beyond the open door of the caravan, the mobile phone started up again, like a distant ice-cream van.

'Grayle? Little Grayle? Little Grayle Underhill, with the eye of Horus earrings? Well, well, well . . .'

'Cindy, hi . . . uh, I didn't expect to get through so easy.'

'Why, because I am a big television star? A glittering celebrity with no time for his friends?'

'Uh, no, I just . . .'

'Are you all right, Grayle?'

Of course she was not all right; the radio waves were fairly crackling with an unexpected tension.

'Well . . . good to hear your voice, lovely,' Cindy said lightly. 'So direct. So focused. So devoid of the omnipresent *hidden agenda*. A rare virtue, almost unknown at the BBC, where the truth lies buried under a thousand unintelligible memos.'

'You're saying you don't have much time and you want me to be direct and upfront, right?'

Cindy laughed. 'Grayle, I am alone in my humble caravan, my mystic's cave. Kelvyn is in his case, recharging his batteries of bile. Outside the glorious St Bride's Bay is serene to the horizon. We have for ever. How is Marcus?'

213

'Recovering from three weeks' heavy flu. He sends his, uh . . .'

'Germs?' said Cindy.

Grayle laughed nervously. 'It's about Marcus I called. I called for some advice. I'm using my cellphone in the yard. I told Marcus I needed some air, so if I start calling you Charlie or something you'll know he just showed up.'

'One moment. I shall settle myself on my bed-settee. There we are. Now. Tell me.'

'OK. This is about a spiritualist medium. If a medium came to you and said she was like too scared to go into trance any more, on account of every time she did she was faced with this like heavy-duty, dark entity that crowded out all the rest of the, uh, spirits . . . what would your reaction be to that?'

'My.' Cindy blinked. 'You do come up with them, don't you, Grayle? This would be an experienced medium? One not easily fooled by the Great Cosmic Joker?'

'Fifteen years, plus.'

'And what does it want, this . . . entity?'

'She doesn't know.'

'Didn't she ask it?'

'It doesn't speak. She says it's real distinct, more solid than anything she ever saw before and therefore scary as hell. But it's like . . . mute.'

'Well,' Cindy said, 'I accept that not all presences are chatty in the accepted sense. But with a medium, a sensitive, there is virtually always some form of communication – else where's the point?'

'It just exudes stuff. Smells. Cold. A suggestion of hostility, violence. Maybe sexual.'

'Like an incubus?'

214

'Well, you know, it has a clearly human identity. Like, it's wearing a suit. Oh, Jesus, why am I telling you this stuff when I don't even know if I believe the half of it?'

'Because it bothers you. Why does it bother you, Grayle? Who is this woman?'

'She came on to Marcus. It messed her up, this experience. She thinks she needs Marcus as a kind of spiritual father-figure. Like, she first came into his life years ago, when she was just a kid and he was a teacher at her school and looking for something to believe in, and he believed in her.'

'And you don't.'

'It's Persephone Callard, Cindy.'

Cindy was silent.

He watched the sea through the window.

'*Well*,' he said at last.

'Your paths ever cross?'

'To date, no. I have read of her exploits in the papers, of course, over the years. Indeed, I've found myself sympathizing, on more than one occasion. Considering common ground – misfits, outsiders . . . albeit, in her case, a somewhat privileged outsider . . .'

'Gets nearly as much space as you nowadays, huh?'

'Ha ha. So, am I to understand that this is where the elusive Miss Persephone Callard may now be found?'

'Castle Farm, in the parish of St Mary's. You recall the dairy building where Bobby Maiden stayed? He'll be here too, presently.'

'Bobby also? A little reunion, then.'

'Kind of.' Little Grayle was suddenly sounding *terribly* down. 'Cindy, I figured . . . maybe if you were . . . like, if your schedule allowed . . .'

'But Marcus doesn't know of this?'

'I thought if you just kind of turned up, that Marcus would be . . .'

'Furious,' Cindy said.

'But secretly grateful. Long term.'

Cindy smiled. 'And the troubled Miss Callard?'

'What I was hoping is you would probably be able to establish one way or the other. If this was the real thing. You know what I'm saying?'

'Yes, lovely, I think I sense the direction in which you are tentatively travelling. My problem is that I have, as you know, commitments in London . . .'

'I'm sorry. I understand. It was stupid of me.'

'. . . at least, until tomorrow evening. Would Sunday be soon enough? If I were just passing through, as it were. Staying at the Ram's Head in St Mary's, with my dear friend Amy Jenkins?'

'Oh Cindy . . .' almost a sob, this was '. . . I would be *so* grateful. See, I would hate for Marcus to have to deal with this on his own. He's been sick, he isn't as young as he used to be. And he's getting kind of disillusioned about his own worth, you know?'

A wave of tenderness washed over Cindy. He remembered his first meeting with Grayle, a wan little figure in the bar of the Ram's Head, searching for her missing sister in a strange place. Exceedingly strange, as it turned out.

'Well, let me see,' he said positively. 'I usually arrive back here quite late on Saturday night, so if I drive up there early in the morning when we are all fresh?'

'Thank you.'

'Thank *you*, Grayle. It will be an intriguing experience. I'm sure. I would relish the opportunity to meet the extraordinary Miss Callard. And to see you again, of course. And Bobby. And . . . Marcus. A little reunion of what we might call the St Mary's Circle. Perhaps it is meant to be. Right. I shall see you on Sunday, then.'

'Well, I might not be here,' Grayle said, almost brusquely.

'No?' Oh. Getting to something. Cindy felt a considerable darkening. 'And why not?'

'I may have to go away. I don't wanna talk about that. Marcus'll tell you if . . . if I'm not here.'

'Grayle . . . ?'

'I have to go. I see, uh . . . I see Marcus coming. Bye, Charlie. Thank you.'

Grayle stabbed the *end* button, stood under the smashed tower, shaking with the knowledge of her own doom. It had come on to rain – mean, squally stuff.

The ominous figure coming towards her wasn't Marcus, it was Persephone Callard with the hood of her black sweatshirt pulled up. She looked dark and witchy under the jagged walls, and the whole scene sang with foreboding.

'Grayle, you can't stand out here like some fugitive.'

'Fugitive from justice,' Grayle said miserably. 'Don't I know it.'

'Look,' Callard said, 'I've been thinking.' She guided Grayle back to the shelter of the curtain wall. 'It's going to be a lot easier if I say it was me.'

'What?'

'If I say I did it. I hit the man, I cut him with the knife. I came down and found them and they attacked me and I grabbed the knife from the wall. I was in a state about it afterwards, obviously, and you brought me back here.'

217

Grayle blinked at her. 'Why would you want to do that?'

'Because you're a foreigner and it could be more difficult for you. And I can afford a good lawyer.' Callard pushed back her hood; her face was dry and calm. 'Grayle, if you hadn't been there, if you hadn't done what you did, I don't know where I'd be now. I don't know what would have happened to me.'

Grayle shook her head. 'It's a generous offer. But no. What if they find the other guy? He's gonna know it wasn't you, and then it'll all be much worse.'

Though she didn't see how it could be much worse. She felt cold rain on her face, glared bleakly up at the castle walls – this huge defensive stronghold once, but what did it keep out now? Not even the rain which spattered into her eyes. It was a good time to cry.

'I killed a guy. I'm not gonna run away from that. What I'll do is I'll go back with Bobby. We'll go to the cops in Stroud or someplace. I might get manslaughter, I even have a case for self-defence. Besides . . .' She fought for a weak smile and almost got there. 'I have an excuse. I'm a New Yorker. I was raised in a violent culture.'

21

St Mary's was the last village in England, so close to the border that on some signs the name was given in Welsh, *Llanfair-y-fynydd*. St Mary's in the Mountains: the Black Mountains, lumbar vertebrae in the spine of Wales.

Here the mountains
Here the Sky
Here the Earth
Meeting place
HEAR the Earth (THUMP)

Bobby Maiden's heart began thumping like Cindy's shamanic drum as Grayle's Mini went chugging into the main street.

Under the overhanging wooden sign of the Ram's Head, known as the Tup – domain of Amy Jenkins, glittery, garrulous divorcee from the South Wales valleys. Two cars and a Land-Rover outside the Tup, but no other vehicles on the move and no people about. A marmalade cat strolled along the wet pavement and hopped on to a wall.

That feeling of returning to a spiritual home. Or

somebody's spiritual home; whenever Maiden came back here, it always seemed to be related to death.

Out of the village into pink soil country, up to where the sign said, *Capel-y-ffin: mountain road, unfit for heavy vehicles.*

Under the tree branches locked across the narrow road like the antlers of fighting stags, the road dipping and the Black Mountains sinking out of sight because they were so close. But you would still feel them there, an underlying dark weight.

Or maybe that was the sombre weight of the crime-scene pictures in his head. The dispassionate police mind having photographed it from many different angles. A file of sickening images to flip through.

And one maverick factor preventing the drawing of conclusions.

When he finally drove between the wings of stone at the entrance to Castle Farm, Maiden allowed himself to start worrying seriously about Grayle and how it was no surprise at all to her that Justin Sharpe was lying dead in his own garage.

She came out alone to meet him, head bowed. A small, hesitant shadow in the darkening yard.

First, patting her Mini like it was a dog that came home, looking up at him from across the bonnet, big eyes behind those unruly tresses glistening with rain.

'Hey. Bobby Maiden.'

'Grayle Underhill.'

She straightened up, stood awkwardly, a couple of yards from Maiden.

'Thanks for collecting the car.'

'Pleasure. Well. Not all of it. Obviously.'

'No.' Grayle smiled wanly. 'But, uh, thanks for

220

bringing the car away without reporting whatever it was you oughta have reported.'

'And that would be . . . ?'

'Uh huh.' A shake of the head, spray flying from her hair. 'This is interview-room stuff, right? Could we skip that part?'

'Whatever.'

'Right. OK.'

She had her small hands crossed in front of her, like ready for the handcuffs.

'So, uh . . .' She took a big breath. 'Well, it was me, Bobby. I killed him. I killed Justin. There you go. That's it.'

'You killed Justin Sharpe.'

'Yes, I did. OK . . . OK . . . I realize . . .' pushing her hands up at him '. . . I realize there's no way you can cover this up, with your job and all, but I'm grateful you brought the car out of there because obviously that would complicate matters on account of being a link between us . . . like, if they could prove I already knew Justin, then they'd be less likely to believe I just struck out at him with the chopper out of total fear – which was the truth of it, so help me – and they'd think there was some history to this, which is *not* true because the history between Justin and me goes back no further than . . . Wednesday, was it only Wednesday, Jesus, it's like . . . What?'

'Grayle, sorry . . . what did you kill him with?'

'Uh, it was like . . .' holding out her hands to demonstrate the length of it '. . . it was a hedging tool. Big, heavy knife? Like a butcher's cleaver?'

Grayle shuddered.

'And you chopped him . . . where?'

'In the face.' She swallowed. 'Obviously. It was . . .'

'Where was this?'

'At Call . . . in a cottage about three miles from the garage. He ran out with his head pouring blood. See, I knew he was hurt bad, but I didn't know—'

'Grayle.'

'See, I would've told you before you went there, Bobby, if Marcus hadn't—'

'Grayle.' Maiden put up both hands to stop her. 'The thing is Justin Sharpe was crushed to death underneath an old Volkswagen Beetle.'

'Wh . . . huh?'

'If anybody hit Justin with anything resembling a butcher's cleaver, all I can say is he heals well. It was his chest that was crushed. His face was unmarked.'

Grayle stood there for a moment in the grey rain, blinking, gulping in air and rain.

Her face collapsing like a wet Kleenex, she fell, sobbing, into Bobby Maiden's arms.

With Marcus – no matter how long since you'd last met – it was always like you'd just been out for fish and chips and returned without the mushy peas. You came to accept this.

However, he had more of an excuse than usual: he'd been unwell. But getting better, Grayle said, although this year's flu was a mean and lingering virus.

'This makes no bastard sense, Maiden.' Marcus was pacing the low-beamed study like a rhino in a pigpen. 'If Underhill didn't . . . then *who* . . . ?'

Grayle said, 'Where did Callard go?'

'Went to change into something dry.' Marcus sat down heavily, snatched off his glasses, pushed his palms over his face and through his battleship-grey hair. 'Maiden, I . . . Bloody sorry to hear about

Clutton. Didn't really take it in on the phone this morning, too concerned with my own agenda. Owe the man my life. Thought I'd had it that day. Will you, ah . . . will you get whoever did it?'

Maiden shrugged.

Grayle said, 'Did I meet this guy? I don't recall.'

'Don't think you did, Underhill. Poor bastard lived a shadowy kind of life, I'd guess. Now the shadowy death. Seems to be this whole stratum of society functioning quite oblivious of the law. I always relished the idea of other levels of existence. Appreciated anarchy.' Marcus watched the logs burning in the stove. 'All rather frightening now. Getting bloody old is what it is. Feeling helpless.'

'Bugger off, Marcus.' Maiden sat on the sofa. 'These are just toerags, as my dad would say. Can't let yourself be intimidated by toerags.'

This was all wrong. He should be furious at being set up, being dropped into an alien crime scene, discovering a suspicious death he couldn't report, driving away in what might have been evidence.

Feeling sorry for Marcus – this was unnatural.

'Bobby . . .' Grayle came to sit next to him. She was still looking limp with relief. 'Where's this leave you?'

'That's an interesting question.'

'Hang on,' Marcus said, 'how do you know it wasn't an accident? Dangerous places, vehicle workshops, especially when you're on your own.'

'Well, the original idea might've been to make it *look* like an accident.'

The top of Justin's big, black moustache had been visible under the tail of the VW. His skin tinted green from a mossed and mouldy skylight. His eyes glazed into a forever kind of desperation. He'd lain face up, hair in the grease, squashed like a cockroach under the heavy ruins of a car with no tyres. Two-thirds of him under the car, ribs crushed, the spirit squeezed out of the body like toothpaste from a tube, the tube left flattened in the middle. Maiden could still smell, under the pervading oil, the stench of Justin letting every-thing go, into his overalls. Questions thumping down in his head, drab packages he didn't want to open: how long had the body been here? Was it possible he was already dead when they dumped the car on him?

Or was he lying here, face up, screaming as it came down?

Got all these hard friends.

'There was one of those hydraulic jacks about two feet from the rear end of the car. I think someone jacked the car up and made him lie down underneath.'

Grayle was white. 'How could they make him?'

'Gunpoint? There are situations where you'll do anything you're told.'

Marcus said, 'If they had the car jacked up and then let it down on him . . . it had no tyres, you say?'

'Without the tyres, it was going all the way down on him.'

'God almighty, Maiden.'

'Maybe it started out as torture. Perhaps they wanted some information.'

The Volkswagen lowered inch by inch, Justin screaming until he had no breath left, telling them everything he knew, gabbling it out, and they probably knew he'd told them everything, but they just went on lowering the car. Maybe quite interested in how it would go because they'd never done it like this before.

'Who . . . who were they?' Grayle's relief at not

224

being a killer was no longer apparent. 'Jesus, this is even more awful . . .'

Maiden shook his head. The air had felt thick with agony and suffocating terror. Of course, he realized he'd generated this atmosphere himself, standing there transfixed, smelling Justin's last moments. Building up, in the polluted space, images so real that he'd felt like a voyeur, guilty that he was virtually seeing it happen and could do nothing to stop it.

'You'd better tell me about him,' he said to Grayle.

As the afternoon closed down, Grayle explained why she'd been in Gloucestershire on Wednesday. Glad that Callard was not in the room. Presumably, having made her kind offer to admit guilt falsely, she'd decided to contain what curiosity she had about Justin, keep a low profile while Bobby was around.

'Hang on.' Bobby looked up from fondling his old pal Malcolm. Blinked. 'This is Persephone Callard, the psychic?'

'No, Persephone Callard, the hairdresser.'

'Right. Sorry.'

'Old friend of Marcus's.'

'I never knew that.'

'Marcus Bacton,' Grayle said. 'Confidant of the stars.'

Without going into the Cheltenham stuff, Grayle and Marcus précised the background and Grayle told Bobby about the fraught final leg of her journey to Mysleton House. And what had happened that night.

'Christ,' Bobby said. 'These guys. Do you have any—?'

'I have no idea. If not Justin, I have no idea at all.'

'They sound . . . professional.'

'What I felt at the time. Kind of SAS-looking.'

'Whoever killed Justin, that was also . . .'

'Jesus, you think there might *still* be a connection?'

'Can't think there'd be too many outfits of that kind operating in one small area of the Cotswolds within the same day or so. Can you, Marcus?'

'Well . . . I suppose the fact that Sharpe was also at Mysleton Lodge within hours of these bastards turning up . . .'

Bobby said, 'A bloke in the village told me Justin had hard friends. In Gloucester and Cheltenham.'

'Cheltenham,' Grayle echoed. Bobby looked at her. 'Just keeps coming up, is all. Go on.'

'Justin likes making money without actually working. Plus, as you said, maybe he's worried about his clock running down. So he's putting himself about, getting into excitingly bad company. Leaving cards in phone boxes with a view to ripping off stranded motorists and helping ladies in distress into the back of his van. And when he finds out Persephone Callard's in the area . . . OK, I don't suppose even Justin thinks he's got much chance of scoring there, but . . .'

'Unlike with cheap-looking Holy Grayle. Thanks, Bobby.'

'Aw now, Grayle, I didn't . . .'

'Just kidding,' Grayle said unsmiling. 'OK, Justin figured he might've been able to make some money out of the information is what you're saying, with everyone looking for Ms Callard. Me, I'd just go to the press, bargain for a swift ten grand. But unless reporting's gotten even less responsible these days, those guys were not like any journalists I ever worked with, so I guess—'

'You're not Justin,' Bobby said. 'What Justin does is

brag to his mates, and maybe one of them passes it on to someone he knows is interested, or somebody overhears Justin relating how he had sex with Persephone Callard.'

'Someone in Cheltenham?'

Bobby shrugged.

'So Persephone *was* the target,' Marcus said. 'Who, then? Why?'

'And why did they find it necessary to kill Justin afterwards? That's just a theory.' Bobby Maiden's eyes trapped Grayle's. 'I think you've got to decide what you want to do about this. Whether you want to bring the police in.'

'Rather thought we had,' Marcus said.

'In your back-door kind of way.' Bobby was clearly still pissed off at the way Marcus ran him round the block, blind.

'Be reasonable, Maiden . . .' Marcus doing injured innocence with overtones of sick old man. 'I couldn't have told you all the background over the phone, now could I? Besides, I saw you as a friend, not . . .'

'Anyway, how do you want to play it? You can't have both of me.'

Marcus humphed. 'Can hardly make a decision on something like this without consulting Persephone.'

'With Marcus,' Grayle said, 'Callard always gets to call the shots.'

'What's she like?' Bobby messed with Malcolm's ears. 'I just think of Doris Stokes, but not as cosy. How sure are you that *she* didn't know those blokes?'

Grayle looked over at Marcus. 'You can't be sure of anything with Callard. Sometimes you think you're getting to kind of like her, sometimes you even think you're starting to understand her. Then she comes out

227

with something so off the wall, and it's like, hey, come *on . . .*'

She tailed off, becoming aware of that dark, slim shape in the study doorway. A woman who'd been too long around ghosts.

Callard glided into the room and put on the lamp. She was wearing the grey cardigan she'd had on when Grayle had first seen her in Mysleton Lodge. The one she didn't over-button.

Grayle was depressingly aware of Bobby catching his breath.

22

Saturday morning, Grayle was so irritated, she just hurled herself into work.

It should have been a really good morning. Another bright, overcast day, the first suggestion of a light green haze over the deep Border hedgerows. And, for the first time in over two weeks, they were working together in the editorial room – Marcus at the trestle table, catching up on most of a week's papers, Grayle burrowing in back copies of the magazine. Doing what she figured she did best.

And trying, God damn it, to avoid thinking about Bobby Maiden and Callard.

An elderly correspondent called Hedges over in Norfolk had sent in an update on one of those hitch-hiking spook stories: dead of night, guy in old-time clothing pops up in front of your car with a hand raised and when you stop he's disappeared. Grayle thought she might use it to nose off a composite piece, collating a bunch of other hitchhiking ghost stories from the past ten years. It was an old scam, but it filled space, which was what they needed right now, with all the time lost.

'Try autumn eighty-nine,' Marcus mumbled, head in the *Mirror*.

'OK.' Grayle started prising apart fifteen-year-old *Phenomenologists*, which were all moulded together. 'Marcus, you're looking better, did I say that?'

'I may not die,' Marcus conceded. 'Not imminently, anyway.'

'Got it,' Grayle said presently. 'Hampshire. Old lady in a shawl. Excellent. Thank you, Marcus. Two more, and I can get a double-page spread out of this.'

'Doesn't seem honest somehow.'

'It's how magazines get filled, with no staff. How's this for a headline? "Road Wraiths" . . . Marcus, are you listening?'

'What?'

'Like road-*rage*, only . . .'

'Bloody hell, you seen this about Mars-Lewis and that smart-arsed hypnotist?'

'Huh?' Grayle came around to his side of the table, read over his shoulder about 'Cindy's Trance of the Seven Veils'.

'Sometimes,' Marcus said, 'if you're not obliged to have any personal contact with him, you can almost admire the creature's nerve.'

'Yeah.' Grayle read the story through. 'Wow. Hey, if this was Wednesday's show, we oughta have it on tape. If you remembered to press the buttons.'

'Of course I remembered. But you can watch it on your own.'

'You gotta accept it, Marcus. Cindy's on a roll.'

'Hmmph.'

'Uh . . .' She hesitated. 'You know, it did kind of occur to me that if anybody could help Callard . . . like where a church minister or a psychiatrist would totally fail to get a handle on the phenomenon, from either of their narrow perspectives . . .'

'Don't even *contemplate* it,' Marcus said, mildly enough to suggest that he didn't think she would do that to him, not in a million years. 'Besides, if Maiden can help her unravel the origins of the whole disturbance, it'll be a start.'

'Yeah,' Grayle said with no enthusiasm.

Last night, she'd finally gotten to return home to her own bed, leaving the sofa to Bobby Maiden. Home to the cosy little cottage behind St Mary's Church.

Where she should have slept the sleep of the exhausted, drifting off to the sound of the night breeze in the windchimes, her amethyst crystal (cleansing and spiritual protection) under her pillow, her last conscious thought one of major relief that she was not overnighting in the slammer.

Funny these days how, when one anxiety went into remission, something else always arose to fill the space.

Bobby had come on at first like a straight cop – had Callard received any threats, been aware of anyone watching her, ever felt she was being stalked?

Callard shaking her head – this was a cop; what would he want to know about the ethereal, the otherworldly, the *matters of spirit*.

So it was Grayle herself who had responded to Bobby's question about Cheltenham – did Callard know anyone there?

'Oh, I think *so*.'

Callard giving her the hard stare that said, *You want me to tell this to a* policeman?

'There are cops,' Grayle replied, 'and there are cops.'

And there was Bobby. Whose past experiences had

shifted his whole perspective way beyond the cop-norm. The last time Grayle had seen Bobby he'd been asking her how crystals worked.

So when he was listening to Callard relating the seance stuff, about the cold atmosphere and the foul smell and the three-button grey suit and the long scar, it was without scorn, or veiled mockery. Grayle had noticed a little grey in Bobby's dark hair. Poor baby; midlife crisis, intimations of mortality.

When Callard's story was over he'd said, 'But they can't harm you, can they?'

'They can steal your energy,' Callard said, sliding on to the desk chair. 'They can keep you awake like a young baby keeps its mother awake. Because they require your energy.'

'What are we talking about here?' Bobby asked her. 'I mean, when the physical body dies, it's said that what Gurdjieff called the *kesdjan* body—'

'The what?' Callard's eyes opening wide. Oh God, she just could not believe this was a cop.

'He means astral,' Marcus said.

'That the astral body remains alive for a while,' Bobby said. 'Is *that* what we're talking about? An astral body kept alive by some earthly obsession?'

'Hey,' Grayle said lightly. 'Technical, or what?'

'I really don't know.' Callard leaning closer to Bobby, the woolly sweater coming open a little more, showing off those flawless brown tits. God-*damn*. 'I don't think the astral body and the spirit are the same, although one may inhabit the other. Certainly I've never seen anything quite so clear as this before. So fully defined, such presence. If it wasn't such a nega-tive presence I'd want to know more. As it is, I just want it out of my life.'

232

'So it's getting its energy from you.'

'I don't know.'

'You dream about it?'

'I'm not sure. When I'm asleep, I can't . . .' she smiled '. . . police my consciousness. I thought at first that, in some perverse way, I was *inviting* it. Now I think it only comes when I open myself formally. Other essences may come through when I'm not trying, but never this one. But if I go deliberately into trance it's there. Immediately.'

'Every time?'

'I'd say so. Which is why I couldn't work, even if I wanted to. This is something that's become attached to me because of what I am. What I do.'

'Like a computer virus,' Bobby said.

'Or a vampire?' Grayle standing up and crossing to the window. It seemed to have stopped raining. 'Like the undead? Something that either doesn't know it's dead or doesn't want to *be* dead.'

'Does anybody?' Bobby said.

Marcus said, 'Maiden had a negative death experience.'

'Really?' Callard looking at him with awfully serious interest. 'I've heard of that. But not all that often – most people, when they're across, seem to wonder why the hell they spent so long trying to put it off.'

Grayle moved away from the window. 'Anyhow, Seffi and I are going over to Gloucestershire tomorrow to talk to this woman who was at the party. Whose husband fucked the son's girl.'

Bobby frowned. 'Is that wise?'

'What's wise gotta do with it?'

'Just that if you find the woman's husband has a slice out of his face . . .'

233

Grayle started to say something, fell silent.

'Those blokes had an agenda,' Bobby said. 'They didn't complete it. Right now, they don't know where you are. Either of you. Unless they got Grayle's name out of Justin before . . .' He stiffened. 'You didn't give him your address, did you?'

'Oh. Did I? No . . . wait . . . I didn't. I gave him my name was all. For the bill. I didn't even write anything down.'

'Nothing in the car with your address on it?'

'I don't think so. Bobby, you think we could be in danger *here*?'

'It's unlikely, but we can't rule it out.'

At which point Callard had actually said, 'Aren't we pushing the bounds of credibility a little here?' And Grayle had thought, didn't it ever occur to you that this is the first time tonight we *haven't* been doing that?

She'd been drawn back to the window. The uneven castle walls looked like a grey army keeping vigil until dawn. Except the castle walls couldn't even keep the damn rain out.

'Look,' Callard said, 'I don't want to put you in danger. I ought to leave.'

'That's ridiculous.' Marcus was half out of his chair.

'If we go over to Cheltenham tomorrow, that gets both of us out,' Grayle said.

Bobby shook his head.

'Two defenceless women, huh?' Grayle snapped.

Then Callard was turning to Bobby, saying, 'All right then, if you think there's a risk, why don't *you* go to Cheltenham with me?'

*   *   *

234

'And I suppose, Underhill, that you're glad to get rid of her for a day,' Marcus said, getting it all ass over tit as usual.

Grayle said tightly, 'Might freshen up the place a little.'

'All right,' Marcus said. 'What's the problem?'

'No problem.'

'Underhill?'

'Forget it,' Grayle said.

23

Well, they hadn't been expecting the husband, but it had always been a possibility. It made it harder, but the rewards were potentially greater.

He was a big man in his fifties. Wide chest straining his mauve polo shirt. Wide face.

Unmarked, as it happened.

He was standing, arms hanging loose, under the veranda of the spacious, colonial-style bungalow in a scrappy, semi-rural village five miles outside Cheltenham. He was staring at Persephone Callard as if he just could not believe this.

Seffi was summery today in a cream woollen jacket over a turquoise silk top and off-white jeans. The ensemble said, *Whatever you've heard, I'm still a woman.*

'Ah, Mr Hole.' She stood no more than a couple of feet from him and did not back away. 'I really came to see your wife.'

'Or maybe you come to see if I've still *got* a wife.' Mr Hole had a rounded Gloucestershire accent. 'You got some flaming nerve, lady.'

The bungalow was in a choice spot at the top of a

rise. There was a long gravel drive, about half an acre of lawn between the veranda and the road. Security gates seven feet tall at the bottom, but one had been hanging open.

They'd parked the Grand Cherokee on a grass verge about a hundred yards away and sat there a while discussing how to handle this. How angry *was* the husband? Maiden had asked.

Called me a black slag.

Mr Hole's face was smoothly shaven. But not, it would appear, with a hedging knife.

'Like you haven't caused enough trouble,' he said.

'It's been troubling me, too,' Seffi Callard said smoothly. 'Look, sometimes these things just come out, yah? And are not invariably accurate. One can never entirely guarantee that what comes through is going to be the absolute truth.'

'Oh, *can't* one? Then why . . . ?' His cheeks reddening. 'Well, we both know why in this case, don't we, lady?'

Anger there, genuine outrage.

'Coral does two afternoons a week at a charity shop in Cheltenham,' he said, 'which is not a suitable place for you to talk to her. So you can talk to me or you can fuck off.'

He wasn't being friendly, he wasn't ready to be talked round. But he was curious, Maiden thought. There were things he wanted to know.

Inside, there were low sofas in bright spacey colours. Potted palms, yellow roller blinds, a Spanish-looking TV cabinet. The picture windows framed flat, scrubby farmland. Mr Hole nodded at one of the sofas but

237

didn't sit down himself. Maiden wondered where the money had come from.

'This is Bobby Maiden,' Seffi said. 'My fiancé.'

Mr Hole didn't smile, making it clear he wasn't mellowing. 'I accept the material compensations might be considerable,' he said bluntly, not looking at Maiden, 'but how does he stand it?'

'I've got no imagination, Mr Hole.' Maiden sat next to Seffi on a sofa with a banana pattern. He was somehow reminded of Consuela's sitting room in Elham.

Mr Hole kept on looking at Seffi and came directly to the point. 'My wife wrote to you.'

Seffi's eyes widened. 'You know about that?'

'Of *course* I bloody know about it. Twenty-six years of marriage, a phoney stage act don't destroy that, lady. We did a lot of talking and we decided we ought to take steps to find out who put you up to it.'

'*Put me—?*'

'We came to the conclusion', he said, 'that it was somebody's idea of a joke.'

'Doesn't strike me as that funny, somehow,' Maiden said.

'Some people have a mighty strange sense of humour.' Mr Hole came to sit in a sofa opposite them. It had a citrus fruit design. He'd never stopped looking at Seffi. 'You could save a lot of trouble, Miss Callard, if you just told me who it was. And don't give me any of that spirit world crap. I don't take any moral stance on how you make your living, but I know a set-up when I see one.'

'Now, *look* . . .' Seffi Callard began to rise. Maiden put a fiancé's hand on her arm.

'Let's hear what Mr Hole has to say. You see, what happened, Mr Hole, was that Seffi was given a lot of money by Sir Richard Barber to come along on the night, and she—'

'*Quite* a lot of money, I'd guess.'

'And she doesn't really know what that was all about. So if you're talking set-up, perhaps she was the one set up.'

Hole still didn't look at him. 'I would like a name. I think you owe me a name.'

Seffi said nothing.

'Not Sir Richard Barber, that's for sure. What about Gary?'

'Gary?' Maiden said.

'You stay out of this.'

'Gary who?' Seffi said.

'You know who I bloody mean, you're not that stupid. Listen, if it's Gary I won't tell him. I won't tell him you told me. I just need to know. If it's Gary, it's all right. You know what I'm saying?'

'Oh,' Maiden said. '*That* Gary.'

And Mr Hole finally turned and looked at him. It was a long, hard look designed to tell Maiden he might have just made a mistake.

'Who *are* you, my friend?' Mr Hole said coldly.

'You're a mate of Gary's then, Mr Hole?'

Mr Hole came slowly to his feet.

'Only, if Gary—'

'Out,' said Mr Hole.

'Is there a problem?'

Mr Hole's fists bunched. They were big, hard fists which had been bunched before. 'Problem's gonner be all yours, boy, you push it any further with me.'

Maiden rather thought he meant it. This was where you had either to blow your cover and bring out your warrant card or leave quietly.

Seffi Callard prodded the Jeep back on to the road. Big, solid clouds were walling up the sky in the east; over the hills a weak sun was trying to get its fingers in the cracks.

'He's interesting,' Maiden said. 'He's *extremely* interesting.'

'Well, I'm glad you think so, Bobby. I found him merely repellant. What the hell were you talking about? Who's Gary?'

'Don't know. But he frightens Mr Hole.'

'Detective games,' Seffi Callard said.

'And how many times did he tell you how wrong you were about him and his son's girlfriend?'

'No. He didn't, did he?' She took a right, signposted for Cheltenham. 'Go on. Get it over.'

'Sorry?'

'You need to ask if I was pre-informed, by anyone called Gary or anyone else about Hole and this girl.'

'Were you?'

'No. Do you believe me?'

'As a copper or as me?'

On the way here, she'd asked him if his death experience had made it harder to be a policeman. A very perceptive question.

'But that's irrelevant right now,' he said. 'Hole evidently thinks this Gary might have given you the information, but he's saying if it *was* Gary, then that's OK. He just wants to know. So Hole's relationship with Gary is a bit risky. Uncertain. He doesn't know where he is with Gary, but if it's Gary playing a little

240

joke, then Mr Hole's going to laugh along with him.'

'A psychologist, too.'

'And consider Mr Hole. Is he a wimp? Is he a big softy?'

'No.'

'What's that say about *Gary*, then?'

'What sort of people are these, Bobby?'

'Iffy.'

'You mean criminal?'

'Well . . . Most people, if they want you off the premises, they start threatening to call the police. He didn't.'

'Now just a minute . . .' She suddenly swung the Jeep into the side of the road, half on the grass verge, stopped with a judder. He saw she was sweating lightly. 'I don't *mix* with people like that.'

'Oh dear,' Maiden said.

She closed her eyes tight, moistening her lips. 'And I didn't mean that how it sounded. This . . . this is a complete nightmare.'

Maiden thought about Justin with his chest pushed in like a toothpaste tube. He thought about someone having Grayle's name, trying to find her. He nodded.

Seffi turned in her seat to face him, breathed hard, all that world-weary, languorous cool in rags. 'I . . . swear . . . I swear to God, Bobby, if there's something bad going on, involving me, I swear to you I don't—'

She put out a hand to him and then drew it back; her skin was glistening like dark honey.

'I know Grayle thinks I'm holding out. I am not. What I do . . . OK, it's a profession full of frauds and liars and self-deluded people and mad people. But I haven't lied to Grayle or Marcus and I'm not lying to you now. I *don't know* what's happening. I don't

241

know where to turn. I don't have any . . . mystical insights about it. I'm scared. I'm scared in this world and I have no refuge . . .'

'. . . anywhere else,' Maiden said softly. 'I wouldn't claim to understand about that. Or maybe I would, I don't know.' He reached on to the back seat for his jacket, pulled out a scuffed notebook, a mobile phone. 'Let's find out what we can.'

'Who are you calling?'

'DCI in Gloucester, Ron Foxworth.'

'Is that altogether safe?'

'It's taking a small chance.' Maiden prodded out the number. 'But we shared secrets once. Back in the Met.'

Meaning Martin Riggs; knowing about Riggs still constituted a kind of bond. He asked Gloucester Police for Foxworth's extension, gave his name.

'Might be a waste of time, of course. It's just a feeling.'

'You're going to tell him about Justin Sharpe?'

'God, no. Let them find Justin in their own time. Or if it looks like dragging out too long, maybe we'll give them an anonymous nudge. I'll have to tell him this is informal. I'm on leave, helping a friend. Though whether he'll be in this time on a Sat . . . Ron?'

'Bobby Maiden? You pick your bloody times, son. Is this anything urgent?'

'It's just a quick question. Off the record.'

'What bloody record's that? Nah, see, I've got a murder on, Bobby. I hate murders at weekends, don't you? Where are you?'

Justin?

'No problem, Ron. I'll call you again. I was only going to ask if you knew a bloke called Hole.'

Brief silence.

242

'Where?'

'Cheltenham area. Well-off bloke. Nice bungalow with a long drive. I've just left there, as it happens.'

'Les Hole? You've bloody—'

'Could be.'

'Well, I'll tell you what, Bobby,' Ron said, collecting himself together. 'I've got a press conference at half-seven. Want to do that myself, make sure we get the right points over. I'll be free about . . . eight, eight-thirty? Where'd you wanna meet up? Somewhere quiet, yeah?'

'Wherever. I don't know this area too well.'

'We're setting up the incident room at Stroud, so . . . Look, gimme your mobile number, I'll call you back. I really do have to do this presser.'

'You won't get much in the Sundays, Ron. Not at that time.'

'Bobby, I'm desperate for an ID, and there's gonna be no nice, peaceful pictures of this poor bugger to show around.'

'Oh.'

'Axe job, it looks like. Geezer found in a ditch, face split like a bloody walnut.'

'Right,' Maiden said. 'Mmm.'

24

'Well, we'll be having a holiday first,' one of last week's Lottery winners says – this is a syndicate of five school-dinner ladies from Basingstoke. 'Taking the kids to Disney World. And, of course, we've already bought ourselves a BMW.'

'*Yaaaaaaaak*,' Kelvyn Kite shrieks, stabbing a scornful talon at the monitor.

The audience whoops. The apparent need of so many Lottery winners to rush out and buy a BMW has become a running joke of Kelvyn's ever since the appalling Sherwin family, from Banbury, immediately bought *five* of them – his, hers, teenage kids', granny's . . . and granny didn't even drive.

'Stop it, now.' Cindy frowns at the bird, pointedly ignoring the autocue. 'It's none of your business. People are allowed to buy whatever cars they like when they win two million pounds.'

'Watch it, Cindy,' Jo says in the earpiece. 'I think you've taken this one far enough, don't you?'

'This has gone far enough,' Cindy tells the bird.

'Awk,' says the cynical Kelvyn Kite.

'Anyway, I *like* the Lada,' Cindy says.

Laughter. Kelvyn sulks, beak in the air. Cindy ignores him, turning to the autocue.

'But one of last week's big winners has gone one better than a BMW. Colin Seymour is the headmaster of a school in Shropshire for children with learning difficulties. He's also a newly qualified pilot . . . So what was the first thing Colin did with his one point seven million . . . ? Why, he bought the very plane in which he'd learned to fly!'

Cue VT. Up it comes on the monitor. A little Cessna winging in to a rural airstrip. Stirring music. Cut to genial Colin Seymour stepping out, grinning. He is tall, lean and bearded and wears a Second World War flying ace's leather jacket.

'Just under two minutes for this one, Cindy,' Jo reminds him. 'And – remembering what he does for a living – *no jokes at all.*'

'Wilco, chief.' Cindy is relaxed about this. Reckless he might be, but he's not stupid. Camelot, the BBC and BMW, however, are *big* targets; they might not like it, but they can't appear mean-spirited enough to censure a man in late middle-age and a midnight-blue diamanté evening dress.

Cindy goes for a little sit down, off set – you don't want the audience laughing at the wrong time, even if they aren't being transmitted – until Jo says, 'Thirty seconds, Cindy. Get ready to brandish the bird.'

Cindy slips his right arm into Kelvyn and walks out, an eye on the monitor. Colin Seymour is surrounded by happy children from his school. He's showing them his plane. Finally, in close up, Colin says, 'And what I'm planning to do this summer is to buy a slightly bigger aircraft in which I'll be able to take small groups of the kids up for short flights. Which will, you know, be a really fantastic experience for all of us.'

Jo says, 'Five seconds . . . Kelvyn.'

Colin Seymour turns to an engaging gap-toothed youngster. 'What are we going to do, then, Charlie? We're going to fly like . . .'

Charlie beams. 'A *kite*!'

And Camera One goes in tight on Kelvyn, who snaps his beak modestly.

Cindy can't resist it. He looks dubious.

'Fly like him, lovely, and you'll never find the blessed airstrip!'

Kelvyn shuts his beak and sulks; the audience roars.

With his habitual sigh of satisfaction at being able to drive west, beyond the hard lights of London, Cindy tossed Kelvyn's pink suitcase on to the back seat of his new saloon car. A Honda Accord, it was, he could never have a BMW now.

However, before leaving the car park, he put on the Honda's interior light and tore open the bulky envelope which had arrived for him, care of the BBC. Young Jo had handed it to him with something of a grimace.

For, at the foot of the expensive, parchment-coloured envelope was inscribed,

Overcross: experience it.

Inside was a leaflet and a small, stiff-backed book. No covering letter, so perhaps he was just one person among several hundred on some marketing firm's mailing list.

The leaflet showed a photograph of towers against a red sunset. It was headed,

Overcross Castle:
The Veil is Lifted

On page two there was a brief explanation.

Overcross Castle, in the foothills of the Malverns, was built in the 1860s (on the site of a medieval castle) by the Midlands industrialist Barnaby Crole, who made his fortune from the South Wales mining industry.

The Victorian Gothic castle was named Overcross after the nearby hamlet, but for Crole this had a deeper meaning: it was a place where, he believed, our world and the world of spirits might overlap.

With its romantic towers and turrets looming from the woods, Overcross quickly became famous for weekend gatherings, at which distinguished mediums of the day, including the revered Daniel Dunglas-Home, would conduct seances attended by the likes of Sir Arthur Conan Doyle, creator of Sherlock Holmes and an ardent spiritualist.

The eminent scientist and psychologist Dr Anthony Abblow, himself an experienced trance-medium, became so enamoured of Overcross Castle and its unique atmosphere that he took an apartment in the castle, where he spent many years engaged in experiments into the meaning of life and death.

Huge and increasingly difficult to heat, the castle ceased to be a private home, became a school and

then a hotel and was then derelict for many years before being purchased by the celebrated consultant-mesmerist, paranormal investigator and television presenter Kurt Campbell.

Now Kurt Campbell is ready to reopen Overcross to continue the work begun by Crole and Abblow in the Victorian heyday of psychic studies.

And from Wednesday 18 March, when Overcross hosts its first Festival of the Spirit for over a century, you can join an exclusive house party, a recreation of a Victorian spiritualist gathering with Kurt Campbell himself and one of the world's most celebrated mediums as guest of honour.

Cindy's eye travelled to the very much smaller print at the foot of page three, where he learned that one might become a privileged house guest on the night of this extraordinary psychic soirée for a mere £500 for a double room.

Perhaps this reflected the deficit in Kurt's finances, resulting from his failure to become the most expensive presenter in the history of the Lottery Show.

Barnaby Crole would turn in his grave.

And indeed, perhaps Kurt was hoping for that. Or for some kind of psychic fireworks, anyway.

Cindy glanced at the booklet. It was a reprint of a small history of Overcross Castle and its founder, originally published in 1936. He pushed book and leaflet back into the envelope.

On reflection, he suspected the mailing list had been drawn up prior to Kurt's appearance on the Lottery Show. He wondered what Kurt's reaction would be if he actually turned up.

*   *   *

Meanwhile . . . home.

Only a humble caravan, mind, but think of the location. And the bonus, this time, of a visit to little Grayle and her irascible employer – that somewhat lesser known castle owner – with rather an intriguing purpose. For which one would require energy and attunement.

Therefore, at first light tomorrow, taking his painted shamanic drum, he would follow the shining path to the gorse-prickled hill overlooking the sea on one side and, on the other, the Preselis. Perhaps even as high as the great magnetic centre Carn Ingli, which he was presumptuous enough to consider his power base.

He would stand alone in the stiff, wiry, sheep-munched grass and give thanks to the elements, to the forces of earth and air, sea and sky which, together, became something approximating to God.

And pray. In his fashion.

Avoiding the horrors of the M25, Cindy found his way to the M4, the motorway of the west. Before the junction, as usual, he put on the radio to catch the ten o'clock news on 'Five Live'.

And with that shamanic flair for pinpointing the moment which, in more pleasant circumstances, would be termed serendipitous, the switch clicked on this:

'. . . and it's just been confirmed that the pilot who died when his two-seater aircraft overshot a runway and smashed into a barn in Shropshire has been named as Lottery jackpot winner, Colin Seymour.

'42-year-old Mr Seymour was headmaster of a special school for children with learning difficulties, and earlier tonight millions of viewers of the BBC's

National Lottery Live saw him showing pupils the plane he'd bought with his one point seven million pound win . . .'

Cindy drove numbly into the mesh of lights at the M4 junction.

He was tasting the bitter tang from the sea.

25

Ron was waiting for them in a layby above Stroud, as arranged. Seffi flashed the headlights and Ron lumbered across from his Rover, a bulky bloke in an old anorak. Maiden got into the back of the Jeep so he could stretch his legs in the passenger seat and appraise Seffi by the interior lights.

'They were right about you having exotic friends these days, Bobby. I'm sorry, love, you don't mind exotic, do you? Ron Foxworth, my name.'

'Hello.' Seffi a touch guarded.

'You're the one I been reading about. The one who's disappeared.'

'Psychic Seffi,' she said with distaste.

'Better watch what I'm thinking then, hadn't I?' Ron said.

'It doesn't work like that, Mr Foxworth.'

'Oh, really? A little limited, my knowledge of these things. Nuts and bolts rationalist, me, I'm afraid. Where we going then, Bobby? I don't think I feel like a drink, and I'm sure our famous friend here doesn't want to be seen in a pub with a battered old bugger like me. Can we just drive around? Cotswolds by night?'

Maiden had almost forgotten what a tricky bastard Ron could be. He started frisking for holes the story he and Seffi Callard had concocted in the harsh light of the discovery of a second body, with a hacked face and few doubts this time about the origin of the wounds.

'So you and Miss Callard, Bobby . . .'

'Friends,' Maiden said.

'Quite close friends.' Seffi pulled out of the layby.

'I *see*. Well . . .'

'We met when Bobby was gathering background information in connection with the Green Man murders. I was able to explain a little about the psychology of people who believe they're being influenced by elemental forces. Working together on something essentially frightening can be curiously . . . intimate, as I'm sure . . .'

Seffi let the sentence hang. Maiden sensed her smile.

How fluently she lies.

'So when I was feeling rather threatened recently, I asked Bobby for advice.'

Telling Ron how, in this line of work, one received endless crank mail. Mostly from fundamentalist Christians warning that the fires of hell were already being stoked in readiness for one's arrival. A very few implied that physical retribution might be exacted on the earthly plane.

Seffi sounding loony enough for Ron to take it all less than seriously, but looking alluring enough for him to see why Maiden had stuck around.

Below them, the lights of Stroud formed a glowing bowl.

She told the story of the party, but only as far as the Kieran Hole incident. When they were into the countryside again, Ron said, 'Yeah, I can see how that would offend Les Hole. This was a message you had . . . on the, er . . . ?'

'A spirit message.'

'Ri-ight.' Ron nodding sceptically. 'From the boy, Kieran, you say?'

'He did hang himself, then,' Maiden said.

'Oh indeed, Bobby. No note, no clothes on. We had it down as a wanking job.'

'I'm sorry?' Seffi said.

'Sexual hanging. Auto-erotic strangulation. "Come Dancing" on the end of a rope. Commonplace enough, but occasionally a bit difficult to prove medically, so coroners often tend to be merciful and put it down as suicide. It affected Coral very deeply, as you obviously realize. And Les, of course. So you're saying Les blamed the, er, messenger.'

'There was a letter', Maiden said, 'from the wife. Trying to set up another meeting with Seffi. But it was the phone calls . . .' Lying now. 'Late at night, nobody there. And this sense of being . . .'

'Stalked,' Seffi said. 'Although I never got a good look at him.'

Ron leaned back against the side-window, getting a good look at her. 'So all these stories about you packing it in . . . ?'

'This was just a part of it. I've been feeling generally vulnerable. No-one likes to be on the receiving end of scorn and hostility.'

'It seemed to me we ought to go and see Mrs Hole,' Maiden said. 'She wasn't there, but he was. He didn't know I was a copper. He was aggressive. He seemed to think someone might have set him up and he wasn't looking at Barber. He mentioned the name Gary.'

253

'Oh, *did* he?' Ron's voice thickening with satisfaction.

'That means something to you, Ron?'

'You don't know?'

'Should I? I got the feeling he was a little scared of Gary.'

'Well, of course he is, Bobby, of course he is. Everybody's a little bit scared of Gary.'

'I feel I should know who we're talking about here, but I don't.'

'Bloody right you should,' Ron said. 'Oh, yes.'

Cindy pulled into the Severn Bridge services and went in for a coffee. Sat in the restaurant, unrecognized in his blazer and slacks, gazing across the dark water to the Welsh side. His mobile phone, switched off, felt like a housebrick in the inside pocket of his blazer. So many people attempting to contact him in the past hour; he could always feel the weight of them.

Back at the car, he sighed and switched on the phone, sat back, closed his eyes and waited.

The first call came through within four minutes.

'Oh, Cindy, hi, this is Simon Tremain at BBC Radio News in London. Really sorry to bother you at this hour, but I was told you always drove through the night after the show. I hope that's right, and I haven't disturbed you during—'

'No problem, Simon, *bach*.'

'Great. Well, look, it's about this poor guy, Colin Seymour, who crashed his plane tonight. Obviously, we'll be running clips from the Lottery Show on all the morning bulletins, and I'm putting a package together for "Five Live".'

'What is it you want then, lovely?'

'Well, I *was* asked to see if you could go into our Haverfordwest unattended studio, but obviously you're going to be a bit knackered, so maybe we could record a short interview on the phone?'

'Fire away, boy.'

'Right . . . can you hold, or should I get plugged in and whatnot and give you a call in a couple of minutes?'

'I'll hold.' Knowing that if he cut the line there would be another call.

Presently, Simon Tremain said, 'OK, I'm rolling. Cindy, if we can start with the obvious . . . this must have been a shock.'

'A terrible, *terrible* shock. I was driving home when I heard the news, and I had to stop. You know, when you're doing the show you feel you come to know the winners personally . . . and, though I never met Colin, it was clear that this was a man who would put his good fortune to good use. He wasn't going to retire to the south of France, he wanted to continue working with these children and use the money to bring some excitement into their lives. An utter tragedy, it is.'

'And I suppose the bitter irony of it is that when Colin and his young friend said they were going to "fly like a kite" you commented that if they did that they'd never find the runway. Which, unfortunately, seems to be roughly what happened.'

'Ah. Yes.' *This is the bit they'll use.* 'Well, you know, you make these flip comments without a thought for the brutal hand of fate, and when something like this happens your own words go echoing in your ears and you'd do anything, you would, to take them back. But I suppose if I really *could* rewind time,

255

what I'd do would be to have Colin Seymour put off his flight until the next day.'

Afterwards, Simon said, 'Sorry, I had to ask you that, but I suppose I won't be the last. I mean, with that guy who had the heart attack and everything . . . bad week for Lottery winners.'

'Indeed,' Cindy said, resigned. He asked the reporter when exactly the accident had occurred and learned that it was actually *before* the Lottery Show. Less than an hour before.

Perhaps poor Colin had been in a hurry to catch himself on television.

The proximity of retirement could take them different ways. Some coppers nibbled away the final year as if they'd already been put out to grass, the crime reports on the desk separated by estate-agent particulars of cottages in Cornwall.

Others were really driven that last year . . . racing against the calendar, determined that a certain piece of business was not going to be *unfinished* business when they collected the Teasmaid with the built-in radio. Driven by the sour certainty that if they didn't finish it nobody ever would.

This, it emerged, was Ron Foxworth. The business in question: Gary Seward.

Ron's obsession. So little time left. Ron abandoning discretion as they cruised through the Cotswold night.

It was a generation thing. He and Gary were about the same age. When Gary was gone, the youngsters wouldn't give a shit. To young coppers, old villains were teddy bears. It was like Reggie Kray and Frankie Fraser – regarded with amusement, even affection if you were too young to have mopped up after them.

'He laughs, you see,' Ron said. 'Laughs all the time. Laughing Gary. Whenever you see him on some bloody chat show, he's laughing his balls off.'

Ron Foxworth, white-haired and big-bellied, did the laugh, slow and measured, like a nasal duck.

'And whenever I hear that laugh, Bobby, it's personal. He's laughing at me.'

Ron and Gary. Coincidence upon coincidence, from the start. Ron was still a probationer in south London when he walked in on Seward doing an off-licence at knife-point. Ron nearly losing an eye.

'In it for the excitement,' Ron said. 'I knew that from the first. This is a villain does it for the buzz. The money's always been secondary. And that's why I think he can't stop. Where's the excitement in addressing Rotary Club lunches?'

Protection and muscle, these had been Gary's business. Usually hands on, Ron said. Gary was never going to be the chairman of the board, delegating, subcontracting. Except, of course, to long-time close associates.

'Sometimes there'd be some poor sod cut to ribbons or bits shot off him. Minimum life-threatening injury, maximum pain. And some big dummy'd go down for it. But you knew, you just *did*, that Gary'd done this one himself. Stubbed out his slim panatella, climbed into his Daimler, drove well within the speed limit, parked outside some mean little terraced house, gone coolly in and done it. For the buzz.'

Seffi Callard said, 'It always amazes me how people can go on getting away with this kind of thing for years and years, never getting caught – when you quite obviously know who they are and what they're doing.'

'What they've *done*,' Ron said. 'Past tense. There's a

257

big difference. Now if only we were clairvoyants like you—'

'I'm not a clairvoyant.'

'Yes, it's odd,' Maiden said hurriedly. 'The thing is, sometimes they're tolerated by certain officers. For a number of reasons.'

Ron grinned. 'What's Martin Riggs doing now, Bobby? Still with Forcefield?'

'Far as I know.'

'Makes you think,' Ron said. 'Riggs would've been at the Met in Gary's day, wouldn't he? But then we all thought Riggs was straight as they come, back then. You didn't, Bobby, but you were just a boy, no clout. Me, I was ready to nick Seward twice and both times the rug was pulled. Makes you think.'

Seffi said, 'But Seward *was* eventually arrested, wasn't he? If it's the one I'm thinking of.'

'Gary Seward did seven years for extortion, my dear, compared with the three life sentences he'd've had if it was *me* who'd pulled him. But it wasn't me, and when he comes out he gets together with a Sunday newspaper journalist and writes his memoirs, name-dropping every famous villain since Jack the Ripper.'

'Oh yes. It was called . . .'

'*Bang to Wrongs*. Serialized in the *News of the World*, sold quite well, but not well enough to furnish him with his current lifestyle. Even allowing for all the chat shows. No. The boy's still at it.'

'Up here?' Maiden said.

'It's where you come when you've made it. It's Beverly bloody Hills UK. When I left the Met – in something like disgust, I might say – to take command of Gloucester CID, who should I find in his gracious Cotswold retreat . . . ?'

'Must be irksome, Ron.'

'And he's at it, Bobby. The bastard is *at it*. All right, he's got laundered money in a bunch of business ventures, but where's the excitement in that?'

Seffi pulled off the road into one of those hilltop viewpoint parking areas. All you could see now was a vast scattering of lights over four counties. She stopped the Jeep and switched off.

'So who exactly is Mr Hole?' Maiden asked.

'Les Hole. Import and export. Mainly import.'

'Porn?'

'Not now. Least, nothing severe. No kids, no snuff. A bad boy in his youth, mind, but that was a long time ago. Long enough that two years ago he qualified for a conditional discharge from Gloucester mags on a few dozen Italian videos. Course, Les's mistake was to do it again too soon. With me watching closely by now. Because of Seward.'

'Associates?'

'Shared investments – legit – and crossover social lives. So, with the conditional hanging over him, he was more than amenable. You know?'

'Amenable?'

'*You* know.'

And Maiden did. Knew why the mention of Mr Hole over the phone had turned everything around, Ron making sure the two of them met up that very night.

'You're saying Les Hole's your *informant*?'

Ron looked at Seffi. Who expelled a short breath of irritation. '*I'm* hardly going to tell anyone am I?'

'All right.' Ron leaned right back against the door so he could see them both, if only in shadow. 'Seward-watcher, I'd call it. He tells me what the boy's up to, the stuff he's party to, and I store it up. Waiting for the moment. I don't want Seward on chickenshit, I want . . . Anyway, the longer it goes on, naturally, the more paranoid Les is that Gary's on to him. Every little remark makes him tremble, every little practical joke. Next thing it might be the exploding petrol tank – he said that to me once.'

Maiden said, 'The odd practical joke? Like setting up a medium to deliver a devastating, humiliating message from the dead son?'

It was dizzying looking down at four counties of lights. Like being on a cliff edge.

'Hang on, let me get this right,' Ron said. 'Les Hole's wondering if Gary bunged Miss Callard serious money in order to make it clear to Les, in public, that he'd better watch his step. On account of somebody knows all his little secrets and won't hesitate to use them. Right? I think this poses an obvious question, Miss Callard.'

'Well, of course I didn't take any money from Seward. I don't *know* Seward.'

'Don't you?'

'No, I bloody don't. Nor have I read his stupid book.'

'Well, I'm sorry,' Ron said. 'Just seems odd to me that he hasn't sought you out, that's all. You being in the same part of the world. And interests in common.'

'What's that mean?' Maiden said. 'What interests in common?'

'You don't know? It's in his book.'

'I haven't read his book either. I know he likes to collect celebrities. Actors, sports personalities . . .'

'And not all of them still alive, Bobby.'

'You're kidding.'

'I'm telling you. He visits bloody . . . he consults spiritualists.'

There was a silence. Maiden watched the lights of a silent airplane over the horizon.

'Why?' Seffi said.

'Started when his mum got run over by a drunk. Took it very personally. Nobody takes something *away* from Gary. You don't *take*. Not even if you're God. I believe it was an auntie or somebody who got him to see a medium, try and calm him down. Seems to have had the opposite effect. Seen various mediums all his life since. Claims it was what got him through his stretch: daily workouts in the gym and regular spiritual counselling. Prison visits from some old lady passing on messages from his old mum, all that kind of cr—' Ron coughed. 'Excuse me.'

'Which old lady?' Seffi said sharply.

'I can't remember her name, you'll have to get the book. See, it comes down to this: Gary's got this enormous appetite for life and the only thing really frightens him is the thought of losing it. Gary Seward vanishing into nothingness, the finely tuned body rotting in the grave. Nothing left but a Cheshire cat grin on some old photos.'

'Midlife crisis?' Maiden said.

'*And* some. Gary needs to believe Gary's going *on*.'

There was a period of silence.

Then Ron said, 'So if it wasn't Gary . . . who *did* tell you about the boy?'

Maiden saw Seffi slowly shaking her head, felt the steam rising. He said hurriedly, 'For what it's worth, Ron, I believe her. I believe she does this . . . thing.'

He could just about make out Ron's faithless smile. 'Forgive me, Bobby, but, from what I've been

261

hearing, that's what you would say. These days.'

Maiden made an effort to disregard it, concentrating on what he needed to know. 'Sir Richard Barber. Where's he come into this?'

'No idea, mate. Never had cause to look into him. But I will now. This has been interesting. A bit weird, if you don't mind me saying, but it's given me a few things to think about.'

'How gratifying,' Seffi said bleakly.

26

During the ten or so minutes it took to drive Ron Foxworth back to his car, Maiden quizzed him politely about the murder inquiry at Stroud. Making conversation, talking shop.

Learning that the dead man had been found by a farmer, near the village of Bisley. The body was tumbled into a ditch with about six inches of water in the bottom so that, at first, the farmer thought this was some drunk who'd drowned. Until he turned the bloke over and was sick.

'So . . . confirmation,' Seffi said when Ron was gone and they were sitting in the Jeep, in the layby above Stroud, with the engine running.

'How far would that be from your place?'

'Bisley? Three, four miles, I suppose.'

'So how did he get *there*?' Maiden demanded. 'And what happened to his mate? There's something missing. It doesn't make sense.'

'It's going to make some awful sense to Grayle,' Seffi said. 'Just when she thought she was in the clear. I'd almost be inclined not even to tell her.'

'What, so she can read about it in the papers?'

At eight-thirty tomorrow they'd be out there in

force, Ron had said. A roughly regimented march through the fields in search of a weapon.

'Could be about six years, however, before they get around to putting divers into the Wye at Ross,' Maiden said morosely.

He saw that Seffi was bent over the steering wheel, her shoulders heaving. He thought she was sobbing then realized it was wild, unhealthy laughter.

'Oh Christ!' She raised herself up. 'Bobby, there's a gap on the wall.'

'What?'

'Back at the lodge. There's a bloody gap on the wall . . . probably with the perfectly etiolated outline of an antique hedge hacker. Do you see what I mean?'

'At the lodge?'

'Mrs Dronfield, the cleaner, comes in on a Monday. I've never thought of her as a deductive genius, but she can certainly gossip for Gloucestershire . . .' She looked across at him, those lush lips slack with dismay. 'Police combing the fields for miles around, everybody talking about it, being careful to lock their doors . . . and here's a perfect outline of the murder weapon set up for Mrs Dronfield. It's not *terribly* funny, is it?'

Cindy was not a person who believed the press was there to be avoided. Had he complained when all those articles appeared commenting on what a refreshing change he had wrought upon the previously tedious Lottery programme? No, he had not.

In sickness and in health.

He sat upon the clifftop, meditated for ten minutes in the sea-haunted silence and then went into the caravan and switched on the mobile phone for the first time since recording his BBC radio interview.

It bleeped within twenty seconds.

'At last. Is that Cindy?'

'No, Kelvyn here. Who wants to speak to Cindy?'

'Ho ho. Listen, mate, it's Greg Cook at the *Mirror*.'

The showbiz editor, or whatever title they gave them these days. At past midnight on a Sunday morning? What on earth was this?

'Good heavens, boy, are you in the office?'

'No, I'm at home, actually, Cindy. I know it's late, but the reason I'm ringing . . . Are you listening, Cindy? Because I know it's late and you're probably knackered.'

'Listening most intently, I am.'

'Because I'm ringing to warn you.'

'A tidal wave, is it, bound for the Pembrokeshire coastline?'

'Er . . . ha ha. No, it's a bit of information that's come our way just quite recently . . . well, tonight, actually . . . that another publication, which shall be nameless, is planning, not to put too fine a point on it, Cindy, to shaft you.'

'*Hello!* magazine?' Cindy said. 'My, there's worrying.'

'We both know who we're talking about here, mate. And, yeah, it *is* worrying.'

'For me or for you?'

'For both of us. You know the *Mirror*'s always been on your side. I mean, you do know that, don't you?'

'I would trust the *Mirror* like my own mother, Gregory,' said Cindy, whose mother had abandoned him, newborn, on the steps of the Bethesda Chapel in Dowlais. 'How do they propose to, ah, shaft me?'

'That crash tonight, Cindy. Yeah?'

'Poor man.'

'Tragic. And the heart guy. And other incidents. Allegedly.'

'I don't understand.'

'Also, stories going round about you. I wouldn't repeat them, but somebody's been looking into your past.'

'Indeed.'

'And offering certain material for sale. Came to us, first. Naturally, we refused point-blank. Showed him the door.'

'Asking too much, was he?'

'But he went straight to the opposition, and we understand a deal's been made. You can expect to read about it next week. It's almost certain to cause a storm. And inevitably put the world's media on your back. Unfairly, in our belief.'

'You . . .' Cindy became aware that the hand holding the phone was shaking. 'You're having me on, I think, Gregory.'

'Cindy, I wish that were the case.'

'But I don't . . . I don't . . . I have no idea what this can be about.'

But he was rather afraid that he did. Some of it, anyway.

He began to breathe harder and covered the mouthpiece to conceal it. He was what he was; he had never attempted to cover it up. He was renowned as an eccentric – this was accepted. He had no sexual secrets – well, not many. But yes, the ammunition was there, he had always been aware of that.

But people *liked* him. He was *popular*. On the stormy seas of controversy, was not popularity the greatest ballast?

266

'Cindy, I want to help you,' Gregory Cook said. 'No bullshit, all right? I personally contacted the editor – rang him at home, tonight, not two hours ago – and, as a result, I'm empowered to offer you . . . let's call it sanctuary. We'll move you to a luxury hotel, a secret destination. We'll give you a sum of money, precise details of which I can discuss later. And we'll let you tell your side of the story – in effect your life story – to an experienced writer, probably me, which we'll publish exclusively and *simultaneously* – that's the key point – thus negating the damage caused by our dockland friends. Are you with me?'

'I may be just slightly ahead of you. You want me to co-operate in the manufacture of what I believe is called a "spoiler".'

'Yes,' Gregory Cook said. 'In a word. We can have you away from your little tin shack before those bastards are out of the pub. What do you say?'

'Gregory, it's . . .' Cindy took a breath, thinking fast. 'A magnificent gesture, it is, on your part.'

'Thank you.'

'I would like, however, a few minutes to peruse my BBC contract. To make absolutely sure it contains no clause precluding my acceptance of your generous proposal. I don't think, for one minute, that there *is* such a clause, but I would like to be certain.'

'No problem, Cindy. Bring the contract with you. We'll get our lawyers to run through it.'

'Please. It will take me ten minutes. Just give me your number and I shall call you back.'

'Cindy, these fuckers could well be on their way. They'll certainly be there by morning.'

'Just a few minutes, Gregory. A few short minutes.'

*　　*　　*

A few short minutes it took him to unpack his cases and repack them with fresh things.

And gather his drum and his cloak of feathers.

And Kelvyn Kite in his pink case.

And load them all into the Honda, which he drove to his lock-up behind Dai Gruffydd's lightless service station on the Haverfordwest road.

Why? Why this? Why this *now*?

In the lock-up was nested his Morris Minor. Unthinkable, somehow, to flee in the Honda. Cindy hoped she would start for, if she did not, it would be the very worst of omens.

27

There was even a metal bracket which had supported the hacker. And, yes, a pale patch on the wall which, even in the meagre glow of a single lamp, gave Bobby Maiden a clear guide to the size and shape of the implement.

'What now? Get rid of the lot?' Seffi Callard said. 'Take out all the brackets, paint the wall?'

'So that your Mrs . . .'

'Dronfield.'

'. . . is faced with the smell of fresh paint and—'

'OK, forget it. No wonder people get caught. They must get *themselves* caught half the time.'

'Tangled webs.' Maiden thought it was incredibly unlikely that Mrs Dronfield would make connections, but . . . 'Perhaps if we move the saw across so that, instead of hanging down, it . . .' lifting the part-rusted blade '. . . fits horizontally, occupying the vacant bracket and covering the space, where . . .'

'Very good,' she said when he'd repositioned the other tools to close gaps. 'You realize what you've done.'

'Become a serious accessory. This gets out, end of career.'

'The feeling I'm getting from you is that that might almost be a relief.'

'Dunno. How would I make a living?' He stood in the dim corner between the door to the kitchen and the bottom of the stairs, forming a picture of how it happened. 'What were your first feelings when you came down and found those guys?'

'What do you *think*?' He couldn't make out her face, but he saw her shiver. 'You any good at lighting fires, Bobby?'

'Did you feel they were expecting you? Waiting for you? Knew you were around?'

'It was Grayle they didn't expect.'

Maiden bent over the hearth, picked up a poker and raked at the cinders. Found a pile of old newspapers and a box of firelighters. Wondered where she lived the rest of the time, what classy apartment she'd abandoned for this dim cave.

'You plan to stay here tonight?'

'Too late to go back. Do you want to ring Marcus and tell him?'

'Did you tell anyone else about what happened at the party? Apart from Marcus and Grayle and me?'

'Only Nancy. And as I was already wondering how far I could actually trust her, I told her no more than she'd learn from anyone who'd been there. The vase breaking, that kind of thing. Nothing about *him*.'

'Well,' he said carefully. '*He* could be a bit irrelevant. To someone else.'

'Despite your liberal attitudes. Despite your death experiences . . .' ice in her voice '. . . this is the one part of it, I suspect, you'd still rather wasn't there.'

'I try to understand,' Maiden said.

She came across the room, stood over him as he

270

knelt at the hearth. 'Imagine you're a woman. You're in a lonely house and every time you pick up the phone to make a call there's some sickening heavy breather on the line.'

Maiden built a pyramid of coal around a firelighter.

'Or you're in a two-roomed apartment,' she said, 'and there's one room you know you can't go into. A door you can't open. What do you do?'

'Perhaps you move out of the apartment.'

'And how would I make a living?' He looked up at her. She didn't smile. 'Is that really all you think this is?'

The cramped, flagged forecourt of the cottage behind St Mary's Church was big enough for a Mini and virtually nothing made since. There was a feeling of security about this. Anyhow, Grayle had always felt safe here.

Even though it was only a few miles from where Ersula had died.

This hadn't mattered, somehow, the way it would have if she was living in some modern condo and her sister had been killed in the next block. All to do with the age of the settlement, how many violent deaths it must have absorbed . . . while the old stone homes huddled snugly together and the church bells still rang out over the rich, pink soil.

Grayle drew the curtains. Checked the door – one lock and a small bolt; in New York she'd had four locks and a big chain and a peephole.

She was OK here, on her own. She'd lived alone, most of the time, in New York. Where was the difference?

Although it was late, she put a match to a wood fire

271

in the living room. Like a campfire in the woods, to keep the bears at bay. The flames lit the inglenook, shadows leaping and shooting up the stones. Living light was caught by the crystals hanging from the big beam, was glinting in the seraphic eyes of the brass Buddha in the hearth.

Bobby and Callard hadn't returned to Castle Farm.

Which was like . . . none of her business. Right?

Because she was OK. Grayle sat still and glum. She was fine.

Very tired, Cindy parked the Honda in the little cindered courtyard behind the Ram's Head and immediately switched off the lights.

The Honda, yes.

The Morris Minor, his totem car, his shamanic chariot, having failed to start. Of course it had. All that time in storage. What did he expect? It meant nothing.

Cindy crept around the side of the pub. He had no wish to disturb Amy. If she had retired for the night, well . . . resigned, he was, if necessary, to sleeping in the car. It would not be the first time.

The merest glow from the interior. A security lamp, perhaps, for even St Mary's was no longer too remote to be immune from the predatory attentions of itinerant thieves. Cindy peered through the bevelled glass into the churchlike glimmerings within the public bar.

A searing pain almost paralyzed his spine.

'*Freeze.*'

'Oh my God,' Cindy croaked.

'Turn around . . . *ve-ry slowly.*'

'Amy, my love,' Cindy wheezed, 'if you wanted me

272

to turn round quickly, we would require the services of an osteopath.'

'Cindy! Oh my God!' Amy dropped the yard-brush.

Amy Jenkins: little and dark and warm and crinkly, a refugee from the next valley to Cindy's own in the broken heart of Glamorgan. Divorced these many years from the man known only as *That Bastard*. Now queen of the Tup.

'You only just caught me, see,' she said, as if this wasn't past midnight and she might have gone to the shops. 'Just having a last look round, I was. Weekend night, you get them in from all over the place – Hereford, Abergavenny. Strangers, and some thinking they can see an opportunity. Always like a last look around, I do, on a Saturday night. And there you was, like a burglar. Well . . . I can't get over it – Cindy Mars-Lewis, and so famous now. Wait till I tell—'

'Nobody,' Cindy said firmly. 'Tell nobody.'

'Oh. Like that, is it?' Amy was leading him to the oak settle in the woody dimness of the deserted bar then putting more lights on, giving him the once-over. 'Looking tired, you are, Cindy. Not quite your old self.'

'I'm fine, lovely. Fine as I could be.'

'That poor man. The Lottery winner. Did you hear?'

'Yes, I did.'

'Money,' Amy said. 'Money makes people careless. Feel invulnerable they do, in the first flush of it.'

'Yes. That is a profound observation, Amy.'

'The usual room, is it?'

'That would be wonderful. I'm not yet sure how many nights. Two, three . . .'

'You stay as long as you like, Cindy. And if you don't want me to tell nobody, nobody gets told.'

'Little Amy,' Cindy said wistfully. 'Marry you, I would, if I was normal.'

'I've been thinking about that laugh,' Persephone Callard said.

They were drinking whisky by the coal fire. Side by side on the hard Victorian sofa.

'Ron isn't best known for his impressions,' Maiden said.

'It was just the general tone. On one level. Quite a strong laugh, but one that wasn't reacting to anything funny, do you know what I mean? It was there. I heard it at Barber's party.'

'But you don't remember Seward. You weren't introduced?'

'Wasn't introduced to anybody. Quite odd, now I think about it.'

'Having a celebrated villain at your party,' Maiden said, 'wouldn't that be a bit dangerous for a politician?'

'*Ex*-politician. Ex-villain, for that matter.'

'Probably no such items. Like you can't be an ex-alcoholic. Just because Seward's doing after-dinner talks and guesting on quiz shows . . .'

'You ever encountered him, Bobby?'

Maiden shook his head. 'He'd have been doing his seven years when I was in London. Listen, say he engineered himself an invitation from Barber because of his interest in spiritualism. He was there because *you* were going to be there. Why no introduction? Seward loves celebrity. Unless—'

'There was something else. Now I think about it . . .' Seffi hunched up on the Victorian sofa, tapping a knee with stiffened fingers. 'I'm remembering him from another context. Damn.'

'Unless it was *his* party,' Maiden said.

'What?'

'Unless Sir Richard Barber was figureheading Seward's party. Say Barber knows Seward, or Seward has something on him. Seward wants you – but if you'd been invited to conduct a sitting at a soirée hosted by Gary Seward the East End villain, would you have done it? Even for twenty-five K?'

'*No* chance.'

'There you go, then.'

'Yes. It makes sense. It would explain why Barber didn't appear to know anybody particularly. The fact that they didn't seem to be his kind of people.'

'Could they have been Seward's kind of people? We know Les Hole was, for a start.'

'I suppose.'

'Gary Seward's party,' Maiden said. 'The place full of iffy entrepreneurs and general villains. All those people with bad secrets. All those bodies buried. And you were the floorshow. Why?'

There was silence. She sat very still, her face sheened in the firelight, heavy hair down one side of her face like a hawser.

Remembering the commitment he'd made, telling Ron Foxworth, *I believe she does this . . . thing.* Which had been said mainly to support her against Ron's impending sneers, and not necessarily because he . . .

If you *believed* she did this thing, that she truly had access to the dead, the implications were vast. Thinking about it now, just the two of them here, it was as though the walls of the room had dissolved and the night was in.

'Persephone,' he said. 'She was the woman who married the king of the Underworld, right?'

275

'And spent half her life among the dead,' she said.

Whenever Maiden thought of the dead, he thought of Em.

Seffi looked at him, firelight flickering in her eyes.

'And if that's what you were about to ask, it *is* my real name. My mother chose it.'

'She was psychic too?'

'I don't know. I ask my father, he just smiles. Yes, of course she was. I know she was.'

'So, have you ever . . . ?'

'Had contact? Not for a long time. I think she's moved on, beyond my reach. I think she was there in the few years after she died, when I was a child. Guarding the portal. From adolescence, I guess I was on my own. Which was when it became disruptive.'

He said, 'Are you still afraid to die? Knowing what you . . . know?'

Her faint smile twisted. 'Oh, come on, Bobby, what do I know? What do I really *know*? It's all too big in there, a huge, endless factory. I'm just standing there, looking at all this strange machinery.'

He had a scary image of unmanned conveyor belts, chemical reprocessing.

'And most of the ones who come out to me, they don't know either. They're the ones who don't realize they're over. Or they have unfinished business here and because of that – this really petty crap – they can't see . . . the fullness of it. Sometimes I can help them deal with that, clear the blockage. But I don't *know* . . . I couldn't tell you what happens to them afterwards. Perhaps they evaporate into pure energy. Go for recycling. Perhaps – God help us – perhaps they don't exist at all outside my head. I . . . I was never one of your evangelical mediums. Never tell anyone it's

276

going to be all springtime and church bells. I don't know.' She paused. 'And neither do you, apparently. No glorious lights when you died, Bobby.'

'No.'

'Depressing, or what?' She started to laugh, bleakly. He thought about Gary Seward who he'd never met – and pushed him away again.

Quite soon, the laugh went out of Seffi's voice but remained in her big amber eyes. Where it reflected a different mood: lighter, untroubled.

Maiden felt a peculiar tingle in his gut.

Seffi Callard's eyes were shining with irony. *Not her eyes*, he thought, and a featherlight shiver started in his spine, a small, tremulous excitement, a feeling of someone coming towards him, weaving lightly through the trees.

And she said, '*It's all right, guv. It's all right now.*'

Her eyes very much someone else's eyes.

The room around them was curtained with shadows and he heard the cracking of the trees in the wind, as though there were no walls.

No walls. The warm shiver enveloped him; he was aware of them both inside it.

She put out a hand and he took it.

She said, '*Come on, guv, help yourself to the sweet trolley.*'

Bobby Maiden began to weep.

Part Four

From *Bang to Wrongs: A Bad Boy's Book*,
by GARY SEWARD

It amuses me when people say, 'There ain't no justice.' In my world there is, every time. One thing we have always believed in is that people should get what is coming to them, by whatever means may be appropriate at the time.

Let me tell you the story of Billy Spindler.

Billy was the scum of the earth. A rapist. By which I don't mean the kind of poor sod what goes down for seven years on account of getting a bit pissed and not hearing her say no. I mean a real pervert what gets off on degrading ladies. (As you may have gathered, I hate perverts of all persuasions, but that is by the by in this instance.) Another reason Billy was scum was on account of being a grass, and when he was nicked for sexually assaulting a schoolteacher, while wearing a black balaclava, on a building site at Chiswick, he was quick to take the Coward's Way Out by striking a bargain with the police, as a result of which three of his neighbours were arrested in connection with a very clean raid on a branch of the Bradford and Bingley Building Society, as it was then known. Naturally, the whole community was up in arms about this, but the scum was hard to get at, without an element of personal risk, due to police protection, which was an outrage in itself.

Now, justice works in peculiar ways and you can't make

an omelette without breaking eggs. What happened was in some respects regrettable, but the law of karma does not require permission from the Crown Prosecution Service to take effect.

What happened was that, two months later, to the day and the hour, the same schoolteacher was raped by a man wearing a black balaclava.

Well, most of the police had been well choked by that deal with Billy Spindler and, alibi or not, there was no way Billy was walking away from this one. He was convicted in record time and done eleven years, and not very pleasant years by all accounts, mostly in Parkhurst, where he ended up in solitary for his own safety and even then discovered he was not totally safe after a screw was bribed to look the other way.

Billy Spindler learned the hard way that certain behaviour cannot be tolerated, especially if perpetrated by a pervert.

And in case you were thinking this was hard on the poor schoolteacher, soon after she received an envelope containing ten thousand pounds in clean money from 'a wellwisher'. So, there you are, everybody was happy, apart from Billy Spindler, which is how it should be.

28

Awakening into half-light from the cell-like window, Cindy put on the bedside lamp and his eyes met the eyes of Kelvyn Kite, sullenly shambling in the chair by the wall at the bottom of the bed.

You cowardly old tart.

'Yes, yes, I know.' Cindy's voice was morning hoarse. 'You don't have to rub it in.'

What the hell are you doing *here?*

'I ran. I ran away, all right? Ran away, I did, from the bitter tang of the cold sea.'

You never learn, boy. Never realize when you're on top. Always looking down, you are, into the darkness.

'Leave me alone,' Cindy said. 'Too early for the inquisition.'

He never wore a watch. He guessed it was not yet seven. Too early, also, to get up and disturb Amy. He reached for something to read and discovered the small, stiff-backed book sent to him in Kurt Campbell's promotion package: *The Mysteries of Overcross Castle* by G.L. Mirebrook.

A ring of Enid Blyton, that title. The facsimile edition from 1935 had fewer than fifty pages. Cindy flicked it open near the middle.

for Abblow, it appears, was both jealous and suspicious of Daniel Dunglas-Home who was, by this time, acquiring an international reputation arising from the extraordinary phenomena which were said to gather around him like moths to a lamp. Home was able to produce not only spectacular visual effects but also sounds, evoking in one instance the tumult of waves and the creaking of a ship's timbers; he also was able to levitate and had been seen to float around the room; he could even, it was attested, assume the physical size and shape of a particular spirit, appearing, furthermore, to increase his own height by several inches.

Crole had met Home at Malvern Spa, where the spiritualist was receiving the hydropathic cure for an illness of the nerves brought on by difficulties and upset in his personal life. In the two years up to 1871, Home was a regular visitor to Overcross, where he said he found the atmosphere most conducive to the physical manifestation of spirits.

This, it should be remembered, was a period when spiritualism was considered by many to be a legitimate extension of science, and when science was advancing in so many other daring directions that many people believed it was only a question of time before mankind was able not only to prove the existence of life after death but to engage in regular meaningful intercourse with the departed. Such a development was felt to be imminent, and Anthony Abblow, who had practised for some years as a medical doctor, was determined that it should be he, a scientist and scholar as well as a medium, and not the likes of Dunglas-Home with his 'carnival tricks', who proved the validity of survival on a spiritual plane.

When Daniel Dunglas-Home ceased to be invited to Overcross, it was widely believed that Barnaby Crole had been 'poisoned' against him by Abblow, who had become intimate with Crole to the extent of being invited to set up his own apartment within the castle. It was here that the two men began to experiment in earnest – and in secret. Many were the rumours that circulated in Overcross and the neighbouring villages and even in Great Malvern itself, it being alleged that Crole and Abblow had experimented on animals. However, this was dismissed as nonsense by Crole, who invited the vicar and senior parishioners to dinner with Abblow and himself to explain that their activities were in no way irreligious and would be seen, when ultimately published, to have made a substantial contribution to the sum of human knowledge. However, nothing was ever published and the experiments seemed to have ceased shortly after the death of a gamekeeper, John Hodge, as a result of the misfiring of his shotgun, and the rumour that his ghost was haunting the castle grounds. These rumours persisted even after the departure of Abblow and the eventual death of Crole, who became a recluse but continued to make large donations towards the upkeep and development of the community.

Cindy smiled. How many people would be prepared to pay dearly to watch whichever medium Kurt Campbell had hired go strolling through the midnight woods attempting to have 'meaningful intercourse' with the restless spirit of Old Jack, the gamekeeper?

Hadn't told little Grayle this, mind, but even as a shaman he'd always been a touch contemptuous of spiritualism. The shamanic way was to achieve intercourse with the elements and the spirits of the ancestors – in a more abstract sense – in order to attain

285

continuity and oneness with the earth. The nurturing of a sticky relationship with a dead individual was unnatural and usually led to psychological problems. Indeed, *something* must have caused Daniel Dunglas-Home to have his nervous breakdown . . .

In fact, Cindy's own research had indicated Dunglas-Home to be, for the most part, quite genuine – the Uri Geller, or the Matthew Manning of his day.

Or even, perhaps, the Persephone Callard?

Miss Callard. Yes. Cindy rose. Remembering also that he needed to buy some newspapers, he felt a plummeting of the soul.

Kelvyn Kite glared spitefully from his chair.

Grayle collected the Sunday papers and by nine was driving between the castle walls to find . . .

. . . still no Cherokee in the yard! *Shit.*

She found Marcus in his study, delving into a book. Grayle tossed her raincoat on the sofa, dumped the string-bound bundle of papers on the desk.

'So they didn't come back.'

'Appears not,' he said, like this was of only marginal consequence.

'I knew it.'

'Knew what?'

'From the moment she was showing him her tits, right there on that sofa.'

Marcus looked up from his book, shocked. 'Maiden and *Persephone*?'

Doing that tone of voice again. Like Callard was serious royalty, or – worse – sacred and untouchable. How could he possibly have read all those magazine stories about her and failed to take in any details of a rich, varied and predatory sex life?

'One assumes they hit on something interesting. Stayed in a hotel.'

'Oh, *right*.'

'Man's still a policeman, Underhill. Just about.' Marcus began untying the papers. 'And Persephone, I fear, was probably glad to get out of here, for all the use I was being.'

'Jesus.' With some effort, Grayle calmed herself. 'Uh, no-one else called, did they?'

'You mean apart from the anonymous man asking if there was a small blonde with a hatchet on the premises?'

'Don't joke, Marcus.'

'No,' he said. 'Nobody called. Neither did the dog bark in the night. And neither . . . bloody hell, look at this . . .' laying the *People* flat on the desk. 'Some poor bastard Lottery winner died after crashing his plane, around the same time that Mars-Lewis was virtually predicting it on television.'

'Huh?'

'Obviously, that's not what it says *as such*, but the inference is pretty clear.'

Grayle leaned over Marcus's shoulder. The main piece was a straight news story about the airfield tragedy. There was also a sidebar:

CINDY'S KITE QUIP FALLS FLAT . . .

'Fortunate for him that they didn't know of his . . . *precognitive powers*,' Marcus said heavily.

287

'Aw, Marcus, he doesn't claim to *have* precognitive powers. Read it. Look, it was just an off-the-cuff one-liner. It's all a piece of crap.'

'If they knew the creature's history,' Marcus said, 'they'd be making rather more of it.'

'Aw, he never actually *hides* his interests. Anyhow, what kind of big deal is that any more? If you're famous, you're expected to have off-the-wall beliefs. Like Shirley McLaine and her spooks, Travolta's Scientology . . . I used to write about that stuff all the time, nobody was *shocked*.'

But, yeah, maybe it was a little odd that nothing so far seemed to have been written about Cindy's Celtic wizardry. Maybe this was what was meant by the shaman's cloak of invisibility.

'Well,' Grayle said, 'who can say?' Keen to get off the subject of Cindy lest, when he showed up right out the blue, Marcus might suspect collusion. It was gonna be real perilous anyway. And at this rate there'd be no Callard around when Cindy showed. It was just too bad of Bobby Maiden not to have called. Also unlike him.

She had this awful image: a naked, post-coital Bobby, all doe-eyed and compliant, his brain turned to gloop by the witchy woman.

Marcus was looking at her, his face still pouchy after the flu.

'What?' she said warily.

'Hmm,' Marcus murmured, as though he'd read her thoughts, which like, no way, not in a million years . . .

'What?' she snapped. '*What?*'

She was standing in the doorway. She wore a pale-blue robe, like a sari, and the small glimmering was a pendant around her neck, a tiny golden cross he hadn't noticed before.

Maiden swung his legs down from the Victorian sofa, sat up. The orange sun came out of the diamond-paned window and into Seffi Callard's amber eyes.

'I think . . .' She looked half-asleep and vaguely unsatisfied. 'Susan, would it be?' She wrinkled her nose. 'Not quite right, is it?'

Something slid heavily to the floor over his feet. A yellow and red striped duvet. He didn't remember there being one last night. He sat on the edge of the sofa, naked apart from his briefs – feeling exposed now, but still bathed in strangeness.

'To be quite honest, Bobby, she was becoming rather irritating.' Seffi smiled at his unease. 'Made her first moves within an hour of us meeting. You and I. Tiresome. How on earth is one supposed to compete with a pale, fragile little hand reaching delicately through the veil?'

She made a weaving motion with her left hand, and the memory came back like a silver thread winding up his spine. She came and sat next to him on the sofa.

'I do tend to forget. Sometimes it can be even *better* than sex. The afterglow. Ah . . .' She glanced up. 'What about *Suzanne*?'

Bobby Maiden almost leapt from the sofa.

'Good.' She clapped her hands lightly. '*Good.*'

'Oh God,' Maiden said. 'What are you *doing*?'

Seffi did a small, rueful smile, touched his cheek with a forefinger. 'Suzanne, yah? And she made you cry. I tell you, Bobby, that was a hell of an aphrodisiac, but it . . .' she smiled wryly '. . . it might've ruined everything. Not worth taking the chance.'

He remembered reaching for her, and she was

289

gone. He remembered her waving goodnight, a small wiggle of the fingers at the doorway. Sometime in the night she must have come down and put the duvet over him.

'And, to be honest, it kind of gives me the creeps. Wouldn't have been . . . me, would it? And I'm such a proud bitch.'

'Oh God,' Maiden said.

'Come on, guv,' Seffi said softly. 'It's only fucking spiritualism. *Tell* me.'

He blinked, shook his head. 'Her name was Em. Emma. But the first time I met her she was calling herself . . . Suzanne.'

She nodded.

'She liked to put on this cockney persona . . . TV cop-talk. *Guv.* What's happening, guv? You know?'

'Sure.'

'We met . . . erm . . . in the course of the job. Kind of.' Maiden closed his eyes, his throat tightening. 'Nothing happened. But it was going to. About to. That night. We booked into this hotel in South Wales and—'

'*No.*' The tips of her fingers on his lips. 'Don't. Don't talk about that.'

He wanted her to know about the sweet trolley. How, in the hotel dining room, he and Em had agreed to dispense with the sweet trolley, the last thing before . . .

Him coming back into the room. Too late. Coming back to blood-soaked sheets.

Seffi said, 'All right. Let it go.'

'Where . . . ?'

He wanted to ask, *Where is she? Where is she now?* Powerfully aware, for the first time, of why people went back to mediums, kept on going back, in a delirium of longing.

'I felt it was all right. For the first time, I felt she . . .'

Wasn't blaming me.

'Slept like . . .' Without dreams about her.

'You mustn't want her,' Seffi Callard said. 'You mustn't want her back.'

'No. I mean . . . I know.'

He wanted Em to go on, to fly, never to look down at him floundering.

'Thank you,' he said. Half-amazed at himself.

Seffi stood up.

'By the way,' she said, 'there never was a Mrs Dronfield.'

29

'You alone, Bobby? I mean, really alone?'

To try and improve the signal to the mobile, Maiden moved out from the wall towards the Jeep, which had been parked all night, half-concealed, on the edge of the wood.

Nine-fifteen. Seffi upstairs, bathing and changing.

'I'm alone.'

'You all right, Bobby?' Ron suspicious.

'Mmm,' Maiden said uncertainly. 'Sure.'

Was he alone? *Was* Em gone? Was he no longer carrying her death? Did he believe that?

Or had his need for her been transferred . . . to someone else?

A slippery slope. More things in heaven and earth. Oh God.

'I'm sorry, Ron. Not been up long.'

'I bet. Fucking hell, Bobby, you picked up a package there, my son. Everybody was saying you got religion or something, into weird beliefs, but, this . . .'

'Seffi Callard,' Maiden said.

Who, for wild, incandescent moments, had been . . . someone else.

Ron said, 'See, you hanging out with a notorious

voodoo lady who takes money off people for another chat with Uncle Horace who's passed on, that's a potentially difficult situation. The Archangel, bless him, is very much on your side right now. You don't want to blow it.'

The Archangel: Alan Gabriel, noted lay-preacher and Chief Constable of West Mercia. Who, as head of CID, had gathered his whole team for prayer before a major drugs raid, in order to imbue the troops with the spirit of the crusaders of old.

'After your remarkable recovery from death, Bobby, and then the Green Man result, closely followed by the discreet departure of Riggs – who everybody says they spotted was a wrong-un even though nobody *did* – well, you were up there and gliding. Plus, Bradbury likes you. And when word floats up to Mr Gabriel that you're *religious* – am I telling you something new here, Bobby?'

Maiden groaned.

'Mr Gabriel takes it as a sign from the *Almighty*. A holy *vision* . . . All right, I exaggerate, but he says to Bradbury, "I want that man bundled into the lift without delay. To the roof".'

'The roof.'

'Unless the cable gets cut. I'm just flashing danger signals, Bobby. On two counts. *One*, Mr Gabriel is a team manager and so takes an extremely dim view of a player breaking formation. *Two*, Mr Gabriel's definition of religious observance is unlikely to include sticking it into a notorious pagan goddess. So, a question. As you are out of your playground and well into mine, is there anything you want to tell me you couldn't tell me last night?'

'About what?'

293

'About anything. All right, never mind, I'll tell *you* something. It appears Sir Richard Barber leases his nice new apartment from Bright Horizon Developments. Bright Horizon is Gary Seward and an otherwise reputable builder called Stuart Etchison, who purchased this rundown block in Cheltenham last year, turned it into quality, no expense spared.'

'You're saying Seward is Barber's *landlord*?'

'Thought you'd like that. I like to be helpful when I can.'

'Can you do anything with that?'

'Can *you*? Let me know. Don't forget. Oh, and Bobby . . . another passing coincidence. We have an ID on our axe victim in the ditch. Well, I say *axe* victim – the PM makes it more complicated. What actually killed him was a massive blow on the head *not* from an axe. Or possibly delivered with the blunt end of the axehead.'

'Really?' Maiden trying not to show more than professional interest.

'Probably from behind. But that's by the by. We'll know a lot more when we find the implement. Geezer's name was Jeffrey Crewe. Big boy. Twenty-six years old. Fit.'

'So what's the coincidence?'

'Oh, yeah . . . Young Jeffrey had a good job. In Worcester. At the Midlands depot of an expanding security firm. Which one, Bobby? Go on, try a reasonable guess.'

'*Really?*'

'Forcefield Security, indeed. Making him an employee of your old guv'nor. Although seemingly off duty at the time of his demise.'

'Is that the coincidence?'

'Perhaps *you're* the coincidence, Bobby. You showing up like this and having that very special relationship with Martin Riggs. One of whose employees gets his head decisively beaten in.' Ron paused. 'Only kidding, son.' He laughed. 'Only kidding. You have a nice day with your exotic friend, wherever you are. And, er, if there *is* anything else you want to tell me, make it quick, eh? It's just not the same if I find out from other sources. Know what I mean?'

Seffi Callard stood at the bottom of the stairs. She wore a black sweater, looked like cashmere, the gold cross hanging outside it. Her hair was bunched on one shoulder; over the other hung the strap of her black leather bag.

She surprised him by kissing him slowly on the lips, holding his face. Her hands were very warm. But when she stepped away, he saw her smile was cool.

'Worked it all out, have we? Grayle – what about *her*?'

'Grayle?'

'She could've told me, couldn't she? Just as she told me all about your peculiar death experience. Or Marcus. Marcus knows all about you and Emma, surely? Perhaps it was Marcus.'

'Marcus doesn't know about the sweet trolley,' Maiden said quietly. 'Nor Grayle. Nobody else knows about the sweet trolley.'

'What sweet trolley?' Insouciance. 'I don't remember saying anything about a sweet trolley. Perhaps *you* said it. Perhaps you heard it in your head. Perhaps you imagined it.'

He stared at her. 'What on earth are you doing, Seffi?'

'Giving you a get-out.'

'I don't want a get-out.'

'There always is one, you know.' The smile was warmer, the eyes were sorrowful. 'There's always a get-out. Who were you talking to?'

'Foxworth.'

She wrinkled her nose.

'Seffi . . .' He glanced at the wall, where the set of hedging tools looked complete again. 'How many times did Grayle hit that guy with the hacker?'

The suddenness of the question made her wince. She turned away from the wall.

'You did see it, didn't you? You saw the blade go in?'

She nodded. Swallowed.

'How many times, Seffi?'

'Once.'

'You're sure?'

'Once . . . seemed to be quite enough.'

He breathed out. 'She didn't kill him.'

'Grayle?'

'He had another head wound. Somebody else killed him.'

'When?' Seffi let her shoulder bag fall to the carpet.

'I don't know. Didn't like to ask about the time of death, or seem too interested in any of it. But somebody hit this lad very hard on the head, probably from behind.'

'He was driven away. By the other man.'

'Which kind of narrows it down.'

'I don't understand.'

'Pretend you're the other man for a moment. What would you do if you were with someone who'd just been badly injured and was bleeding all over your car?'

'Take him to hospital. Or call for an ambulance.'

'Of course you would. That's how you were brought up. Only, suppose this bloke had got the injuries as a result of something seriously criminal you and he were into, what would you tell them at the hospital? Midnight gardening accident? Give them his name and your name? Wait around while they call the police?'

He stopped talking, letting her work it out.

'Oh *no*, Bobby.'

He shrugged.

'You're suggesting the *other* man killed him. To save . . . explanations . . . embarrassment.'

'And a prison sentence. It also suggests they weren't close, of course.'

'Why couldn't he simply have taken him to a hospital, left him outside or something?'

'And risk being seen? And risk being fingered by the damaged bloke when the police got at him? The guy's already incapacitated, he's in a lot of pain, he doesn't really know what's happening. And you know you've got a hammer or something in the boot . . .'

'That's utterly *barbaric*.'

'Well it . . . it might have been a panic thing. I mean, I hope it *was* panic. Otherwise, yeah, the kind of person we're looking at . . .'

'This is a nightmare, Bobby. This is a continuing bloody *nightmare*.'

'Mmm.'

'You'll have to tell him, I suppose. Foxworth.'

'Or you and Grayle will.'

'I don't want to do that.'

'It might be for the best.'

He was thinking: Crewe and his partner came here because they wanted Seffi Callard, and when it all went pear-shaped Crewe was chopped without a second thought. And then Justin was killed. Perhaps to get information, but perhaps also because Justin would know enough to finger someone when Jeffrey Crewe's body was found.

So what was he going to do next, whoever he was? Was he going to walk away at this stage?

Maiden realized how unwise he and Seffi Callard had been, spending last night in this place. He realized he hadn't been taking any of this quite seriously enough.

'We'd better go,' he said. 'We need to talk to Grayle. Give her the good news.'

And the bad news.

30

'What's happening?' She was screaming. 'What's going *on*? Cindy, why are they doing this to us?'

Near hysteria. The poor child.

Within a mile of Castle Farm, he was, when the phone, against all rural odds, had managed this tiny gasping bleep, a faint whimper. Cindy pulling over into the hedge – if it had turned out to be his friends from the *Mirror*, he would have had to hang up without a word.

'Doing it to us, Jo?'

'I've just had a call from the BBC Press Office. You wouldn't believe the questions they've had fired at them.'

'I rather think I would,' Cindy said sadly.

'The Press Office've drawn up a statement saying it's complete nonsense. But they want to clear it with you before it goes out. Yes?'

'And to what does this statement react?'

'The *Mail*, the *Express*, the *Mirror*, the *Telegraph*, the—'

'Yes, yes, but what are they saying?'

'In the statement? Well, obviously, the BBC is rejecting any suggestion of you being involved with witchcraft.'

'Well, *good*. That's . . . er . . . that is quite true. In essence, but what I meant—'

'Or the occult in any respect.'

'And, indeed,' Cindy said carefully, 'depending upon the interpretation of the word "occult", this also could be considered broadly accurate.'

'Cindy . . . ?' A sudden remote quality to young Jo's voice. He imagined her in the lovely Notting Hill flat she shared with her boyfriend, a writer of TV screenplays. Another lazy, idyllic little Sunday over the arts pages. Until this silliness. 'Cindy, I don't like the way you said that.'

'Too Welsh?'

'Cindy, for Christ's sake! You're only half denying involvement in the occult. *This is not funny*.'

'No. No indeed.' He was watching a buzzard alight upon a telegraph pole. 'Not funny at all.'

Refusing to dwell on how important the programme had become in his life. Not only financially – he had no pension, no savings to speak of – but the way the buzz of live television twice a week had heightened his everyday consciousness, his being in the present moment, to an unexpected degree. He'd been flying, as never before.

'Cindy, listen to me, you know there've always been people who want you out.'

'Jo—'

'*Nobody* wants the show to be dangerous, that's the issue. Or anything other than genial, superficial crap, and all the winners buying their BMWs and flying off to the West Indies for a couple of months, and all living happily ever after. They never liked the idea of you satirizing the myth and they were all attuned for the first indication that what we were doing wasn't working any more. Right?'

'Jo, it . . . it's little more than a hobby.'

'What do you mean?'

There was, inevitably, a devastated silence.

Cindy sighed deeply and told it as it was.

'Many years ago, while working in North Wales, I stayed with a family, the Fychans. Two of whom, father and son, were . . . well, *dyn hysbys* is the Welsh term, meaning "wise man". In other parts of the Celtic world they've tended to be women; in Wales, for some reason, more often men. Anyway, the family had followed this particular path through many generations – making little of it, I have to say; it was entirely normal to them. But I was a young man and fascinated. And although I did not have the Welsh language, they were kind enough to say I had a peculiar aptitude for . . . this art.'

'I'm not sure I understand,' Jo said, evidently with some residual hope that it would all have been herbal cures and the odd love potion.

'Shamanism is the technical term I tend to prefer. The Welsh descriptions, when translated, tend to invoke images of, er, wizardry.'

'It's not just like Mystic Meg then, is it?' Jo said aridly. 'Oh, Jesus Christ. Why have you never told me all this?'

'I never hid it, lovely, but I always detected that you were a trifle impatient with those people usually termed New Agers and, indeed, Kurt Campbell and his research into the paranormal.'

'What about the bird? One of the papers said . . . oh, *God*, this—'

'The truth of that', Cindy said patiently, 'is that a shaman often adopts what is sometimes called a totem

301

beast – well, the beast, it is, usually, which adopts the shaman. In his . . . let's call it his *reverie* . . . he will perhaps find himself accosted by a particular species of creature – it might be an owl or a fox or a hare – with which he will develop a relationship. In my case, it was the red kite which, at the time, was confined to an area of the Cambrian Mountains. Kelvyn was a humorous diversion. A shamanic in-joke, if you like.'

'Cindy, I . . .' He could hear the air being expelled in a thin stream between Jo's little teeth. 'I don't believe I'm hearing this. Cross-dressing is fine . . . being gay is fairly cool . . . having a rubber fetish is just about acceptable. But a ventriloquist having an un-natural relationship with his *doll* . . .'

'Communications between shaman and totem crea-ture occasionally are founded upon hostility rather than sympathy.'

'This is a dream, isn't it?' Jo said. 'This has got to be a bloody dream.'

'It sounds to me', Cindy said soberly, 'as if the feeding of this background information to the press has been quite cleverly orchestrated.'

'By whom?'

'Not sure. Look, we both knew it was never going to last for ever, Jo.'

Jo gave a kind of yelp. 'What are you *saying*? Listen . . . *Listen, listen, listen!* Just you stay out of the way. All right? Wherever you are, *stay* there! Don't talk to anybody. I'm going to tell the Press Office I couldn't get hold of you. Meanwhile, I don't care how you do this – lie, cheat . . . deny, deny, deny . . . but you *have* to think of a way out of this. You're smart, Cindy, you can talk your way out of anything. Look at the Campbell incident.'

302

'Ah, yes,' Cindy said. 'The Campbell incident.'

He's obviously just extremely vindictive, Jo had said.

'Just think about how you're going to get us out of this, Cindy.'

The line went dead.

In a big roadside pub, its bar like a deserted factory floor, they took a distant table, ordered coffees. Maiden laid on the table the brown paper bag from the bookshop in Gloucester. They'd stopped in Gloucester because Seffi needed a chemist's. On his way back from the bookshop Maiden had seen her standing against a concrete wall, talking into her mobile.

He tipped out the book. On its cover was a smiling face. A cheery face under a slab of pavement-grey hair. One tooth off-centre, giving the smile that dangerous edge, that Jack-the-lad, lock-up-your-daughters, cross-me-at-your-peril kind of gleam.

The force of the smile gathered in all your attention so that you didn't really notice the eyes, not at first. You didn't notice how cold and fixed they were, like the eyes of a big fish packed in ice; all you saw was the cheery smile and the cheery title.

Maiden turned the book round, pushed it in front of Seffi.

BANG TO WRONGS
A BAD BOY'S BOOK

'Good God.'

'You recognize him? From the party?'

'Yes. Yes and no. All I remember from the party is

hearing the laugh. Not the face. I'm not aware of seeing him at the party, so he must've been keeping well away from me. Maybe another room, I don't know. But, yes, it was nagging at me last night, where I'd heard that laugh *apart* from the party.'

'And?'

'This was Barber's driver,' Seffi said. 'He picked me up at the hotel.'

'The *chauffeur*? The chauffeur was Seward himself?'

'Peaked cap, the whole bit. Very friendly, very jovial, big smile. This smile. And, yes, the laugh, for heaven's sake . . . *that* was what I was half remembering. The chauffeur had the laugh.'

'What did you talk about with the chauffeur?'

'He told me how seriously interested his employer was in the spirit world. Suspicious in retrospect because Barber obviously couldn't care less.'

'Is it possible Seward knew that something . . . extraordinary . . . was likely to happen to you that night, at that party? Did you get that feeling when he was driving you there?'

'I wasn't particularly . . .' Her phone went off in her bag, like a small police warbler. 'Yah.' Brusquely.

The female voice in the phone was animated, insistent.

Seffi said, 'Nancy, look, I'm going to have to call you back . . . No. No, I don't. Yes, I will. But when *I'm* ready . . . I'll call you back.'

She tossed the phone back into her bag, biting her lip then forcing a smile.

'My agent. In a state of some anxiety. Wondering if she's ever going to make any money out of me again.'

'She know about the . . . trouble you've been having? The nature of it?'

304

'She seems to know too much,' Seffi said, 'but that's not your problem.'

Before they left the pub, she went to the lavatory. She was gone more than fifteen minutes and didn't explain. Maiden guessed she'd been on the phone in there. Very evidently, now, there was something she didn't want him to know about. He was feeling uneasy as they took the road towards Ross-on-Wye and the border.

After a while, she said, 'I won't stay. At the farm. I'll just pick up my stuff. Perhaps you could explain to Marcus.'

'Oh.' He watched her biting her upper lip as she drove, hugging the wheel.

'It was a mistake, anyway, Bobby. I've brought him nothing but hassle.'

'Marcus likes hassle.'

'When he's well. But he's not well. I'd never have written to him if I'd known that. I just wanted someone to tell it all to, who wouldn't be judgemental.'

The Jeep rolled into a sandstone village with a Norman church. He saw how she'd tightened up, pulled back into herself. Like last night was something which had happened in a different time-frame.

Which bothered him. He'd felt so close to her. She was right: what had passed between them was as intimate as sex. Not casual sex, either.

'What's changed, Seffi?'

'Nothing's changed.'

'You sure? You go to Marcus for advice after twenty years, because he's the only person you feel you can trust. And then you just walk out. You know, it's going to make him feel like a useless old bugger.'

305

She slowed as the road narrowed. She cleared her throat. 'I've got to be somewhere, OK? Tomorrow, probably.'

'You could stay tonight, then?'

'No.'

'Only there are things we need to discuss. All of us. Like the fact that there's someone out there who wants you.'

A truck loaded with gravel came grinding and clanking past, making even the Jeep shiver.

'That's no-one's problem but mine,' Seffi said.

31

'Because you'd've said *no*!' Grayle backed towards the door of the study. 'Am I crazy?'

'Yes!' Marcus roared. 'Also irresponsible and treacherous! How the fuck *dare* you go behind my back, you devious bitch?'

'Like you had better ideas? The hell you did! All you could say was how you'd failed her, and stomping around in the hair shirt, scourging yourself.'

'You called me . . .' Marcus was stabbing a stubby finger across the desk '. . . a self-righteous old phoney.'

'But a self-righteous old phoney with *good contacts*. We aren't either of us psychics, but you're the guy who knows people who *are*. The best people.'

'Mars-Lewis.' The name came out at last, like Jello from a mould, floated there, quivering, between them.

'It was always gonna need someone who works on Callard's level,' Grayle said. 'Spirit level. Whatever.'

Marcus said grimly, 'Where is he?'

'Out back. In his car. He won't come in till you say it's OK.'

'Excellent. That solves everything then. He can bloody well sleep out there.'

'Marcus!'

'What do you want *me* to do? This is your project, Underhill.'

'Go out there and talk to him. It's gonna take you to convince her this is a person she can trust.'

'How can I convince *her* to trust him, when—?'

'You trust what he *does*. Come on, Marcus! OK, he offends you as a person, that's neither here nor there.'

'And . . . and neither is *she* . . . in case you hadn't noticed! We don't know where she is or when she's coming back. According to your theory she could be in some hotel bedroom with bloody Maiden and a do-not-disturb sign on the bloody door.'

'You just . . .' With some difficulty, Grayle controlled herself. She held open the study door. '. . . go talk to him. Tell him what we need. You can do this.'

But when they got outside, Grayle came to a sudden halt.

'Uh oh.'

Two vehicles nose to nose in the yard: Cindy's Honda and the Grand Cherokee.

'You *knew*,' Marcus snarled.

'Marcus, so help me, I had no idea! How could I know they were on their way? What am I, psychic?'

Callard stepped down from the Jeep, Bobby Maiden climbing out the other side. Cindy didn't move from behind the wheel.

Marcus turned to Grayle, the volcano in him only smoking. 'You'd better get that mutation out of here for at least two hours.'

'You're gonna talk to her, right?'

'You *devious* bitch.'

*　　*　　*

Up beyond the castle, where the pink fields lay quiescent under the glowering Black Mountains, the small late sun poked out of quilted cloud, like a kid's torch under the bedclothes. And Cindy unpacked his case.

Grayle said, 'No birdsuit?'

Cindy had this cloak thing with feathers all over it that you'd think would make him look real silly, but actually it was kind of dramatic if you saw him against the light. And somehow, when he was wearing that cloak of feathers, Cindy was always against the light.

'Today, I think not.' He brought out the drum, the goatskin bodhran with the maze-like patterns representing various journeys of the soul. He was wearing slacks and a tweed jacket. The kindly uncle who took you hiking.

'You figure on taking Callard up to the Knoll?'

'No, little Grayle, but I shall take myself for a while. Originally planned to go up to Carn Ingli, I had, to recharge the inner batteries, but circumstances dictated otherwise.'

He looked up towards the hills, shading his eyes.

'Of course, the problem with the Knoll, as an energy centre, is that it is oriented to the sunrise and at eventide is itself a touch depleted. However, if I can still my own personal fears, it will be a start.'

'I never think of you as having fears.' Her own worst fear had been assuaged a good deal by what Bobby Maiden had told her quickly, before she'd followed Cindy into the fields. But not totally. The guy was still dead.

'It's nothing,' Cindy said. 'Trivial. Strange, it is . . . I had never imagined that piffling career problems would ever weigh on my mind. I suppose it's the thought of getting old, in poverty. Losing friends.'

309

Grayle was shocked. She'd never heard Cindy talk like this or seen him looking so down. Never even thought of him as old. Was he sick or something? Had he found out about some encroaching disability?

'We're your friends. Even Marcus.'

Cindy smiled sadly.

'And your career's soaring.'

'Like a kite,' said Cindy. 'Like a light aircraft.'

Grayle frowned. 'This have anything to do with that Lottery guy who crashed his plane?'

He didn't react. Grayle watched a layer of deep grey cloud forming over the mountains like smoke from a grassfire.

'Cindy . . . uh . . . how exactly do you plan to handle this, can I ask that? Is it gonna be some kind of exorcism?'

'If you mean the gentle detachment and sympathetic redirection of an energy form, then . . . perhaps. We shall have to see what's there, isn't it?'

'Will you have to treat her? Rather than . . . it? I mean, if this is a purely psychological blockage, how will you approach that?'

Cindy spread his hands.

'The medium speaks of spirits, the psychiatrist of syndromes.'

That was an answer?

So Cindy went off to the Knoll, minus birdsuit, and Grayle carried his shaman's case back to the farm-house. She found Bobby Maiden hanging around the yard. He was in a curious state. Restless, looking a touch bewildered. He said Marcus had taken Callard into the study.

Bobby was unshaven. Which inevitably got Grayle

310

thinking about why he was unshaven. And, again, about where he and Callard had spent the night.

They walked in the ruins. Bobby told her about the Cheltenham guy who screwed his dead son's girl-friend, how he'd figured someone called Gary had set up Callard to reveal his secret at the seance. Bobby said he believed Callard when she denied this, but it had brought this person Gary into the picture. Later identified by this cop friend of Bobby's as a well-known former big-time criminal, now on the talkshow circuit.

Grayle said, 'Gary Stewart?'

'Seward. Was a regular London villain. Wages snatches, stuff like that. Then protection. Then drugs, then protecting major drug dealers against other major drug dealers. And then he got rich and then he got nicked. Did seven years. Came out, let somebody ghost his memoirs and got richer. Last year he had his own quiz show on one of the cable channels. It was called "The Loot".'

'You know, I think I heard of this guy. Would he have toured his book in the States, couple years ago? Letterman? Jay Leno? One of those shows. I guess nobody took him too seriously – joke English hood, charming grin, quaint London accent.'

'That's how America sees our villains? A joke?'

'Oh, *yeah*. English crooks are like Robin Hood. Quaint. Steal the country-house jewels. They get outsmarted in the end, but only by Hercule Poirot, on account of all English cops are either idiot toffs who ride to hounds or dumb, potato-faced guys with big boots. Sorry and all, Bobby, but we need our stereo-types. How, uh, how did you get along with Callard?'

'She's . . . interesting.'

'Uh-huh.'

'Impressive.'

So you made like rabbits the whole night, huh?

'She told you stuff?'

'Yes.'

'Uh-huh.'

'Told me stuff about . . .' Bobby looked uncomfortable. 'About Emma.'

Oh, Jesus, his major point of vulnerability.

'Stuff she couldn't've known?'

'Unless you or Marcus told her.'

Grayle sighed. 'No. We just told her you were a cop who was not as other cops. Like more of a fruitcake.'

'Thanks.'

'I kind of think she could've told me stuff too. About Ersula. Only I declined. I guess you didn't . . . decline.'

'No,' he said. 'No, I didn't decline.'

Goddamn New Age cop. They stood at the base of the headless tower. The wind seemed to be rising.

'Bobby, did I do wrong, calling Cindy?'

'He got me through a very bad night once.'

'I know. That doesn't answer the question.'

'He makes connections we wouldn't even think of. No, I'm really glad you called him. It was inspired.'

'Let's not go overboard, Bobby.'

'She says she's going to leave tonight.'

'She does? To go where?'

He shook his head. 'She's not saying. There are things she isn't going to tell us. And once she drives away from here . . .'

'You're a tad scared, right?'

'Bit. These guys are not Robin Hood, and they'd spread Hercule Poirot's little grey cells all over the

312

ceiling.' Bobby smiled sheepishly. 'Sorry. I didn't mean to . . .'

The wind began to rattle in the tower.

'The *Lottery* person?' Persephone laughed – a brittle, jittery laugh – at the utter absurdity of it. 'This person, this shamanic therapist of yours is . . . that Lottery person?'

Marcus felt his face go red.

'I watched it once,' she said. 'As a kind of social exercise, I suppose. It was . . . bizarre.'

'One word for it.'

'He's transsexual or something, isn't he? Flaunts that ghastly . . . bird thing.'

'Kelvyn Kite,' Marcus said through his teeth.

Persephone was sitting on the sofa in the study, dressed rather demurely, wearing no make-up, reminding him of how she'd looked in school uniform. Even plaited her hair; it hung down one side of her like a cathedral bell-rope.

'I think', Marcus shuffled, 'that we should forget the whole thing. It was a mistake. If you have to go, you have to go.'

Persephone cupped her chin in her palms. 'Tell me about him.'

'No, it's stupid. I'm just being a . . . self-righteous old phoney.'

'*Tell* me.'

Sydney Mars-Lewis. Madman. The red kite. The aboriginal mentors, in North Wales.

'Tradition goes back to Merlin. *Allegedly*. In that, if Merlin actually existed, he was probably as twisted and deranged as Lewis.'

Marcus explained, as best he could, the role that Lewis had accepted for himself: the misfit, the outcast who had grown up reviled, scorned, shunned. The walking duality of the man – male and female, sanity and madness, reality and fantasy. A foot in two worlds. At least two.

Watching her eyes appear to darken and knowing she was remembering her schooldays and the taunts of her peers. *Witch doctor. Ju-ju woman.*

He told her that Lewis had been an actor, an end-of-the-pier entertainer, a long-time occasional contributor to *The Phenomenologist* . . . and, as it happened, the first to suspect that a number of apparently unconnected murders in the British countryside bore the hallmarks of a single perpetrator: the Green Man.

'Despite his high-camp demeanour and that irritating Welsh whine, he does seem to possess what I can only describe as a dowser's sensitivity to . . . well . . . to the nearness of evil, I suppose. To be quite frank, Persephone, basically I can't stand to spend too much time with the ludicrous bastard. Pains the hell out of me to admit he has abilities that will always be beyond me, but there it is.'

'The Lottery man.' She thought about it, with a watery smile. 'Must be my day for light entertainers.' She stood up, sudden rain flecking the window behind her. 'Sure. What the hell? Let's do it. Thank you, Marcus.'

'If, when you meet him, you don't like the look of the bastard . . .'

'I'm sure I'll *love* the look of him. But', she took his hand, 'whatever happens, I shall have to leave tomorrow.'

'Where will you go?'

'Oh . . .' For a second, she looked nakedly unsure. 'There's an appointment to keep. And then perhaps I'll go abroad for a while. I need to think about things. Perhaps do something different, find some other way of using whatever abilities I possess before it's too late.'

Too late?

'Persephone, if people are looking for you . . .'

'Then I'll go somewhere they'll never find me. India or somewhere. Join a bloody ashram. I'll send you a postcard. Don't want to lose touch again. I'll write . . . an article or something, for your magazine. Something you could print. That'd make Grayle feel a little better about me, do you think?'

'I think', he said, 'that that would somehow be desperately unsatisfactory. I mean you going off on your own. Into hiding, as it were.'

'I'm sorry.' Persephone shrugged awkwardly and twisted away. 'I've behaved like a clinging child. I've imposed on you inexcusably. I've put a strain on your working relationship with Grayle . . .'

'No,' Marcus said. 'Not at all. No . . .'

Suddenly, she seemed so much smaller and even more vulnerable than she had as a teenager. Marcus was afraid for her and all she represented.

He doubted Mars-Lewis would be able to help her.

The sky was starting to darken when Grayle and Bobby Maiden watched Cindy return. He looked like a member of a mature persons' hiking club back from the hills for his hot broth and his bed in some hostel. He seemed a little brighter.

The new wind carried a spattering of rain. They

stood in the shelter of the curtain wall. Cindy looked up at the sky and nodded, then turned to them.

'Bobby,' he said. 'Good to see you again, boy.'

'How are you, Cindy?'

'I'm good. Good, yes.'

Grayle frowned. 'What's the schedule, Cindy?'

Cindy patted her arm. 'Begin soon after dark, we will, I think. As the first . . . occurrence was at night. We need to appear to be dancing to his tune.'

'*His* tune?'

Grayle recoiled at the way the wind was rolling at the castle wall. Although it was not a particularly cold wind and even blew a gruff promise of spring.

The dog Malcolm ambled towards them from the back of the farmhouse, pausing to sniff in all the usual places where the grass grew in clumps through fractured flagstones.

'Keeps his distance from Callard,' Grayle said. 'Even Marcus commented on it.'

'You're saying this is a sign of what she carries, little Grayle?'

'How would I know?'

She looked up at him, his face tilted towards the last of the light, the sawn-off tower rearing over him.

'Right, then.' Cindy patted Malcolm. 'Let's go in. Lead the way, my boy.'

32

'Ms Callard.'

Cindy met her at last just after seven, when she emerged from Marcus's study into the ill-lit, stone-walled passageway. He took her hand, bowed formally over it.

He wore his tweed jacket and slacks with crisp creases. His hair was conservatively brushed and carried only a hint of its usual mauve. Bobby Maiden thought he looked like the manager of a slightly faded hotel, approaching retirement. *Not really a celebrity*, the clothes said. *Not quite a loony*. But they were just as much of a costume as those spangly frocks.

'Mr Lewis,' Seffi Callard said.

The two hands parting civilly.

Seffi, joined now by Marcus, was calm and seemed distant – as though something had been agreed, Maiden thought, but it would be no more than going through the motions.

Seffi didn't look at Maiden. He watched, with Grayle, from the doorway of the kitchen across the passage. He thought of Em, but she was far away now.

He looked at Grayle in her jeans and a lime and lemon baseball sweater too big for her – a defiant statement; none of this solemn Victorian formality for her. She looked very pretty, her blonde hair bunched like bananas. But also forlorn, Maiden thought. He didn't think he'd ever met anyone with less to hide, less to feel bad about.

But his gaze, inevitably, was drawn back to Seffi Callard, evoking a longing as strange and raw as the one he sometimes felt for lonely places – long beaches, estuaries, ante-rooms to infinity.

'I'm getting the feeling you'd rather keep this formal.' Cindy's accent, like his hair, was smoothed down. He and Seffi looking at one another almost like opponents. Not fighters, but maybe international chess champions: same game, different language, different names for the pieces.

'It's your show, Mr Lewis,' Seffi said.

Cindy shook his head gently. 'No, lovely, *your* show it is, tonight. You are walking the tightrope. Think of me as a safety net. Or, rather, don't think of me at all.' He smiled and ushered her into what had been Mrs Willis's healing room.

They might have been going in for dinner.

The first time Maiden had been in here, Mrs Willis was recently dead and although he'd never met her there'd been a poignancy about her stripped-down daybed and the rickety shelves still loaded with jars and old Marmite pots full of herbs and potions. Now the shelves were sagging under stacks of back copies of *The Vision*.

The size of the place, its height, surprised him. Perhaps a partition wall had been taken down since he was last here. It was clear now that the room had once been a small barn or a cowshed attached to the farm-

318

house. Rafters were exposed where a short hayloft had been; there was a long window which had probably been a doorway, and you could see the ruins out there and hear the wind whining like a trapped banshee in the derelict castle's sawn-off tower.

A computer, unplugged, had been pushed against a wall on its table. In the centre of the room was a circle of six wooden chairs, some brought in from the study and the kitchen. On a small, round table in the middle of the circle, an earthenware bowl held a stubby candle.

Maiden said, 'Six chairs, Cindy?'

'Are there really?'

'There are five of us.'

'Hmm,' Cindy said. 'A little corny, do you think?'

One time, while she was with the *Courier*, Grayle had been given special permission to cover a seance given by the exclusive New York medium, Morgan Schuster.

She was real ghostlike: small, white-haired, wore white woollen dresses. She had an apartment in the Dakota Building, the turreted and gargoyled Central Park château where Polanski shot *Rosemary's Baby* and Mark Chapman shot John Lennon. It was, she said, perhaps *the* most resonant location in the city, a major spiritual *node*, a focus of psychic energy, a great amplifier for the inner voice.

Morgan used to operate out of her front parlour in Queens until not too long after Grayle's column broke the story about her psychic contact with the spirit Beatle. Which – whatever the likes of Lyndon McAffrey said – had seemed genuine enough to Grayle at the time. And, even if it wasn't, where was the harm? Morgan was a wise, good-natured person who helped people find their true selves. Just that she used to help poor people and now she helped mostly rich people, and had a way of making Grayle feel good about what *she* did.

See, Grayle, to people all across the nation – distressed, grief-laden people and those who're just looking for some kind of celestial light in a gloomy world – you've become very essential. You are a crucial conduit in a data flow which begins in the unseen world, passes to people like me and reaches the material world through your column. What you're doing transcends mere journalism.

Grayle nodding weakly, figuring Lyndon McAffrey might see it from a different perspective, regarding her column as a useful conduit through which large amounts of money were siphoned into the bank accounts of people like Morgan Schuster.

And then . . . *So Lucas, the art dealer, is no longer close to the centre of your world*, Morgan had said.

I tell you that?

You didn't have to. Morgan looking up, through half-closed eyes.

There you go. Just when you start putting them down as phoney, up pops a winning number.

'Grayle.'

'Huh?'

'Are you with us, lovely?' Cindy said.

'Sorry, just . . . a little nervous. Trying to ground myself.'

'Grayle, I would like you and Marcus to sit on either side of Persephone. But, remember, don't touch her!'

Like she was gonna be live with electricity or something? Grayle looked at the dark, sombre Callard and compared her with the flitting, Caspar the friendly

320

ghost figure of Morgan Schuster. She thought, *I set this whole thing up. What am I, crazy? Am I sick?*

'OK,' she said.

'And try not to move, whatever happens.'

'Sure.'

Cindy lit the wick of a tin oil lamp with a match, lowered the glass and placed the lamp on the low window ledge behind Bobby. Next he lit the candle in the bowl on the table. When he put out the lights, shadows leapt and the room shed centuries.

Grayle heard the normally stoical Malcolm whimpering from the study.

An explosion of glass in Marcus's head. Young girls' trilling screams in the dormitory, then the baying of the headmaster, scared even more witless than usual. *What the hell are you doing, Bacton? How dare you let her out?* The long, dull-panelled corridor, meagrely lit by economy night lamps. Marcus proceeding slowly along it, as though edging down a railway carriage, to where the child was crouching like a small, wild animal . . . *Don't move . . . It wasn't your fault . . . Do you understand? . . . Don't move . . .* Half expecting her to leap up at him with claws out, like a half-grown, feral kitten.

'Ah, Marcus, my sweet . . .'

Lewis's limp paw on Marcus's shoulder. He jerked back, as though stung, his fists tightening. The whole situation slipping away from him and into the hands of a madman.

'Try to *relax*, Marcus,' Lewis soothed. Like the smarmy, phoney hospital consultant the night his little daughter, Sally, lay dying. 'Was I not sent here by cunning circumstance?'

Marcus gripped the seat of his chair. 'Don't fuck this up, that's all.'

And then, somewhere on the creature's person, an electronic ululation began. The fool had brought his mobile phone in here.

Cindy walked quickly out of the room, snatching the phone from his pocket. Forgotten about the thing, he had. Taken it up to High Knoll with him in case there should be a further need to reassure young Jo.

He moved to the end of the stone passage.

'Lewis here!'

'Cindy, Christ . . .'

'Jo, I must call you back.'

'Cindy, listen to me . . . this is like a sick joke . . . this is the sickest joke you ever heard.'

'Give me two hours, lovely – two hours.'

'No, you listen!' Jo shrilled like a raging child pulling at its father's knees. '*Listen, listen, listen* . . . the Sherwins of Banbury. You remember the Sherwins? Started the whole BMW thing when they bought one each, even the old granny? The Sherwins, Cindy – all the news programmes are asking for the tapes of the Sherwins with their BMWs and their top-of-the-range Barrett home. Oh, God almighty, I can't believe any of this.'

'What are you saying?'

'Happened around lunchtime today. The Sherwins had been out to dinner last night with loads of guests and freeloaders and hangers on, as usual, and they didn't get back until late and so they all slept in, in a big way, and it's thought one of them got up, still half-pissed, wandered into the kitchen for a snack, left something on the posh built-in cooker hob, or the built-in bloody spit . . .'

'And?'

'And they're all *dead*, the stupid irresponsible bastards! The Barrett home's a smoking ruin, the BMWs are reduced to blackened shells in the quadruple garage. You do *remember* the Sherwins, Cindy? You remember Kelvyn Kite cackling on your arm. *It'll all end in tears, mark my words, it'll all end in tears!'*

Cindy walked out into the treacherous night, through the uncaring wind, the spiteful rain. Crying to the elements.

What was happening?

He pushed his forehead into the cold, wet castle wall, sensing the blood and the flames of its history, the screams and roars of some small medieval massacre mingling with the screams of the burning Sherwins, the roar of the fire. Had they been screaming, trapped, or were they quietly suffocated in their beds, mother and father and daughter and son? And granny, owner of a silver-grey Series Seven BMW that she would never drive.

Above the screams and the blood and the shrivelling, crackling flesh rose the shrieking of the Kite.

End in tears, end in tears.

End in the cardiac unit . . .

Cindy pulled the mobile phone from his pocket and hurled it high over the smashed castle wall.

Fly . . . fly like a kite . . .

He thought he could hear the tinny techno-treble of its call as it fell among the ancient ramparts.

33

Debussy's sirens call him back.

Oh, he knows Debussy. Poor Claude – now *there* was a frustrated shaman. Called him an impressionist composer, they did; he hated that, although, yes, his music responded to light.

The light below the surface.

Cindy slides damply, uncomfortably, into the candle-lit barn room, where no-one is speaking, the ethereal music wafting from a boom box on which the legend XtraBass is inscribed, silver on black.

Marcus glances suspiciously up at him, twin candles in his glasses. But Marcus, for all his rage, must be calmer here than anywhere, for this is Mrs Willis's room.

Cindy prays silently for the essence of Mrs Willis to be here with them tonight. Mrs Willis and all her healing. For Cindy knows that the old woman was once Annie Davies, the child who met the Lady who stepped from the sun up on High Knoll on a midsummer morning. Up on the Knoll, Cindy called to Annie to join him on his meditative journey to gather in the last of the light. And then collected seventeen small stones in his case.

The stones are now placed unobtrusively around the room, creating a second, larger circle around the chairs. Going to need all the light they can get tonight, for there'll be none from Persephone Callard.

Cindy approaches the boom box, turns down the volume until the level of the music is no higher than that of the wind, then seats himself in the chair nearest the door, next to the empty chair which, on his instruction, is directly opposite Persephone Callard's.

Cindy clears his throat.

'We should have a few more minutes' quiet, my friends. Then we shall begin. Calling on the Brightness to surround us as we summon, from another place, the presence clinging to Persephone. When we begin, try not to look at one another. Particularly, try not to look at Persephone.'

Who sits, in all her sphinx-like beauty, with her hands upon her knees, so still – and yet he senses a great activity around her, like a cloud of moths around a garden lamp.

Bobby Maiden gives her periodic sidelong glances.

Oh dear.

The poor boy. Afraid for her. And, of course, besotted, like many before him – Cindy's view is that the men she's been with over the years will have fallen generally into two types: the ones who are a little scared of her, who *like* being scared of her – some Gothic masochism thing – and the ones who want to get *into* her . . . sex being only the beginning of the supernaturally enhanced relationship they are going to have.

Cindy, however, is feeling for common ground – yes, the shaman's role is also to commune with spirits, but in a less claustrophobic sense than the medium. To channel unseen energies, to ride the green ray, to connect people with the spirit of their ancestors and of their place, in a healing way, a connecting way, thus overcoming the acute sense of alienation which so afflicts modern societies. All rather less, shall we say, *domestic* than the spiritualist. Less domestic and perhaps less – Cindy would never dare say this aloud – *mean-spirited*.

Which is to say that the Celtic shaman would not normally consider it seemly to communicate with the essences of dead individuals.

Tonight, however . . . Well, tonight Cindy's role may be one of interception. If it comes through, he must catch it, hold it within the circle. No pussy-footing. He wants answers.

Debussy has finished. All is silent. Cindy lets it lie for a moment.

'Persephone?' he whispers at last.

She nods.

'When you are ready,' he says steadily.

She does not respond at once. Cindy glances at Grayle's soft, candlelit blondeness. She is looking past Persephone at Bobby, half lit by the hurricane lamp behind him. Grayle's face is solemn. Probably since a night of thunder and lightning and death at the Rollright Stones, little Grayle has been hiding, even from herself, certain feelings for Bobby Maiden. *Oh dear, oh dear,* so many complications. Such an emotional tapestry is hardly the safest backdrop for the theatre of souls.

'The . . .' Persephone's voice is cracked 'the line . . .' She swallows.

The calm is fractured, Cindy sensing a sudden acute

trepidation in the part of her – the personality – which must now allow itself to be pushed into the back seat. He closes his eyes and opens his hands in his lap, sending her the steel-blue light of fortitude.

She breathes out once, through her mouth, a long and hollow breath, like the sound from a seashell or a cave.

'*Haaaaaaaaaw.*'

Cindy opens his eyes, focuses on the middle distance.

'The lines are open,' Persephone Callard states. Though it is little more than a croak.

Seconds later the first indication is from the dog. Malcolm howls once, pitifully, far away in Marcus's study, another world.

Marcus's eyes flicker up at once, in concern, and Cindy gives him a hard look – *stay*.

Marcus subsides. Malcolm subsides, but Cindy knows the dog is panting now, in fear, as some animals do during an electric storm. He will crawl under Marcus's desk and lie there, trembling.

The air in here feels thin – like the air, it is said, on the top of a high mountain. It is a sensation Cindy has experienced – for reasons, of course, other than altitude – upon Cader Idris, the sacred mountain of Snowdonia and, most joyously, on little Carn Ingli, near his home.

It is not so joyous here. The candle flame grows longer and, under the whine of the wind, there is a scratching, like rats, at the wall, from outside.

Next to him the sixth chair creaks. '*Oh God,*' Grayle whispers.

Marcus frowns. Cindy's eyes meet Grayle's and he

sends a shushing across the space between them. *Don't look at the sixth chair.*

But Bobby it is who stirs. Standing up quickly. Looking confused, glancing from side to side. He walks out of the circle.

Stop him?

Wait a moment.

A tiny chittering voice in the corner of the room becomes louder, passes through the chair circle, is gone like a breath of wind. Perhaps only Cindy has heard it. But, no . . . there's a sharp glance from Marcus; he has picked up the sound and Cindy can almost read his growling thoughts.

You and your bastard ventriloquism.

Marcus will always be the first to suspect Cindy, but Cindy knows that the little, chittering voice was the voice of the spirit which draws back the curtain.

And that the lines are indeed open now.

He sees that Bobby has returned. The boy has on his knees one of the office jotters. He's watching Miss Callard most keenly, his hand moving on the pad.

The rain beats on the long window. Reminds Grayle how, one time – the only time – she saw what might have been a ghost. Or something.

Not so very long ago, on an autumn day, she was alone in the rain up on High Knoll and she saw this little girl, who could not have been there. A little girl in blue who ran in the rain, was part of the rain – ran and ran in the same patch of crystal rain, getting nowhere. Not existing outside of the rain. And Grayle ran, too, terrified, all the way down the hill, to where Bobby Maiden found her and brought her to Marcus and Marcus's whisky. A day of destiny, though she couldn't have known it, her future being shaped around her as she shivered in the rural rain.

Through the rain noise, she's heard Callard say,

The lines are open.

Well, sure, big deal.

The candle flame is, like, two inches long. Grayle looks away from it, down at her sneakers. Though she feels safe with these people – with *most* of these people – one thing she isn't gonna do is look at that goddamn sixth chair, get into some stupid hallucination trip, like no *way*.

Marcus ponders. Those small voices, meaningless as twittering birds . . . certainly possible that Lewis could have been doing that; in this light he needn't even worry about being seen to move his lips. Equally – there was a radio, wasn't there, in that ghetto-blaster thing of Underhill's? Perhaps it had activated itself when the CD ended. Or perhaps Lewis himself . . . Yes, it was Lewis who turned the music down. The creature was a conjuror for a while wasn't he . . . devious bastard.

Lewis says, 'It's here, isn't it, Persephone?'

Marcus stares through the candle at Lewis and then, boldly, angrily, at the sixth chair.

Seeing nothing there but a fucking chair.

The nearness of Seffi Callard. The erotic sound of her breathing in a darkened room. Bobby Maiden can't stop thinking about Seffi Callard and he wonders if she can feel his longing, rising like the candle flame.

His right hand, tight around the pencil, moves across the pad. Across the space between their chairs, she seems to reach out and touch his hand with one long finger.

Bobby Maiden shudders with a sudden rush of passion for her that's far more complex than desire. He needs to draw her face, convey the weight of her hair, the dark lamps of her eyes.

And Cindy's brain pulses with the sudden sense of something violently squalid, poisonously shrivelled.

Assailed now by the stench of a lavatory lust, so strong and physical that he wants to run from the room before it sucks him into that steaming, sordid pit on the edge of which – more than once, to his shame – he has teetered.

Cindy is badly shocked, close to panic, almost wrenches his chair away from it, from whatever monstrosity is forming like a gas in the chair next to his own. It is with enormous difficulty that he keeps his voice low and steady.

'Talk to it, Persephone.'

'I can't.'

'Try,' Cindy hisses, teeth clenched.

'I don't know what to call him.'

'Ask for a name.'

Persephone sits with her spine straight, her hands clasped in the lap of her skirt.

She says, her voice robotic, 'What's your name?'

Cindy urgently visualizes the seventeen little stones – under the window, at the foot of the shelves, beneath the computer table – and, with a burst of will-power, makes them glow.

Persephone says, stronger now, 'What's your *name*?'

Cindy conjures in his head the sound of a drum

330

beating, his own drum, his painted bodhran (knowing that the drum, lying on the back seat of his car, will now be vibrating).

'Who are you?' Persephone cries in anguish. 'Who are you, who *are* you, WHO ARE YOU?'

The drum is beating on its own, Cindy thinking rapidly: this business of No Name indicates not so much the *absence* of a name but that Persephone *refuses to hear it*. Refuses to confront the possibility – Grayle, it was, suggested this and Grayle might well be right – that she may, in the time-honoured, deliberate formality of the seance, be conjuring a personification of her despised art at its most foetid and contemptible, summoning a spirit of the lowest order, comprised of spittle-like strands of sick longing.

You and I, we are prisoners in the same old, mildewed tower.

'Ask its name, Persephone!'

'He won't . . . tell me.'

He. Always *he*. Part of the denial. Giving it maleness, giving it a hard, damaged face.

'All right. All right then . . .'

The drum beating louder in his head, the circle of seventeen stones glowing brightly there, Cindy braces himself, aware that what he is about to suggest is not terribly wise. It will bring with it pain and suffering, awaken memories of old, foul dreams.

'Throw it to me,' Cindy says lightly, and turns to look directly at the sixth chair. 'Throw him to me, lovely.'

His hands, both of them, moving rapidly on the pad, Maiden is becoming aware of a surge of enthusiasm, a sense of violent arousal. His thumb is smudging the

331

freshly laid pencil shading into misted whorls as he sculpts the face.

He's in Justin's garage, rich with the smell of oil and fear, and Justin is sobbing, '*Please . . . I don't know . . . I've told you . . . for fucksake, man, I don't . . .*' There's a silent, gloating presence suspended in the vault of grimy light from the roof.

'*Nice one.*' A low and guttural sigh. A rasp. Rapture.

Seffi Callard screams. 'He's touching my face!'

Maiden jerks at once to his feet, the pad and pencil falling to the floor, and moves towards her, but it seems a long way, like swimming through dark, muddy water, his hands clawing at the soup.

Hearing Cindy, sharply, 'Bobby, sit *down.*'

Maiden feels frustration. Anger. An old resentment running as deep as a sewer. Hate. Then Seffi—

'He's touching me—'

Seffi draws in a huge breath and her body rears back, shuddering, and then it goes still and tight and Maiden waits for her breath to come out, but it doesn't. She's frozen, arched and rigid, an abandoned sculpture in bronze.

Maiden throws himself at her, but there's something in between, something that hones the air, makes it vicious like a blade. Far away, Malcolm's howl is close to a scream.

'The smell!' Grayle blurts. 'Oh Jesus, it's coming . . . it's coming *off of her.*'

Maiden tries to touch Seffi but his hands don't reach, and Seffi, though still rigid, starts to vibrate, as though there's electricity forking into her, and there's sweat forming like a second, bubbling skin on her face, and when Maiden's hands hover over her shoulders he

332

expects the electric charge to go through him like a sizzling knife, and he doesn't care.

'Please,' he whispers.

And they're all dead, the stupid irresponsible bastards!

'Not now!' Cindy shouts. 'Leave me alone, can't you?'

The drumming has lost its rhythm and the seventeen small stones from High Knoll have lost their lights, and – despicably – all Cindy can think about is his own predicament, the dissolution of his brilliant career. In a sick, dispiriting moment, he finds himself looking at the sixth chair.

It is empty but, above it, he would swear he sees Kurt Campbell's sharp face projected into the window, in the light of the oil lamp.

And then the window itself collapses, a waterfall of glass.

34

The bulkhead bulb came on, awakening shadows in the castle walls, as if the explosion had summoned to the surface all the violent drama locked into its eight hundred years of history. Grayle stood in the yard in the rain and the irritable wind, hugging herself to squash the shakes. Feeling the banging of her own heart, like an iron bucket against the sides of a deep, deep well.

Marcus stumbled out through the fan of light, slivers of glass shining like snow crystals in his hair, an open cut on his forehead.

'Just don't say it, Marcus!' Grayle's voice rising like an elevator out of control. 'Just like the old days. Just like the old freaking school. Only difference is, this time it's *you* got to explain to the insurance guys.'

And then she was sorry because Marcus, barely free of the flu, looked like shit. Looked like he'd been beaten up on.

'Should be some . . . chipboard.' He was looking around vaguely. 'In the old pigsty, round the . . .'

'Huh?'

'To board up the window. Got to keep . . . keep the rain out.'

A fog behind his glasses. The sour chill in the air, the smell, the sound, the *taste* of it, and all of it right there in his own back yard, within his own castle walls. The shock of invasion.

Grayle took his arm. 'We'll deal with it, Marcus. Bobby and I will handle it. You come back inside. Let's get you a big glass of something strong. Get that cut cleaned up.'

'Cut?' A nerve tweaking his cheek. 'Where's . . . where's Persephone?'

'I guess she's still in there, with Cindy and Bobby. Leave it, huh?'

'I have to talk to her. She'll be distressed. She needs reassurance.'

'No, Marcus,' Grayle said patiently. 'That was last time. That was twenty years ago. She grew up. She knows precisely what she did.'

Cindy came out, followed by Malcolm the dog, loosed from the study. Then Bobby.

'Marcus? You OK? Grayle?'

'We're fine, Bobby. Just deciding which of the all-night glaziers in St Mary's we should call out.'

A bubbling giggle forming. Here we go, that old hysteria, welcome home. Some glass splinters fell out of her hair.

Bobby was looking at Malcolm, who didn't move. Grayle shook her head hard, watching more glass fall around her feet. Bobby bent and patted his thighs. Malcolm looked uncertain. Grayle thought, *What is this? Did Bobby collect something in there?*

Malcolm gave a slow wave of his stumpy tail, ambled over. Bobby crouched. He and the dog bonded under the bulkhead lamp.

335

Cindy nodded. Whatever it was, it was OK now.

'Where's Persephone?' Marcus demanded.

Bobby looked up. 'I thought she came out with you.'

'I don't think so.'

'She was ahead of you. She ran out of the room. When it happened, she ran out, hands over her ears.'

'Then she's out here, someplace.'

'Persephone?' Marcus stumbled out into the yard. '*Persephone!*'

Stopping and listening and getting no reply. Only the wind against the castle walls. Marcus strode to the dairy. Hammered with a fist on the door.

'Persephone! Are you in there?' He turned to them, blood oozing down his forehead. 'What if she's in there with . . . with . . . ?'

He couldn't say it. But Grayle knew she wouldn't have laughed at him this time if he had. She breathed in hard to cancel the memory of the feral, male smell.

'Stand back,' Marcus said.

'Aw, Marcus—'

Marcus hurled himself sideways at the door. Bounced off, moaning, holding his shoulder.

'Bloody hell, Marcus.' Bobby putting himself between Marcus and the door. Malcolm started barking, figuring this was a fight.

'She's in there . . . don't you see, Maiden? She's locked herself in. She's trying to deal with it herself. Bloody Lewis screwed it up, and she—'

'All right.' Bobby pulled hair out of his eyes; he was sweating, anxious. 'Before we kick it in, you've got another key to this place, haven't you?'

'Lost it. Months ago. Persephone's got the only key. *Persephone!*' Marcus kicked the door, under the lock. '*Please . . .*' He rattled the handle and the door sprang open. Marcus crashed through like an old bull, flung down on his hands and knees inside the dairy.

Bobby moved to help him up. Grayle pushed past them both, putting on the light. Marcus was shaking Bobby off, ramming his glasses into position.

'Oh,' Grayle said.

On account of there was no-one else in the dairy.

She saw the bed was half made, the duvet turned back. A lone silk blouse hung limply on a hanger on the closet door.

But there was no sign of Callard's bags. Grayle went quickly into the other rooms. She opened the closet: empty. No personal stuff in the kitchen, in the bathroom just a tube of toothpaste and a toothbrush on the shelf over the basin.

This *Mary Celeste* feel about the whole place.

'What's going on?' Marcus demanded. 'What's happened here. Underhill?'

'Looks like she checked out.'

'I don't understand . . .'

'Hold on. Let's . . .'

Bobby Maiden had run out into the night, Grayle trailing behind him across the yard, towards the entrance. When they got there, they found the wooden farm gate unlatched, the wind smacking it against the post.

Grayle looked back, rain in her face. She guessed the Cherokee was also gone. They hadn't heard the motor start up. Probably on account of the wind.

337

Part Five

Part Five

From *Bang to Wrongs: A Bad Boy's Book*,
by GARY SEWARD Preface to the paperback edition

CLARENCE JUDGE – A TRIBUTE

*As you may have read in the papers, since this book first
come out, my dear old mate Clarence has been taken from
us . . . taken from behind, in cold blood.*

*This has gutted me, I don't mind admitting, like no other
incident in my rich and varied life.*

*Doing it like that is not only the coward's way, it's the only
way they'd have got Clarence. Right to the end – and he was
nearly fifty-eight years old – this was a geezer people didn't
ever mess with if they could avoid it. You knew where you
were with Clarence and if you was on the opposite side,
Gawd help you.*

However, he was a decent man.

*Now I know a lot of moralistic gits out there will be going,
What?!!! But I stand by what I just said. There's no denying
this business is full of evil double-dealers what would stab
you in the back and lift your wallet in a single move. But
Clarence was a man of honour, a staunch ally and a faithful
friend. Even his enemies, Clarence done right by them – if
you was going to be 'visited' by Clarence, he would look
you in the eyes in the street and tell you to your face, and*

that was that, because Clarence believed in being fair and upfront at all times. At least one piece of scum, possessed of this advance information, took the opportunity to top himself first, and you can't say fairer than that.

Sadly, Clarence Judge never had much luck the whole of his life. He was too honest. If the filth accused him of a crime, he would put his hands up straight away – usually to damage a couple of them first, but that was Clarence, an angry man sometimes.

As a result, he spent more than half his adult life in prison.

'A stupid man, too, then,' some smirking young talkshow host in a shiny suit remarks to me late one night on BBC 2. I felt like redecorating the set with his face in memory of Clarence, and I would have too if my fellow guests Kurt Campbell and Barry Manilow had not been sat between us in nice clean suits.

Was all the war heroes, the VCs, what went over the top on their own with a rifle, was they stupid men?

Because this is what Clarence was . . . a brave foot soldier who would lay down his life for his comrades. He never mugged old ladies for their pension money, nor did he give heroin to eleven-year-old schoolkids. The people what Clarence hurt – and yes, all right, he did hurt them, he hurt them grievously, usually – was the scum: the grasses, the snouts, or the cowards what drove off in the getaway car the minute they seen the filth and left their mates to face the music. Like me, Clarence knew what could and could not be tolerated and he stuck by his principles.

But, in the end, it seems, one of the scum got at him, in the cowardly way they operate. So far the police have failed to apprehend the guilty party. I do not know how hard they have tried, but as they are unlikely to offer much of a reward for apprehending the murderer of a 'notorious criminal', I shall do so myself. If any reader of this book has information fingering Clarence's killer and would like to write to me, care of my publisher, I personally will pay them the sum of between ten and twenty thousand clean ones, according to the strength of the information.

Naturally, as a law-abiding citizen these days, I shall immediately hand over anything of value to the police.

35

Cindy ate a small breakfast in the otherwise empty, wood-walled bar, the place as quiet as the morning of a funeral.

The wind had not died with the dawn. Cindy had awoken into cold light and the rocking of the inn sign, with its grim, grey, curly-horned ram.

Amy collected his dishes. She wore one of her little black dresses, very Juliette Greco. Quite sexy, he thought sadly. Too late now for him to appreciate such qualities. The course was set; whichever way he turned would leave him leaning suicidally over the abyss.

'How can they say those things?' Amy said. 'They don't know you. That brother, he've got no brains. Just hit out, they do, without a thought.'

Cindy was silent.

'You mustn't let them get away with this.'

Cindy smiled with a sorrow which, in the gloom of the bar, Amy would be unlikely to discern.

'Not as if they've *sacked* you, Cindy, is it? The BBC would not be so daft! You're a big star!'

'A big star. Yes.'

The *Sun* lay folded by his plate. He poured himself a coffee, picked up the paper.

'Don't . . .' Amy said anxiously. 'Don't torture yourself.'

'A little late for that, my love.'

Cindy spread out the *Sun*.

THE CURSE OF
KELVYN KITE

The enormous front-page headline displayed like an official public warning.

Cindy briefly closed his eyes, opening them to the sub-head:

Brother blasts Cindy as horror
blaze kills Lotto family

This angle came from Brendan Sherwin's brother, Greg, who did not, Cindy judged with unusual bitterness from the photograph, look like a man who might qualify for Mensa.

> Greg, 34, said: 'My sister in law was very upset when Cindy made that bird come out with all those comments about the new Barrett home and the BMWs.
>
> 'Brendan and Sharon were both demoralized. It had got that they were scared to come out of their new house because of the remarks people made.
>
> 'One day last week, two little kids were standing at the edge of Brendan's drive flap-

ping their arms like birds' wings and shouting, "It'll all end in tears!"'

Greg added, 'I hate that Cindy now for what he's caused. It's like he's sneering at ordinary people's good luck.

'He tries to blame it all on Kelvyn Kite, but everybody knows it's what he really thinks.

'Cindy is sick. If you ask me, he should quit now.'

Oh, how cleverly it had been done. Perhaps some hungry freelance journalist had initially put the words into Greg's mouth: *So how do you feel about Cindy now, Greg? I expect you hate him.*

'Er, yeah.'

And the use of the beautifully ambivalent line, *I hate Cindy for what he's caused*. Causing people to deride Lottery jackpot winners or, in fact, causing their deaths?

Nobody was suggesting such a nonsense, of course. Nothing so direct.

The piece continued across pages four and five. Page four referred to the plane crash and the heart attack. The National Lottery death toll. The paper had spoken to a consultant psychiatrist, whose portentous comments began, *If people are constantly warned to mistrust good fortune achieved without any effort on their part and told that such luck will inevitably bring repercussions, then . . .*

Page five was all about Cindy.

Oh God.

He could not read it.

He should leave quietly. What use was he here, having failed Marcus and Grayle, failed Persephone Callard and – what was worse – damaged her

347

equilibrium, driven her away in fear and despair? No, he was not the world's most popular man this morning. Not at Castle Farm in the parish of St Mary's. Nor, by the looks of the morning papers, anywhere in this impressionable country.

Sydney Mars-Lewis, I am arresting you for complicity in the deaths of Gerry Purviss, Colin Seymour, Brendan Sherwin, Sharon Sherwin . . .

But let's not get carried away.

Leave that to the *Sun.*

Around eight-thirty in the morning, Bobby Maiden had the lights on in the editorial room, formerly a treatment room, now a mess. With no window, you needed all the lights all the time.

He and Grayle had pulled out the jagged glass from the frame, boarded up the space as best they could with chipboard panels from the stable – Marcus shouting instructions, cursing a good deal to cover up how unnerved he was, while Maiden was thinking, *She'll come back. She just wants to drive around for a while, clear her head.*

Only she hadn't come back. She'd grabbed most of her stuff in a hurry and taken off, just as she'd apparently done from Barber's party.

Fled from it.

Obviously likes to go out with a bang, Grayle had said laconically before she went home around midnight, leaving Maiden to bed down on the sofa. Marcus had offered him the dairy, but he couldn't bring himself to sleep there. He'd lain awake for a long time, Malcolm sleeping on his feet. Maiden listening for the sound of an engine in the wind.

All right, she was unpredictable, *famously* unpredictable, and she owed him nothing, perhaps not even an explanation. But this wasn't right. He had to find her. How could he not try to find her?

Marcus came in, still in his dressing gown.

'She hasn't . . . ?'

'No.' Maiden picked up a shard of glass they'd missed last night.

'No phone call?'

'Nothing.'

'It's not like her, Maiden. People don't change that much, whatever Underhill might say. She wouldn't leave the way she did, leaving us in the bloody wreckage, if she hadn't got a good reason.'

'Other than wondering what else she might do to the place if she stuck around?'

'Did you feel anything, Maiden? Did you feel a build up of energy?'

'I don't know. Maybe I wouldn't know what a build up of energy felt like. Not the kind of energy you mean.'

'Last night,' Marcus said, 'before we let the damnable Lewis take over, she and I had – I mean, you couldn't call it a heart to heart exactly, but she did go on about the trouble she was claiming she'd caused. All this about coming between Underhill and me. Which was nonsense. She said she'd made a mistake coming here.'

'She said that to me. She also said she couldn't stay because she had an appointment to keep.'

'You ask her what it was?'

'Should have, but I didn't.'

'Don't suppose she'd have told you. Went on to me about going to a bloody ashram, something of that nature. Bullshit, probably. This has been a total

349

disaster. She was in a state of torment and we probably made it worse. She couldn't stand it any more. Buggered off.'

'She was going anyway. She was already packed.'

Marcus waved a dismissive hand, went off to get dressed.

Maiden prowled the room, picking up more glass. He wondered if maybe they hadn't *all* made the window explode – all sitting there nursing their private fears and longings.

Under the computer table, which he and Grayle had pulled back into the centre of the room, he found a writing pad. He froze.

Cindy searched for his phone for a while before remembering that he'd hurled it, in his agony, over the castle wall.

At nine, from the payphone in the hallway of the Tup, he rang Jo's direct line at the BBC. No answer. No point in calling her at home; she'd be on her way to the office. Cindy returned to the bar and his table, bare now. Except for the *Sun*.

No excuse any more. He looked at page five. Saw a picture of himself wearing a cunning smile and a pointed hat.

Underneath the picture, the caption read:

Cindy the sorcerer: '*communes with spirits*'.

The smile on the face was real, but the hat was a clever and convincing computer graphic. Perhaps a legitimate liberty, under the circumstances.

The feature story had it all. Twisted and sensationalized, of course, but, in essence, true. The *Sun* had even sent someone to confront one of the Fychans, young Sion, at his farm in Snowdonia. Not that this had proved entirely helpful. Sion had invited the reporter in for tea and generously answered all his questions. In Welsh, of course. Only in Welsh. Cindy allowed himself his first and probably final smile of the day.

The sources of the information which did not require translation were given as 'close friends' and anonymous people said to have 'worked with' Cindy.

Only one person was actually named in the piece.

> TV hypnotist Kurt Campbell, who recently discovered the hard way that Cindy was no easy subject, said last night, 'I didn't know any of this, but to be honest, it doesn't surprise me.
>
> 'You can tell that behind all that camp stuff the guy has iron will-power.
>
> 'Sure I could believe he's studied magical techniques. It could explain a lot.'

'Thank you, boy,' Cindy murmured grimly. He returned to the payphone in the hallway, redialled Jo's number.

This time the phone was answered almost immediately. The voice was male and young and cool and assured.

'I'm sorry, Jo Shepherd isn't coming in today.'

'Unwell, is she?'

Jo was always at work on Monday, planning Wednesday night's show.

'Far as I know, she's absolutely fine. Who's this?'

'That's all right,' Cindy said. 'Call her at home, I will.'

'Ah.' Pause. 'That's Mr Mars-Lewis, isn't it?'

Cindy considered hanging up.

'Glad you called. My name's John Harvey. I'll be taking over as producer for the next few weeks.'

Cindy's grip on the phone grew tight. 'I may be wrong, but I don't recall Jo mentioning that.'

'Oh, Jo didn't know until this morning.'

And could not reach Cindy because his phone was lying in some soaking nettlebed at Castle Farm.

'Swift decision from On High,' John Harvey said. Smoothly. Triumphantly. 'They wanted someone more experienced to take over for a while. I don't think I need to explain the reasons, do I?'

'Perhaps not,' Cindy said, then regretted it; these people never thought they needed to explain, they just dictated memos.

John Harvey, sounding all of twenty-six, said, 'Look, Cindy, I'm going to have to call you back, I'm due—'

'In a meeting?' The hand gripping the telephone now shaking.

'You've been in the business a long time, matey. I think you know how these things work.'

'Not really, boy. Perhaps you can enlighten me when we meet at rehearsal tomorrow.'

John Harvey laughed nervously. Cindy remained silent.

He was going to make the boy say it: that his presence at tomorrow's rehearsal would be very far from essential.

Grayle had come in with a whole pile of papers, all this crazy stuff about Cindy, portrayed as some kind

352

of jinx figure bringing down darkness and retribution on innocent people for the crime of winning the National Lottery.

What the *hell*?

Insanity all around her. Hadn't gotten any sleep until must've been four a.m. Lying there, hearing Callard whispering, *He's touching my face*. And then the window disintegrating, the exclamations, the scraping of chairs, the stumbling, the feet skidding on glass.

And now here was Bobby Maiden staring in disbelief at the office pad they used for telephone notes.

A drawing on it, another relic of a wild and crazy night.

She hadn't seen Bobby like that since Emma, his girlfriend, was savagely killed, when he was groping for the light of understanding under the deadening pressure of a lingering head injury.

'OK . . . let's . . . let's be calm.' Easing the pad out of his fingers. 'Let's look at it by daylight. Let's consider the rational options before we get carried away.'

She bore the pad quickly to the back door and out into the farmyard, Bobby following in silence.

The main options were that he was lying, that he'd done this as a scam to give Callard some credibility. Or that Cindy had done it after they left him alone in there last night. She didn't know too much about Cindy's level of artistic ability, but the design work on his shamanic drum had some style.

It was good that Marcus had not reappeared. Better not to complicate this by introducing the Big Mystery option.

The wind was blowing, the sky was heavy but there

was no rain. Grayle leaned the pad against the stump of an old gatepost. She didn't like to hold it. She was glad to get it out the house. Well, Jesus, a face like *that* . . .

The drawing was rough, done with the kind of broad, scrubbing strokes that Lucas, her old art-dealer friend, might appreciate. She could almost hear Lucas now: *Yeah, yeah, bold, confident . . . what it lacks in finesse it makes up for in raw energy.* The pencil shading had been smudged, like Bobby had licked a finger and rubbed at it.

Damn it, this face had life.

Bobby and she stood together examining the picture, like they were figuring whether to buy it.

'You never said you saw him,' Grayle said.

'I didn't . . . see him. Grayle, I don't remember doing this.' Rubbing hard at his eyes. 'What the *fuck* . . . ?'

'Calm down. Jesus, were you like this when you found Justin's body? Believe me, this is . . . this is just . . . I've seen this stuff before, Bobby. It's just an anomaly.'

'It *was* me who did this?'

'Sure it was. I was vaguely aware of you drawing. I didn't even think much about it at the time. I must've thought, yeah that's what he does when he's all strung up. He draws.'

She remembered something else then, something that had gotten wiped from her memory in all the chaos of Marcus trying to break into the dairy.

'What were you doing in there with Cindy? Afterwards.'

'Well, he was just . . . it was a cleansing thing. Didn't he do it to you?'

'No. A cleansing thing?'

'A banishing. He made me stand against a wall and he drew shapes in the air in front of me.'

'Pentagrams?'

'I don't know. I was a bit shaken. Lost track of time. And then,' Bobby thought back, 'he told me to stay there and he went off and came back with Malcolm.'

'*Right.* He was checking if you were clean. If the dog had growled and backed away or taken a piece out of your ass, there'd still be a problem. He was scared you'd become possessed.'

'By what?'

'By . . .' Grayle jerked a thumb at the drawing. 'Look, like I said, I've seen this . . . well, I've seen so-called spirit drawings and . . . I guess none of them were like this. They were all kind of two-dimensional. Or do I mean one-dimensional? Whatever, they didn't have this level of . . . of . . . expression. I mean like the expression on that face. That is . . . that is some . . . expression.'

The wind peeled back the page of the flimsy pad – the page made even flimsier by the pencil-scraping and thumb-smudging. Grayle moved to stop it getting torn off, blown away.

'Leave it,' Bobby said.

'It might be important. Don't you . . . think?'

'It doesn't prove anything, does it? There's nothing to show exactly when I drew it, is there? Nothing to show it was me who drew it at all.'

Grayle looked at him. Bobby was way off-balance. Bobby was scared.

'Grayle . . . I attacked her, didn't I?'

'Naw . . . hey . . . What happened, she starts saying it's . . . *it* . . . is touching her face. You try and grab her . . . or maybe you're trying to grab *him*. It was confusing.'

355

'That's why she ran away, isn't it?'

'That's ridiculous. She ran away because there were things she didn't want to explain.' Grayle looked back at the picture; she hated it. If it was her who drew that she'd be setting light to it then burning incense. She said tentatively, 'I guess if we kept it . . . and we showed it around . . . like, I don't know *where* we'd show it around . . . but maybe there's somebody somewhere who could like attach a name to this person. Like if there *was* someone who looked like this.'

Bobby said, 'Oh, there was.'

'*Bobby?*'

He bent down and helped the wind take the drawing of the guy with the thin, mean face and the slicked-back hair, the Roman kind of nose and the watery-looking eyes and the scar that cut horizontally across from eye to ear, like half of a pair of glasses.

'That's the thing,' Bobby said. 'I know who this is.'

The paper got scrolled up into a funnel, and the irritable wind hurried it across the yard towards the castle walls.

36

The plump woman in the eight-till-late store in St Mary's stared hard at Cindy. She was thinking, Was it? Could it be? *Surely* not?

Cindy was in his blazer and slacks. Perhaps he should also be wearing dark glasses and a false beard. Come to buy another paper. A *Times* or a *Telegraph* or a *Guardian*. Wanting to know how the broadsheets had treated the story of the Sherwins' fatal fire. Trying to tell himself tabloid hysteria was not necessarily the end of the world.

Even though the new producer, John Harvey, had said it had been decided that Wednesday's show should be compèred by Carl Adams, the stand-up who occasionally stood in for Cindy. A breathing space, Harvey had claimed. They'd be in touch soon. And after all, Cindy's contract had another three months to run, did it not?

Oh, three whole *months*! And the very fact that Harvey knew how long the contract had to run . . . what did *that* tell you?

Cindy had tried to contact Jo at her home, but there was no answer. She must be somewhere inside the warren of the BBC. Trying to call him, no doubt. But he was unreachable now, a man with no mobile – unthinkable in London, might as well be dead.

There was just one *Telegraph* left. The shop woman, unsmiling, eyed Cindy as he bent to lift the paper from the rack.

From the front page of the *Sun*, at the top of the rack, his own face leered at him, all lipstick and long black lashes. Next to it, the pop-eyed profile of Kelvyn Kite. The photograph had been printed hard and contrasty, making Cindy look demented and the bird positively demonic.

Cindy scratched his ear, put on a querulous cockney voice. 'Looks like that geezer's gorn too far this time, dunnit, love?'

The woman looked relieved. Not him at all, then. Just an early holidaymaker on a Saga tour, or someone here to visit his grandchildren.

'Well, I must say, I never liked him myself,' she said. 'People like that, they've always got a chip on their shoulder, haven't they?'

'Size of half a brick,' Cindy agreed. 'Bleedin' perverts.'

He paid for his paper. In the doorway, he turned back.

'Oughter get treatment for it, I reckon. Compulsory. They says this whatchacallit, electric shock, sometimes works. Attach a couple of wires to their privates, that'd teach 'em to wear ladies' frocks. Few hundred volts up the goolies, madam. Yes, indeed. Good mornin'.'

Shattered, he was, however. Everywhere he'd been, in the past months, people had smiled, made jokes, tossed Kelvyn's catchphrases at him. *It'll all end in tears*, they'd chorus as he sat in some café with a cup of tea and a Bakewell tart.

Cindy Mars-Lewis: lovable, irreverent, saucy in his backless cocktail dress. An institution. Who could even remember the Lottery Show without him?

He crossed the street back to the pub, feeling hunted, glancing at cottage windows for furtively twitching curtains, turning his head the other way when a car came past.

If this was the attitude in St Mary's, what would it be like in more populous places? In London, he'd have to start taking taxis door to door to avoid the vengeful public, and thus endure the cabbies' crunching wit.

And back home, back home on his lovely piece of the Pembrokeshire coast, it would be a return to: *What have I told you about going near that creepy old man?*

Tears sprang into Cindy's eyes.

Grayle said, 'This is so crazy. The British press has no sense of responsibility.'

Papers all over the table in the editorial room.

'Underhill,' Marcus produced this infuriatingly knowing smile, 'it's practically a British tradition. Back to Tutankhamun, Macbeth. The British love a curse.'

'For Chrissakes, it happened just a coupla times. That's a curse?'

'Three times. Inside a *week*, Underhill.'

'Aw, this is bullshit. What do the others say?'

She pulled the *Independent* off the pile. There was a page one story about the fire, noting it was the third tragedy to befall a jackpot winner in a few days, but no mention of Kelvyn Kite.

Walking into the shop this morning, thinking about last night, wondering if Callard had returned, she'd come face to face with Cindy and the kite, in triplicate across the daily paper rack. His face was big on the front of the *Sun*, the *Mirror* and the *Star* but just a single-column shot on page one of the *Daily Mail*, where the big picture was the burned-out house with one surviving BMW in the drive. The *Mail* still had the line about the brother claiming Cindy had punctured the family's joy, it just wasn't making such a big deal about it. But then the *Mail* didn't have the stuff the *Sun* had about Cindy's mystical pursuits.

'Where's Maiden?' Marcus asked.

'I think he went to look up something in a book,' Grayle said cautiously.

'Like what?'

'How would I know?'

'Maiden behaved particularly strangely last night, I thought.'

'We all did, Marcus.'

She hadn't told him about the drawing of the face. Kind of hoping Bobby Maiden would come back wearing a bashful smile because the guy he'd been thinking of looked nothing like this, had a completely different kind of scar. *Delayed shock, Bobby. We all jump to crazy conclusions in stressful times.*

'You see, the point is', Marcus said smugly, 'Lewis the Lottery Man was a tabloid creation. Tinsel thin. Essentially inconsequential. And those who the tabloids create, they reserve the right to destroy. Of *course* they know all this curse stuff is complete balls – that's why they're not actually saying it.'

'I know what they're not actually saying, Marcus. I used to be a tabloid journalist.'

'American tabloids are rather tame in comparison with ours.'

360

'Jesus, most American *porn* is tame compared with your tabloids. What nobody seems to realize is this is a career they're wrecking. Guy struggles along for years, bit-part acting, summer season, finally gets his break when he's looking at a cold and lonely old age—'

'That's show business,' Marcus said heartlessly. 'All the same, one can't help wondering who gave them the crucial background information. Obviously no use asking who particularly has it in for Lewis, when the entire entertainment industry's riddled through with jealousy and back-stabbing. The answer is: every bastard who isn't making as much money.'

'Including you.' Grayle dragged the phone over. 'I'm gonna call the pub. Get him to come over here right now. Time like this, a guy needs friends. Even friends like you.'

Marcus snorted.

''Sides, we need to talk about last night.'

'Nothing to talk about. Lewis blew it. It was beyond him. He hadn't the faintest idea what he was doing. And when Persephone realized it, she just got out. A little too late, unfortunately.'

'Marcus, that is just so simplistic.'

Marcus hit the table with the heel of his hand. 'Well, I'm *feeling* fucking simplistic.' He came to his feet, walked to the wall, began to pick at a piece of crumbling plaster near the door. 'I just hope she's all right.'

'Jesus, Marcus . . .' Grayle stood up, too. 'What's it gonna *take*? What is it gonna take to actually make you feel sore at Callard? The woman stays in your house, eats your food, borrows your friends, turns me into a murder suspect, then drives off without a damn

361

word, leaving a pile of glass, and it's still like *poor Persephone*. Jesus Chr—. Oh. Hi, Bobby.'

He wasn't wearing a bashful smile. Or any particular expression at all. He carried a paperback. He put it on the table. There was a vaguely familiar face on the front of the book, guy with a raffish smile but cold eyes. *Not*, Grayle was supremely glad to note, the guy in the drawing that the wind blew away.

She glanced up at Bobby.

'Page one hundred and ninety,' he said.

Grayle picked up the book. 'You're kidding, right?' Flicked over the pages. Around the middle of the book was a stack of photo-pages all together. Pictures of newspaper headlines, reproductions of news pictures – guy in handcuffs being led to a police van, bunch of guys in bow ties getting showered with champagne around a dinner table.

'Over the page,' Bobby said.

Grayle turned the page to find a police mugshot. Underneath, the caption said,

> **Believe it or not, this is the only photo I could get of Clarence. He always hated having his picture taken.**

'Holy shit,' Grayle said.

362

37

'Well, well,' Marcus said sourly. 'If it isn't the Angel of fucking Death.'

And Cindy, while hurt, could understand the dismay. Marcus's heart would have done a small leap when he saw a flash of blue skirt. *She came back.* Flinging wide the door to welcome back the prodigal daughter. Only to find, instead, his favourite deviant in twinset and pearls, hair fluffed out, with a fresh mauve rinse.

Cindy and Marcus looked at one another for two silent seconds before Cindy smiled his gentle, ironic smile, an old clown painting out his sorrow.

'If I am going to be hanged, it seemed beholden on me to present a more tasteful figure upon the scaffold.'

Wearing men's clothing last night had been a mistake. He had wanted to present to Miss Callard an image she could not deride, which would give her confidence. How foolish to allow his psychic responses to be inhibited by image and taste and diplomacy. The result was an overload of masculinity in the room, an imbalance. Cindy's nose twitched in memory of the stench of the urinal sharpened with soiled lust, an unmistakable odour of male evil.

But the clothing had been only one of his errors. All of them the result of giving into material neuroses, worldly apprehensions, fear of public hatred, fear of penury.

Marcus, for once, was right to be suspicious. He scowled.

'Suppose you'd better come in.'

At once he detected an electricity in the room. A dreadful excitement. At first falsely attributing it to the stack of morning papers on the table, the evidence for the prosecution.

Little Grayle, at least, seemed glad he'd returned. She rose, hugged him.

'Jesus, why are they doing this to you?'

Cindy was stoical. 'When things happen to us which we clearly cannot alter, little Grayle, we must ask ourselves what is to be learned from them. What they may be telling us about ourselves that we were unwilling to recognize.'

'Oh sure. Like you've been chosen as God's tool to break the hold of the National Lottery on the public's consciousness? Did the BBC respond yet?'

'My career with the BBC is, you might say, in a state of cryogenic preservation. Someone may perhaps consider thawing me out in five years' time.'

'Cindy, can they just do this?'

'I fear they have done it, lovely. Some years ago, the mandarins might have stood by me. Those days are gone.'

Bobby Maiden looked up from the *Mirror*. 'This didn't just happen, did it?'

'Perhaps not.'

'Somebody had to start it, didn't they?'

'I also tend to be sceptical about spontaneous combustion, Bobby, but I rather suspect we have something more important to discuss than the descent of Kelvyn Kite.'

He had seen the exchange of glances. Oh yes, something else had occurred in the aftermath of the explosive exit of Miss Persephone Callard.

Grayle said, 'You better tell him, Bobby.'

This was the standard mugshot issued to the papers when Gary Seward's long-time enforcer, Clarence Judge, escaped from police custody in 1976. Used many times since because Clarence always hated having his picture taken.

'You could argue', Maiden pointed out, 'that I came across it browsing through Seward's book, and it just stuck in my head. A famous picture of a minor gangland celebrity.'

'Which was subconsciously stored', Marcus said, 'and surfaced in a moment of heightened consciousness during a meditative state induced by sitting around in the dark with a group of people who—'

'Hey, whose side are you on?' Grayle demanded.

'Just giving the psychological explanation, Underhill.'

Maiden smiled to see Grayle setting up in opposition to Marcus, the way she often did, without realizing this was what Marcus intended.

Cindy examined the photo in Seward's book. 'It's a face which seems to convey a brutal distrust of the entire human race.'

'A criminal stereotype, in fact,' said Marcus.

'And another stereotype', Grayle said, 'is bad guys always having scars. I don't see a scar in this photo.

365

Otherwise, yeah, it's very like the face you drew. Got the scar when he died, maybe?'

'He was shot in the back of the head,' Maiden said.

'Oh.'

'I believe he got the scar in prison.'

'So he *did* have a scar.'

'If not several. According to Seward, another inmate with a long-standing grudge surprised Clarence in the prison library. With a fish slice he'd nicked from the kitchens. And sharpened.'

Grayle winced. She was probably thinking about hedging tools and a dead man in a ditch. Maiden hesitated.

Grayle took a breath. 'Just finish the story, Bobby.'

'It's really about what Clarence did next. He's half-blinded by the blood, according to Seward, but still manages to push the guy's head through the back of a free-standing bookshelf. OK? Leaving his face sticking out among the books, like in a pillory?'

'Uh-oh,' Grayle said.

'And he can't get free, and he's hanging there. And then Clarence goes around the other side and props up these leather-bound encyclopedias against the guy's ears on either side for further support. And then he starts hitting him. For . . . well, for a long time. It was said the blood spread so far that the library had to throw away more than a hundred books.'

'This was in the pen? Where were the . . . wardens . . . the guards?'

'Oh, well they were attending to a small disturbance elsewhere. It probably didn't even involve a bribe – none of the screws would've lost sleep over something unpleasant happening to Clarence. They hate people prison life doesn't seem to bother, and nothing ever got to Clarence. If you spat in his food, Seward says, he'd eat it all up in front of you and ask for seconds. And then he'd bide his time, but eventually he'd come and "visit" you, as he liked to put it.'

'Jesus. And this is what . . . visits Callard? I take everything back. No wonder she's so fucked up. Jeez, I only have to look at that drawing and I'm . . .' Grayle shuddered.

Marcus said, 'You ever come across this man personally, Maiden?'

'No, I didn't know him at all. Clarence would've been doing his bird when I was at the Met. I've just been having a quick look at Seward's book. Looked up Judge in the index. Lots of references. Clarence has rare qualities, Seward says. Possibly the only person he truly admires, apart from Lady Thatcher.'

'Hold on,' Grayle said. 'Let's get back to the scar. Were there *no* pictures of him with this scar from the fish-slice attack?'

Maiden thought about it. 'I don't know. None that I'm aware of. With a scar like that you can understand him keeping a low profile.'

'So you can categorically state that you never saw a picture of it?'

'Not categorically. But I'm pretty sure. It could be artistic licence, though, couldn't it? We're never going to know for certain unless we dig him up and call in a facial reconstruction expert.'

'So, Bobby – let's just get this right – you only know what the scar looked like from Callard's description, that it was like half of a pair of glasses. In fact it may not be quite like you've drawn it here, but we'll never know. OK, let's deal with the other rational explanation. What if Callard deliberately fed us this image of the face, with the glasses' scar? Maybe planted the whole idea of this Clarence. And even Seward, with his peculiar laugh.'

'Except that it was Les Hole who first mentioned Seward,' Maiden said.

Marcus looked pained. 'Underhill, why would she anyway?'

'I have no idea. I'm exhausting rational possibilities, is all. It still makes no sense to me why she suddenly skipped out last night, and it doesn't to you, Marcus, if you'd only admit it.'

Marcus was silent.

'So let's look at the crank stuff,' Grayle said. 'Spirit drawings. It's a common enough thing for an artist to be present at a seance, right?'

Cindy, who'd been absorbing all this stuff in silence, said, 'And the artist does not necessarily have to be a medium. Sometimes he or she works the same way as I believe police artists do, creating the face according to the instructions of the medium. And on occasion,' Cindy coughed lightly, 'this is done without them even speaking.'

'The image gets transferred mentally,' Grayle said. 'It sounds crazy, but I've seen this happen.'

'Usually, I think,' Cindy said softly, 'when there is, er, a close personal link between the medium and the, er, artist.'

Marcus stiffened, directed a hard look at Bobby. Grayle made no comment.

Cindy said, 'What were your feelings, Bobby, when you were doing this drawing? What sensations were you experiencing?'

'I can't remember. I can't remember doing the draw-

368

ing. All I have a clear memory of is Seffi saying, "He's touching me", and me diving at her. And then the window bursting.'

Grayle wondered what might have happened at this point if the window *hadn't* exploded. 'This gets us nowhere,' she said hastily. 'What actually happened to Judge?'

'From what I can remember,' Bobby said, 'his body was found in a rubbish skip somewhere. He'd been shot in the back of the head. It was assumed it was a gangland killing. Only one shot, close range. Looked professional. No-one was ever caught.'

'When was this?'

'Over a year ago.' He opened the paperback. 'I assume this edition's only just out. In the front here, Seward's written a ridiculous kind of eulogy to the old thug, also offering a large reward for information leading to his killer. He says he'll hand any new information over to the police immediately. I think that's where we're supposed to laugh.'

'What exactly was Clarence to Seward?'

'Minder, enforcer. Basically, what he did to that bloke in the prison for free was what he did professionally to people on the outside.'

'Oh boy,' Grayle said sombrely. 'If we believe Callard, both of them were present at this Sir Barber's party in Cheltenham. One of them alive, one—'

'Quite.' Marcus gave a short cough. 'Er . . . no matter how bizarre it seems, we probably have to consider this is what we're looking at. The planned reuniting of the ex-criminal, Seward, and this . . . this Clarence Judge . . . across the, ah . . . the, ah . . .'

'I think the word you're groping for, Marcus, is, uh, grave. Question: was this Seward intent on using

369

Callard to reach his dead pal, Clarence? Was that what this whole Cheltenham charade was about?'

'We know he is obsessed with spiritualism,' Bobby said. 'We know he has used mediums to try and contact his mother because it's in the book. And we know he was shattered and angry – almost *affronted* – by Judge's murder.'

'And we *know*', Grayle felt suddenly very excited, 'that he was real determined to find out who the killer was, because he was offering . . . *how* much, Bobby?'

'Up to twenty grand.'

'Strange, huh? That's close to what Callard was paid to put on a seance.'

'Right,' Bobby said, 'we also have reason to think that it was Seward, not Barber, who was putting up the cash that night. That Barber was a front, presumably because Seward suspected Seffi would refuse to do it if she knew she was being employed by someone like him.'

'Right! Hey, this is cool. Seward, who believes firmly in this stuff, is investing twenty grand in Callard being able to put him in contact with Clarence so that – this is *it*, guys – *so he can find out from Clarence who it was shot him!*'

'Good God,' Marcus said.

'It adds up,' Bobby admitted. 'Seward's making no secret of being determined to find out who killed his friend, but the underlying truth there might be that Judge and Seward have the same enemies, and Seward's watching his own back. He's thinking: they got Clarence, am I going to be next? Yeah. I can accept, given his beliefs, that he would set this up.'

'I can see this whole thing,' Grayle said. 'Seward stays in the background until Callard says, "I'm getting a guy coming through with like weird eyes and a funny scar. He's got a message for Gary. Do we have a *Gary* in the house?" And up steps Seward with some heavy questions. Who did it, Clarence? Who blew you away? Just gimme a name.'

'However, the man presumably doesn't realize', Marcus said, 'that the most useful piece of information ever gleaned from a denizen of the bastard spirit world is that the brown socks mislaid by Uncle Tom in 1946 may be found behind the fucking hot-water tank.'

'Ah.' Grayle lifted a finger. 'I think he does know that. I think that's why he wanted Persephone Callard.'

'Only the best,' Bobby said.

'Plus . . . what about this? . . . all the people at that party, with the possible exception of Sir Barber, had one thing in common. They were all people who knew Clarence Judge! It was like *Clarence's* party! How could he – Jesus, this is eerie – how could he not turn up for his own party?'

'Underhill, I would hate to think you're getting carried away . . .'

'It's a hypothesis, Marcus, but I think it's a good one. Callard kept saying how like a fish out of water Barber seemed among these people. He didn't know them, he was a little nervy in their company.'

'I figured that too,' Bobby said. 'These were mostly, if not all of them, decidedly iffy people.'

'It's still a bloody gamble, Maiden.'

'So? Seward's a gambler. He loves risk. Also, he put himself very close to Seffi earlier on, when he posed as Barber's chauffeur so he could pick her up at the hotel. So he could get close to her. Would he see that as establishing a link – with someone who wouldn't normally handle pond life like Gary Seward?'

Grayle stood up. 'There's clearly a whole lot we don't know, but we have a working theory. So let's follow it through. Callard gives out real indications that she's in contact with Clarence. But then it all goes wrong because Callard's this loose-cannon kind of medium. The breaking of the vase, all this chaos . . . and then she runs out on them.'

'Taking Mr . . . Judge with her?' Cindy said delicately.

'Right! And then', Grayle grabbed his hand with a jangling of bangles, 'she goes off into the night . . . with this dead guy . . . attached to her. And she can't get rid of it.'

'Why, though?' Marcus said. 'Why can't she get rid of it? She's an extremely experienced medium, she's done all this before.'

'Yeah, well, I can't explain that. Except maybe there's something different here. Something she *hasn't* done before. Or, of course . . . she may know more than she told us.'

'The point about all this', Bobby Maiden said, 'is that most of it remains valid even if you don't believe in ghosts. All you need to accept is that Seward himself is a complete believer. Also a gambler, chancer, ruthless bastard . . .'

'Because of what comes next, right?' Grayle said.

38

What came next was the Mysleton Lodge incident.

And the dead guy, Crewe. And Justin.

Bobby hypothesized that Seward wasn't about to give up on Callard, even though she'd put herself out of the picture.

Grayle took up from here.

'Seward's getting real antsy. He's thinking: Shit, does this woman now know what *I* oughta know? After all, he's paid this broad twenty grand, he's *entitled* to that information. What's he do next, Bobby, how's he go about this?'

'He puts out feelers. Among his own people, to begin with, and maybe some of his showbiz friends. His network. On the fringes of which, maybe, are Justin Sharpe's "hard friends" in Cheltenham. So when Justin happens to find out that Seffi's at the lodge at Mysleton . . .'

'It gets back to Seward in like no time at all, and Seward, he's through with elaborate scams, arranging smart parties. It's down to basics. He sends these guys out to fetch her. Bring her in.'

'That could be it. We know that one of them was an

employee of a security firm doing a bit of moon-lighting, like they often do.'

Marcus looked appalled. 'The man was having Persephone kidnapped, to make her attempt to re-engage with . . . Is that even possible, Lewis? That she could be *forced* to do it? Go into trance, under duress?'

Cindy considered. 'Perhaps we should be asking ourselves not what is possible, but what such a man as this might consider possible.'

'And when it all goes pear-shaped and one man winds up dead,' Bobby said, 'Justin's hard friends go back to make sure he doesn't implicate them. Maybe one of them is even the other Mysleton guy. The one who felt obliged to put Crewe out of his misery.'

Grayle thought of something. Wished that maybe she hadn't. Felt queasy.

'If they made Justin talk, there's, uh, one thing he could've told them. Which is my name.'

'Oh,' Bobby said.

'I told him my name. I didn't write it down or anything, I didn't spell it out, but . . .'

'This is madness!' Marcus howled. 'It's got completely out of hand.'

'Yes,' Cindy said, 'perhaps it has.'

'What if the bastards turn up here?'

'Just a name?' Bobby said. 'No address?'

'No. No address.'

'She'd be hard to track down from just a name, Marcus, even if Justin remembered it correctly. All the same . . .'

Marcus pushed his chair back. 'We should take it to the police.' He glanced at Bobby, coughed. 'I mean . . .'

'You mean the real police,' Bobby said.

Grayle thought about having to make that full statement, tell the cops about the hacker at the bottom of the River Wye, take them to the spot where they tossed it in, stand by while the divers went down. Oh God.

'They gonna believe us, Bobby?'

'Do *we* believe us?'

Marcus came to his feet, paced the flagged floor. 'We've been here before, I think. What the holy fuck are we going to do, Maiden?'

'If this is Seward,' Bobby said, 'it would be naïve to assume that he's going to stop now. He's still going to want Seffi.'

'We need to find her first, right?' Grayle now had that jumpy sensation around her middle.

'Well, at least I know a senior copper who's prepared to believe anything of Gary Seward. If we can spend an hour or two trying to harden all of this up a bit, I could take it across to Gloucester and dump it in his lap. That would be the sensible solution.'

'I guess.' Any residual excitement seeped out of Grayle, leaving only the queasy feeling. If they were right, at bottom this was just a sordid tale of underworld obsession, revenge, cover up. Which, as Marcus said, had gotten way out of hand.

And yet was still glowing darkly under the halo of Big Mystery: the imploded window, the drawing – where did you get by taking stuff like this to the cops? You got disbelieved. Derided. Suspected. Accused. Referred for psychiatric reports, like all those creeps who said, *I heard a voice telling me to do it.*

'All right.' Marcus cleared his throat. 'I think we all probably agree that before doing anything hasty we should spend some time attempting to locate Persephone ourselves. She needs to know about this possible Judge connection.'

'Assuming she doesn't already,' Grayle said. 'And that's one of the reasons she hightailed it into the night without so much as an offer to pay for the glass.'

'Yes, all right, Underhill. So how do we go about finding her?'

'We could call in a medium,' Grayle said.

'Or we could simply call her agent,' Maiden said. 'She was talking to her yesterday from this pub we called at on the way over here. Whatever it was about, she didn't want me to know. She took the phone into the loo. Afterwards she started saying there'd be no point in coming to St Mary's, and that she had to be somewhere tomorrow – that's today.'

'She didn't want us to know where she was going,' Grayle said. 'Why?'

'Do we have the number of the agency?'

Grayle smiled. 'I guess Marcus does.'

Marcus called from his study. He was quivering with the kind of adrenalin charge he'd thought he'd never experience again. 'Want to speak to Nancy Rich,' he told some lofty bitch.

'Ms Rich is in a meeting. Perhaps you could call back later.'

'Just get her,' Marcus rasped.

'I don't know whether you heard what I—'

'Well get her *out* of the bloody meeting!' Marcus roared. 'This is *crucially important*.'

'And you are?'

'Marcus Bacton, my name. Tell her—'

'Does she know you?'

'Tell her it's about Persephone Callard.'

'Are you a journalist?'

'What I am', said Marcus, 'is a man with very little

time to fart about, so you can tell Rich that if she doesn't want to lose her principal meal ticket, she'd better get off her complacent arse and drag herself to the fucking phone. Am I making myself clear?'

'Explicitly,' the woman said coldly. 'Hold the line, please.'

Marcus waited. The agency's phone played Mozart to suggest you were connected to people of taste and intelligence. Marcus drummed his fingers on the desk. Outside, the wind was still battering the castle walls.

Nancy Rich came on the line.

'You have one minute, Mr Baxter.'

'*Bacton*. Look, I'm calling because I believe you're still in fairly regular contact with Persephone Callard.'

'I'm her agent.'

'It's imperative I speak to her. Without delay.'

'Mr Bacton, have you any idea how many callers say precisely that?'

'And half of them are dead, no doubt. Madam, I don't care how many bloody crank calls you get, this is not one of them.'

'Had to play the Winterstone card, in the end,' he told them. 'That's the school. Which, inexplicably, is still in existence. Says she'll call me back. Wants to check me out, I suppose. I think she's still afraid I'm a bloody journalist.'

'You are a bloody journalist,' Grayle said.

'Hmm. Yes. One forgets.'

Grayle smiled. The only good thing about this weird, uncomfortable situation was that Marcus had been galvanized.

The rest of the morning they drank coffee, nibbled toast, tossed around wild theories. Cindy tried, in vain, to call his producer. Grayle stashed all the dailies out of sight because of the way he kept going back to stare in distress at those big headlines. In the end Cindy said he'd walk up to the Knoll, give himself a retune.

Around two, a call came through.

Bobby's mobile.

Foxworth. Maiden took the phone outside.

'Information for you, Bobby. Show you what a helpful fellow I am.'

'I always knew that, Ron,' Maiden said warily.

'Sir Richard Barber, Bobby. Still interested?'

'Sure.'

'Barber and Seward. It's a yes. Barber retired at the last election, yeah? Afterwards, gets divorced from his missus. Papers are thinking, hello, what's been going on there? But it's too late now, he's nobody special any more, so they never tried too hard to find out what he'd been up to in his nice new flat. Which, as it turns out, he'd been renting from Seward for quite a while before he bought it. Only for girls, mind, nothing sordid – Gary hates perverts. Just nice, clean, grown-up girlies.'

'So, Gary's flat and Gary's girls? Where'd you get this, Ron?'

'I'm a member of the Conservative Club. For the cheap beer. Always a comfort after the kind of day I've had.'

'No developments, then.'

'Oh yeah. Just the kind of development you need with my budget. Another one. Even nastier.'

'No!' Maiden wedged himself into the doorway, out of the wind.

'Woman gets round to reporting her boyfriend missing after the other side of the bed's been cold the best part of a week. Local bobby makes a routine visit to his place of work – he has a garage – finds somebody's dropped a bloody car on the poor sod.'

'Like from a crane?'

Ron explained.

'What are the Cotswolds coming to?' Maiden said neutrally. 'No leads?'

'How many d'you want? For starters we've got about half a dozen blokes whose wives this lad reckoned he was stuffing, so the regular girlfriend's also worth a glance. Oh, yeah, lots of angles and about two spare bodies in CID for the legwork. I was *trying* to link it into this other one seeing it wasn't far away, but they won't quite gel.'

Maiden said, 'You talk to the late Mr Crewe's employer yet?'

A chuckle.

'I was waiting for that. Yes, I have indeed. In person. Lovely office in Worcester. Charming view of the Severn. *Mr Martin Riggs* on the door, gold lettering. And what a nice chap. Out comes the twelve-year-old malt. "What a tonic to see you, Ron, talk to an old-fashioned copper again."'

'He offer you a job when you retire?'

'Blimey, son, that's positively uncanny. Must be with poking the psychic.'

'What else he have to say?'

'Crewe? According to Mr Riggs, Forcefield is such a big organization nowadays that it's appallingly difficult to keep tabs on all the staff. However, he's done some checks and this does seem to be a regular lad, absolutely no reason to suspect, etcetera, etcetera.'

'You believe that?'

'What difference does it make? Where are you at present, Bobby?'

'Staying with friends, out past Hereford.'

'You and the lady?'

'Just me. She had some business.' Maiden decided there wasn't going to be a better time to pump Ron on the subject of Clarence Judge. 'Leaving me with lots of free time to read Gary's book. Oh . . . I take it you know about the new paperback – the reward for a name on Judge?'

'You what?'

He had Ron's full attention. He took the phone into Marcus's study, found the book, read out the relevant part of the Preface.

'I may be wrong here, Ron, but do you think maybe he doesn't trust you to investigate it properly?'

'I don't doubt that would be true, if it was my case, Bobby, but Clarence was found on a building site down near Abingdon. Where he was done, that's another matter, but Abingdon was where they found him, so it's Kiddlington's migraine. Especially now. Well, the cheeky cunt.'

'Still a big shortlist, is there?'

'Extensive. Not counting the ones excluded on account of having fingers too arthritic to hold the gun steady.'

'Is Seward really that upset?'

'Think of Clarence as a not-over-bright brother Gary felt responsible for. Vicious as a cobra, but not over-endowed up top. You gave him a gun, knife, spanner . . . pointed him in the right direction, waited for the screams. And he never knew when it was over. The one time I nicked him, I sent six bobbies in with batons. When I got there, four of them were sitting on Clarence, the other two getting helped into an ambulance with half an ear in a paper bag and that much blood around they weren't sure which of 'em's it was. Never a domestic animal, Clarence Judge.'

'What was it he went down for last?'

'Rape and attempted murder – sadly, nothing to do with Seward. Clarence's night off. Took the barmaid home, but she changed her mind. Naturally, the Met offered him a deal for Seward, but Clarence is too loyal.'

'Matter of honour, for Seward, then, seeing the killer go down?'

'Seward has no honour,' Ron Foxworth said coldly. 'Matter of pride. And talking of pride . . . let me say one thing, my son, and let me say it very clearly. If it were to turn out to be your delicate, artistic fingers on Seward's collar, as distinct from my gnarled old digits, I just can't tell you how upset I would be. Just can't *begin* to tell you.'

Marcus snatched up the phone. 'Yes!'

'Mr Bacton, it's Nancy Rich. My secretary's done some checks with the school, where there are still people who remember you. Having spoken to you herself she says you simply have to be the same person. I'm therefore inclined to accept that you have Seffi's best interests at heart.'

Marcus grunted. Could imagine how people at the bastard school had described him.

'So perhaps I can ask *you* some questions,' Rich said. 'What was Seffi's state of mind when you last saw her?'

'Erratic,' Marcus said. 'Confused. She stayed here

381

for a few days, now she's missing. Listen, I do know the background. I just don't know how much of it you know, but I understand you spoke to Persephone on the phone yesterday morning.'

'Yes. But that was about a contractual arrangement. It's not something I would normally discuss.'

'Look,' Marcus said. 'I don't know what other clients you have—'

'Let's just say that none of the others are in this particular line of work.'

'Quite. And I don't suppose any of them would find themselves in the position of being used by a man with an extensive criminal record to try and contact a violent psychotic who's been in his grave for over a year.'

A considerable hush.

'Oh my God,' said Nancy Rich. 'Are you serious?'

'No.' Marcus eased himself on to the desk. 'I'm entertaining my fucking self.'

'That's impossible.'

Underhill came into the study then. And Maiden. Marcus was inspired.

'Look, Rich, this is a police matter now. I have a detective with me. Would you like to speak to him? Name's Maiden. Inspector. I can put you—'

'Absolutely not!' Rich said, aghast.

The sun struggled against heavy, muscular clouds, strings of vapour twisting like tendons. A meshwork of illusion and lies obscuring the light.

Lies. Lying to himself. Sheltering behind the confusion of his identity, flailing in the dark and swirling soup of his motivations, his impulses, his ambivalent sexuality. This way, that way, insubstantial, capricious.

382

His bangles rattled cheaply, his pearls were paste, his Oxfam shop woolly jumper a mass of plucks, his bra full of bubble-wrap.

'*I hate that Cindy now for what he's caused. It's like he's sneering at ordinary people's good luck.*'

Taunting voices carried on the wind.

'*I must say, I never liked him myself. People like that, they've always got a chip on their shoulder, haven't they?*'

'*Angel of fucking Death . . .*'

'*. . . chosen as God's tool to break the hold of the National Lottery on the public's consciousness?*'

Cindy's mouth stretched into a silent scream. What if this flip remark was on target? What if he had become a channel, a conduit? But not for God, not for good. He thought of Colin Seymour, who planned to introduce handicapped youngsters to the thrills of flying, rising above nature's blackest jokes.

Cindy laid his hands on the collapsed capstone, massaging its ancient heart, until the stone and his hands grew warm.

Give me knowledge, give me inspiration, give me truth, give me direction, give me clarity of mind.

He straightened his spine, breathed deeply into his abdomen for a hundred seconds. Then he closed his eyes and set up an earth rhythm on the drum until it began to sound in his solar plexus beneath the waistline of his blue skirt. The beat vibrating directly through his body, emerging in his spine. Ascending the spine

(*dummm*)

. . . to *her* head

(*dummm*)

. . . to *his* shoulders

(*dummm*)
. . . down *her* arms
(*dummm*)
. . . into *his* fingers
(*dummm*)
. . . and into the stone.
'Old stone.'
(*dummm*)
'Strong stone.'
(*dum-dummm*)
'Strengthen me.'
(*dum-dummm*)
'Hold me hard.'
(*dum-dummm*)
'Against the dark.'
(*dummm*)

Marcus put down the phone.

Maiden and Underhill were standing on either side of the unlit woodstove. Marcus shook his head.

'Surprising how educated, law-abiding people are so reluctant to get involved with the police. Oh, she said, that would put her in a very difficult position. Client confidentiality, all that bollocks.'

Underhill said, 'They found Justin, Marcus. The cops finally found Justin. Bobby just talked to—'

'Where's Lewis?'

'Up at the Knoll.'

'Hmm,' Marcus said. 'How much do either of you know about this fellow Kurt Campbell?'

384

39

In the early evening Bobby Maiden borrowed Marcus's truck and drove down to the village, to Grayle's cottage. He'd never been here before. The windchimes gave it away – two sets, hanging either side of a lantern over the old, studded door.

The cottage was in the middle of the terrace which lined one side of the short street, with the church wall on the other. The tiny forecourt space was filled by the Mini. Maiden parked the truck in the rutted road.

It was dark; the wind had died but the air was colder. There was a dim light in the squat-towered church. It was all very quiet, no kids around, no dogs barking. The lantern came on and by the time he reached the front door Grayle had it open.

'Isn't New York, is it?' Maiden said.

'Guy in the shop says the last time the council retarred the village street it was for Queen Victoria's carriage.'

She wore a dress tonight: woollen, red, long-sleeved. Maiden guessed that after today – Grayle in the baseball jersey, Cindy in the twinset – she was reclaiming her gender.

He paused on the threshold. 'You really feel you belong here?'

Grayle frowned. 'You know how much I hate small talk, Bobby. Why don't you ask something heavy?'

'You annoyed with me?'

She didn't smile. 'I'm annoyed with everybody. Why I came home early. Put it down to time of the month. Like, it isn't, but it tends to satisfy guys, you tell them that.'

'There many guys around here?'

'Sure. Farm guys. Retired guys. Rich guys with weekend cottages and two kids. Who needs guys anyway? All guys are stupid. Come in.'

He saw crystals on the windowsill, a brass Buddha in the small inglenook fireplace next to a bed of ash. Reflected in a long mirror opposite, he saw, to the left of the front door, a plaster statue of Anubis, dog-faced Egyptian god of the dead, wearing a jewelled poodle collar.

Grayle said, 'Cindy still up there with Marcus?'

'Examining the psychic history of Overcross Castle. Driven men. It's like they're planning a siege. I needed to get away for a while.'

'Maybe this is a good thing for Marcus, I don't know. Anyhow, welcome to the bijou dwelling. Siddown, grab a crystal, strengthen your vibes. I have water boiled for herbal tea. Or you can have coffee.'

'Herbal tea? Wonderful.'

'New Age freaking cop. Oh boy.'

Maiden didn't sit down; he followed her into the kitchen, where bunches of dried hops hung from the ceiling beams.

'Speaking as a cop, I don't know whether it's a good thing for Marcus or not. A psychic festival run by a

386

TV hypnotist doesn't worry me a lot. But if the spiritual input somehow involves Gary Seward . . .'

'You feel that, in spite of two killings and all that horrific violence surrounding Clarence Judge, Cindy and Marcus are not taking him seriously enough.'

'The whole nation doesn't take him seriously enough any more. If you smile on TV, people think you're their friend. As for Marcus and Cindy, is there an age after which you just don't care any more?'

'It's my fault.' Grayle poured boiling water into a small brown pot. 'I wish I'd never remembered we'd had an invite to that thing.'

How YOU can be part of
The Overcross Experience...

Grayle had found the leaflet in the boxfile she'd marked *Probably junk, but who knows?*

The leaflet said the organizers of the Festival of the Spirit were offering the magazine a unique opportunity to meet its public face to face by taking a stand at the most prestigious event of its kind ever staged on British soil.

Marcus had gone ape when he saw what they were charging for a stand. *Bloody grasping little con-man* – all this and more. Which was just as well, far as Grayle was concerned. The way she saw it, if they took a stand at the festival, readers would indeed have a unique opportunity to meet with Marcus. After which *The Vision* would have no circulation worth a damn.

The leaflet promised a world-famous medium for the re-creation of a Victorian seance. Today Callard's agent had confirmed to Marcus that she was the one

387

and now under heavy pressure from Kurt Campbell not to renege – Campbell even suggesting he might be able to *solve her problem*.

How did *he* know what the problem was?

Because he used, until recently, to sleep with her. Ah. *Right*. Well, no big surprise there, given Callard's reputation and that they were both tied into the entertainment industry – tight enough in the States, over here it was claustrophobic. Also, Campbell was a male person under ninety years of age with links to paranormal research.

And also, in a negative kind of way, to Cindy.

Oh boy. When Cindy came down from the Knoll and heard about Callard and Campbell and Overcross, he became real weird, weirder than last night when he'd come out with all that stuff about getting old and washed up. It swiftly became clear that Cindy figured it was Campbell who had fucked him over with the papers.

The upshot was that Cindy had offered to pay half the fee if they could still hire a stall for *The Vision* at the Festival of the Spirit. Which started, as it happened, in two days' time, Wednesday through to the weekend.

Like this was part of his destiny. He'd been up to the Knoll to ask for an answer, and when he got back to the farm, there they all were around a marketing circular headed,

Overcross Castle:
The Veil is Lifted

Some kind of shamanic signpost.
Jesus.

'This Kurt Campbell,' Grayle said, putting down the teatray in the living room, 'he isn't really known in the States. He's like David Copperfield?'

'He's not a magician,' Bobby said, 'he's just a hypnotist. Has his own consultancy. But also does TV. These shows where people come on to be made to do humiliating things. Bit like Paul McKenna?'

'Right. So the thing he did with Cindy – or tried to do – on the Lottery Show . . .'

'That was his routine act. But there's also a serious side to the hypnotism. And this interest in the paranormal, which led to the Overcross project.'

'So apart from that Seward's into spiritualism, do we know of a connection between him and Campbell?' Grayle put the pot on the tray between two mugs with Cottingley fairy faces on them. 'I've been trying to read his book, but it's all written in dialect and jargon, so presumably ghost-written from taped interviews. Jeez, I don't even understand the title.'

'Clumsy pun on London villain-speak. The only mention of Campbell is a passing reference to him and Seward once appearing together on a TV talkshow.'

'So?' Grayle shrugged. 'Showbiz is a small world. Seward's plugged into the same circuit. It means squat.'

She thought Bobby looked tired. Sitting there by the inglenook, all dark eyed and unreadable. Was his agenda linked to amber eyes and brown breasts and hair you could use to tie up a boat in a storm?

She poured pink tea. 'So what's gonna happen at this seance?'

'That's what bothers Marcus. What happens when she goes into trance and Clarence – if it is Clarence – takes over?'

'But if Seward's behind this, isn't that what he wants?'

'But if this Victorian seance is a highly public event . . . I mean really public, as distinct from an invited audience of Midlands villains.'

'It's a conundrum, Bobby. I guess you want to be there, too, don't you?'

'I don't know. I hate going into anything blind.' He drank some herbal tea, didn't wince. 'I wondered about going to see Kurt Campbell.'

'Now?'

'Well, tomorrow.'

'On what pretext?'

'I thought that I could take a temporary job with *The Vision*. Request an interview about the festival, with its founder.'

'Sure. Except the next *Vision* doesn't come out till next month.'

'He doesn't know that. I could say it's out on Thursday, and I've just got time to get an article in.'

'You don't know too much about production schedules, do you, Bobby?'

'Yeah, well, he probably doesn't either.'

'And interviewing? What do you know about interviewing?'

'Done thousands, Grayle. In depth.'

'Oh, yeah, sure. Like, "Where were you on the night of the fifteenth and don't give me no shit or I'll slap you around the cell?" What are you, crazy? He'd have you sussed in like four minutes. Listen, I'll go. I shoulda thought of this. I'll do the interview. Which is why you came here, right?'

'It is *not* why I came. Besides, they very likely know your name.'

'So you think this would, uh, expose me to some risk?'

'Well, no, not particularly. That just happens in movies, but—'

'Like the movies where they crush you to death with an old car? What the hell, the way I'm feeling I could use risk.'

'Bad attitude, Underhill. Consider yourself off the case.'

'Screw *you*. Listen, OK, here's what's gonna happen. We both go. I'm Alice D. Thornborough of *The Vision*. And you could be . . . you could be like Lenny Lens, the photographer. You can handle a camera, aside from mugshots and pictures of DOAs in chalk outlines?'

'I can handle a camera. We don't do chalk outlines.'

'Well, as it happens, I have a camera here. A Nikon, ex-*Courier*. Convincingly professional. We'll do it. Hell, let's go interview Seward too. Let's stir some shit.'

'That's a *very* bad attitude,' Bobby said.

'Yeah?'

Grayle caught sight of herself in the long mirror, amid the crystals, the Tree of Life poster, the Egyptian dog of the dead. For all the tough talk, she looked small and lonely in her red frock, a lost kid in a fairy grotto. She was just four miles from where her sister was murdered.

She coughed. 'This herbal tea's making me feel sick. Let's get some serious coffee. Old-cop strength.'

40

'Guy's a saint, it appears.'

On the editorial room table, Grayle gathered together the cuttings on Kurt Campbell. Say what you like about Marcus, he was assiduous in compiling files on anything and anybody connected to the paranormal.

Just that these clippings were hardly firming up the image of a man who would facilitate a not-necessarily-ex criminal's plan to contact the spirit of his psychopathic buddy.

'Seems Campbell once flew to Belfast to give hypnotherapy free of charge to a kid of four who'd become mute after both his parents were shot in front of him by the IRA.'

'Worked too, as I recall,' Marcus said.

'Apparently.'

At nine a.m., she'd called the PR firm handling the Overcross Festival and left a message requesting an interview with Kurt. In case *The Vision* sounded too smalltime, she'd given the name of the *New York Courier* – well, they *had* invited her to submit freelance pieces after she quit.

'Also, Campbell gives his services to all kinds of

youth charities, and he's worked with terminally ill people to calm their minds, and ease pain to the extent that some of them no longer needed drugs. Gee, Cindy,' Grayle looked up in dismay, 'you're a guy really knows how to choose his enemies.'

'Indeed,' Cindy said gloomily. 'Even though – as all too few will now remember – the saintly Kurt, it was, who chose me.'

He still wore yesterday's twinset, but without the pearls and fewer bangles. No defiance today, Grayle thought, this was comfort-dressing.

None of today's papers actually said he was finished. They didn't have to.

The *Mirror*'s lead headline was

Lotto-phobia!

The angle was that outlets and agents all over Britain were reporting that the sale of Lottery tickets had slumped to an all-time low because so many people were now 'afraid to win'.

'It gets worse,' Bobby said glumly. 'Look at this.'

Grayle peered over his shoulder. One of the tabloids had found another bunch of 'victims' of the curse of Kelvyn Kite, two pages' worth.

'"I haven't had a day's luck since I won two million,"' Grayle read out. '"The day after we were featured on the Lottery Show, I discovered my wife was having an affair with her boss. Now we're getting divorced and she's demanding half my money and the new house."'

Bobby said, '"My partner's health seemed to break down all at once, and we had to cancel the cruise . . ."'

'". . . and the money meant we were able to fly to Houston, Texas for the fertility treatment, but it all went horribly wrong . . ."'

'Stop,' Cindy cried weakly. 'I can take no more.' He passed a limp hand over his forehead, half-hearted theatrics. Tried to call up his former producer again this morning. No answer, no machine switched on. Like she was avoiding having to speak to Cindy or call him back.

'Well, I've seen this happen before,' Grayle said, as brightly as she could. 'You plant the idea of a jinx and all these jerks suddenly realize they never knew what bad luck was till they got lucky. Perverse. People are assholes. And, you know, it snowballs for a couple days and then it's just like it never—. Oh, Jesus, will you look at this? The *Sun* just opened a Lotto Curseline. You believe that?'

'Interestingly,' Marcus said, 'the broadsheets barely mention Lewis. The *Guardian* quotes a psychologist who says a major surge of disillusion with the Lottery was inevitable after a few years and people are simply using this nonsense as a vehicle for expressing it.'

Nonsense? This sounded like Marcus actually trying to cheer Cindy up. Wow.

'Hey, they actually use the word nonsense, Marcus? Gotta be a step toward sanity.'

'I'm afraid, my friends,' Cindy said in a voice full of finality, 'that it doesn't matter *what* they call it now.'

And Grayle knew he was right. The BBC would fire him, change the show around and everything would be just fine again inside a couple of months . . . except, of course, if you were Cindy, for whom the Lottery Show meant more than he was ever going to admit. He loved it when people loved him despite that he was weird.

394

And he knew that this time he was too old to come back.

Cindy straightened his cuffs, half-smiling like some elderly maiden aunt with no stake in the present, no hope for the future. The future was Kurt Campbell – a couple years younger than Grayle, a lot of money and a reputation that was firming up again after a minor hiccup. Caused by an old guy who wasn't coming back.

The phone rang.

Kurt Campbell's PR firm, for Grayle.

'It's gonna be tight,' she told Bobby, hanging up. 'Kurt's doing an interview at BBC Pebble Mill in Birmingham late morning, then he's over to Radio Gloucester this afternoon. Bottom line is he can give us twenty minutes at his hotel, early evening.'

'Which is where?'

'Cheltenham, ironically. Twenty minutes isn't much, but I told them we'd be there.'

It was ten-thirty, just gone. Marcus had his tweed hat in one hand, Malcolm's lead in the other. 'Thought we could go in your car, Lewis. Leave Maiden the truck.'

Grayle shook her head at him. 'I don't see this. I don't see why you had to hire the damn stall. Why not just go in as a visitor, tomorrow, when it starts? Mingle with the Tarot readers and the palmists and the Kirlian photographers.'

'Because, Underhill, visitors asking too many questions attract attention, whereas someone who's invested in the thing has a right to want to know what the fuck's going on. Anyway, we've arranged to go and look this morning, and if we like the pitch we'll take it. Also thought we might open ourselves to the ambience of the world's only purpose-built haunted house. See if we can uncover what this bastard was up to.'

He placed in front of Grayle and Bobby a weighty volume from his reference section, *The Encyclopedia of the Unseen*.

> **Abblow, Anthony (1846–1928)**
> Controversial spiritualist whose aggressive atheism led to frequent quarrels with his contemporaries. Abblow, a former medical practitioner, insisted that religion was a barrier in the path of worthwhile research into the existence of life after death, in which he remained a firm believer. He was reviled by the Church after publishing a paper in which he argued that the spirit world was a parallel plane in which individual status was principally determined by the force of personality and strength of character developed in this world, rather than humility and purity of heart.
>
> In the 1870s Abblow came under the patronage of a wealthy industrialist, Barnaby Crole, who funded his research, accommodating him at his palatial home, Overcross Castle, in Worcestershire. The nature of their experiments remains a mystery as the results were never published. Abblow died in Italy, to where he retired after leaving Overcross.

'Man of his time, then,' Bobby said.

'Jeez.' Grayle raised disbelieving eyes to the beams. 'Sounds like he just about stopped short of telling the rich they could take it with them. Surprising he didn't get rediscovered in the 1980s.'

'Be interesting . . .' Marcus clapped his hands to summon Malcolm, '. . . to see how many of the New Agers at this fiasco realize the kind of man whose memory the event appears to be commemorating.'

'Marcus . . .' Cindy looked down, self-consciously removing some fuzz from his jumper. 'Marcus, I don't think I can go.'

Marcus looked up so quickly his glasses wobbled. 'What did you say?'

'I . . . don't want to go. Not today, anyway.'

'What the hell are you talking about?'

'I suddenly feel quite uneasy. I'm sorry, this is most unlike me. Never before felt the weight of fate and circumstance so heavily against me. I'm not ready to go out there. I need more time. Why don't we go tomorrow? There'll still be time to set up the stall. What I thought . . . I thought I would walk up to the Knoll again. Dwell for a while. Consider. Uneasy, I feel. I'm so sorry.'

'Uneasy?' Marcus changed colour. 'It's me who should be feeling bloody uneasy! Do you think I *want* to be seen around with a blindingly obvious transvestite?'

'I'm sorry . . . perhaps a breath of air.' Cindy brushed at his skirt. He truly was agitated, Grayle thought. This wasn't acting.

Marcus expelled breath. 'Just go and get in the bloody car, Lewis. You've got to face the damned public sometime.'

Cindy bit his lip, pulled down his jumper. Made his way down the passage. 'S'truth,' Marcus said through his teeth.

397

'He's got big problems, Marcus,' Grayle admonished. 'His career just took the final dive.'

'I know he's got problems.'

'He's also receptive to things.'

'Don't start *that*,' Marcus snapped.

They walked out to the yard. The wind had changed and the sky over the ruins was heavy with clouds veined and yellowed like mature Stilton. Something had clearly altered since yesterday. Or maybe it was just wrong to use Cindy as a weather-vane.

'Why do I feel that if Kelvyn Kite was out of his case,' Grayle said to Bobby, 'he'd say this was all gonna end in tears?'

41

Chatterton Mansions was an impressive mongrel. Georgian origins, maybe a little Regency, a lot of Victorian.

There was a furniture van parked outside on a yellow line, two blokes loading a heavy red fireside chair into the back.

The street was lit by unexpected mid-afternoon sun. All the buildings were three, four storeys, the stone not quite Cotswold but mellow, certainly. Quiet, too, although there was a roundabout and a busy shopping street not two hundred yards away.

Maiden followed Grayle up the steps of Chatterton Mansions. This was her idea; it had meant Marcus making another call to Nancy Rich for the address, which Marcus was not too pleased about, but Grayle thought it would be crazy coming to Cheltenham without taking a look at where this whole thing began.

Inside, the building was less grand than you might have imagined. A central staircase, but fairly narrow, and several big doors with quiet nameplates on them – a solicitor, an architect.

'Upstairs, I guess, Bobby.'

He was looking around. 'No doorman. Thought there might've been *some* security.'

'Huh? Oh, I get it. This could get to be an obsession, Bobby.'

Mindful of what Ron Foxworth had said about other hands on Seward's collar, Maiden had called Gloucester HQ – if they were invading Ron's playground today it would be wise to tell him. Ron wasn't around; Maiden left a message.

They were bypassing Gloucester in the truck when Ron had got back to him. Maiden had pulled into a petrol station.

'You know, Bobby, forgive me . . . but it seems to me you're being a mite too nosy for a man just trying to find out who's been leaning on his girlfriend.'

'It's since you mentioned Seward. Hate him to have an interest in her.'

'And do you think he has, Bobby?'

'Can I roll another name past you? Kurt Campbell?'

'Who?'

'He's a hypnotist. On the telly. He's just bought a Victorian castle in the Malvern Hills. They're holding a festival there this week. The Festival of the Spirit.'

'And your interest is?'

'Seffi's appearing. My information is Seward's likely to be in the audience.'

'Well, given Gary's interests and how fond he is of celebrities, I wouldn't be inclined to rule that out.'

'I wondered if you knew of any connection between Seward and Campbell, that's all. Or if there'd be any kind of police presence at the festival.'

Ron had sounded suddenly amused. 'Not my problem, son, even if it was on my patch. Festivals are

Uniform's headache. And generally wasteful of manpower and overtime, in my experience, for the handful of thieves and dealers you nick.'

'It's not a rock festival.'

'Be full of weirdos, though, won't it? That's not to demean your new friends, Bobby. As a matter of fact, I did hear a mention of this event. In the context of them not actually requiring a police presence. Having arranged their own security.' Ron chuckled. 'Go on. Do your psychic intuition bit.'

'It's coming to me through a kind of mist, Ron. Word beginning with . . . F?'

'Your powers blind me, son. Don't suppose she's got an older sister, has she, your psychic?'

'You never did answer the question about Seward and Kurt Campbell,' Maiden said.

Grayle had gotten Bobby to remind her about former Superintendent Riggs and his arrangement with the 'entrepreneur', Parker, Emma's father, now also dead. She hadn't thought corruption on this scale could happen in English towns, undetected, but if the detectives were taking a slice, who was there to do the detecting?

Bobby had told her that Vic Clutton, just before he died, had said Riggs blamed Bobby for making it too hot for him to stay in the police. Riggs was still real sore. Grayle figured Bobby was becoming just a little paranoid, seeing Forcefield, therefore Riggs, everywhere.

They went up the bronze-carpeted stairs of the mansion house. No-one tried to stop them.

Grayle said, only half-seriously, 'Well, I sure hope we don't run into any of Riggs's guys. On account of they aren't going to feel too well disposed toward the woman carved up one of their colleagues.'

Bobby glared at her to shut up, but there truly was no-one around, no-one at all. At the top of the stairs was a big, bright, Georgian window with a terrific view across rooftops, with church towers, pinnacles and such.

And more doors.

'This is it,' Bobby whispered, pointing to the left-hand door. 'Apartment Six.'

It was weird, standing outside the wide, cream-painted, Georgian-style door out of which an uncharacteristically panicked Persephone Callard had rushed on a dark February night, the bronze velvet drapes drawn across the Georgian window, the wall lights on, the corners in shadow, footsteps behind her.

'And it's open,' Bobby said.

It was true. The cream door was open a crack. Like, pulled to.

'Sir's back home?'

Or maybe had never left. Callard had told Bobby he was in France, but how true had that been?

There were big footsteps on the stairs behind them. Bobby spun around as two of the removal guys appeared, a young one and an older, foreman-type guy with a bald head and glasses. The young guy pushed open the door of Apartment Six, walked straight in.

'Excuse me,' Bobby said to the older guy. 'Sir Richard isn't moving out, is he?'

The guy stopped, looked at him. 'I wouldn't know, pal.'

The young removal guy had left the door open, and they could see a short hallway and then another door opened into what seemed like a big room, with dust covers visible.

'So you're just kind of taking his furniture out for a while,' Bobby said.

'No. We're taking *this* furniture.'

'Out of Sir Richard Barber's flat.'

'No, pal. Sir Richard Barber's flat's the next floor up. I know that for a fact, on account of we moved him in.'

'So whose is this?'

The foreman stood with his hands on his hips. 'With all respect, pal, what's it to you?'

'We're supposed to see Sir Richard,' Bobby said. 'We were told to come here.'

'Well you were told wrong, because Sir Richard . . .'

'Next floor up, yeah. But I was definitely given this number. So who lives here?'

'What you got here is a show apartment for Bright Horizon Developments, and if you don't mind we've got half an hour to get this room cleared.'

'You're moving the stuff to another apartment?'

'You want to know everything, don't you, mate?'

'Uh, Barber,' Grayle said, 'that is Richard, was getting us some information about this block. See, we were hoping to get an apartment here ourselves . . .'

The removal guy relaxed. The American accent seemed to make it all right.

'I, uh . . . I'm having a baby,' Grayle said.

'Congratulations.' The guy started looking for the bump.

'In late summer . . . Uh, I just thought. Honey, if this is the show apartment, maybe that's where Richard said he'd meet us. My husband, he's a lawyer,' patting Bobby on the arm. 'He gets things wrong a lot. Could we . . . ?'

403

The guy sighed. 'Yeah, all right . . . just for a couple of minutes.'

'Oh, you are so good,' Grayle said.

And so they walked around all the rooms, Grayle clinging to Bobby's arm and looking thrilled. The bedroom, the bathroom and the kitchen were all fully equipped and furnished. The bedroom had a four-poster and a faint but unmistakable smell of marijuana. Grayle and Bobby exchanged glances.

The main room – the parlour, the drawing room – was almost cleared. Just a few small tables, two boxes full of ornaments and framed photos and bric-a-brac and a Cotswold village watercolour in a gilt frame. The two Georgian windows had the same view as from the top of the stairs.

'This is wonderful.' Grayle looked blissfully around, her gaze coming to rest on an empty alcove with a tasteful plaster moulding. 'Oh, look, honey, wouldn't that be just the perfect place for the big Chinese vase?'

'Perfect, darling.' Bobby gave the removal guy a *these women* kind of long-suffering smile.

'Used to be one there last time we was here, I think,' the removal guy said. 'Maybe it got broke.'

'It happens,' Bobby agreed.

It happened so bloody quickly, you would not have believed it.

Marcus and Lewis had parked in Malvern Link, no more than five miles from Overcross Castle. It was a straggle of mainly modern shops hanging loosely from the famous priory town on its steep hillside. Marcus needed money from a cashpoint, also an Ordnance Survey map of the area. Never liked to go anywhere without a large-scale OS map.

He could have been away from Lewis's car no more than seven minutes.

As he turned away from the cashpoint, squinting at his receipt, he heard a young chap say, 'Oh yeah, *sure* it is . . . and that's the Pope cleaning them windows.'

'No, honest to God,' another man said excitedly, 'I'm not kidding. It bloody *is* . . .'

Marcus stuffed the notes into his wallet, pocketed it crossing the street. Couldn't see any shop likely to sell maps. Never mind, he'd get one somewhere else.

Lewis's charcoal-grey Honda Accord was parked on a corner of the shopping street and a side road leading to a housing estate. When Marcus returned, there was a small crowd around it, as though it had been in an accident.

Marcus groaned. God almighty, Lewis had been discovered. You tended to forget he had a famous face these days. There'd be bloody autographs and jokes about Kelvyn bloody Kite and this curse nonsense, and they wouldn't get away from here for a good half-hour.

But as he drew closer, it became apparent that the situation was not quite like that. There was a woman shouting at Lewis through a gap in the driver's side window. She was in her thirties, buxom, in a green leather coat. A teenage boy with her was grinning inanely.

But the expression on the woman's face, Marcus saw, was one of explicit, self-righteous rage.

'. . . ripped them up, my mother did! Ripped 'em up! Twenty quid's worth! She says, "I'm not taking no chances." Two weeks after her operation, this is, you swine. That's what *you've* done – destroyed a simple pleasure for ordinary folk. Destroyed their only little

405

dream. Twenty quid's worth of tickets! That's nothing to you, is it? That's small change to the likes of you!'

'What the *bloody hell* . . . ?' Marcus tried to squeeze between two pushchairs.

'Yow won't get him, mate,' a man said. 'He'll not come out, he won't. He's locked the doors.'

Marcus looked at the man's reddening face and, in an appalled moment, realized that this was not just one belligerent bitch, but the whole bunch of them. He could see tomorrow's tabloid headlines: *Lottery Rage.* Virtually overnight Lewis had become – in other circumstances this would have been almost bloody funny – Britain's most hated man.

The great British public.

'Lewis!' Marcus pushed through, wondering why the silly bastard didn't wind up his window. Then he saw an elderly chap with his walking stick jammed in the gap. Over the heads of two jeering women, he glimpsed Lewis hunched down in his seat, the stick waggling back and forth over his ludicrous mauve hair, Malcolm barking furiously, bumping around on the back seat.

'You should give this lady her twenty quid back,' the old bastard shouted. 'Least you can do. Go on, get your wallet out, you bloody cream poof!'

'Now look—' Marcus stopped. He'd heard a long, rending squeak. He turned to see the teenage boy's fist juddering down the Honda's flank.

Lurched at the kid. 'You little *sod*!'

The kid stepped back and the penknife dropped into the road and Marcus flung out a foot and kicked it under the car.

'You leave him alone!' the harpy in the leather coat shrieked. 'He's off school with his asthma!'

'Don't you worry, madam,' Marcus snarled, veteran of a hundred confrontations over the castle walls, 'if he's having trouble breathing, I shall be delighted to perform an emergency tracheotomy with his own bloody knife. Now get back, all of you. Are you *insane*?'

Noticing then, to his alarm, that his own breath seemed to be jammed in his chest. Legacy of the bloody flu.

'Hello, his boyfriend's turned up now.' Some oaf from behind. Laughter. Marcus's fists tightened, nails digging into his palms; he tried to turn, but he was wedged between the car and two youths in reversed baseball caps.

'You want your money back, love? We'll shake it out of him, shall we do that? Nathan?'

'Just get out of my way, sonny,' Marcus snarled. 'I have to find a police—'

Hands seized him from behind. 'That's right, mate, don't turn your back on the bugger,' the old man crowed. 'Bloody ole shirt-lifter, bloody arse-bandit.' Marcus, flailing, was prodded and jostled as the Honda began to move. Four of the bastards bumping it up and down.

'Shake him out of there, boys!' The pensioner joyfully wagging his walking stick through the window of the bouncing car. Malcolm standing in the back with paws on the front seat, snapping at the stick until the old bastard jabbed it to the back of his throat and he squealed in rage and pain and fell back.

Marcus leapt. 'I'll break that fucking stick over your fucking—'

The sentence dying as he was pushed back against a streetlamp and the breath seemed to congeal in his chest. He sank down the lamp standard, down to his knees, as if a great force beyond gravity was pulling him into the pavement.

He thought, *Broad bastard daylight on the edge of a respectable English spa town.*

His glasses had gone. He heard them click and rattle on the pavement, the world a grey haze of hostility. He scrabbled around, encountering dust, a pebble . . . glass . . . yes. The first thing he saw as he fumbled the glasses back on was a bloody advertisement, outside a newsagent's, for the National bastard Lottery, and he heard what he thought was Lewis yelling, '*Marcus! Marcus!*' before his senses were savaged by the enormous pain which spread through his chest like a jagged lightning tree with many hard, bright branches and his vision closed down on the Lottery sign.

Maybe . . . it wheedled.

Just maybe . . .

Part Six

From *Bang to Wrongs: A Bad Boy's Book*,
by GARY SEWARD

Religion, eh?

No doubt, the way I was going on before, about trashing that church and everything, you all probably reckoned Gary Seward was dead against the very idea.

Not so. The only word I have a problem with is 'faith'. It don't wash with me, never has. You go through life, everybody's telling you you got to 'Stand on your own two feet', 'Don't let the bastards grind you down', 'Get a life.' Everybody except the Church. The Church is bleating, 'Put your trust in the Lord', 'Let the bastards kick sand in your face and turn the other cheek' and 'Forget life . . . Get a death instead.' Leastways, that's my understanding of theology: if you don't go through life as a total mug, you can expect to get the shit kicked out of you in a big way after you turn belly-up.

I had many an argument with prison chaplains about this. I say, Listen, mate, you give us all this old toffee about the sinner what done a U-turn being guaranteed a special place at the top table, but HOW DO YOU KNOW? And he'll say, I got faith, Gary, and I say, But suppose you're WRONG . . . suppose you got it all COMPLETELY TO COCK . . . you've wasted your life, ain'tcha? He says, That's very narrow thinking,

411

*Gary, if you don't mind me saying so . . . on account he
knows he ain't got an answer.*

*And all the time I'm thinking, I bet I could get a bleedin'
answer . . .*

42

'Is he *harmless*?' Kurt Campbell caught the question with both hands. 'Well, of course he is, Alice. How anyone could think otherwise is entirely beyond me.'

White-suited Kurt leaning back in the leather chair, dropping his left ankle on to his right knee, throwing his arms out and his head back as though it was surrendering to the pull of his lion's mane of golden hair. Bobby Maiden went down on the soft pile carpet of Kurt's hotel suite and took a picture of him like that, like he was intended to, with arms out, expansive St Kurt.

'Look ... Yes ... all right ... on one level he's this absurd anachronism, an old-fashioned mumbo-jumbo man. Do you know anything about Shamanism, Alice?'

'A little,' Grayle said, her tape machine spinning on the low yew table between them. She'd told Kurt she was doing a major article for *The Vision* and filing a shorter piece to the *New York Courier*.

'The shaman used to "contact the spirits" on behalf of his tribe,' Kurt said. 'Shaking bones and banging drums and all that rubbish.'

'You think it's rubbish?'

'It was for effect, it was to overwhelm people, it was saying, "Hey look at me, I'm a big magic man and you'd better be scared of me, you'd better be in awe, because *I'm different*." So, what you had was this funny, unbalanced, psychologically screwed-up guy who, instead of skulking on the fringes of his society, was projecting his skewed sexuality and his strange fetishes upon an ignorant and superstitious public only too ready to—'

'So you think this is what Cindy Mars-Lewis is doing, with the cross-dressing and stuff?'

'Oh, hey,' Kurt said good-humouredly, 'I was talking about the primitive old tribal shamans. Cindy's a modern-day entertainer, a comedian, this is part of his act. For many people, he's just a very funny guy, and when I was on the Lottery Show with him I was expected to play along with that, play the straight man, and I was happy to do that and *pretend* to hypnotize him . . .'

'Yeah, but aren't you—?'

'Alice . . .' Kurt raised a forefinger, fixed Grayle with that relaxed, pellucid blue gaze. 'I really don't want to talk about this guy any more, if that's all right with you. He's having a hard time and I don't want to compound that. I think it's ridiculous to suggest that he's been using some kind of black magic to darken the image of the National Lottery.'

'I don't think anyone's actually . . .'

'The only point I'm interested in making is that the so-called Way of the Shaman was a primitive way, in that it was a smokescreen designed to prevent ordinary people discovering the truth about life and death and what may lie beyond. The shaman was saying, "Listen, *ordinary people*, this is *my secret world* and you'd

414

better stay out of it *for your own good*." Now I'm a mesmerist, a hypnotist, and what I do is scientifically proven, and I'm anxious to sweep aside all this mystic nonsense in favour of a more scientific approach . . . and that's really what the Festival of the Spirit is about.'

'But you know you're gonna attract the New Age crowd.'

'Absolutely. And maybe they'll learn something. Yes, sure we're going to have a few fortune tellers and alternative healers and people selling crystals. But I'm interested in finding the scientific truths behind all this. Which is how it all began at Overcross, with Barnaby Crole, who rebuilt the castle, and Anthony Abblow. The whole point about Victorian spirituality is that it was science-based.'

'So perhaps you could explain how hypnotism ties in with spiritualism?'

'Yeah. Right. Absolutely. That's a very good question, Alice. You know, it's really great to be interviewed by someone who knows enough about these things to ask the right questions.'

'Well, thank you,' Grayle said and Bobby Maiden, down on the floor with the Nikon, decided his initial dislike of Kurt had been far from misplaced.

Kurt dropped his ankle from his knee, leaned forward. 'Hey, Alice, you *are* coming to the festival, aren't you?'

'Well, I hadn't . . .'

'Alice, you've just got to. You'd find it so enlightening. You'd be able to see for yourself that . . . You've got press tickets, yeah?'

'Well, not yet, but—'

'And you'd like to come to the first Victorian seance tomorrow night?'

415

'Oh, gee,' Grayle said.

'You would. You would like to come.'

Kurt's head very still. Like he had her in a trance, Maiden thought, quietly impressing his enormous will on her. Kurt was young and confident of his powers.

Grayle said, 'Well, uh . . . I'm not sure *The Vision* is gonna be able to run to five hundred pounds.'

Kurt waved a boyish hand. 'Hey, that's not what I meant. You can come as my *guest*,' he smiled, 'Alice.'

Which was when Bobby Maiden realized there was more to this than spreading the charm like soft honey.

Kurt Campbell actively fancied Grayle.

Which was . . . understandable. Grayle was extremely fanciable. In her little red dress. With her hair up, fastened by one of those Indian-type things with a stick through it. With her small face and the sparkle in her eyes and that loose, easy smile, the quick, nervous gestures, the animation of her.

Maiden concentrated on altering the exposure on his camera. He changed lenses and took a picture of Kurt from floor level, all groin and his head reduced.

'I, uh . . .' Grayle turned over her tape, clicked it into the machine, set it running again. 'What I have to do at this point, Kurt, is get some nuts and bolts stuff, OK?'

Kurt's PR woman appeared in the doorway. Severe, business-suited, clutching a mobile phone. Probably no older than Kurt, Maiden thought, except in attitude.

'Kurt, you have another appointment at—'

Kurt looked up only briefly. 'Delay them, Francine.'

Francine nodded, scowled at Grayle, disappeared.

'Sure,' Kurt said. 'What do you need?'

'Well, about the organization of the festival. Like, is

416

it just you putting up the finance, or do you have backers?'

'I've been able to raise most of the finance myself, but sure, there are some people with a strong interest in the subject who've given us some . . . padding.'

'Anyone we've heard of? Like anyone famous?'

'Shouldn't think so, Alice. I mean . . . look, this is not a political movement collecting supportive celebrities. This is in the nature of a serious inquiry.'

'Right. Uh, the medium you've got for the seance. Who's she . . . or he . . . gonna be? I've heard a few names on the grapevine . . . Betty Shine, Eileen Drewery, Persephone Callard . . .'

Kurt sat back. 'What I should say here, Alice, is that the name of the medium is not important. It's the event itself. And the location. We believe there's a resonance at Overcross because of its history and its actual situation – whether you're talking about the juxtaposition of so-called leylines or the geophysical properties of the site itself, the rocks the castle's built on—'

'But this is not the actual castle, is it?'

'It's a Victorian house built in the castle grounds, in the neo-Gothic style. Built on the site of a medieval chapel, we understand.'

'So, the house itself doesn't have what you'd call an extensive history.'

'It has what you'd call a *concentrated* history.'

'It's haunted?'

'There's evidence of that, certainly. For instance, a gamekeeper accidentally shot himself with his own gun and his ghost is said to prowl the grounds.'

'John Hodge, right? I, uh, read the booklet. Is your medium gonna try to contact him?'

'He's one of our projects, yes.'

417

'Cool,' Grayle said. 'You worked a lot with mediums before, Kurt?'

'To an extent.'

'Which brings me back to my question of a few moments ago . . . which, uh, kind of got lost . . . What *is* the connection between hypnotism and mediumship?'

'Well, trance, Alice. They have trance in common. Mediums operate in trance, and the huge interest in hypnotism – which began in your own country, of course – happened to coincide with the Victorian spiritualist boom. Hypnotism was also used for healing, as Mesmer himself did back in the eighteenth century, and this began to be tied in with spiritual healing. What it comes down to is that, at the time, these were two fields of study approached in the same spirit of adventure, and I think the fusion of psychology and spirituality is a good, solid base from which to explore the human condition.'

'So, do you possess mediumistic powers yourself?'

Kurt smiled. 'Sadly not. Obviously, I've practised self-hypnosis but I've never been approached, while in trance, by . . . outside influences.'

'You've been a . . . friend of Persephone Callard. I think that's widely known.'

Kurt shifted.

'Not *so* widely,' he said.

'Yeah, well, we – the magazine – have connections.'

'Evidently. Sure, yeah, Seffi and I were close for a while and we still have a professional liaison going from time to time, but that's all.'

'But she's not one of the festival's backers?'

'Certainly not. You're pushing here, aren't you, Alice? Look, the backers are entitled to their

418

anonymity. There's still, unfortunately, a stigma attached to spiritualism.'

'But you're clearly not afraid of that yourself.'

'I'm not afraid of anything,' Kurt said. He glanced down at Maiden, like he'd noticed a bluebottle on his trousers. 'That's enough pictures, OK, matey?'

'Bloke thinks he's a god,' Bobby Maiden said, unlocking the truck.

'Well, you know,' climbing in, Grayle hid a small smile, 'he undoubtedly has – to use Mesmer's own term – a certain animal magnetism.'

Bobby switched on the lights, pulled away from the parking area into the centre of Cheltenham. 'I'm not entirely sure about you going to this seance.'

'Oh, you're not, huh? The little defenceless female walking into the dark castle?'

'We don't know that he hasn't realized who you really are. That he wasn't bluffing.'

'Oh, he wasn't bluffing, Bobby. Women can tell this kind of thing.'

Smiling into the darkness.

Bobby said nothing.

'It's a real shame they won't allow photographers in, but you can understand that – all those flashes.'

She decided not to bring up the question of whether they should doorstep Seward – she had no idea where he lived, guessed Bobby did but that he'd had enough for tonight.

They headed out of town through sparse traffic.

'Curious Callard never mentioned Kurt.'

'Why should she?'

'No reason, I guess. Unless there's still something between them.'

'Blokes try to use her', Bobby said, 'in all kinds of ways.'

'Aw, poor kid,' Grayle said.

They approached the roundabout in the area known as the Rotunda, where Chatterton Mansions was.

'You worked it all out yet about the apartment, Bobby?'

What with talking to the removal guys and getting to look around the place, then dashing directly over to Kurt Campbell's hotel, they hadn't had much opportunity to discuss what they'd found out at Chatterton Mansions.

'If it wasn't even his flat,' Bobby said, 'it's just further proof that Seward was using Barber as a respectable front to get Seffi to do the seance.'

'We established that. But why not use Barber's own apartment if it's in the same building?'

'Probably because he didn't want all those people – people like *that* – in his home.'

'But if Seward was in a position to put the bite on Barber, was Barber in a position to argue over details?'

'What other reason could there be?'

'I don't know,' Grayle said. 'Hey, you get a whiff of the dope in that bedroom?'

'Tart's boudoir,' Bobby said. 'Wardrobe full of handcuffs and rubberwear.'

'You looked?'

'I'm guessing, Grayle.'

'What did those guys call the apartment?'

'A show flat.'

'Like, an example of what you could expect if you bought an apartment in the block?'

'It's bollocks, isn't it? But why are they moving the furniture?'

420

'Somebody actually bought the place?'

'One room only?'

'You're right,' Grayle said. 'That doesn't add up. It's like they were getting rid of all the stuff in there on account of it was messed up or something.'

'Tainted by bad vibes,' Bobby said.

'You're spending too much time with Cindy.' She leaned back, watching the lights of the town receding in the wing mirror. 'I guess we're no further forward, Bobby. We're just collecting more questions. Maybe some of it'll hang together with whatever Cindy and Marcus discovered at Overcross.'

When they got back to St Mary's – around nine p.m., this would be – the wind was up again and a branch had snapped from one of the old trees which clashed like antlers over the mountain road.

The heater in the truck didn't work. Grayle had on her raincoat, and it was too damn thin.

She thought Kurt Campbell was slick and arrogant and, for all his mastery of the techniques of hypnotism and his knowledge of the history of spiritualism, probably dangerously superficial. She wanted to go to this expensive Victorian seance tomorrow night about as much as she wanted to revisit the place where Ersula's body had been found.

And there was the problem of Callard. She'd need to get in fast with the Alice D. Thornborough if they came face to face. Be kind of interesting, she supposed, to see how Callard reacted to Kurt's guest.

For reasons of perversity, Grayle had allowed Bobby to go on thinking she'd found Campbell intriguing, attractive, magnetic, all of that.

They drove through the castle gate. Cindy's Honda

421

was parked in the yard. She was relieved they'd gotten back.

Then she spotted Cindy himself waiting under the bulkhead light with Malcolm the dog.

Cindy looked bedraggled in his twinset and tweed skirt, truly the maiden aunt fallen on hard times. The truck's headlights threw his face into hard relief: deep lines and no make-up, the mauve hair blown on end by the wind.

'Something's wrong,' Bobby said.

43

You could see Overcross Castle from a distance of maybe a mile, across countryside which would be lush in summer. Signs told of cider farms and a vineyard a few hundred yards and at least a whole season away. The light-green glaze of new growth on the trees looked like an illusion in the scrabbling wind.

'I just knew it was gonna be like this.' Inside the heaterless truck, Grayle rummaged in her bag for her long, woollen scarf.

The house had towers and turrets and battlements and all those other *Son of Robin Hood* features. Viewed through the spiky trees, it looked stark and threatening, more like a true medieval castle than any of the actual ones she'd seen. Made Marcus's ruins look like garden ornaments. Behind it you could see, in the distance, the hill of Great Malvern with white houses and hotels strung along it like a necklace of teeth.

Billionaires in California had erected mock castles like this, and she'd marvelled at a couple when she was a kid and her father was lecturing out west.

But California was California and didn't have the weather for it. Jesus, the first day of spring tomorrow, the vernal equinox, and was that *snow* on the truck's windshield?

'Bobby, is that snow?'

'It's not volcanic dust,' Bobby Maiden said. He looked unhappy and unsure about everything.

As Grayle supposed they both were, since Cindy gave them the news about Marcus. *'The curse is come upon me', cried The Lady of Shalott*, Grayle thought drably. Wishing she was anyplace but here, as they came to an old brick wall, about ten feet high, with trees hard against it and a long sign along the top.

Experience . . .

THE FESTIVAL OF THE SPIRIT.

MARCH 20–25

And then a gatehouse. There was a cop on duty behind a barrier. Except, when he came over, Grayle saw he wasn't a cop, although the uniform was damn close; Bobby thought so too, muttering something about take away the red armband and you could have him for impersonation. Bobby wound down the window and Grayle handed him the press passes she'd been given by Francine, Kurt Campbell's haughty PA.

'We also have a stall,' she told the almost-cop, leaning across from the passenger side. 'Stall thirty-eight?'

'Hang on a moment.' He studied the passes before pushing them back. He was a big young guy with an impassive, military kind of look, and Grayle saw the word **FORCEFIELD** on his red armband. 'Bacton, is it? Somebody's already there. Came about an hour ago.'

'Yeah, we know.'

'Right – Avenue Three. End of the drive, turn right by the tape and the arrows and you'll see the way it's divided – stalls one to fourteen, and so on. It's your third, right at the end.'

'Thank you, Constable.' Bobby wound up the window. You could see an angry fire had been re-kindled inside him, could almost smell the smoke.

'Oh, I really don't like the way you said that,' Grayle said.

'I'm sorry.'

'This is your private obsession taking over. At bottom, you're just as bad as this guy Foxworth. You have a tenuous connection here between Campbell and this Riggs and Riggs is your personal bogeyman, so you're thinking like maybe if you can build Seward into the picture . . . right?'

'The only picture I'm getting', Bobby said, 'is Vic Clutton lying dead outside the house he was finally happy to call home.'

'Oh boy.' Grayle wound the big scarf around her neck and tightened the belt of her raincoat as the truck entered the grounds of Overcross Castle.

At close to eleven a.m. on a working day and the festival not due to open until that evening, there were probably fewer than a hundred people there – most of them around an expensive-looking restaurant marquee which, presumably, had heating, and was the only part of the site that looked remotely inviting.

The festival was set up in three sloping fields which might once have been parkland, leading up to the stone terrace surrounding Overcross Castle. Most of the hundred or so stalls were open-fronted display tents

425

with room for about five people. One was being fitted out as an esoteric bookstore, another was figuring to sell aromatic candles which, with the wind and snow and all, nobody could hope to light.

They left Marcus's faded blue truck next to Cindy's Honda on a cindered parking lot reserved for stall-holders. Hundreds of yards of wooden decking-track had been laid across grass which was destined otherwise to become a boot-churned bog.

Avenue Three was right under the highest part of the castle, a round tower with a conical roof and a lightning conductor which prodded the bruised low cloud like an old-fashioned hypodermic syringe in a junkie's arm. Stall thirty-eight marked the furthest point of the festival campus and was right next to the toilet block, a line of white Portaloos – already the source of a seriously acrimonious dispute, as Grayle and Bobby approached.

'. . . don't care if it was a late booking, this is not bloody good enough, is it, sonny?'

Young guy with a clipboard backing off. 'Look, it's the best we—'

'Four yards . . . *four yards* . . . from the stinking toilets? Can you imagine the state those makeshift shithouses are going to be in by next Sunday? I mean, have you thought for one bloody second what this *means*, from our point of view? Well, I'll tell you . . . It means that whenever anybody who's been here comes across a copy of *The Vision* in future, they're going to associate it immediately with the stink of stale piss and probably steaming vomit.'

'Now look, those loos are the most hygienic—'

'Makes no odds, sonny. By Saturday morning we'll still all be swilling diarrhoea from the canvas.'

426

'I can definitely assure you these toilets will be cleaned every—'

'Pah!' And Malcolm the dog barked once, as if in support.

'Look, if you've got a complaint, you'll have to put it in writing.' The boy tucking his clipboard under his arm, turning away. Bad move, Grayle thought.

'Don't . . . think . . . you're . . . walking . . . away . . . from . . . this.' The force of nature in the glasses and the tweed suit, and the dog, advancing on the poor kid, planting a foot in front of his. 'I want another site.'

'I keep telling you, we haven't *got* another site.'

'In that case, I want two hundred pounds off the charge. Or I'll be obliged to take this to Kurt bloody Campbell himself.'

'What?'

'*I'll* show the smarmy bastard what a hypnotic trance feels like.'

'Did you really say two hundred pounds?'

'Seems eminently bloody reasonable to me. And I'm sure you wouldn't like the good vibes to be soiled by the sound of me telling everyone, including the press and the local television, what a shoddy little sideshow this is, organized by a slimy tosser with no—'

'All right!' The kid held up both hands, dropping his clipboard in the mud. 'I'll go across to the admin office and see what I can do.'

He started to walk back along the decking then turned around. 'I'm sorry, I've forgotten your name.'

Grayle fought for control as the bottle blonde in the tweed suit glared at this hapless kid through plain-glass spectacles.

'Bacton,' Cindy snarled. 'Imelda. *Miss.*'

*   *   *

A short while later Grayle went back to the cold comfort of the truck and called the infirmary in Worcester on Bobby's mobile.

'Are you a relative?' the staff nurse demanded.

The snow had stopped. It was never going to stick, but it was so bitter that Grayle's hand was numb around the cellphone.

'Well, I . . . Yeah, I'm . . . I'm his niece. Alice Thornborough.'

'Well, all I can tell you, Miss Thornborough,' the nurse's voice was unexpectedly clipped and frigid, 'is that he's as comfortable as can be expected.'

'And in plain English, that means?'

'It means', the sister said, 'that everything about him is weak except his language.'

'Uh, yeah, that figures. He kind of hates hospitals and doctors. Doesn't even have a thing about nurses in uniform.'

'He wanted to discharge himself this morning, but when he found out how much pain was involved in getting out of bed, I think he finally understood that he needed us rather more than we need him.'

'But he is gonna be OK? Isn't he?'

'If he accepts this as a severe warning.'

'Yeah,' Grayle said pessimistically. How was this woman supposed to understand that if there was anything to which Marcus Bacton reacted badly, it was a severe warning?

'Can I see him?'

'Tonight, if you like, but only for a short time. We've had to put him in a side ward, for the sake of the other patients, so if you ask the nurse who—'

'Tonight could be a problem,' Grayle said quickly.

428

'But if you could tell him not to worry, that everything's being looked after this end?'

And his sister sends her best wishes?

Maybe not.

'He wanted to be here. Cindy sat on the counter, hitched up his tweed skirt, lit a cigarette. 'And so he is. The shamanic solution, I suppose you might call it.'

'Nothing to do with you not wanting to be recognized, then,' Bobby said, patting the masterless Malcolm, poor confused creature.

'Well, that too, naturally.' Cindy blew a spontaneous smoke ring into the cold air. Cindy didn't smoke, but Imelda Bacton apparently did.

Subtle padding made him stocky. His blond wig was shoulder-length. His foundation cream was a deep bronze, his lipstick scarlet, his glasses black-rimmed and businesslike. He was sitting on one of the packing cases they'd fetched from the truck. It contained a couple of thousand copies of *The Vision* and, for display purposes, a set of atmospheric colour photos of High Knoll taken by a woman called Magda Ring, who'd been Bobby's girlfriend for a – mercifully, in Grayle's view – short time. In one of the pictures, blown up big, a formation of white clouds resembled two praying hands. The picture had been taken just after the Green Man killings had ended.

'You saw it coming, didn't you?' Bobby said.

'I don't . . .' Tears threatened Cindy's make-up. 'I felt *something* coming. I didn't realize it was going to be Marcus. Marcus was . . . invulnerable.'

'A force of nature,' Grayle said.

'It was one of the absolute worst moments of my

429

life. About to try mouth to mouth, I was, until I saw the look in his eyes.'

Cindy found a smile. Last night he'd been a mess. Prowling the windy ruins, a ragged spectre of despair. He'd killed Marcus, just like he'd killed the BMW family and the plane guy and the guy who'd married a gold-digger less than half his age. Killed them all. Cindy, the walking curse.

After talking it over with Bobby, Grayle had called the hospital at midnight, learned that Marcus was sleeping. She'd told Cindy that Marcus had whispered to a nurse to tell Lewis that it wasn't his fault, that he had to pull himself together, see it through. A necessary lie.

This morning they'd had a call from Amy at the pub to say Cindy had left for Overcross before six a.m.

'We're gonna have trouble with him, though, Cindy.'

'Marcus? Yes. Taking it easy, obeying doctor's orders . . . not his way. Mind, I didn't even know he had a heart problem.'

'Nor did he,' said Grayle. 'He hadn't seen a doctor in twenty years. He just saw Mrs Willis. Like, if he did have a heart problem, maybe it didn't matter with her around.'

Bobby looked at Cindy, who really didn't look at all like Cindy. 'Does he *have* a sister?'

'I have no idea, Bobby.' Cindy pulled up a wrinkle in his tights, flexed a leg. 'But if he did, this is what she would be like, and if she doesn't achieve a fifty per cent reduction in Marcus's stall rental, she won't consider herself worthy of the family name. Now, listen to me, children – close those tent flaps – there are things you need to know.'

Arriving early was always useful, Cindy said. It was barely light when he got here and freezing cold and the restaurant marquee wasn't open. So Imelda Bacton had gone up to the house, where the woman who cleaned the kitchens had taken pity on her.

This cleaner was one of the temporary staff hired for the festival, a big, cheerful cockney lady called Vera, who made coffee for Cindy and herself in the vault-like kitchen where dinner was to be prepared each night by a catering company from Worcester. And, of course, they'd gotten talking and Imelda had said she was only managing the stall for her brother, who'd had a heart attack, and Vera said she'd been forced to take this miserable job because her husband had died recently, leaving her short.

Like old friends, the two of them, in no time at all. Vera was cynical about the Festival of the Spirit and appalled at the amount being paid by the house guests attending the Victorian seance.

And the thing was, she said, it was all going to be a complete con. She'd taken Cindy up to the baronial dining hall where, behind screens and false bookcases, all was revealed.

'Projection equipment,' Cindy said, 'for the creation of ghosts. Hidden spotlights to illuminate the muslin and chiffon gauze used to simulate ectoplasm. Tables with mechanical rapping devices built into the legs, a platform with a floorboard that rises when a foot pedal is pressed, thus causing the table to rock. Need one go on?'

Grayle's eyes widened. 'A scam? The whole thing's gonna be a scam?'

'And a rather obvious one, it seemed to me. Obvious

431

to us, today, that is, but convincing enough, evidently, to the likes of Sir Arthur Conan Doyle and other believers in the early part of last century.'

'But – hold on – how does this equate with all the bullshit Campbell's giving us about seeking the scientific solution?'

'Perhaps he wishes to demonstrate how those early researchers were frequently fooled, which they undoubtedly were. Such was the craving for mystical experience that there was considerable money to be made in those days.'

'In New York', Grayle said, 'there was a woman had a hole in the front of her dress, used to pull this glowing ribbon from a roll she kept up her snatch. Sure. All kinds of scams. But why would Campbell wanna bother with this garbage?'

Cindy moved to the tent flap, peered out to ensure they were alone. He took a small notebook from his fitted tweed jacket, opened it.

'A look at tonight's guest list – which the delightful Vera showed to me with a certain contempt – offers a possible explanation. I copied down a few names. For instance, we have the Chairperson of the Heart of England Tourist Board, the MP for Worcester, officials of the Malvern Chamber of Trade, the Elgar Society, the Chief Executive of Forcefield Security. Also, Lord . . .'

Bobby looked up, like a bird just took a shit in his lap.

'. . . and Lady Colwall. I don't think I need go on. It's a collection of local dignitaries and notables to launch the event. None of them will be paying, of course, they're here to bestow upon it Establishment credibility. And, because attitudes have changed considerably since Victorian times, one can't imagine any of these people accepting the invitation if they thought it was to be a *real* seance.'

'So they're not even gonna *pretend*?'

'Of course not. It's to be a civilized after-dinner entertainment, an exhibition of deception and human folly. We see how the magic lantern was used to project phantoms, how sound effects and the deployment of light and shadow would simulate the atmosphere of a haunted house . . .'

'Big deal.'

'Ah, but then . . .' Cindy laid down the notebook '. . . what if, at some point in the evening, there is an imperceptible change? What if we shift from simulation to an invocation of . . . who knows what? What if the obviously fake gives way to the semi-convincing and then – in front of this august assembly – to the terrifyingly inexplicable? And what if afterwards, as the somewhat timid applause dies down, the guests come to realize that what they have just witnessed is . . .' Cindy raising his hands, fingers moving like undersea creatures '. . . the reality of it?'

'This is where Callard comes in?'

'I don't know, little Grayle. I won't be there. Only you will be there, among the dignitaries.'

Grayle moistened her cold lips.

Bobby said, 'But that's just what you *surmise* will happen?'

'Of course,' Cindy said lightly. 'And if nothing happens but the fakery, nothing is lost, no reputations are damaged. But if it does, particularly in front of this distinguished group, think of the kudos for Kurt's venture.'

'Hold on here,' Grayle said. 'Are we talking about

433

Clarence Judge? Because that's what they're gonna get from Callard. Just Clarence freaking Judge and his slimeball smell. That doesn't make a whole lot of sense, Cindy.'

'No,' Cindy said. 'Perhaps it doesn't.'

'Maybe we put two and two together and made sixteen.'

Bobby said, 'I don't suppose Seward was on that guest list?'

Cindy looked disparaging. 'I know he's a popular figure now, but is that really likely, Bobby? Even rejected for the Lottery Show once, he was. I think it was the idea of the big money balls in the hands of a known felon . . . Hush a moment . . .'

Cindy lifted a finger. There came the unlikely sound of ragged, unaccompanied singing. Bobby stood up, walked over and spread the tent flap. Grayle went to peer over his shoulder.

'Aw, this always happens.'

Over on the cindered parking lot, a minibus had drawn up, a bunch of people gathered around it. They were singing a hymn. Two of them carried a banner between two poles. In black stencilled lettering, it carried a not unfamiliar appeal.

IN THE NAME OF JESUS, STOP THIS EVIL!

The banner took some holding steady in the wind, but maybe they had support from above.

'Whenever you advertise any kind of big New Age event, you get these militant evangelicals,' Grayle said. 'Happens a lot back home.'

Cindy joined her and Bobby in the opening. Quite a few more New Age stallholders had emerged, so there was some kind of audience – if not the kind likely to be on the side of the protesters.

'Open your minds, why don't you?' yelled this woman in a long, grey woollen cloak. 'There's more than one narrow little way to God!'

The evangelicals carried on singing, led by two guys in clerical collars.

'How long will they keep this up?' Bobby wondered.

'Oh hell, Bobby, they'll be here all day and then I guess another bunch'll take over. Less, of course, the security guys move into action, but that's not too likely. Throwing out a Christian on his ass is not what you'd call good PR.'

'Now there's interesting,' Cindy said.

'Huh?'

'See the person on the end with the handwritten placard?'

Small guy in a suit and tie, not singing, just standing there holding up his placard.

'What's it say? Oh.'

The sign said

THEY MURDERED
JOHN HODGE

'The gamekeeper?' Grayle said. 'The shotgun accident?'

Cindy turned to Bobby.

'Go and have a word, boy. You are the detective, go

and detect. Grayle and I will mind the shop.' He seemed suddenly alive with an excitement Grayle hadn't seen in him in such a long time. 'This is what we've been waiting for. The answers always lie in history. Get him out of here, Bobby. Don't let anyone see you.'

44

He had a long piece of sticking plaster diagonally across his forehead.

'Oh, yes, they did that,' he said diffidently in the snug, panelled bar of the Unicorn.

'The security men?'

'Well, you see, I landed on a piece of barbed wire. This was when they slung me off the site. I don't suppose they meant it to happen, but they never came out to help me. I could've lost an eye, I suppose, for all they cared.'

'Just let me get this right. This is the Forcefield men?'

'Is that what they're called? Anyway, I came back. I paid my entrance fee and I came back. And when these religious people arrived, I decided to attach myself to them. I explained that this was an example of the kind of evil that resulted from all this meddling. Had to say I was thinking of joining their church, but at least it meant I could make my protest without getting assaulted. Stand there a while and hope someone would come along who'd take a bit of notice. And now here you are, sir.'

He raised his glass to Maiden.

Get him out of here, Bobby. Don't let anyone see you.

They'd thrown his placard face-down in the back of Marcus's truck and then Maiden had driven him through the gates, the man's face turned away from the Forcefield gateman, and four miles to the Unicorn, which was three pubs distant from Overcross and almost empty, thankfully.

'I'll go back again,' he said. 'Got to keep it up, sir. I promised.'

He was a slightly built man about Marcus's age, gingery-white hair and a small, pointed face as inoffensive as a hedgehog's. His name was Harry Douglas Oakley. John Hodge, gamekeeper to Barnaby Crole, was his great-grandfather.

'You really are the police?' He spoke quietly, the way informers spoke in pubs, the way Vic Clutton would speak, only a little more refined and with none of Vic's irony. Mr Oakley had a small bicycle shop in West Malvern.

Maiden displayed his warrant card. 'But, I'll be honest, this is not my area. And I'm on leave, anyway.'

'So, can I ask what your interest is, sir? Do you mind?'

Maiden hesitated. 'This would be in confidence?'

'Surely.'

'I don't know about John Hodge being murdered, but people have certainly been killed since and I'm looking for connections with some friends. We're not sure what we're after. I'm sorry to be so vague.'

'If you're sincere, that's good enough for me, sir.'

Maiden said, 'Would you mind not calling me "sir"? I have a bit of a problem with it. My name's Bobby.'

'Certainly, Bobby,' said Harry Douglas Oakley.

438

*　　*　　*

By early afternoon many more vehicles had entered the site and the tents were taking on a new allure, signs going up proclaiming palmistry, crystal-healing, Tarot readings and a big caravan, where you could attach yourself to devices that altered your brainwaves. There were practitioners of Reiki and a *feng shui* adviser. An Asian band with a range of hand drums set up in a corner of the field and beat away the cold.

Cindy and Grayle finished laying out the stall. Even with the dramatic colour pictures of the Knoll and one oblique photo of Castle Farm, home of *The Vision* (silhouetted against the sunset, its location un-identified; Marcus would kill them first), it all still looked a little sparse, even for a cover, a smokescreen.

Grayle had brought a small case containing the long black skirt and the high-necked Edwardian-style blouse she guessed she'd need to wear for the period seance. 'I'd be lying if I said I wasn't feeling uneasy about tonight, Kurt Campbell coming on to me and all. And what happens if . . . when . . . Callard spots me?'

They were standing with Malcolm the dog in front of the tent, watching the build-up of cars and vans. Grayle was looking for a Jeep Grand Cherokee with a woman at the wheel. She'd already checked the cordoned off exclusive parking lot up by the castle. Was Callard coming here at all, or had Marcus got it all wrong?

'She won't give you away.' Cindy lit a cigarette. 'She wants an end to this. It's been going on too long. Longer than she knows.'

'What's that mean? What are you saying?' Puzzled by this new animation around Cindy. Everything he

439

said seemed pointed and penetrating, like a needle teasing a splinter out of the skin.

'I think', he said, 'that Bobby may be able to complete the picture when he returns. But ponder this, Grayle: the only purpose-built haunted house? What does that *mean*?'

'Means they were ambitious. They were aiming to call down spirits at will. Scientifically.'

'But how many ghosts is it reputed to have? You'd think a hundred, wouldn't you? And yet . . . John Hodge, the gamekeeper. The sole apparition. Just poor John. Accidentally shot, here in the grounds, with his own gun. I wonder where, precisely.'

'They probably put the damn toilets over the spot.' Grayle glanced briefly over at the Portaloos. 'You're saying you think there's a connection between the death of John Hodge and what's happening now? Or is that shamanic intuition?'

'If we think of Anthony Abblow as the Kurt Campbell of his day . . . a man whose interest in the paranormal had little of the mystical about it. A man who—. Something wrong, is it, Grayle?'

'Sorry, I just saw . . .' Grayle was staring at a big vehicle heading up the main drive towards the castle. 'Cindy, you see that van? Wait till it comes out the other side of that clump of bushes . . . OK, you see the symbol on the side panel?'

'A blue rose?'

'Right. Well, this is probably nothing, but I would swear that is the same firm we saw taking stuff out of the flat we thought was Barber's. In Cheltenham.'

'You're sure about this?'

'I'm almost sure it's the same company. It may not be the same van. I mean I wouldn't recognize the licence plate or anything. Maybe this is the outfit everybody uses in these parts. Coincidence.'

'You are saying this could be the van which departed carrying furniture and effects from the room in which Persephone Callard conducted a seance for Sir Richard Barber?' Cindy's eyes flared. 'Grayle, in such a situation as this, there can be no such thing as coincidence.' He clipped on Malcolm's lead. 'Come on.'

'What about the stall?'

'Would all these spiritually developed people help themselves to free copies of *The Vision*?'

'Only if they haven't read one before.'

Grayle followed Cindy and the dog up towards the castle. It looked bloated against the light.

'My mother died earlier this year, Bobby,' said Harry Oakley. 'She always used to say to me, "The truth won't come out in my time, there's still too much prejudice. But perhaps before the end of your life it might." So I promised her, you see, that one way or another I'd make sure it did come out. Not quite on her deathbed, but it was a promise.'

'What did she mean by too much prejudice?'

'Prejudice in his favour. Nobody in the locality would hear a word against Barnaby Crole. You see, not only was he the local benefactor, he was the only one there'd *ever* been around here. He built almshouses for the old people. Built the school. Turned a blind eye, the locals, out of pure self-interest, Bobby.'

'So . . . how do you think your great-grandfather died?'

'How much do you know?'

441

'I've read that little book. It says he had an accident with his shotgun.'

'Aye, and no-one's ever going to prove otherwise now. I'd be happy, and I think my mother and her mother would rest in peace, if it was just accepted locally that they probably murdered him. That's all we want.'

'Crole and Abblow?'

'They were doing experiments', Harry said, 'into what happened at the moment of death. I remember my grandmother talking to my aunt – in that hushed way they talked when there were children about – about Mr Crole and Mr Abblow coming to see their neighbour when he was dying. They wanted to be with him when he died, you see. Crole even offered to pay for the funeral, with an expensive memorial in the churchyard – oh, he was made of money was Crole. But they still wouldn't let him go into the bedroom that last night because they knew he just wanted to watch what happened when the old man passed over. Watch the light go out of him.'

'It was said they took animals.'

'I believe it. Though that wouldn't satisfy them for long.'

'You think they experimented on John Hodge? Or did he see too much and they killed him to stop him talking?'

'Oh, he'd already talked,' Harry said. 'Or his dreams had. These terrible nightmares he couldn't properly remember. But he knew he was going to die, my mother said they were all convinced of that. By day he was very quiet and withdrawn. At night he'd scream. My grandmother remembered those screams and they disturbed her own nights all her life. That's how bad it was.'

'What were the actual circumstances of his death?'

'They heard a shot and then Abblow was said to have found him in the woods with half his face blown away. They claimed he was unfit to move, so they made him as comfortable as they could on the grass, Crole laying down his fine jacket and Abblow tending him – Abblow was a doctor, you see.'

'What year was this?'

'Eighteen eighty-seven. This month. This day.'

'This actual *date*?'

For an instant Maiden was aware of himself being vibrantly aware of the moment – as though he was standing behind himself and Harry Douglas Oakley seated at a round, mahogany table in the small, dark-panelled bar.

'Those evil beggars,' Harry said. 'Myself, I don't think they were tending him so much as prolonging his agony. Dragging out his death so they could study him and make him tell them what was happening. Perhaps they'd got gadgets attached to him.'

'Gadgets?'

'I don't know. Like Frankenstein. They always had gadgets in those days. Kept them in the dungeons, most likely.'

'The castle has dungeons?'

'Well, cellars with thick walls. Nobody been down there in years. All the years it was derelict, it was well fenced off and barb-wired, and no-one ever went there because it was always private land. Except for my poor old great-grandfather. Who never went away.'

'You mean his ghost.'

'Aye.'

'That was seen quite often?'

'At one time. So it's said.' Harry looked down into

his beer, as though the face of John Hodge might materialize there. 'Poachers and so on. But even the poachers got nervous. The last time . . . well, that would be a young couple, staying at the Crown for a night. Ramblers, with backpacks. Walked into the pub at sunset, all ashy-faced. Strangers wouldn't know, you see. Ninety-seven, this would've been.'

'What did they say they'd seen?'

'They'd found one of the paths through the grounds and they were getting as close as they could to the castle and up strolls a man in a cap, with a shotgun under his arm – so clear and sharp they thought he was a real, living person. And they stopped and wished him good evening and hoped they weren't trespassing . . . and he walks within a few feet of them and never took them on and just disappeared into the air. Been a few like that.'

Maiden took a slow sip from his glass of cider. He was hearing Seffi Callard.

. . . certainly, in my experience as a medium, I've never seen anything quite so clear as this before. So fully defined. Such a physical presence.

'A few like that? Were they always so clear?'

'There's ghosts and ghosts, aren't there, Bobby? Some you hear of, it's just a wandering light, no shape, no features. People who've seen this one, they could identify my great-grandad from old photographs. And *did*!'

'You've never seen it?'

'And never wanted to, Bobby. Never wanted to. Besides, it's better coming from others, isn't it? Old John Hodge, he's doing no more than I am today – drawing attention to a murder.'

'Why did the place become derelict?'

'Well, it didn't happen overnight. Abblow left – went abroad, it was said. Crole never came out much after that, although you'd apparently see his wife sometimes, on her own. When he died she sold the castle, and then it went through the usual things – a school, a hotel. Before this syndicate put in an offer, it was owned by Arthur Slater, the farmer. His dad, he bought it with a hundred and fifty acres in the Seventies. They ploughed round the castle.'

'Why do you say syndicate?'

'Well, I don't know if it was or not. This young man, Campbell, he always makes out it's his castle, but I do know Arthur slightly, and he reckons it was a Gloucestershire firm made the initial approach. Bright's? Would that be it?'

'How about Bright Horizon Developments?'

'That's it,' said Harry without much interest. 'Bright Horizon Developments.' He finished his beer. 'You got what you wanted, Bobby? Only I wouldn't mind getting back. They reckon there's Midlands television coming to film the festival taking shape and I wouldn't mind getting my sign in front of the camera. P'raps they'll want to interview me. Do you think?'

'It's always possible.'

'I'm not a nutter, you know,' Harry said. 'It's funny – my grandmother used to say it was a big joke in the family that one day her father was going to be the ghost of Overcross. Because he loved that place so much you couldn't get him away. Dawn till dusk and then half the night, building up that estate from nothing. Part of it, you see.'

Vera, the cleaner from the kitchens, was a large woman with white hair tied up in a bun and kind of

445

knowing eyes. You could tell, somehow, that nothing would get past her.

Grayle and Cindy sure didn't. They went in through the kitchen door, round back of the castle. It didn't look much like a castle this side, the door and the woodwork modern and utility.

'You're back again, Miss Bacton.'

'It's *bloody* cold out there, Vera.'

Wasn't too warm in here. The kitchen was the size of a hospital ward and all white tiles. Vera said, 'You'd like some tea, I s'pose.'

'That would be splendid,' said Cindy. 'This is my assistant, Thornborough. And this is my poor bloody brother's dog, Malcolm, who would appreciate a bowl of water and a chocolate digestive.'

Had to hand it to Cindy; he was good, could switch personalities in the blink of an eye. Right now, no way would Grayle make the mistake of addressing him as Cindy.

'We got about ten minutes', Vera said, taking this huge kettle to one of four sinks, 'before the caterers arrive to criticize everything.'

'Big dinner?'

'The Victorians stuffed themselves silly.'

'Great,' Grayle said miserably.

'Vera,' Cindy said, 'those removal men . . .'

'Removal men?'

'Bloody big van. Must be around somewhere.'

'I never seen no van this end.'

'Just that I could really bloody use a van that size, if it's coming back. Got a load of stuff for the bastard stall, held up at Cheltenham station. Thought they might have a spare corner, and if Campbell was already paying them . . .'

446

'They've probably gone round the front. Or using one of the side doors.'

'Possibly. Would you mind if . . . ?'

'You have a look around, if you want,' Vera said.

'Excellent. Stay with Vera, Malcolm.' Cindy crossed to a central door, pushed through, beckoning Grayle.

They were in a low passage with some narrow, cramped stairs. Servants' stairs. A row of small bells on a bracket, for Barnaby Crole to summon the butler.

'Quietly.' Cindy mounted the wooden stairs. 'We just want to know what they're bringing and where they're taking it and then we're out of here.'

'What do you think it's gonna be?'

'The furniture, of course. If I'm right, they want to recreate the room where Persephone Callard was introduced to the essence of Clarence Judge. They want her to do it again, see, under the same conditions. And this time she doesn't walk out on them.'

'They'd go to that kind of trouble? Transport the whole room? But that's so crazy!'

Cindy paused at the top of the stairs, looked over his shoulder. 'Is it?'

'Look . . .' Grayle hung back. 'I don't understand this, Cindy.'

Cindy stood above her in his tweed suit and his straw-blond wig now under a black beret.

'That's because, little Grayle, you are not a fanatic. This is about fanaticism. It's also about ego. Egos big enough to want to survive death. The fanaticism and the egotism of Barnaby Crole and Anthony Abblow and Kurt Campbell and Gary Seward. Huge and cosmic, it is, and yet also so terribly small and sordid.'

And he turned and continued to the top of the stairs.

'What kind of freaking explanation is *that*?' Grayle yelled.

'Oh,' Cindy said.

He looked back down at Grayle. His eyes flashed: *caution*.

Grayle went up slowly and joined him where the stairs came out in a square hallway with rough panelling, blotched with old mould.

Kurt Campbell stood in a doorway watching her emerge.

And Persephone Callard, sleek in black.

45

Maiden watched Harry Douglas Oakley tramp off, with his contentious placard, to join his evangelical guardians on the edge of the festival car park.

It was mid-afternoon. He hadn't eaten since leaving Castle Farm. It had started to snow again, flakes fine as flour dusting the windscreen. A few days ago, when he'd driven into Gloucestershire with Seffi Callard, it had felt like early summer.

He sat for a while in the cold truck, trying to form a steady picture from the confusion. It was like one of those magic-eye pictures, that short-lived fad some years back: find the Rembrandt inside the Jackson Pollock.

In no time at all, thanks to Harry Oakley, he'd established the connection. Fact: the purchase of Overcross Castle was the fruit of a collaboration between Kurt Campbell and Gary Seward, whose interest in spiritualism had become an obsession. Seward's other obsession was his need to find the killer of Clarence Judge – because Clarence was part of Gary's history, his yardstick of hardness. And because it was not safe for whoever killed Clarence to be out there.

Seward's fervent, if irrational, belief that this knowledge could be attained through the employment of a good medium – the *best* medium – had led him to Persephone Callard, ex-girlfriend of Kurt Campbell. To conceal from her the involvement of either of them, they'd set up the Cheltenham seance, using Sir Richard Barber as a front.

Question: if Campbell had been so close to Seffi, why hadn't he just asked her to do the seance, the way he'd asked her to do the Festival of the Spirit? As a favour, presumably.

What was the real relationship between those two? *(i.e. has she betrayed us? Has she betrayed me?)*

Unanswerable. He tried not to think about Emma.

So . . . OK . . . the Cheltenham seance had ended in disarray but what it produced was convincing enough for Seward to target Seffi Callard, to do anything to get her back. Resulting in two killings.

And then there was the Riggs connection.

Maiden pushed his face through his cold hands. It was like a mad, holistic dream, unbreakable strands of his experience twisted into a pulsing, fibrous knot. Perfectly logical to the likes of Cindy, who always looked for great and abstract patterns, the Pollock beyond the Rembrandt.

He wished he could talk to Marcus Bacton, that unique blend of the impressionable and the incisive.

The thought of Marcus made Maiden suddenly so absurdly anxious that he pulled out his mobile and rang Worcester Royal Infirmary. Even while he was being transferred to the ward, he heard a voice in his head asking if he was a relative, then saying, gently but firmly,

I'm afraid Mr Bacton died this morning.

450

His hand was shaking. The snow collected like icing sugar on the rubber wiper blades. He heard the staff nurse answer, heard his own voice identifying himself as Marcus Bacton's nephew, heard the nurse say that Mr Bacton was making satisfactory progress. Heard Seffi Callard, as Em, purring, *Come on, guv, help yourself to the sweet trolley.*

'I'm sorry, sir, did you hear what I said?'

'Would you mind not calling me *sir*?'

'I beg your pardon.'

'I'm sorry.' He was coming to pieces. 'Oh God. Sorry.' Get a grip. 'Would you . . . tell Marcus everything's OK. And we'll be in to see him just as soon as we can.'

'I said, would you like to speak to him?'

'What?'

'Because I think he'd like to speak to *you*.'

'Well, I don't think . . .'

'Hold on a moment, would you? We'll get the phone to Mr Bacton's bedside.'

Damn. He didn't need this now. He knew what he should be doing, what he should have done days ago . . . tell Ron Foxworth everything. You could go mad considering Cindy's shamanic solutions, contemplating Marcus's Big Mysteries, while people were getting killed.

If it were to turn out to be your delicate, artistic fingers on Seward's collar, as distinct from my gnarled old digits, I just can't tell you how upset I would be.

Very sensible. Delicate, artistic fingers weren't equipped to feel collars. He'd call Gloucester police, ask to speak to Mr Foxworth. Report, to begin with, the Bright Horizon connection with Overcross and the festival. Take it from there.

'Maiden?'

'Marcus. How are—?'

'I want you to do something for me.'

'Well, if . . . you know . . . if I can . . .' Maiden said weakly. Marcus didn't sound weak. He didn't sound any different after his heart attack, this big, sobering, life-shrinking experience.

'Maiden, I've just had a schoolboy in a white coat at my bedside offering me drugs. I told him to go and sell them on the street like everyone else. Or, alternatively, shove them up his arse.'

'I see.'

'The kid seems to have called for back-up. So I'm doing the same. Get me the fuck out of here, Maiden. Tonight. All right?'

Marcus cut the line.

Kurt Campbell smiled.

'Looking for me, Alice?' The deep, smoky voice, the voice of a much older man. Like *whole lifetimes* older, Grayle thought.

But Kurt was smiling out of a young hunk's face. That well-washed tawny hair. And, down below, the tight tawny jeans.

'Oh hi,' Grayle said. 'Listen – this is awful; I'm really . . . you know, I'm really not that kind of journalist – but we saw this door open and we just had to take a peek, I mean, this place . . . this place is so awesome. Like, real . . . like Mervyn Peake . . . like Gormenghast, you know? I'm a big . . . big Peake freak. You know? I . . .'

'Alice . . .' Kurt raised a hand to stop the flow. 'You're excused.' Using the hand to introduce the woman at his side. 'This is Persephone Callard, by the way.'

452

Those amber eyes met Grayle's. So she was doing it. Ms Persephone Callard in from the cold to climax a phoney Victorian seance full of dry ice and ectoplasm.

'Oh . . .' Grayle widening her eyes. '*Hi!*' Lurching forward, hand out. 'I'm Alice D. Thornborough, representing the *New York Courier* and *The Vision* magazine. Wow. Hey. Persephone Callard. I can't believe this. You're looking so . . . good.'

Stupid thing to say to someone you weren't supposed to know, but maybe OK for a journalist who'd read all the stuff about Callard being washed up. And she *was* looking good. Looking, in the simplicity of black – the long skirt, the simple, scoop-necked top, no make-up, no jewellery – like the queen of this place.

And she nodded, like a queen does, and she said nothing, like a queen does to journalists.

However – a whole lot worse – Kurt was looking intently at Cindy, like there was something about this tall bottle blonde in the glasses and the country tweeds that he couldn't quite identify. Oh, Jesus.

'Kurt,' Grayle said quickly, 'this is Imelda Bacton, of *The Vision* magazine. She's here to run the magazine's stand in place of her brother, Marcus, who . . .' flicking a swift glance at Callard, '. . . had a heart attack.'

Seeing the quiver, quickly stilled.

'I'm very sorry to hear that,' Callard said steadily. 'I once met Mr Bacton. How is he?' There was shock in her eyes, and Grayle intuited that she was thinking this must have happened the night she brought Clarence Judge into Castle Farm and then ran out on them, that it was her fault.

Which was OK. It might just as easily have happened then.

'Weakened but recovering,' Imelda Bacton said powerfully. 'Needs more than a cardiac blip to take that old bastard out.'

At the sound of the voice, so abruptly different from Cindy's syrupy south Wales, Kurt Campbell visibly relaxed.

'I was showing Seffi to her room. The problem with this place is that it has about twenty-six bedrooms and, so far, less than half of them've been refurbished. It's an ongoing operation, this house.'

'Like the Forth Bridge, I imagine.' Cindy gazed up at the ceiling from which paper hung in shreds. 'You must've spent hundreds of thousands on this place already. What the hell possessed you to take it on, Mr Campbell?'

'I like challenges,' Kurt said. Grayle saw that he now had no interest at all in Imelda Bacton – too old to screw and probably a royal pain in the ass. 'Look, Alice . . . I'd like a word with you. If you want to wait in the main hall – that's just along this passage – I'll be down in ten minutes. That's next to the main door, so if Miss Backley wants to get back to her stand, that's the quickest way.'

'Well,' Cindy murmured as Campbell followed Callard through a Gothic-shaped doorway with no door, 'that's me in my place, isn't it? We have two options, little Grayle. One, I stay with you and Kurt gets suddenly called away again. Two, I disappear.'

'Has to be two, I guess. We're lucky he didn't spot who you really are.'

'I was careful to keep looking away from him. A hypnotist always recognizes your eyes. Grayle, the more I think about this, a third option might be wiser – we both disappear.'

'No, I'm gonna wait for him. See this through.'

They walked to the end of the passage and when they came out at the other end the architecture appeared to have shed about six centuries. They were in the main entrance hall and you could see this was where most of the money had gone so far. It was the full baronial: a stone staircase, high stone walls with coats of arms and crossed pikes and deerheads on shields and a gigantic wrought-iron chandelier with flickering electric candles.

Not quite tacky, not quite tasteful. More filmset than authentic haunted house. There were five or six people waiting around. Two wore suits, carried brief-cases. One was leaning against a wall by the stairs, talking down a cellphone. Overhead, a black heating outlet pumped out warm air.

There was a big reception desk with wrought-iron legs, three phones on top. Next to a woman with glasses on a chain sat one of the Forcefield guys, looking half-cop, half-paramilitary and wholly bored. A noticeboard leaning up against the desk advertised festival events including an illustrated lecture on Friday evening by the authors of *The Golgotha Manuscript: the Truth about the Crucifixion* and a session by Ronan Blaine, the revered hands-on healer from Ireland.

'This is the real thing, isn't it?' Grayle said des-pondently. 'It isn't a front for anything. It's gonna build up year by year, become an institution and make piles of money. Turning Kurt into some kind of New Age Bill Gates.'

The original Victorian Gothic castle door, twelve feet high, hung open. A smoked-glass conservatory had been built on the front, and there were people sitting at tables with computers, selling tickets to events like the Golgotha guys. New Age big business. Exploitation of the seekers after truth.

Grayle suddenly felt angry.

'We're wasting our time. If Campbell has anything to hide, he's got a million places here to hide it. And Callard's looking all cool and distant and fully in control.'

'I wonder how.'

'Hypnotherapy?'

'Grayle . . . ?'

'Anyhow, not our problem. I don't even know what we're doing here any more, now Marcus isn't part of it. In fact, unless Bobby has anything meaningful to tell us, I say we close up the stupid stall, go over to Worcester, try to cheer Marcus up and tomorrow we don't come back. Marcus is our problem now.'

'Hmmm.'

Cindy was standing looking up the stone stairs. A window on the landing was long and churchy, with stained glass depicting two knights in armour. The guy leaning up against the wall by the stairs put away his cellphone and walked off smiling, and Grayle half-recognized him from someplace. He was in baggy jeans and a grey polo shirt with a short row of black battlements and Overcross Castle printed on the pocket.

'The notorious Gary Seward, as I live and breathe,' Cindy said mildly.

'Oh, shit, you're right!'

'Don't *look*, child. Might be as well if he didn't remember us.'

'Are we sure it's him?'

'A few more lines than the face on the cover of the book, a little less hair, a little more jowl. So unless he has a slightly older brother . . .'

'Shit, we gotta tell Bobby.'

'It doesn't *prove* a meaningful link, him simply being here.'

'The fuck it doesn't!'

It was like a psychic experience. The manifestation of Seward by the stairs changed everything – made the great hall darker, full of shadows, turned the electric candles in the iron chandelier from sparkling orange to a menacing blood-red.

Cindy appeared unmoved, squinting out through the conservatory. 'No sign of the furniture.'

She remembered what Cindy had said before they met Campbell and Callard. About egos and survival. *Huge and cosmic, it is, and yet also so terribly small and sordid.* She looked up at the window and the walls and decided she really hated Victorian Gothic. She needed fresh, cold air and trees and sky. She pushed her hands into her raincoat pockets, kept her eyes fixed on the stairs.

Cindy said, 'I wonder if Miss Callard knows what she's really here for.'

'You mean you *do*?'

. . . yet also so terribly small and sordid.

Grayle saw Kurt Campbell come around the landing and start descending the stone stairs. 'You were right,' she said. 'We shoulda gone while we had the chance.'

Arriving back at *The Vision*'s stall, Bobby Maiden found it deserted. A few copies of the magazine had been blown away and were stuck in the mud, pages fluttering miserably like seagulls in an oilslick.

'I've been trying to keep an eye on it,' a woman called from the next tent. 'I don't know where they've gone.'

The sign on this tent said,

Lorna Crane, Etheric Massage.

Lorna was fiftyish and fit-looking. She had close-cut red hair and lip rings. She wore apple-green sweats.

'They – is it your wife and her mother? – they went off with the dog, must be nearly an hour ago. I mean, I can understand them not wanting to hang around here. We'll do bugger-all business if the weather doesn't improve. Bloody stupid idea starting midweek, this time of year, but if you're getting four days for your money you think it's worth it, don't you? You want a cup of tea, love? I've got a big flask inside.'

'Oh. Thanks.' Maiden followed her into the tent, which was bigger than *The Vision*'s, better carpeted inside. There was a table with leaflets on it, a couch covered with Mexican blankets, a Calorgas heater. The polythene window was tinted red, putting a warm blush on the canvas walls.

Lorna Crane said, 'Buggered if I'm forking out what they're asking for a cup of tea in the restaurant. You been in there? Ridiculous! And we're expected to pay the same as the *punters*. Ye gods, the stall fees were enough, they never told us there were gonna be surcharges and overheads.'

'Market forces.'

'*Dark* forces. I never liked the look of Campbell.' Lorna grinned. 'I'm quite fond of *The Vision*. It's quirky. What do you do?'

'Take pictures.'

'They pay you?'

'Sometimes.'

'That older woman,' Lorna said. 'You know, for a

minute, I thought that was Cindy Mars-Lewis. Because he did used to write articles for you, didn't he?'

'Cindy Mars-Lewis is my mother-in-law? No wonder I never have any luck.'

'It's a load of crap, isn't it?' Lorna said. 'All that Lottery hoodoo. Papers must be desperate for something to write about.' She poured tea from a chrome flask into two white china mugs. 'It's Earl Grey. Got no milk or sugar, I'm afraid.'

'That's fine.'

Lorna handed him a mug. 'Not your mother-in-law then?'

'A friend.'

Maiden sipped his scented tea. He felt reality receding again. The police at Gloucester were saying simply that Superintendent Foxworth was unavailable. They'd offered to put him through to someone else. He'd asked when Foxworth *would* be available. They couldn't tell him. He assumed there'd been a development on one of the two murder inquiries. But what development?

'What's etheric massage?'

'I work with the aura. Healing and relaxation. Does it work? Yeah, course it works. Sometimes. Can I see auras? Too bloody right, and it isn't always a blessing, when you look at people and see they haven't got long.'

'Can you see mine?'

'Yep.' She bit off the word, held out a packet. 'Ginger biscuit?'

'Thanks.'

'You're hungry. Take two.'

'What do you charge?' Maiden asked.

'When I'm working, twenty-plus for fifteen minutes.

459

'I'm not doing you, though, you'll never relax long enough. I'll just give you some advice. Stop thinking about it, you'll not work it all out on your own. Go home. Lock the door. Go to bed.'

'What will I not work out?'

'I dunno. Seriously, go home.'

'What colour is it? My aura.'

Lorna shook her head.

A voice outside shouted, 'Hello?'

'Sounds like it's from your place,' Lorna said. 'Could be a wholesale newsagent wants to place an order for ten thousand copies a month.'

Maiden handed her his cup, stuck his head outside the tent.

'Excuse me, sir . . .' One of the Forcefield men, standing by the fallen *Visions*. 'The little blonde American lady? You with her?'

'What's wrong?'

'You might want to come with me, sir.' Big, stolid-looking bloke, greying beard. 'She's had a bit of an accident, nothing to worry about.'

'Accident?' Maiden stumbled out.

'She's just over in the first-aid tent.'

'Where's that?'

'This way, sir.'

He led Maiden around the side of the toilet block, where a second Forcefield man was peering non-chalantly at the grass around his boots. He looked up when Bobby Maiden appeared.

'Shit,' Maiden said.

The bearded man hit him in the gut. As Maiden doubled up, the other man hit him in the face. At the same time, Maiden felt a foot pulled from under him.

He was lying, hurting, with his face in the cold mud.

He couldn't move; there was a heavy boot on his neck. Something which felt both hard and sharp, like an axe, went agonizingly into his back.

He felt very cold. *I've been stabbed*, he thought. *I'm going to die.*

It was as quick as that.

46

'You wanted to look around,' Kurt wore a baggy, collarless shirt – snow-white but creased up, to show how loose and expansive he was, 'so I'm going to show you around.'

'You sure you can spare the time?'

'Hey, I'm touring the States in the summer. A little advance publicity in the *New York Courier* will do no harm at all.'

Cindy had melted away as Kurt approached. Kurt acting like this was to be expected – what did he need with an old broad?

'Well, I'll sure do my best to get you some space,' Grayle lied.

'Yes, Alice, I'm sure you'll try your hardest for me.'

Overcross Castle, when you'd been inside a while, was full of give-aways that it wasn't awfully historic. One was the efficiency with which the rooms had been linked – no poky dead-end passageways, everything fitted and dovetailed. Kurt led her into a huge oblong room to the right of the entrance hall. It also had bare stone walls and two big wrought-iron chandeliers over an oak table, which looked to be thirty or forty feet long, or maybe it was two tables pushed together.

There were also sconces, real ones in iron brackets, which could be lit to send real flames leaping up the walls.

'The banqueting hall.' The heavy door closing behind them with a *thunk-click* which spoke of post-Victorian craftsmanship. 'Now this is exactly how it was in the 1870s. The medieval touch. This is where Daniel Dunglas-Home often appeared.'

'The medium? What sort of things did he do here?'

'Oh . . . summoned endless spirits, obviously.' Kurt sounding surprisingly dismissive. 'Sometimes with manifestation. And on one occasion it was said he levitated from a table, almost reaching the chandeliers. Enterprising guy.'

'Wow. These chandeliers?'

'Similar ones. There were about ten people here at the time – invited guests, like tonight – and several of them swore they'd seen it happen. But some others said that, as far as they were concerned, it had never taken place at all.'

It had begun to get dark outside now. The two Gothic windows were grey-white and there were no colours in the room. Kurt leaned closer to Grayle. His aftershave was subtly suggestive, like a snuffed-out bedside candle.

'So which do you believe?' Grayle asked, like she was supposed to.

'Ah. Well. Interestingly, Dr Anthony Abblow was here that night. A medium and also a very powerful hypnotist. For his time.'

'Oh, really.'

'People sometimes see what, under hypnosis, they're persuaded to.'

'I don't understand.'

463

'Neither do I, Alice. Were some of the guests persuaded to see Dunglas-Home levitate? Or – hey – were some persuaded *not* to?'

'I'm sorry?'

'You read the little book?'

'Sure.'

'It says there that Abblow was responsible for discrediting Dunglas-Home in Crole's eyes, right? Presumably so he could replace him, so that he could become the key man at Overcross, have access to Crole's millions, yeah?'

'Oh. Right. I get it. You're saying, did Abblow hypnotize some of the guests beforehand to blank out Home's act or something?'

'Makes you think doesn't it, Alice?'

'I guess.'

'So guess who our medium's going to be tonight.'

'Well, uh, I just met Persephone Callard. So unless you hypnotized me to like see her when she wasn't there at all . . .'

'Oh she was there, all right.' Kurt grinned. 'But tonight's star is going to be Dunglas-Home himself. Come on. I'll show you the rest of this mausoleum.'

Grayle tightened the belt of her raincoat. *Here we go.*

When Gary Seward left the castle by the main entrance, Cindy followed him. Remaining fifteen to twenty yards behind, studying the man, the way he moved, the art of *being* Gary Seward.

From up here you could see that the festival site was bigger than it had first appeared, covering fifteen to twenty acres. Quite a crowd out there now too, despite the weather – an advance contingent for the psychically ravenous multitude. By the weekend, there would be ten, fifteen times as many, thousands having travelled from Birmingham, even London, to catch talks or a promised visit by fashionable psychics and healers.

Seward walked down the drive towards the three lines of huts and tents, each one a bijou business marketing baubles and trinkets of spirituality like fashion accessories, to be worn and discarded, mixed and matched.

Cindy felt more in control. Had begun to build a picture of what was happening here – even if, as yet, it consisted only of darkening smudges.

Seeing Kurt Campbell up close, for the first time since the unfortunate Lottery Show encounter, he realized that bitter circumstance had led him to overestimate the young man. Apart from ambition, greed, lust and the mastery of a particular technique, there really wasn't all that much to Kurt. Not a profound person, not even a terribly interesting one. His failure to spot the Cindy behind the Imelda suggested that Cindy was, to Kurt, not so much a figure of hate and fear but a mere obstacle to be removed. Hardly flattering – indicative, indeed, of insufficient respect for the shamanic tradition – but at least it reduced Kurt Campbell to something potentially more manageable. And it was to be hoped that the resourceful Grayle would be able to manage him.

Seward, however, was more complex.

Taller than he looked, he was, close to six feet. Excess weight gave him a stocky appearance, and he moved heavily but confidently. As though – Cindy smiled – he owned the place.

Seward was in no hurry. He seemed aimless, in fact,

as though he had time to kill, had left the house for no purpose other than to be out of it for a while.

Cindy kept his distance, always mindful of what the man was known to have done – or have *had* done – to various people. Which, as he admitted at one point in his book, was not the half of it.

Cindy noted how, rather than enter the compound through the turnstiles, Seward braced himself then jumped the barrier, smiling as he landed. This implied two things: that the ageing hard man was proving to himself that he could 'still do it'. And that barriers, in his view, were for ordinary people. Despite the intermittent fine snow, he was not wearing a jacket over his polo shirt, so perhaps his smile was more in the nature of a grimace.

Through the turnstile went Cindy, displaying his stallholder's pass, watching Seward inspect various displays, but not part with any money. No-one seemed to recognize him, which he would find annoying.

The autobiography was buoyant with bonhomie and heavy-handed attempts at humour – made slicker, perhaps, by the former *News of the World* journalist who had ghosted the book. But Cindy could tell now, simply by the way he moved, that Gary Seward was a more ponderous character than the prose suggested – essentially a dogmatic man, with a fixed code of immorality detectable in his repetition of the phrase *I could not tolerate* . . .

A combination of the rigidly self-righteous and the constant need to break rules, jump barriers, was perhaps the essence of Gary Seward. Whichever way he jumped would afterwards be seen to have been the *right* way.

Seward at last went into a tent. One of the larger

ones. The book tent in fact. Cindy waited. In less than three minutes Seward was out again and Cindy was able, for the first time, to study his face.

Which would have been quite handsome but for the thickness of the lips, the way the mouth turned down at the corners, emphasizing the radials astride the nose. Perhaps this was why he smiled so much – he didn't like the way his mouth turned down, thought perhaps that it made him look a little sulky, not so cheerful and accommodating.

Gary certainly wasn't smiling now. Incredible! Had he really imagined that a New Age bookshop, specializing in healing and transcendence, would have copies of *Bang to Wrongs*?

Seward looked up when a vehicle horn bipped rapidly, twice. A dark blue van, like a police van, had stopped at the bottom of Avenue Three. Seward looked up, walked across and opened the passenger door. He bent to enter then pulled back. He leaned on the door and turned his head slowly, his gaze panning the assembly.

Until it came to rest on Cindy. Who froze.

Whereupon Gary Seward's face crinkled into the most carnivorous smile, with a wild glimmering of gold.

All the breath went out of Cindy.

He knew I was there. The whole time.

Seward waited until the van began to move before waving gaily to Cindy and swinging smoothly, in his *I can still do it* way, into the passenger seat. The van went out through the gates and Cindy – shaken now, worried – returned to the castle kitchens to retrieve Malcolm from Vera.

*　　*　　*

467

'. . . *show you the rest of this mausoleum.*'

Except it wasn't going to be the rest of it.

His hands either side of Grayle's waist, Kurt propelled her smoothly through a door into a low-lit room, where there was an electrical hum in the air and a small guy with glasses was messing around at what looked like a recording-studio mixing desk.

'How goes it, Darren?' Kurt asked breezily.

The guy gave him a nonchalant thumbs-up and Grayle asked what was happening here, knowing he must be in charge of the special effects Cindy had mentioned. But Kurt just said, 'Ambience', and manoeuvred her across the room and out through an archway on the other side.

'What's through here?' Grayle asked brightly, suppressing nerves.

'The most interesting part,' Kurt said.

Then they were through another door, to the left, and going up a small, extremely dark, spiralling stone staircase – this place was a warren of stairs – and up and up, scores of stairs, twisting and twisting, Kurt just behind Grayle, and she could hear him flicking switches to put on lights ahead of them – tiny lights set deep into the stone – and, Jesus, for the first time you could really start to believe this was a purpose-built haunted house.

And as she climbed, raincoat flapping, the backs of her legs starting to ache, she was thinking hard about what Kurt Campbell had just told her about the master-medium, Daniel Dunglas-Home, and Anthony Abblow, a man whom Cindy had seemed to compare with Kurt. The use of hypnosis to create or remove the illusion of psychic phenomena. Had Abblow done that? It didn't matter.

It didn't freaking *matter*. It was *now* that mattered ... and Abblow's evident influence on Kurt Campbell.

Grayle paused to get her breath, looking over her shoulder at Kurt's big face with the blond hair flying back.

'Look, I, uh, I'm getting kinda dizzy, you know? Where are we ... where is this ... ?'

'Not far now, Alice.'

They must be in the big tower, the big, fat, dark tower which reared over Avenue Three. The Gormenghast tower.

'Must be, uh ... some view from the top of here, huh, Kurt?'

'Some view,' Kurt agreed.

And then they were out on what surely must be the final landing, a very short, rounded landing with an electric lantern high up. Doors in stone alcoves to either side.

Now Kurt was beside her, a big, tight-trousered presence, a whole head taller than Grayle and his arm around her waist, a little tighter now, like he was supporting them both, still laughing at their exertions. Though clearly he was less out of breath than she was, must have done these stairs many times. Behind many different people.

Usually female, no doubt.

Kurt steered her into one of the alcoves, reached in front of her with a classic castle-type key – about the size of a can opener, black and gleaming – pushing it into a hole in this squat, Gothic door of solid, seasoned oak, waggling it about a little before it turned. Symbolic.

And then they were – wouldn't you know it? – in this bedroom.

469

Well, it wasn't like she hadn't been here before. Occupational hazard for young female journalists. Especially, it had turned out, for one specializing in the spiritual. They all tried to set you up: tantric therapists, from whom you expected it, and pot-bellied 'celibate' swamis, from whom . . . anyway, you learned how to deal with it. It seldom ran to attempted rape.

In the room the last of the stormy light had collected through a small square window in the rounded wall. There was a giant four-poster and a dresser with a small tray on it with whisky and, inevitably, a champagne bottle and glasses.

No closet; this was the kind of medieval bedchamber where clothing was left strewn across the polished, oak-boarded floor, abandoned in passion.

'Must have been a hell of a job getting that bed up here,' Grayle said. 'Does it come apart?'

'I wouldn't know,' Kurt said.

Locking the door behind them.

Sliding the long key into his hip pocket, where it made a matching bulge to the one the other side.

'You know, I think we need a rest after that,' Kurt said lazily.

Aw, for heaven's *sake* . . . this was like Justin level, God rest his greased-up soul.

Kurt crossed to the bed, slid through the curtains, which did not draw all the way, were just there for effect. Eased himself up, with his back against the big, dark headboard.

Grayle stood by the snow-speckled window, with this sheer seventy – eighty, ninety, a hundred, who-knew-how-many – foot drop to the stone parapet around the castle.

'Oh well.' She pulled open the belt, shrugged out of her raincoat. 'You want I should pour the drinks?'

47

'No fooling you, Vera, I can see that.' Cindy peered through the scullery window into a yard with a broken-down wall and, beyond that, outbuildings of brick and stone – a barn, stables – and the wooded hillside.

'No bloody patronizing me, neither, dear.' Vera wiping her hands on her white apron. 'What's going on? What you been up to, Miss Bacton?'

No real escape route through the back. Only hiding places. The real hiding place would be a change of persona. Imelda had been rumbled. The consequences, given Gary's background, were not to be contemplated.

'I believe I have offended the organizers, Vera. Complaining about the situation of the stall, demanding money back, causing unrest among the other stallholders. I think they plan to . . . invite me to leave.'

Which, he supposed, was the most innocent possible interpretation of Gary Seward's wild smile.

'It ain't a police state,' Vera said. 'For all it looks like one, with all these geezers in uniform. They can't just throw you out.'

'They will manufacture a pretext, Vera.'

'So that's why you're in hiding, is it? I ain't too bright, but I can't believe that.'

'I'm sorry.' Cindy looked frankly into Vera's plump, olive-skinned face; an intelligent woman cast into the lowliest of employment situations on some miserable pittance, for the crime of being widowed. 'I didn't want to compromise your position here.'

'*Position?* Don't make me laugh.'

'Vera, how much do you know about your employers?'

'I never even seen my employers. I hear about this festival coming off, walk into that conservatory place where all the admin people are getting it together. I says, you got any jobs going, and this woman grabs hold of me, brung me down the kitchens – looks like a flaming bombsite – and she says, Here, can you do anything with that? So I rolls up me sleeves, works me knees off, fourteen hours non-stop, and I got me a job. That's how you always got jobs in my day.'

'You came all the way from London?'

'I'm not *that* daft. Nah, lived up here for years now. My late husband, he was a Brummie.'

'So you know nothing about the people running this show.'

Cindy was aware that he'd slipped back, near enough, into his normal voice. The shock of being rumbled, he supposed.

'No, dear.' Vera shook her head, opened the scullery door a crack, peered through at the bustle of the caterers preparing a sumptuous, Victorian banquet for the Mayor of Malvern, the MP for Worcester and so on. Closed the door quietly. 'But it sounds like you do. So if you want any more out of me, Miss Bacton, you better come clean, you had.'

'Clean?' Cindy slumped in an unsteady farmhouse chair. The dog, Malcolm, sat as still as a bollard on the flagged floor. 'All right,' he said. 'Consider me an investigative journalist. Consider the *Vision* stall as something of a front, a cover. And your employers . . . consider them under investigation.'

'What for?'

'Let's call it fraud. Misrepresentation. Vera, would you perhaps be amenable to assisting me a little tonight? My movements appear to be a trifle restricted at present. I could make it worth your while . . . in due course.'

'Worth me while? What do you think I am, a prostitute?'

'I didn't mean—'

'All right, listen. I'm not daft, and yeah, I do keep my eyes open. I been making breakfasts for people the past two days, been seeing who's who around here. I seen that geezer always smiling, doing his little laugh and I'm thinking, where've I seen *him* before? On the telly? Played a gangster, some'ing like that? And then I realize . . .'

'Ah.'

'Ain't life strange,' Vera said. 'When I was fifteen I worked in the biscuit factory at Bow, and I had a mate called Paula what went out with a boy called Gary Seward.'

'It's a small world.'

'Not that small. He was putting it about all over east London. She only went out with him twice, mind. Took her to the pictures and when they wouldn't let him in for nothing, he slashed two full rows of seats on the way out.'

'Could not tolerate it,' Cindy mused.

'But that wasn't the reason she didn't go out with him again. It was just she found out he was only thirteen.'

'Heavens.'

'See, his mother died. They'd moved up from the country when he was little. And then his ma got killed in an accident when he was twelve, and he went wild after that, apparently. Nobody could control him.'

'And what is his position here, Vera?'

'Boss man, ain't he? Wouldn't do nothing without he was the boss, would he? They're all terrified of him, for all he's supposed to be straight these days. Course, when he first heard my accent – this is Gary – he made me sit down, gives me a glass of champagne. *Very* friendly. Old East Enders together. I didn't say nothing about Paula, mind.'

'And did he tell you why he was here?'

'He *said*', Vera smiled, more than a trifle cynically, 'that he was Tired of Earthly Concerns.'

'There's spiritual.'

'Tell *that* to the bleeding troops,' said Vera. 'I tell you, Cindy . . . it *is* Cindy, isn't it?'

Cindy smiled weakly.

'Yeah, I thought so. It was the voice done it. I never bought a Lottery ticket in me life, but I always watch the show. Very amusing, you and that bird.' Vera paused meaningfully. 'It's you and him, ain't it? Kurt Campbell. We all saw that bust up you had on the box. Made him look an idiot and he didn't like that. Has he got back at you in some way and now you're getting back at him?'

'I'm really not in a great position to get back at anybody, am I?'

'Seems not. They're all after you now.'

475

'So I imagine.'

'In hiding, eh? I reckon some papers would pay a fair bit to know where you are.'

'A price on my head, is it? I feel like Butch Cassidy. Except, possibly, for the butch part. So . . . what do you propose to do about this opportunity, Vera?'

'Puts me in a funny position, don't it?'

Outside, the snow had stopped, but the fingers of dusk were feeling through the wooded hill behind Overcross. It would be dark in under half an hour.

'I'll make a bargain with you,' Cindy said. 'I'm told I can command a substantial sum for my . . . story. Far far more than anyone could expect for shopping me. Split it with you, I will. Whatever it amounts to. Fetch me pen and paper and I will put that in writing.'

Vera looked at him for a moment and then laughed hugely, clapping her hands to her apron. '*I* don't want your money. I'll have a kiss from that bloody Kelvyn Kite. You tell me what I can do to help.'

'I won't forget this, Vera.'

'Go on! Get on with it!'

'Well, to begin with, I should be most interested to know what happened to the furniture brought here from Cheltenham.'

'Can't help you there. Never seen no furniture. I could try and find out.'

'If you could.'

'Anything else?'

'If I . . . have to go away for a while . . . would you look after my dog?'

'Blimey. Sounds like you think you might not be coming back.'

Cindy laughed.

'I got to work later on,' Vera said. 'Bloody wait-

476

ressing. One of the girls fell down six stairs, twisted her ankle. Muggins got volunteered. If I shut the dog in here with some water and scraps, will he be all right?'

'He has a stoical temperament.' Cindy had taken off the wig concealing the mauve hair, unbuttoned the tweed jacket to reveal the purple woolly.

'There you are, see,' Vera said. 'You were underneath all along. That furniture you're looking for, where would it most likely be? Not something you could easily miss, is it?'

'What about the room where the seance is to take place?'

'No way, dear. Just the big dinner tables, lots of chairs. They won't get nothing else in there now and they'll be starting dinner in an hour.'

'Mr Seward is not on the guest list, then.'

'No way.'

'But definitely Miss Callard.'

'This is the coloured lady?'

'The medium. The one who is to conduct the seance.'

'Nah, you're wrong,' Vera said. 'It's some geezer.'

'I don't think so, Vera.'

'I'm telling you, there's no place been laid for a Callard. Just this . . . Oh, blimey . . . same name as the old Prime Minister. Douglas-Home?'

'*Dunglas*-Home?' Cindy stared at her. '*Daniel* Dunglas-Home? Vera, he's been dead since 1886.'

'Well, all I know is, they've made him a little sign thing for his place at the dinner table.'

'Damn.'

This meant, of course, an actor was playing the part of Dunglas-Home. It meant the *whole* thing was a fake. An illusion. Undisguised trickery.

477

So what on earth was Persephone Callard's part in this? Wasn't going to be in the audience, that was for sure.

An explicit dread seized Cindy.

Of *course*.

There would be two seances tonight. One a sideshow, a costume drama, a parody.

The other – with Seward and Miss Callard – would be the business.

'Vera . . .' When Cindy arose, his legs felt weak. 'One more thing. Would you happen to know which room Persephone Callard is occupying?'

'That's easy,' Vera said. 'Room Three. First landing, turn left.'

'Thank you.'

48

'No,' Grayle said. 'Don't put the light on.'

'Hey . . . you can't be embarrassed, surely. Nobody's embarrassed any more. You're from *New York*, for Christ's sake.'

'I just don't like artificial light, is all.'

On account of, in the light, we can see into each other's eyes, and I don't like what I understand you can do with yours. I don't wanna wake up, if you don't mind, to a snap of the fingers and semen running down my inner thighs.

She sat on the edge of the four-poster bed with her glass of champagne. So far, only her raincoat had come off. Not the jeans, not the baseball sweater.

'Kurt, can we talk?'

'I don't . . .' He gave this kind of exasperated sigh. '*I* don't want to talk. I didn't come up all those stairs for a fucking *light conversation*. Alice, I thought you were *up* for this.'

Grayle looked at the stiff shadow and laughed. 'You big stars, you're so goddamn *presumptuous*.'

Kurt laughed too, softly. 'Hey,' he whispered, 'Alice, I wanted you from the moment you came into my hotel suite last night. You're not the consolation prize,

479

you're my very special present and I would very much like to . . . unwrap you . . .' His hands were on her shoulders now, lips close to her ear. 'Snip the string, peel off the giftwrap, slip my fingers through the tissue-paper . . .'

'Uh-huh.' She stood up, at the same time picking up the champagne bottle.

'Christ, Alice, come *on* . . . what's the matter with you?'

'I have another question.'

'What?' Angry.

OK, here we go . . .

'Down in the banqueting hall just now, when you were talking about Anthony Abblow and Dunglas-Home, you said how people could be hypnotized to see or not see a ghost, right?'

'You want to discuss fucking *ghosts*?'

'Did you ever do that?'

Grayle moved slowly round the bed. Up from the festival site, way below, floated the windy rhythms of an Andean-type band. Through the window you could see lights coming on, on the fringe of the site.

Kurt said, 'Alice, what are you talking about?'

Her foot touched Kurt's pants, on the floor where he'd tossed them. She bent down slowly, keeping the champagne bottle from clinking on the boards.

'Did you ever hypnotize somebody to see a ghost?'

Feeling for the pocket where he'd put the key. A key that size, it should be . . .

'I really don't know what you're talking about, Alice.'

'Well, like . . .' she was being real quiet, in case a bunch of coins or something spilled out '. . . like you could say to someone – under hypnosis – you could

480

plant some kind of auto-suggestion thing, so that every time they came into certain circumstances, like they entered a particular room or something, it would be there, this ghost. And it'd keep happening to them. Scaring the shit out of them. Until you hypnotized them again and took it away.'

'It wouldn't work,' Kurt said. 'You can't make someone do something that would be repugnant to them or see something terrifying they wouldn't normally believe in.'

'But suppose they were the kind of person who . . .' scrabbling at the pants. Got to be in a pocket. *Got* to '. . . who would not be that scared. Who would not think it was so weird . . .'

'Like a medium,' Kurt said.

'I guess.'

'You guess.'

The light blinded her. She dropped the pants.

Kurt Campbell was sitting up on the bed. He wasn't smiling. He wasn't erect. When she was through blinking she saw that the long key lay on the coverlet between his legs.

'Uh . . . right.' She breathed quickly in and out. 'OK, Kurt, here's what's gonna happen. You . . . are gonna toss me that key. You're gonna stay right there on that bed. And I'm gonna unlock the door.'

'Really.'

'Uh huh. In return for this consideration and in light of me perhaps failing to make it sufficiently clear that you were not gonna get laid, I will formally undertake not to write about any of this in the *New York Courier* or any other publication. Or indeed my diary. Hell, Kurt, I will forget about it.'

'You really don't need me, do you?'

'Kurt, in other circumstances, who can say—'

'Because you've just fucked yourself very nicely, haven't you, Grayle?'

Silence. The Andean band had stopped. There was no audible applause, just the wind whipping the window.

'What . . . what did you call me?'

Kurt said, 'Gary recognized you at once.'

'What . . . whaddaya mean?' She backed up against the door. 'Who's Gary? I don't know any Gary.'

'He and a friend were visiting Seffi at Mysleton Lodge one night. You apparently became quite hysterical. Overreacted.'

Oh no. She saw the eyes through the holes in the hood, heard the cold voice, *You . . . are dead*. A numbness began to eat in. *Oh, please God, no*.

'Naturally, he made a point of finding out who you were. But as he didn't get any further than your name and the fact that you were American, it was quite a stroke of luck you turning up here.'

'Oh . . .' Felt like she was going to vomit. 'Oh, dear God.'

'Gary was going to have a chat with you earlier on, but I said, "Gary, the woman's been driving me potty. I've just . . . I've really got to shag her, you know?" Gary was fine about that. He says, "OK, you've got two hours."'

She closed her eyes. She couldn't think.

'You could've been so much less tense by now, you silly bitch. Afterwards, I'd have relaxed you. It could all have been so much easier for you.'

Grayle found that she was still holding the champagne bottle. She lifted it, hefted it like an axe.

'OK. Either you give me that key . . .' her hand was

482

trembling; the bottle was almost full, champagne glug-
ging out, splashing on the floor. 'Or I hurl this through
the window.'

'So?'

'Everybody's gonna hear it. Everybody down there.'

'No, they aren't.'

'Or I'll smash it against the wall and I'll . . . I'll cut
you up.'

'No, you won't.'

'Yeah, I will.' *Don't look at his eyes.* 'I damn well
will. You . . . you better believe that, you asshole.'

'OK,' Kurt said lightly. He picked up the key and
tossed it to her. It fell at her feet. 'There you go.'

'All *right*.' She bent down, still clutching the bottle.
Maybe he was thinking about what she'd done that
night with the hedge hacker, what she could do to his
pretty TV face with a broken bottle. She snatched up
the key, poked around for the lock, glancing back at
him on the bed, but not at his eyes.

He didn't move. He just looked disappointed,
cheated.

She found the keyhole. The key turned at once.

'And don't you come after me, you hear?'

'Christ,' Kurt said, 'what do you think I am?'

And she turned the door handle, and she was out of
there on to the little landing, panting with a mixture of
fear and elation.

OK . . . so what she'd do, she'd go right down the
stairs, but at the bottom of the tower she'd turn
the other direction, away from the banqueting hall
and the entrance hall; what she had to do was find the
kitchen where that nice woman Vera was and maybe
Cindy, also; or she'd get out the back way and if she
couldn't find Cindy or Bobby, she'd avoid the truck

483

and get over a wall, run to a cottage or a farm-house, and she'd call the cops, no messing around this time. *So terribly small and sordid.* Cindy was right. And Kurt, he was mixing out of his league; Kurt was no killer, but he'd downshifted, gotten involved, maybe out of greed, with people for whom killing was a small thing, a tidying up.

Grayle hurried on to the spiral staircase and went down three steps, and then stopped, in sick dismay, the stomach bile really rising into her throat this time.

Two of them.

Just like at Mysleton Lodge, only this time they were in uniform.

And not cops.

Part Seven

From *Bang to Wrongs: A Bad Boy's Book*,
by GARY SEWARD

I done all right.

That's what I always say. I mean, nobody, no matter how they spent their life, is going to say I done all wrong, are they? I've robbed people and I've hurt people, but most of the people I've robbed, well, they had it to spare, didn't they? And most of the people I hurt, they done things what could not be tolerated in a civilized society, in terms of being too cocky and grassing up straight villains and whatnot. All you need to understand is that our world is a rigid and conservative world and we never got around to banning corporal punishment nor, indeed, the Final Deterrent.

Now, I don't want to give you all that Frank Sinatra stuff, but it's true. I done it my way. You'll never hear me bleating, Oh, it's my social background, I was abused as a child and all that old toffee. Everything I done was considered and decided on, and that's the way it will always be.

I suppose that's why death still bothers me a bit. 'Cos you lose control, don't you? I really hate the thought of losing control, and if anything keeps me awake at night it's that.

I just cannot bleeding tolerate the thought of losing control.

49

They were never very rough with her, but when she overcame her initial fear and became frantic and garrulous and started bouncing questions off of them ('How many of you guys *are* there here? Is this your full-time job, or are you just on a retainer for special events? Is it a good organization to work for, Forcefield? Are there fringe benefits? Do you get over-time for this?') they taped her mouth.

The bastards taped her freaking mouth!

Using this stuff about two and a half inches wide, so it covered from her chin to her nose, and she guessed she recognized it from someplace deep in the Cotswolds, and when the bile rose again she was convinced she was going to choke to death on it, on her own puke, a sad, disgusting death.

All this time they were using thinner stuff – electrical tape from a roll, ripping it out and biting it off – to secure her hands, wrist to wrist, tight and chafing behind her back.

This was after they'd all come down the stairs, one in front of her, one behind, and, ironically, had turned exactly the way she'd been aiming to go, and the building was dumping whole centuries again, switching from medieval Gothic to dingy early-twentieth-century industrial.

And then they put a bag over her head.

Which was just so disgusting – slimed and smelling of someone else's sweat and clinging to her face, getting sucked in – that she could hardly breathe and could only make this high-pitched puppy whine in the back of her throat.

All of this happening within a hundred yards of the gentle New Age fiesta, folk discussing the journeys of the soul, to the floating woodwinds of the Andean band. Overlaid in her head by the voice she now knew to be Gary Seward's, coming at the end of a long, awful, blood-misted silence and flat with cold certainty. *You . . . are dead.*

Stumbling, tripping over her own feet, a big hand in the centre of her back, blackness in her eyes. The sounds of doors being opened but no voices; wherever they were headed, people seldom came this way, least-ways not people who might be moved to question the sight of a trussed woman dragged along by two big men dressed like paracops. She tried to bring up a picture of these two men's faces; one had a beard, this was all she could recall.

And then she knew, by the coldness of her bound-up hands and the sound of the wind through the bag, that they were outside, and she recalled horror stories of IRA executions, the hood over the head, the moment of silence before the bullet through the brain, and she suddenly wanted to pee very badly.

A door creaked. Inside again. A close, flat atmosphere. Another door. 'Steps,' one of them said. 'You take it slowly, luv, or you'll gerra broken leg.'

Northern accent, a good deal heavier than Bobby

Maiden's, but the same general area, Grayle guessed – Liverpool, Manchester, Leeds, Newcastle, someplace . . . *don't pee, don't pee* . . .

The steps seemed to be wide and short, but she kept tripping and the big hands went up under her arms. So, if they'd come down from the tower to the ground, then this meant . . . Jesus, just when you thought you weren't claustrophobic . . . they were going underground. Lips taped, head bagged and earth all around, Grayle began to puppy whine again.

'Take it easy. Nearly there.'

Sound of a key struggling in a door. Like the tower room, a big key, a thick door. But an old, resistant lock.

'Stay back, sunshine,' the northern guy said, 'or you'll get your face kicked in.'

Then nobody was touching Grayle any more and there was the sound of the door shutting, the key grinding in the lock.

And this other northern voice, quiet and sad.

'It's OK, Grayle. It's OK.'

The voice really saying, *You're still alive, but it's not OK.*

Grayle went rapidly all around the walls, like a fly, feeling the rough, damp stone, pat, pat, pat . . . but it was no good: no more doors, no boarded-up windows. It was a dungeon, in the original sense; you reached up you could even feel the ceiling – stone or concrete, no boards, no plaster.

'We're screwed, right? We're gonna die.'

A small, black, cold cube, like the hole in the middle of a concrete block, and stinking of earth and mould and some kind of decay.

'They put us down here just until it's like the middle of the night and everybody's off the site, and it's safe to take out the bodies. Our bodies. Like, there's a hundred acres out there to bury us in.'

The one merciful aspect of absolute darkness was that nobody could see you cry, and she let it come, in floods.

'Grayle, listen . . .'

'Oh, dear God, this is not the way I planned to go out.'

'Killing people . . .' his voice came from the corner from which he hadn't once moved '. . . Killing people is no big ceremony for these people. They don't have to wait for midnight, they don't have to worry about getting rid of bodies, they just—'

'Wow. Jesus. I'm so comforted by that, Bobby.'

She sniffed. Her tissues were in her raincoat pocket, up in Kurt's tower; she used the cuff of her sweater.

Bobby said, 'All I'm saying is if they'd wanted to kill us, we'd be long gone.'

If he came out with much more of this crap, he'd be maybe halfway to convincing himself. The instant of relief at finding she was in here with Bobby had been swiftly cancelled by the knowledge that he was no longer out there and able to resume as a cop, call in other cops and move against these bastards.

She still couldn't see him. He'd pulled off her bag and stripped off her tape, and they'd rubbed the circulation back into her wrists and she'd told him about Kurt, how really fucking smart she'd been.

'Where are we?' She'd thought her eyes would adjust, but no light was no light; it was like being in an immersion tank, most of what you could see was

492

what you imagined, the forms your mind gave to the invisible.

'I came in bagged like you,' he said, 'but I'm assuming we're under the house. Crole had these cellars built for . . . I dunno, for his coal, probably.'

'Oh sure, we all lock up our coal.' Grayle breathed in deeply through her nose. 'I'm sorry, Bobby. It's just people in this situation, in the movies and stuff, they sit down and they say, hey, we gotta be practical here. And that's when they find the hidden trapdoor. Or they feel around the walls, and these stones suddenly slide out and there's this secret passage, and, OK, it's waterlogged and full of snakes, but it's a way out. And I just went over the walls, feeling and patting, and there is no way out of here except through that door for which we do not have a key. Oh *God*.'

The pressure that wasn't going to ease.

Bobby said, 'Erm, if this is . . . I mean, obviously I can't see you or anything.' His voice was stripped down to the accent you weren't that much aware of when you could see him. 'All I, er . . . I mean, would it help if I was to put my fingers in my ears?'

'Uh . . . yeah,' she said. 'I guess that would help.'

'OK. I'm doing it. I can't hear anything.'

She went tight into the opposite corner from where he was sitting, and laid down the bag she'd had over her head. At least that would absorb most of it.

When she was through, she stood up and shuddered with relief, and then she went and sat down next to Bobby Maiden and took his fingers out of his ears and gently kissed what she hoped was the side of his mouth.

'Thank you. That was the nicest thing anybody . . .'

She broke out laughing then, for a blessedly insane moment, and they held each other, sitting on his jacket on the stone floor in the cold and the darkness and the ammonia fumes.

After a while, her hands warm in his sweater, she said, 'You know what Cindy said to me earlier? He said this was all about big egos. Egos wanting to survive death. He said you could see it being of like cosmic proportions or really small and sordid. He said it was about Kurt and Seward, but also Crole and Abblow.'

Bobby told her what Harry Oakley had alleged about Crole and Abblow. How they liked to watch the lights go out.

'This John Hodge . . .' she shivered in his arms. 'They messed with him down here? Maybe where we're sitting. What did they do to him?'

'I don't know. But maybe Campbell and Seward do. If we assume that Seward's fascination with spiritualism is the main reason he's bankrolling Kurt . . . because he thinks Kurt's the man who can prove something to him . . .'

'. . . then it's in Kurt's interest to show he can come up with the goods,' Grayle said.

She told him what Kurt had said earlier about Abblow and Dunglas-Home; how some people had claimed to have seen him levitate, others had denied it. About the question she'd put to Kurt.

'I think he wanted me to know. Though he couldn't admit it, he wanted me to know how clever he'd been. I would bet money that he was with Callard until just days before the Cheltenham party and that he hypnotized her.'

'What?'

'I guess it was down to auto-suggestion. He wouldn't even need to be there. You think about this. She's psychic – I'm not gonna deny she's psychic, she's proved it in all kinds of ways.'

'Yes.'

'And . . . and the drawing, right? Sure, I know you could've gotten that from the picture in the book, but I think you got it from her. She has it. Whatever it is, she still has it. She talks about being washed up and all, but she still gets these spontaneous . . .'

'She was Em,' Bobby said.

'You don't have to talk about that. Bottom line is Marcus was right about Callard. She is an extraordinary person. But she's also human and stupid enough to get involved with a slimeball like Kurt. She always said that the men who came on to her, half of them wanted to get into her pants, the other half wanted into her career. Maybe Kurt looked attractive because he already *had* a career, was making even more money than she was, in kind of a similar area. And maybe he was therapy.'

'Hypnosis.'

'Like Campbell said to me just now, he can relax you. Hypnosis can take away stress and make you feel good about yourself, all that stuff. So maybe it started with her submitting freely to it, all strung up with the stresses of communication with the dead. And then he gets into her mind and he can plant all kinds of stuff in there. Plus, all that about how you can't hypnotize someone against their will is just smoke, you ask any professional hypnotist – if you're a suitable subject, they can get you . . . any time they want. So, like, Kurt

495

has this financially fruitful relationship going with Gary Seward – does Seward have an awful lot of money?'

'More than anyone's ever likely to know about. They all have, these guys. The taxman just gets the occasional gratuity . . .'

'So Kurt has this thing going with the most famous and glamorous medium in the Western world. And *he's into her mind*. And he knows what could really blow Seward away. What if . . . what if Callard could be shown to have contact with the newly murdered Clarence Judge? Think about it, Bobby. Callard's still getting the spontaneous spirit contacts, everything's normal . . . until she does a formal sitting. And then, instantly, there he is . . . *there's Clarence*. Every time, on cue. So suppose Kurt put her under one time – maybe this is just after they got laid when she's all compliant and softened up . . . and he shows her a picture of Clarence Judge.'

'There isn't a picture of Clarence Judge with that scar.'

'Just because there isn't one in the book doesn't mean there *isn't* one. So he shows her a picture – or whatever – and he's like, You will see this face every time . . . *Jesus* . . . every time you say the words, "The lines are open."'

'Bloody hell.'

'It's her line, Bobby! Hers and only hers. It's widely known. You go through Marcus's files, you'll see that damn line used as a headline on at least two profiles of Callard.'

'You're saying there's no ghost. No Clarence outside of Seffi's mind?'

'I think that's what I'm saying.'

'So what about the other stuff. The smell? You even said you smelled it, at—'

'Yeah, yeah, the bad dick smell. Well, she's a powerful psychic. She can blow out windows, she can fake Chaucer. To me, that's all entirely rational, and to a lot of scientists also. And, by the same rules, the smell's coming out of her. She's got this obnoxious Clarence so deep in her subconscious she's producing an associated stink. Maybe Clarence never smelled like that in his life, maybe he washed his dick scrupulously every night, I wouldn't know about that and neither would Callard. You have to excuse me here, Bobby. I'm thinking this out as I go along.'

'So this "lines are open" post-hypnotic suggestion thing is angled on the seance which Kurt set up for Seward in Cheltenham, right? You think Kurt was there all the time?'

'Probably in the back room, out of sight. Callard mustn't know it's him . . . what's *that* gonna do to their blossoming relationship? Yeah, the seance . . . it goes better than he could have hoped . . . bad-dick smell, drop in temperature, exploding vase . . . and Callard runs out, leaving Seward knocked out and lusting for more and thinking how right he was to invest in Kurt Campbell.'

'And maybe,' Bobby said, 'under normal circumstances, Kurt would have erased the instruction from Seffi's mind. But it messed her up so much and she ran so hard . . .'

'Whatever, he didn't get to erase it, did he? So whenever she comes out with the trademark phrase, there's old Clarence, in all his filthy glory. No wonder she went half-crazy. Hypnosis gone wrong can screw up ordinary people, hypnosis of a sensitive with

497

psychokinetic abilities . . . that's potentially devastating. *Actually* devastating. I wonder if he told her. I wonder if he told her on the phone . . . told her some of it . . . and that's why she's here.'

'Because he's promised to get rid of it.'

'In return for one special appearance, to put a cool spin on a mock-Victorian seance? Does that sound enough to you, Bobby? Does that sound worth all this . . . *Bobby* . . .' Grayle sat up. 'You moaned. You're hurt. Jesus, honey, they hurt you. You can't get up, can you? That's why—'

'They just kicked me around a bit. I thought they'd stabbed me at first, but they just knew where to kick. Me dad wouldn't even have felt it.'

'You're lying. You can't get up . . .'

Dear God, for a few minutes it had felt real good, putting it all together, talking it all out. You could forget . . . She moved a hand lightly over Bobby's face, feeling the bumps of dried blood.

'Those bastards,' she sobbed. 'They're like some private secret police force.'

'That's what they are,' he said. 'They are a private police force run by an ex-senior policeman who knows exactly how far he can go.'

'This is Britain!'

She felt him smile.

'Doesn't even have to be very secret any more. Several security companies are operating close to the edge. Riggs is quite bitter. He liked being a policeman.'

'He hires out a Forcefield team to Seward?'

'No, to Campbell. It's probably a hand-picked unit consisting of those particular employees he knows are open to a sub-contract, under the table – *that's* from

498

Seward. Riggs also gets a rake-off. Or favours in kind, I don't know.'

'So, like the Forcefield guy Seward brought over to Mysleton . . .'

'*Seward?*'

'It was Seward with the dead guy. He came himself, didn't I say? I forgot what I told you and what I told Cindy. Bobby, why would he do that? Why would he come himself, with all that money?'

'Because he loves it,' Bobby said. 'He needs that old thrill.'

'Jesus. What an unbelievable monster.'

'Or maybe just a sad old bugger,' Bobby said wearily. 'On reflection, though, I do think you carved up the wrong man.'

'Did you see him? Did you see Seward?'

'No. They just kicked me about a bit, tossed me in the back of a van, bag over the head, like you. I'd guess this came from Riggs, rather than Seward. He saw me . . . or somebody else saw me. Some of them will be disenchanted ex-coppers.'

'Bobby, do you wanna try and stand up?'

'I think I'll just lie here for a while,' Bobby said. 'If that's OK.'

Incredibly, Grayle slept.

Incredibly, she had a warm, fuzzy dream in which they were at home in the cottage in St Mary's, with a big log fire, the flames reflected by the crystals and the paste gems in the poodle collar around the neck of Anubis, the tame Egyptian god of the dead.

And this metamorphosed into a lucid kind of dream – a dream of what she knew was a near-death experience. Not the awful kind which Bobby had, but the traditional light-at-the-end-of-the-tunnel kind. The one where you didn't want to go back.

It was wonderful, and when she awoke she awoke into light.

'Both of you,' the Forcefield voice said. 'Get away from each other. Stand up.'

50

The renovation of Overcross Castle was like a half-finished portrait, Cindy thought, the central features blocked in and coloured, the rest little more than a scribble. On the first-floor landing, the paint faded off with the lighting, into greyness, shadows and dust-cloth ghosts.

Vera indicated to Cindy the alcove concealing Room Three, then pointed up at her stiff Victorian waitress's cap and down towards the kitchens to signify she would be needed soon to serve dinner to the visiting nobs. From below, Cindy could hear the sounds of polite laughter, clinking glasses.

When Vera was gone, he moved quietly into the alcove – quietly because the door was ajar and there were voices from within.

A problem. He needed to see Persephone Callard alone.

But, in the end, he didn't.

Standing in the shadow of the alcove, becoming still as a monolith, his breathing as light as a bird's, he heard,

'. . . even have to stay the night. I'll have a car

501

waiting. We'll get you out of here before midnight, I swear.'

Kurt Campbell. In a state.

'. . . can't believe it,' Miss Callard saying. 'Can't believe you or anybody could be so utterly, insanely . . .'

'Look . . . yes . . . all right . . . call me naï—'

'*Naïve?* It's not the word, is it, Kurt?'

'Greedy. Power-hungry. Hey, call me what you fucking like, I'm at the stage I don't really care. All I'm saying . . . if you finish this you'll never hear from me again, you'll never hear from Seward and you'll never . . . be troubled by . . .'

'*Him?*'

'You can unload it. Now you know what it's about, you can unload it just like . . .'

'Oh, it's so easy, Kurt, isn't it?'

'I'll help you.'

'Think I've rather had enough of your help. I just . . . the utter fucking *duplicity* . . .'

Kurt collecting himself into his voice, the mesmerist's velvet purr.

'Seffi, you can't possibly imagine how quickly this happens. You meet on live, late-night telly, you're both high on it, he says why don't we go on to a club . . . and then another club and you're with all these cool, dangerous people, and you're pissed and you're telling him your life story and your ambitions, and you think . . .'

'What a great guy. Yah, I've been there, Kurt. I was there when I was seventeen.'

'Yeah, well, when *I* was seventeen I was a sad kid at tech college doing a correspondence course on hypnotism at night and working bloody hard at it, so call it

502

delayed adolescence, but . . . he was just taking me over!'

'You're a bloody hypnotist and he's taking *you* over?'

'Things just happening, Seffi, like by magic. Obstacles getting moved, difficult people no longer difficult. Contracts, money, meetings, parties – and that's how you get drawn in, it's like drugs. And then one day you realize some of the things he's been doing for you are monumentally illegal – people getting bought, threatened, beaten up and . . .'

'And what?'

'And worse.'

An indrawing of breath by Miss Callard.

'And it's when you realize innocent people are getting . . . damaged to boost your career and get you into his pocket or to satisfy his warped sense of natural justice. Look, there's a story in his book – he's been very clever, he's changed the names and the circumstances so it can't be traced back, but it's essentially true – and it's about a man he's called Billy Spindler, a grass, who they fitted up for rape by actually *having a woman raped*. By Clarence Judge himself, I suspect. And he's done worse than that. People . . . OK, people've died, innocent people, but that's never how he sees it. If somebody gets hurt they usually deserve it because they're not as innocent as they look, or they're stupid . . . or they're just there to serve a higher purpose, which is *Gary's* purpose. He's a psychopath, Seffi, remorse is an abstract concept to Gary. You've just got to help get him off my back before another innocent . . .'

Cindy thought, *Billy Spindler?* The name was set in ice, what it represented.

503

'Kurt, if we do it, as planned, in a large public room, in front of the Mayor of bloody Malvern and Lord Ledbury and whoever, I'll go with that. Squalid, back-room stuff, you can forget.'

'You don't know this guy, Seffi.'

'I know *you*, and I know you're full of shit.'

Billy Spindler, Cindy thought. *The expendability of innocent but stupid people.*

'He's lost it. It's gone well beyond obsession. We have all kinds of rules now, set up because of signs and omens. Like it has to be tonight because this is the day when Crole and Abblow did what they did. And it has to be in exactly the same place. And there have to be the right number of people and there has to be . . . *please*, Seffi. You have to trust me.'

Behind Cindy there was a sudden fusilade of clipped, impatient footsteps. He took a breath, prepared to escape into the spectral netherland of dust sheets and abandoned paint cans.

Too late. He emerged from the alcove facing the woman identified to him as Francine Burnell-Brown, Kurt Campbell's PA and graceful toehold in society. Looking furious; she'd been left on her own to enter-tain minor aristocracy, tedious dignitaries and the local press, while the famous Kurt bargained and wheedled and lied through his white, white smile.

'Who the hell . . . ?'

'Sssh.' Cindy brought a finger to his lips, assumed Imelda's tone. 'It's a delicate moment. Give them a few minutes.'

'What's going *on*?'

'Two minutes, my dear.' Cindy took Francine by the shoulders and pushed her firmly into the passage and then walked calmly down the stairs, through the entrance hall and out into the night.

What Maiden obviously hadn't shared with Grayle was the implication of the Forcefield men operating quite openly, their faces now on show under the old fluorescent strip light in the passageway.

This was the death sentence.

His stomach hurt when he walked. Also when he breathed. He saw the concern in Grayle's eyes and was moved almost to tears. He'd discovered that he cried easily since his death. Not very policemanlike. Would disgust Norman Plod.

They stopped outside a fat oak door. 'Hands, please,' the Forcefield man smiled thinly, 'boss.'

'Oh, bugger.' Maiden recognized slim, narrow-eyed, felt-pen moustached DC Ballantyne, stationed briefly at Elham about four years ago. Ballantyne handcuffed him, hands behind. They weren't police issue cuffs, more like sex shop, but they worked.

'It's Matthew, isn't it?' Maiden said.

'It's sir to you, you fucker,' said Ballantyne.

'What's the pay like,' Maiden said, 'sir?'

Ballantyne looked into his eyes. 'Ever had your legs kicked from under you when you're cuffed? Scary.'

Grayle was watching, concern for Maiden giving way to blank fear for them both, as she was cuffed, too. By the bearded guy who'd worked Maiden over behind the Portaloos. The cuffs looked like medieval manacles above Grayle's small hands.

'Actually, this particular assignment', Ballantyne lowered his voice, 'is a farce. But the money . . .' he winked '. . . the money's great.'

The oak door opened and a man slipped out, closing it behind him. He wore an evening suit: white jacket, with one of those Sixties-style bow ties that fitted under the collar making an inverted V. It was almost an anticlimax to discover who he was.

Older than the pictures; they always were. More wizened, corruption lodged in every line that the camera lenses had blurred. Bags under the eyes, but the eyes were shrewd and bright and merry and cold as a mortuary.

'Bobby Maiden!' Both hands gripping Maiden's shoulders. 'Heard a lot about you, cock.'

'From my old boss, that would be?'

'You signed out a short while back, yeah? How long was it? Three minutes?'

'Four.'

'Fucking amazing.' The eyes never blinked. 'Where you get to, Bobby?'

'Wherever it was, Gary, I was glad to get back.'

'You must be an immature soul, my son. But no matter . . . you was there . . . you was over the fence. It's the experience what counts, know wha' mean?' He turned away from Maiden. 'And Grayle . . . Underwood.'

'Hill,' Grayle said. 'Under*hill*. I believe we, uh . . . met.'

'Nice of you to remember the occasion, Grayle. You also remember what I said to you that night?'

'I guess.'

'Don't guess, darlin',' he said breezily. 'Tell me.'

'You are dead,' Grayle said tonelessly.

'Good girl.' Gary Seward put out a hand, held Grayle's chin gently between thumb and forefinger.

506

She didn't move her head, but Maiden saw her swallow. 'Heat of the moment, sweetheart.' Seward let go of Grayle's chin. 'Heat of the moment.'

Maiden saw former DC Ballantyne smirking in delight at this dear old underworld character from a lost era, as if this was cabaret. He wondered if Ballantyne knew what Seward had done to his colleague, Jeffrey Crewe. He wondered what Seward had told Riggs about the incident.

'But having said that, Grayle, it's incredible how things what comes out in the heat of the moment do turn out to be quite prophetic. I believe in all that stuff.' Seward swivelled, spreading his hands. 'I mean, let's be frank about this, a short time from now, the two of you will have died three times between you.'

The fluorescent tube in the ceiling zizzed and popped along with the famous monotone laugh.

'I mean, you know, how else is it supposed to end? What else can I do, the position you put me in? It's your own fault, innit?'

Grayle looked at him, frozen-faced, her skin blue-white under the strip light, her hair tangled on her shoulders. Maiden wondered desperately how he could get her out of this. Being nice to Seward didn't seem an option.

'I mean this is an omen, yeah? The two of you here: a young lady what was recently told she was dead and a geezer who *was* dead.'

'Mmm,' Maiden said, 'that is really uncanny.'

'What can I tell you? You're gonna die. You *are* gonna die. We all die. Your time has been brought forward, that's all. How I always look at it. Bringing forward the inevitable. That's all it is.'

'I never thought of that before,' Maiden said tonelessly. 'That's amazingly profound.'

Gary Seward tucked a fast fist into Maiden's undefended stomach.

'That the spot, Bobby?'

Maiden retched, folded in agony.

'*You scumball!*' Grayle screamed. 'You knew he was hurt!'

'But I digress,' Maiden heard Seward say, across the pain. 'What I was about to say is, by the time you check out I hope we'll all know more about the actual business of death and what follows. The reality. You ever meet Clarence Judge, Bobby?' Seward bent to him. 'Eh?'

Maiden shook his head.

'We can fix that.' He turned and pushed open the oak door, stepped back. 'Go through, would you, please?'

Ballantyne and his colleague blocked the passage in each direction. Ballantyne signalled Maiden into the room.

Where Maiden saw what he expected to see. A richly carpeted area with a red sofa and five chairs around a table. A little bit of Cheltenham.

What he didn't expect to see, in one of the chairs, was Ron Foxworth.

51

The table was of creamy, polished yew, the seating around it an inelegant mixture: two straight-backed wooden dining chairs, three red brocaded Edwardian fireside chairs. In one of which sat Foxworth.

He barely glanced at Maiden. He still wore his old black anorak with the rally stripes. He looked slightly absurd in this opulently furnished cellar.

But then the island of opulence itself looked absurd. All around, it was still a cellar. The walls had been patched up with cement. A strip light buzzed and flickered near the top of a wall. A dusty unlit bulb dangled from a brown Bakelite rose in the centre of the low, grey ceiling.

It was this hanging bulb, more than anything, which made it look less like a filmset than a display hurriedly flung together in a furniture warehouse.

'He holds this very much against you, Bobby.' Seward tilted his head to peer at Foxworth as though he was a child in a pram. 'Don't you, Ronny?'

Maiden saw that Foxworth was also handcuffed but with his hands in front. He saw a tall, expensive Chinese vase on a table pushed against the furthest wall. On either side of it, two oil heaters faintly smoking below a jacket on a hanger on a hook in the wall.

'All this talk of the Festival of the Spirit, you really whetted Ron's appetite, Bobby. Thinkin' about you and me and how we all fitted into the picture. Had to come over and check it out, didn't you, Ronny?' Seward smiled at Foxworth and then at Maiden. 'It's his obsessive personality.'

Ron Foxworth didn't speak. Ballantyne directed Grayle and Maiden into the red chairs on either side of Ron.

'Course Ron sticks out a bit. Not very New Age. Not like you, Bobby, by all accounts. Now, you tell me – what was I supposed to do? It's one of those moments, one of those signs. Detective Superintendent Ronald Foxworth visits the Festival of the Spirit. Life's too short to ignore it. You know you got to react quick or you miss it. So . . . soon as we established he was on his tod, we had him. Lifted him clean, banged him up.'

Ron cleared his throat, didn't look up. Maiden thought he'd never seen a man look so destroyed.

'Surprised?' Gary Seward slid into a wooden chair, crossed his legs, did his one-tone laugh. 'Very surprised indeed, wasn't you, Ronald? I mean, it don't happen, do it? A senior officer, a distinguished detective? Should have heard the bluster, Bobby. *You really done it this time, Seward.* Big, powerful detective, this. Spent half his life trying to pull Gary Seward. Now I've pulled him. Exquisite. But it goes deeper, don't it, Ron?'

Foxworth looked up. His eyes were pale and blood-shot. He didn't look at anybody, his focus point seemed to be in a haze about eighteen inches from his face. But, at some stage since he was lifted, Ron had learned about the consequences of failing to answer direct questions.

'Gary thinks I was once uncivil to Clarence Judge.'

'Masterly understatement, Ron. What happened was . . . there was a siege situation yeah? Late Seventies, Ron? Seventy-nine, eighty, around then. Clarence, I think he done a post office for pocket money or alimony, some minor cash-flow thing. Course, Ron looks at Clarence, sees Gary Seward, know wha' mean? Obsessive. Goes in mob-handed, SAS-style. Absolute overreaction, utterly uncalled for. Poor Clarence thinks he's for the jump, killed trying to escape, some'ing like that. Thinks he's fighting for his life. Well you would, wouldn't you?'

Ron rallied. 'He had a copper's ear between his teeth. DS Earnshaw. Took four men to tear his bloody face away. Had half the ear in his mouth and if they hadn't made him cough it up he'd have eaten it.'

Seward ignored him. 'So, back at the station, what does Ron do but invite three of DS Earnshaw's colleagues to pay their respects to Clarence in his cell.'

'He was smashing up his cell,' Ron said to his chest. 'He was also in danger of injuring himself. Judge had no pain threshold.'

Seward half-turned, pointed the finger. 'You, Ron, are a lying toerag. What are you?'

Maiden closed his eyes. *Don't make him say it.*

'Nah,' Seward said. 'He knows what he is. He humiliated Clarence that day. He stood and watched while those pigs hurt my poor friend in all the places what didn't show. But, worst of all, they hurt his pride, and that's the severest thing you can do to a man like Clarence, and it cannot be tolerated long term. I says, leave it, Clarence, don't do *nothing*.

'Cause he never had no finesse, see, the poor love. You leave it, I says. But one day I will see to Ron for you, I promise. And Gary Seward keeps his promises, and this is that day and Clarence is going to be here to see it. Matthew . . . ?'

Ballantyne closed the oak door.

Oh God, Maiden thought.

'Let's make ourselves comfortable.' Seward bent down the side of his chair, came up nursing black metal. 'We're gonna get cosy. There will be no resistance, otherwise the inevitable gets brought forward, know wha' mean?'

Shotgun. Sawn-off. Maiden estimated that if Seward let that thing off in here he could kill one of them, maim the others with a single shot.

'Stand up, Miss Underwood.'

Seward ambled over, placed the twin barrels against Grayle's temple. '*Oh* God.' Her voice was like a startled bird taking flight from a branch. Maiden began to breathe hard.

'You too, Ron, Bobby. Up. Now, what we do, we close our eyes and we keep the fuckers closed.'

'I can't,' Grayle said.

'Oh, you can, darlin'. Just consider the alternatives.'

'Oh God. Oh God.'

'Thank you.'

Maiden stared into the blackness, telling himself that if Seward was going to execute them he wouldn't use a sawn-off shotgun.

Would he?

A fumbling behind him. For a moment his hands were free. His heart leapt, his body tensed, he wanted to lash out, go for it.

'Stay still, cock!' Seward, hard-voiced. 'No resistance.'

512

Maiden's right hand hung by his side. His left was jerked up. Handcuffs snapped.

'You can all open your eyes now,' Seward said.

Maiden opened his into a grotto-like gloom. The strip light was off, the cellar was now feebly lit by the hanging bulb. Seward was hunched on the hard chair, he and the shotgun fused into the same bulky shadow.

'And you can leave us now, lads,' he said to Ballantyne and his mate. 'Go and find Kurt. Tell him I want that toffee-nosed bitch down here asap.'

A tug on the left wrist told Maiden he was hand-cuffed to Ron Foxworth. He saw that Ron was handcuffed on the other side to Grayle.

Foxworth glared angrily at Maiden. 'You know why else I came down here, you tosser?' Like them being bound at the wrist had unblocked him. 'Because a lad called Scott Ferris was telling us how a bloke with copper's ID was asking after Justin Sharpe. Described you to a T.'

'You had me in the frame for Justin?'

'I had you in the frame for a lying bastard. Had you in the frame for pissing up my leg.'

'Ron, I tried to call you . . .'

'Stop bleedin' whingeing, Ron,' Seward said. 'I never took to you, you know that? You was always such a miserable git.'

Maiden said, 'Why the chain gang, Gary?'

'It's a circle, Bobby. Or it will be. Put your hands on the table, palms down, little fingers touching. It's incomplete, but that'll be rectified.'

'It's a seance,' Grayle said softly. 'He wants to hold a seance.'

'Give the little girl a coconut,' Seward said.

* * *

Cindy stopped at the edge of the parapet and looked back at the golden light in the tall, Gothic windows, and didn't know how he was going to get back into the house now. Little Grayle was in there alone. He had to find Bobby.

He hurried down into the festival site, lit up below him like a fairground, strings of coloured bulbs between the bare trees. The punters were thinning out, drifting away. Soon the stalls would close, the stall-holders returning to their hotels and guesthouses in Great Malvern, some to their camper-vans on a site near the road.

There was an arc of applause from the main marquee, where a writer on alien abduction was concluding her lecture. Or was it the demonstration of pendulum dowsing?

While, inside Overcross Castle . . . two spiritualist gatherings: the mock seance in the banqueting hall, some actor-magician performing the stunts of Daniel Dunglas-Home, as he would tomorrow and the rest of the week for paying audiences. And, somewhere in the heart of the house, the secret ceremony over which Persephone Callard was being pressed to preside – to preserve foolish Kurt from the wrath of the vicious Seward. Poor Kurt, who lived in such fear of this man. Awakening one morning with the horrific realization that he was in partnership with a still-active dangerous criminal.

Crap. Kurt was a liar. He was very deeply into this. He needed Persephone Callard here as much as Seward did but, because she would have knowledge of at least one murder, he would be obliged to build up Seward as the dangerously unbalanced instigator.

514

As he hurried through the lights, Cindy became aware of a few people staring at him, pointing. His blond wig was gone, his glasses were gone. And even New Age followers watched television.

By the time he reached *The Vision* stall, it was more than just a few people. He remembered the jokes with Vera about a tabloid reward.

'It'll all end in tears, you mark my words!' a man yelled, and there was laughter. Images battered Cindy: the car siege in Malvern Link, the jeering, the taunts, the anger, Marcus slumped under a lamp post.

'Please! Leave me alone!' he yelled helplessly. *Bobby, Bobby, where are you?*

Flinging himself into the tent, where he stood gasping, appalled at his loss of control. But he couldn't cope with this now. Let them all tear each other to pieces in the race to the phone, to be the first to finger the fugitive Cindy Mars-Lewis and claim their blood money.

'Well, well,' a woman said dryly. 'I thought it was, all along.'

'What are you doing here?'

It was the woman from the next tent, the etheric masseuse, Lorna something.

'Lorna Crane.' She was standing, hands on trim hips, under the photos of High Knoll, spotlit now. 'And what I am doing here, Mr Cindy Mars-Lewis, is helping you out. I've sold a hundred and three copies of *The Vision*, between clients. Also seven subscriptions. And taken the addresses of two women who would like to correspond privately with Marcus Bacton. One left a photo of herself. Taken fifteen years ago, if I'm any judge. Money's in a cashbox

515

under my treatment couch, it's all quite safe.'

'Thank you,' Cindy said, bemused. 'It's very good of you. We must . . . pay you.'

'Nah,' Lorna said. She shouted at the small crowd gathering outside. 'Piss off, eh? He'll be out later.' She grinned. 'Must be amazing, having fans, being adored.'

'I fear you misunderstand. They want to tear me apart. The bogeyman, I am now. Baron Samedi. Kali the Destroyer.'

'What *are* you on about?' Lorna took from the sleeve of her multi-hued jumper a sizeable spliff and a book of matches. She got the spliff going, inhaled joyously, offered it to Cindy, who declined. 'Don't need this stuff, I suppose, when you're a shaman. That all true, Cindy? The Celtic shaman bit?'

'I never have denied an interest,' Cindy said cautiously. 'Excuse me just a moment.' He pushed into the tiny rear compartment, where Grayle had left the small case containing her dress for the seance. Flipped open the case. The clothing was still there, neatly folded. Cindy went cold.

'She hasn't been back. She hasn't been *back*.'

Lorna stood and eyed him blearily through the smoke. 'That guy, the photographer, *he* came back.'

'When?'

'I dunno. Two, three hours ago. I haven't got a watch. Maybe longer. Yeah, it was light. He come in and had a cuppa, then some guy was shouting for him and he pissed off.'

'And you haven't seen him since? What about the girl?'

'Nah. Nobody else. I tell you, though, his aura looked like shit.'

516

'Bobby?'

'I told him to go and sleep it off and not talk to anybody.'

'Lorna, have you *any* idea where he—?'

Cindy froze over the case. A man had entered the tent behind Lorna.

Blue-black uniform, with silver epaulettes. Cap with black, shiny peak.

He said, 'In here, Gavin. We got her.'

Suddenly it was real eerie.

The bulb was low wattage, you could look hard at it, see its filament, how spidery and frail it was. Like in the early days of electricity, when technology was a small glow in a big fog. When spiritualism was born.

And Seward, all light and shadow in his evening suit, looked out of that era, too. She was recalling him now from the TV talkshow in the States. *Dave! How are ya mate? 'Ere . . . brought yer some'ing . . . Get these dahn yer . . . jellied eels. You'll never go back to pizza again, mate.*

Leaning back in his chair now, the shotgun on his knee. He couldn't let that thing off in here; the honoured guests would hear it booming like an earth tremor under their feet.

Sure. And think it was just another sound-effect, courtesy of Mr Daniel Dunglas-Home and the first age of spiritualism.

Oh Jesus. *Oh Jesus, I never gave you too much respect, you were never enough fun and I only prayed to you when I was in real deep shit, but please, please . . .*

Her wrist, cuffed to the fat, hairy wrist of the big detective, Foxworth, was beginning to ache. Only way

517

she could move it would be to pull his hand down onto her lap. Maybe not.

How long? How long were they gonna sit here, the four of them? Waiting for the *toffee-nosed bitch*. Just pray she never came. Pray she called the cops instead.

Bobby said casually, 'So who did kill Justin Sharpe, Gary?'

Foxworth's shoulder jerked, dragging the handcuffs, hurting Grayle.

'Oh, *that* prat,' Seward said. 'Well, he deserved it, didn't he? He was a pain in the arse. Little big man. Bloody nuisance.'

Bobby said, 'He gave you Grayle's name?'

'Did he? Yeah, could be we had it from him.'

Grayle said hoarsely, 'Why'd you have to kill him?'

Seward shook his head a little, in non-comprehension. 'Darlin', you're talking like this was an innocent member of the public. He dabbled. He had his fingers in the pie, he lost his fingers. It happens.'

'Where do you draw the line?'

'I dunno.' Seward looked thoughtful. 'Maybe I ain't as pragmatic and businesslike as I was. Comes from not needing to do it for a living no more. All them years you spend watching your back and the law and planning everything careful, like a military operation. And then you write a book, do telly, and the money just bleedin' *rolls* in. It's weird – you don't have to do nothing to nobody for it. Get invited to invest in legit business. And suddenly you're just bleedin' *loaded* – you're turning over twice, three times what you used to take off the suckers.'

Ron Foxworth sniffed in contempt. 'Military operation my arse. All you ever were was a grown-up version of the kid that used to take other kids' dinner money.'

'Ronald—'

'Drugs and protection, that was you, Seward. The dregs. The gutter. You never planned a clever job, not ever. You were just this mean, ruthless bastard who never cared who got hurt. That was the whole secret of your success, Gary, you never gave a flying fart who suffered along the way.'

'Ronald,' Seward smiled delicately, 'I rather think, my old friend, that you are beginning to show off to the children. Which cannot be tolerated. I don't think I'm gonna tell you again not to do that, know wha' mean?'

Grayle said, to diffuse the horrifying tension, 'If you're making so much money, Mr Seward, why are you still—?'

Seward shifted in his chair and she caught the cold eyes in the gloom, and it was like coming face to face with a wolf in the undergrowth.

'You're a clever girl. I got to say I never really liked clever women. They ain't never clever enough to know when to stop.'

Foxworth sighed. '*I'll* explain this, if Gary doesn't mind, Miss Underwood. It's because he's got everything he ever wanted and he doesn't feel alive any more. He got addicted to the buzz. And the buzz in having everything you ever wanted . . . for a man like Gary, it starts to fade on day two.'

'You mean like when the body's replete you realize how starved the spirit is.' Grayle frantically recalling a think-piece she once wrote for the *Courier* about why so many billionaires and movie stars and rock stars got obsessively into New Age studies.

519

'But in that case', Bobby said, turning this into some kind of crazy, surreal debate, 'don't you start to reject your material wealth and remember all the people you misused and try to repay them? Don't you start trying to put something into the world to replace what you took out before you saw the light?'

'Yeah. And that's . . .' Grayle sat forward. 'Like, this one time I had a long discussion with Shirley McLaine, and she—'

'*And it is easier for a rich man to pass through the eye of a needle than to enter the kingdom of Heaven*,' Seward said.

'It's a point of view,' Grayle said.

And then cowered back in her chair as Seward rose, snarling, tiny jewels of spit popping out.

'You airy-fairy, nampy-pamby *twats*! You're just fucking *hippies*! You're like them bleedin' doped-up crazies we're fleecing out there! Shirley Fucking McLaine? Listen . . . do you know why the Victorians got closer than anybody has since to proving life after death? 'Cause they didn't fart about wiv peace and love and this shit. The Victorians, the old spiritualists, Crole and Abblow and them . . . they was scientific. They didn't make the mistake of thinking life after death had to do with bleedin' religion. They did what had to be done. Know wha' mean? Nah, you don't, do you? None of you bleedin' *know*!'

There was a pool of silence.

Then Bobby tossed in a rock.

'*I* know what you mean. It's like the way Crole and Abblow realized it was necessary to kill John Hodge.'

'And what do you know about that, cock?'

'I think they wanted him for a ghost,' Bobby said

into a sudden cavern of silence. 'For the first purpose-built haunted house.'

Grayle said, 'Huh?' Then a pulse of pure understanding went through her like white fork-lightning.

'Go on, Bobby,' Seward said.

There was a tap on the door.

'Come,' Seward said.

Grayle turned her head to watch the door. When it opened and the blue-white light fell in, she realized how dark it had been with that one miserable bulb.

With the light came Persephone Callard. Behind her, Grayle saw the thin security guard.

Callard stood there in her dark dress. Her hair was in one long, dense, bellrope plait. She looked slowly round the cellar. From Seward to Grayle to Foxworth to Bobby Maiden, making no response to any of them, giving no hint that she knew them. Then she shook her head. She hadn't seen the handcuffs, but she'd seen enough.

'Oh no,' she said, all quiet and succinct and upper class. 'Oh no, I really don't think so.' She turned to the security guy. 'Take me back. I want to talk to Kurt.'

Seward stood up. He looked suddenly out of condition, like an old-fashioned restaurant manager who ate too many of his own rich meals. Maybe he was aware of this: irritation twisted the fixed smile downwards. He walked into the middle of the room.

Held the squat shotgun at waist-level.

Grayle said, '*Oh*—'

The holes down the shotgun barrels were mineshafts into hell.

'Shut the door, please,' Seward said.

521

52

'Would you come with us, please, Madam?'

'Are you arresting me, officer?' Cindy held a hand to his throat, affronted but dignified.

'You could say that.'

'I don't think you *can*, mate,' Lorna Crane said. 'You got no powers to arrest anybody.'

The Forcefield officer quite clearly believed otherwise. He had the frame of a bodybuilder and the considerable acne of a fifth-former. He carried a rubberized torch nearly two feet long.

'This woman has stolen money and jewellery from a number of stalls,' he said with a certainty the actual police were rarely permitted to exercise.

'Oh.' Cindy began to feel resentful. 'Jewellery *and* money? And do you have the evidence?'

But he knew he was trapped. The youth had at least one of his colleagues behind him. And behind *him*, probably a great many members of the Lottery-following public who would enjoy seeing a disgraced Cindy Mars-Lewis ignominiously led away into the gaily coloured night.

'Get lost, sonny,' Lorna said. 'I'm paying silly money to occupy this tent and as long as I'm doing that you're not welcome here. Go on. Push off.'

'Please stay out of this, madam. It's really not your concern.'

Lorna erupted. 'You got a flaming nerve! You clowns marching round like bloody storm-troopers – you've got less authority than traffic wardens! This is supposed to be a *spiritual* event. You know what that means? I doubt it. I tell you, a lot of things here don't fit and you Gestapo bastards are one of them.'

'I think you'll find, *madam*, that this will go down on record as one of the least troublesome festivals of its kind ever staged. And that will be precisely because we don't tolerate stealing or', he sniffed, 'drugs.'

'Oh, do me a *favour . . .*'

'We don't do favours on drugs.'

'No? Depends who's selling them, doesn't it?'

'That's a lie.'

'What's a lie? Go on, bugger off, you're all bent.'

The boy turned his back on Lorna. A leather-gloved hand went out to Cindy. 'Come on. We don't want a scene. I'm only obeying orders.' Steering him towards the tent flap.

Only obeying orders. God forbid. Cindy was suddenly quite afraid of this humourless boy and his masters, and of where it was going to end.

'Bastards,' Lorna said. 'And you've got an aura the colour of shit.'

Grayle felt a small tug on the handcuff as both Bobby and Ron Foxworth moved to the edge of their chairs. Both pairs of cuffs clinked, and Persephone Callard glanced across and saw the situation for the first time, and her whole body went taut.

Grayle could almost see Bobby thinking that now

would be the time for all three of them to rush Gary Seward, hold him in a chained circle . . . that this would be the last chance they'd get.

And then, what would happen was that Seward would let off the gun.

The sawn-off twelve gauge.

As Grayle understood it, British hoods appeared to hold this weapon in some kind of black affection as part of their criminal heritage. The only time she'd seen one before was last year, with Marcus, when they visited a grisly crime museum in a small town near the Forest of Dean. There were also old police helmets, domestic artefacts from the Kray household and a skeleton in a cupboard. You tried to laugh.

Close up, this gun, like Seward, was about as funny as cancer, as sentimental as Hitler's smile. Close up, you could clearly understand the point of sawing off the barrels more than halfway down. If all three of them went for Seward, whatever was down there would come out like some kind of heavy metal custard pie, and if any of them survived it, it would not be a great life thereafter.

Bobby half-turned and Grayle met his dark eyes and saw that he was arguably more scared than she was, maybe having seen at some stage of his career the carnage a weapon like this could leave. Foxworth stared straight in front of him, but his breathing was faster, and Grayle knew that because of Foxworth, most of all, and the weight of law he represented, there was no way any of them would be walking out of here as long as Seward was in the way with his arms full of death.

Only Persephone Callard looked calmly into the two barrels.

'The way I see it', she said candidly to Seward, 'you could probably also be an actor. Like that idiot upstairs with the whiskers stuck on. I mean, I have, as yet, no reason to think otherwise, yah? You understand what I'm saying?'

The silence lasted long enough for Grayle to try and count, for the fifth time, the filaments in the feeble light bulb.

Callard said, 'You could put that ludicrous thing away, unlock those people, and we could all go upstairs and have a quiet drink and talk over what I can do to help you.'

'That's your proposal, is it?'

Seward walked over to the wall, as though he was giving this serious consideration. He stood with his back to a photograph framed in black lacquered wood. It showed two men posing on either side of an antique microscope. Except it was probably a brand new, state-of-the-art microscope when the picture was taken and the men's watch-chains and yard-brush moustaches were the height of fashion.

'Know who these two are?'

Callard shook her head.

'That's Crole, that's Abblow. That picture was took right here where we're standing. This was their research lab. This basement, where we are now.'

'I guess that's why you couldn't bear to change the bulb,' Grayle said.

'Shut the fuck up, Grayle. Do you feel their presence, Miss Callard?'

'I really don't believe', Callard said, 'that you're stupid enough to think the atmosphere in here at the moment is conducive to any kind of psychic communication.'

'No?' Seward walked round the wall until he and his weapon were somewhere behind Grayle and the others, sending a cold tingle of apprehension through her neck. 'Well, as a matter of fact, sweetheart, I got good reason to think this atmosphere is close to bleedin' perfect.'

Outside a small crowd had gathered, ten or fifteen people. Cindy recognized a number of them as stall-holders and resident psychics. A murmur rippled through the group as Cindy was brought out.

A young man stepped forward. He wore a motor-cycle jacket. A golden ankh hung from one ear and his shaven head was green and red under the coloured lights. He stood in the path of the second and older Forcefield officer. His accent was deepest Lancashire.

'You know who you've got there, man, don't you?'

'We've got a thief.' One of the security guards gripped Cindy's arm, bruisingly, above the elbow. 'Out of the way, please.'

'That is Cindy Mars-Lewis, man.'

The Forcefield man snatched a look at Cindy; his eyes widening momentarily. 'It doesn't matter to me who it is. It's what she . . . he . . . has nicked is what concerns us, so you just—'

'Perhaps,' Cindy said, 'I could meet the person who is accusing me of theft. Or you could simply name the stall from which the items are alleged to have been removed.'

'I think what you do is you let go of him, man,' the young man in the leather jacket said. 'You're nowt but a bumped-up bouncer, anyroad.'

At which the Forcefield men hardened visibly, the

two of them shoulder to shoulder, like riot police.

The older one said, with a formality which was indeed indicative of an earlier career in the police service, 'Under the authority invested in me by the organizers of this event, I must ask you to step out of the way. And I must warn you that if you *don't*—'

The young man smiled. 'And by the authority invested in *me* by the radiance of the unquenchable flame, I'm warning *you* that if you don't let go of Mr Mars-Lewis right now, me and my enlightened brethren will take you and your mate over the field there and shove them bloody big torches where the eternal light never shines.'

A cheer went up. Several other people moved forward. Including, Cindy observed, the mild little man who had carried the placard relating to the death of John Hodge. When the Forcefield officer let go of Cindy's arm so that he might grip his long torch with both hands, the shaven-headed boy grinned in satisfaction, thrust himself between the security men and Cindy and pushed out a hand.

'Maurice Gooch, Federation of South Pennine Dowsers. Glad to meet you, Cindy, man.'

Seward's nasal voice was so close behind Grayle that she imagined she could smell his breath. 'See, what you got in here is Clarence's, as you might say, vibe. Clarence's kind of atmosphere. Put the old love in a dark room wiv a few frightened people and an air of – as you might say – repressed violence, and poor old Clarence, he'd become very excited indeed. Isn't that true, Ronald?'

'You mean, was he sick?' Foxworth said. 'Yes, the man was very sick.'

Callard pointed at a silver-framed photograph on one of the tables. 'Is that him?'

Holding her cool with difficulty now. She'd walked down here, presumably, of her own free will. Convinced that, whatever was going to happen, she would be in control. She was Persephone Callard, she was famous, she was unique; either she got to call the shots or she walked away.

Here, in this half-lit dungeon, Gary Seward, with his sawn-off gun, was calling the shots. Callard's outrage, Grayle guessed, had not yet quite been overtaken by fear.

'Clarence was young then, Miss Callard.' Seward motioned with his gun at the photo. 'And the ladies was fond of him. Sad, really. He never could understand why, as he got older, they shied away.'

'So not too smart either,' Grayle said.

'Grayle Underwood, you get the second warning,' Seward said quietly. 'Now, Miss Callard, you see that jacket on the hanger? Over the heaters?'

Grayle saw that the jacket was black or dark grey. That all three buttons were fastened. Oh Jesus.

'He had two suits like that,' Seward said. 'He was cremated in the other. That one over there is the actual jacket he was wearing when he died.'

Callard made no comment. Grayle saw her glance at Bobby.

'We did have it cleaned. That was probably a mistake. Too late now. Now this shotgun. This wasn't actually Clarence's – he was more of a hands-on craftsman, know wha' mean? – but he was the geezer modified it. Sawed off the barrel for me, filed it down nice, so it didn't rip the lining of your coat.'

'This is the Clarence Museum,' Bobby said.

'A Clarence *shrine*, cock. Now, in my under-standing, Miss Callard, and from what young Kurt's figured out from studying the pioneering work of Anthony Abblow, I think I'm right in saying we could not have a better atmosphere into which to invite the spirit of my dear old friend.'

'That's simplistic,' Callard said, but there was a faint sheen on her face.

'Nor indeed a better person to facilitate the con-nection. You're number one, ain'tcha? The most effective medium in this country, maybe the world?'

'I don't think so. I think I've just had the most publicity.'

'Nah. Don't undersell yourself, sweetheart. See, even Kurt thinks you'd be the one Abblow hisself woulda picked for the job. On account of you got no religion.'

Grayle remembered the heavy cross Callard had worn around her neck. It was not visible tonight; she wore no jewellery with the plain black dress.

'Plus,' Gary laughed his awful laugh, 'Clarence was quite fond of coloured ladies. As I recall. And Ron recalls. Tell the people, Ronny.'

Foxworth sighed bitterly.

'Gary means he raped one once.'

They guided Cindy, somewhat bemused, to a spacious tent jointly rented, apparently, by practitioners of t'ai chi and transcendental meditation. There were cushions and rugs and oriental lanterns, and the central space was swiftly filled by people reflecting that mixture of the quaint, the exotic and faintly menacing which had come to characterize such gather-ings as this.

'Why the disguise, Cindy?' Lorna Crane asked him. 'I don't get it. You're a legend. We were all having a laugh earlier on about the directors of Camelot jumping from the fourteenth floor.'

Cindy was startled. 'They haven't?'

''Course they haven't. But I think everybody here agrees the National Lottery's a force for the dissolution of society.'

'It is?'

'What?' Lorna snorted. 'Millions of people living from ticket to ticket? Gotta be a millionaire by weekend or life's not worth living? Buying more and more tickets, five times as many on a roll-over week, 'cause that's *big* big money? And if they lose on Saturday, they're spiritually comatose until Wednesday, existing day to day on a drip-feed of Lottery Instants. And if they win, everybody who ever knew them expects a piece and it's never big enough, and you've got this dark fog of hatred and jealousy radiating all around them.'

A small Indian gentleman in a white suit told Cindy, 'Sir, you have helped enlighten the populace about this pulsing core of negativity thrusting its black tentacles into every household. You have become the vehicle for a necessary karmic force.'

'Well, I'm not too sure about that,' Cindy said. 'Indeed, it was never my intention to become the vehicle for anything more than a mild irreverence, but . . .'

'Don't knock it, man,' Maurice Gooch whispered in his ear. 'You're on a roll here.' And then, raising his voice, 'Well, it's good to have Cindy wi' us.'

'It's a sign!' someone shouted.

'Aye,' said Maurice, 'but let's not forget the original

530

purpose of this meeting, which was to elect delegates to express our general dissatisfaction to organizers with the exploitative way the festival's being run. First up, Forcefield Security. We've just had an example of the way them buggers operate – law unto 'emselves, private army – and that's not acceptable in a civilized society, least of all in what's supposed to be a centre of enlightenment and human potential. Agreed?'

'Forcefield must go,' the Indian gentleman said firmly.

'Point two – the fees. We all thought the basic charge for a pitch were a complete rip-off, but we thought it were worth coppering up for on account of it were such a prestigious event.'

'Some of us always had our suspicions,' Lorna muttered.

'But what we didn't reckon on were the extras – vegetarian meals at fancy restaurant prices wi' no discount for stallholders. No water on site except for bottled at rip-off prices. And then the campsite fees – seventy quid a night for a bit of sodden grass, size of a hearthrug.'

'Should be free,' Lorna said.

'Aye, it should. Question is, what do we do about it? We've got a proposal on t'table that we elect a delegation to go up t'castle first thing tomorrow wi' a petition signed by everybody as objects to the way we're being treated – with the stand-by threat that, if we get no satisfaction, we all pull out, leavin' 'em completely shagged for the big weekend. Now that makes sense to me. Do we have an amendment?'

Cindy coughed lightly.

Maurice turned to him.

'Far be it from me, Maurice, to intrude upon a private meeting . . .'

'You're a paid-up stallholder, man. Let's have it.'

'. . . but while energies are at this moment running high, a grey morning and a deserted site could well be less conducive to the firing of passions. Also, I wonder how many of you are aware that at this very moment, being formally entertained in the banqueting suite, is a small and elite gathering of dignitaries representing local government, national government, tourism, economic development . . .'

'Fuck me,' said Maurice. 'You're kidding.'

'And while a petition may be taken away for consideration, thus delaying the consultative process by a day or more, it would be less easy for the organizers to brush it under the carpet were it to be presented in full view of the great and the good . . .'

'Embarrassing the piss out of the buggers at t'same time! He's right. Bugger the petition. We should ger up there now.'

'What about the security guards?' someone asked nervously.

'They may well find themselves outnumbered on this occasion, don't you think?' the placid placard man pointed out.

'Shit hot, man,' said Maurice.

'It was how we last put him away,' Foxworth said. 'She was called Priscilla Hall. West Indian. Barmaid at Judge's local, the Dragoon. She was in hospital for three weeks with internal injuries.'

'*Jesus*,' Grayle breathed.

'But she *deserved* it, Ron,' Seward said. 'You forget that. What she would do, she'd lead customers on.

532

Then, on the way back to her place, her brothers would step out the shadows and roll the poor sods, for wallets and watches.'

'The same night', Foxworth intoned, like he was giving evidence in court, 'one Clayton Hall, aged nineteen, brother of the rape victim, was hospitalized with serious abdominal stab wounds.'

'A very silly boy,' Seward said.

'He died three days later, from complications. We never managed to hang that one on Judge, as a murder.'

Seward snorted. 'That was not murder, Ron. That was waste disposal. Those youths was becoming an irritant.'

Persephone Callard had started to back away towards the door. She had her hands clasped so tightly in front of her that Grayle thought she heard a knuckle crack.

'Come back, Seffi,' Seward said lightly. 'You got away last time, just when we was so *very* close. That is not gonna happen again.'

'*Close?*' Callard screamed. 'Close to *what*?'

'Close, darlin', to the manifestation. Come *back*. You know what I want. I want Clarence Judge here. I wanna see my dear old friend. In all his glory.'

'You're insane.'

'Am I? That's your opinion, is it?'

'Think about it, Gary,' Bobby said. 'It doesn't really make any sense.'

But Grayle knew that it kind of did.

And there were photos of the mother all around the walls, and her favourite things scattered about . . . clothes, handbags. And all the family – the husband, the twins, another sister – all of them there. And the room was dense with her before we started . . .

Callard at Mysleton, talking about the most effective manifestation she ever scored.

Bobby said, 'You want Clarence to tell you who killed him? Because if that's—'

'*I just want Clarence!* I wanna *see* him. I want the proof that we go on. Just the way Abblow said we go on. Without any fucking angels with harps on fucking clouds. That we remain what we are. Who we are. That what we made ourselves into is not blown out like a bleeding match, know wha' mean?'

'Life everlasting and no heaven,' Grayle said. 'Jesus, Gary, you're a piece of work.'

Her neck contracted; she was sure he was going to do something to her from behind.

'Sit down,' he said. 'Over there. Join the circle, Seffi. And fetch Clarence for me. I will not ask you again.'

Callard tossed her head like a pedigree racehorse, turned her back on him and walked towards the door.

'Fetch him yourself,' she said, 'you crass little man.'

There was a moment like a chasm.

It was only when the light bulb turned red that Grayle was truly aware of what had happened: the shotgun had gone off.

53

By the time they reached the castle, there were possibly sixty of them. Gentle, peace-loving New Age people: astrologers, dowsers, palmists, Tarot-readers; practitioners of acupuncture, reflexology and reiki; regulators of auras and biorhythms; experts on earth mysteries, geomancy and *feng shui*; members of the New Order of the Golden Dawn, the Aetherius Society and the Subud Brotherhood; followers of Wicca, Rosicrucians and Scientologists. Seers and mystics and healers in suits and saris, patched jeans and ceremonial robes. They carried lamps, they carried candles in glass holders. They held Celtic crosses and wooden staves with archaic symbols carved into them.

At the head of the procession, with the militant Maurice and the edgy etheric therapist Lorna Crane, were Cindy Mars-Lewis, Celtic shaman, and Mr Harry Douglas Oakley, whose great-grandfather was said to haunt the grounds.

Overcross Castle, where the dead had been formally invited to walk, was now floodlit from the parapet, its stone walls gauntly splendid, its tower swollen with the dark charisma of the forbidden.

It had begun to snow very lightly again, out of only a part of the sky, a strange, gritty dust over the cloud-locked crescent moon. Cindy looked up at the high turrets with an anxiety for the most part unrelated to the Forcefield personnel awaiting them at the main entrance.

The Forcefield personnel numbering precisely seven.

None of whom – this was evident – had expected an invasion. Who now assembled on the parapet, exchanging uncertain glances, knowing that if they behaved in a fashion deemed less than formally polite there would be a riot, the real police would be called, and their jobs and conceivably their short-term freedom would be on the line.

'Look, lads,' Maurice Gooch said reasonably, from the bottom step. 'I don't know whether I'm addressing trade unionists at all, but this is a legitimate, peaceful protest relating to conditions on the site, and we would like to put our grievances directly before Mr Kurt Campbell or one of his associates.'

A Forcefield man who, absurdly, wore an arm-band with three stripes, pulled at the peak of his cap and beckoned Maurice to the top of the steps. Cindy followed. The Forcefield man said quietly, 'Come back tomorrow morning, between nine and ten, no more than three of you, and we'll see what can be arranged.'

Maurice smiled at him and turned to the assembly. 'This gentleman would like us to come back tomorrow between nine and ten. How would you feel about that?'

There was a great roar, which in no way could be interpreted as assent.

'Nice try, man,' Maurice said. 'Now go get Kurt.'

Behind the four uniformed men, the conservatory extension was deserted. A small security lamp burned. Carried from inside the house, a full-blown theatrical voice related a story.

'*In 1866, I spent some time for my health's sake at Malvern Spa, where I fasted for several days, partaking only of the mineral waters. It was on this visit that I made the acquaintance of Mr Barnaby Crole and a fellow spiritist, Dr Abblow. And so I came to Overcross . . .*'

One of the Forcefield officers had pulled a mobile phone from a pocket of his uniform and was swiftly tapping out a number when Maurice leapt up the remaining steps and snatched the instrument from his hands, smiling grimly. 'On second thoughts, lads, we'll come in and find him ourselves.' He cancelled the call and handed back the phone. 'Now don't you even—'

Which was when, above – or, in fact, below – the actor's commentary, they heard what could have been nothing but a muffled gunshot.

Maurice stopped. 'What the bloody hell's that, Cindy? A sound-effect?'

'I rather doubt it, boy.' Cindy saw one of the Forcefield employees close his eyes upon an intake of breath which suggested the man had a suspicion of what or who this was about – and a fervent wish that he was no longer a part of it.

Maurice, also, now appeared less ebullient. 'What do we do, Cindy?'

In reply – while holding in his inner vision the glory of the sunrise over High Knoll and praying incoherently to the Lady of the Dawn – Cindy ran up the steps and thrust himself urgently between the uniforms.

* * *

It went on echoing massively in Bobby Maiden's head long after it had died away, repeating itself over the *ulp ulp* of Grayle throwing up.

Maiden fought to swallow his own nausea, to hold his handcuffed wrist steady against the drag. He heard the efficient clack of the sawn-off as Gary Seward finished reloading, came briskly around to the front, not a stain on his suit, not a blotch on his white dress shirt.

'Twice I warned him, yeah?' Seward said. 'You heard me warn him twice.'

Now that the solitary bulb had turned crimson, it was much darker in the cellar, but the reddened glow imposed an illusion of warmth. Three walls were blotched with dark blood, brains, splintered bone, nuggets of foam rubber. Also one side of Grayle's face and her hair. Which she didn't yet know.

Maiden looked away, numb with shock, as Ron Foxworth's stout copper's heart went on pumping arterial blood through the borehole of his neck. He saw Seffi Callard pulling frantically at the door handle before turning back into the room with both hands over her face.

'Come and sit down, love.' Seward hooked a foot around the chair next to Grayle's as Maiden worked out that he and Grayle and Seffi were still alive and uninjured because Seward had confined the blast by shoving both barrels hard into the fabric of the armchair, where it was plumped out into a headrest, the instant before he fired.

Seffi began to scream through her hands. Maiden wrenched in anguish at the hand locked to the dead hand of Ron Foxworth. Seffi bared her stricken face. 'Christ, Bobby, what have I—?'

'It's not your fault,' Maiden murmured. 'Just do what he says.'

'*Bobby.*' Seward smiled again. 'She called you Bobby. So you *do* know each other. Well, that helps no end, Seffi, because if you don't come and sit down and do the business, the next one to go is Bobby hisself.' He levelled his shotgun at Maiden, whose head snapped back instinctively. 'Pffft!' Seward raised the barrel, made like he was blowing away tendrils of drifting smoke. The cocktail of stenches in the room was foul. He didn't seem to notice.

Daniel Dunglas-Home bent and pulled three feet of glowing ectoplasm from the mouth of Lady Colwall.

The cello music swelled to a shivering climax. Dunglas-Home held up the ectoplasm to applause.

It was a farce, a travesty. Dunglas-Home, as Cindy understood it, was slender and a touch camp. He was also very probably a genuine psychic, whose reputation had survived considerable scientific scrutiny.

This man was large and black-whiskered, a vulgar showman, and it was ridiculous and insulting to imagine that Dunglas-Home had done anything as cheap as producing ectoplasm tape from the orifices of a woman assistant, mediumistic or fake.

Tonight's performance was clearly a cynical satire aimed at convincing the potential donors of tourism grants that the new Overcross enterprise was far from sinister and that Kurt Campbell and his associates remained untainted by the mystical gobbledegook purveyed by the stallholders in the grounds.

To genteel applause, Lady Colwall, middle-aged, attractive, endowed with an impressively Victorian *décolletage*, was assisted back into the audience.

From the doorway of the banqueting hall, with the New Age warriors behind him in the passage and the Great Hall, Cindy observed the more formal candlelit gathering.

Two long tables at right angles. The performance taking place in a dark space between and beyond them.

Here, there stood a leather chair and an octagonal table bearing a brass oil lamp, a bottle, a wineglass. The actor, the conjuror, sat down in the chair, laughed lightly as though to himself, poured himself a glass of red wine.

'*I was to make seven further appearances at Overcross, under the patronage of the hospitable, enthusiastic and – fortunately – wonderfully gullible Mr Barnaby Crole. And would have made many more had it not been for the arrival of*', the performer scowled, '*the uncannily perceptive Dr Anthony Abblow.*'

Kurt Campbell was at the head of the nearest of the two tables, his back to the doorway and to Cindy, his golden hair luxuriant over the collar of his white dinner jacket. His glass of after-dinner port half-full. There were about twenty other guests, some in Victorian costume, some in ordinary evening dress, two women in cocktail dresses. Neither of them – a last vain hope – was Grayle.

All right, then. Holding up a hand to restrain Maurice and the others, Cindy fluffed up his hair and padded across to tap Kurt lightly upon the shoulder.

Kurt turned, at first impatient and then exhibiting a delicious, slow-dawning shock.

Cindy smiled in the glow of five bright candles in a silver holder.

'A quiet word, I think, boy,' he said.

In wiping her mouth with her free hand, Grayle inadvertently touched something else on the side of her face and she howled in revulsion and vomited again, while aware of Seward moving silently, purposefully and taking her free hand. And when it was all gone, and her stomach felt sore and she was dry-retching, she looked up into a blurry image of Persephone Callard in the chair next to her and found that this hand was free no longer but handcuffed to Callard's right hand and Callard's left hand was linked to Bobby's right.

And they were a complete circle now. Including the horrific corpse of Ron Foxworth. She couldn't look at him, but she could feel the small hairs on the back of his hand against the back of her own.

This was a nightmare beyond all imaginable nightmares.

'God forgive me, Grayle,' Callard whispered. 'I'm so very sorry. All this, I could've . . .'

'Well, I apologize for that!' Seward boomed. 'It was for Clarence, really. I owed him. Gary Seward promised. You ladies can close your eyes if you want.'

The way he kept referring to himself in the third person. Like putting distance between himself and his actions – as if what *Gary Seward* had promised was already set in stone, out of his hands.

Seward stood outside the circle, his back to the door. Grayle heard Bobby say, 'So you're not joining us, then, Gary.'

'Impractical, Bobby. Plus, Gary Seward, for all his many abilities, is not psychic. Went for these psychic lessons once, but it din't work. This guru geezer, he says I "lacked the requisite humility". Which was a load of old toffee. I mean, you look at Miss Persephone Callard here, how much humility's she bleedin' got?'

Grayle screamed, 'Why don't you just swallow both barrels now? 'Cause you're never, never, *never* gonna cover this one up. This is—'

England, she was going to say.

Seward ignored her anyway, addressed Callard. 'Listen, you'd know about this. Don't they say that lifeblood's the great materializing agent, don't they say that? This is gonna help even more, innit? I ain't psychic but I can feel him coming, pushing at the curtain, know wha' mean?'

Bobby said, 'Why isn't Campbell here?'

'No need. He's done his bit.'

'Nothing to do with him being squeamish. Nothing to do with what he doesn't know won't—'

'Shut up,' Seward said. 'First warning.'

'Oh God.' Grayle set her teeth, fighting for control.

'You surely realize I can't possibly do this now,' Callard said.

Seward broke his shotgun, snapped it back together decisively. 'You fucking will, my dear. Especially as all you got to do is say the words. You know the words. You say the words . . . and he'll come.'

Except he won't, Grayle thought. *He won't come at all. She'll just think he's come. This is what happens. She thinks he's come. Kurt hypnotized her so that whenever she says that famous sentence,* The lines are open, *she believes he's there. Clarence Judge.*

Post-hypnotic suggestion, this was the term. And the rest of it, the smells, the cold air, the breakages were the physical results of what that suggestion triggered in Callard's volatile psychic metabolism.

542

'And because you are the best there is, you'll make it so I can see him,' Seward said.

Except you won't. You can't.

'And when I get tired of waiting, I blow Bobby into the spirit world. Which don't worry him greatly – he knows the way. All right. Hands on the table. Ron, too. Palms down, little fingers touching.'

Resting the gun barrel on Bobby Maiden's shoulder, the mouth against his cheek, Seward began to separate Ron Foxworth's fingers.

Seffi Callard shook her head. 'You're—'

'And the next person here calls me insane, just to make it that little bit different, I'll blow a hole the size of a football in Bobby's stomach.'

He took a step back so that he could see them all. Opened the gun, peered at the cartridges, snapped it shut. *Clack.*

'Persephone . . . don't disappoint me.'

Seffi Callard's mouth tightened. She looked despairingly at Bobby, then closed her eyes. In the silence, under the bloodied bulb, she drew in a long, long breath.

And let it out: 'Haaaaaaaaaaaaaaaaaaaaaaaaaw.'

'OK,' she said after a while. 'The lines are open.'

Kurt Campbell propelled Cindy out of the room, through a black velvet curtain, beyond which a young man at a mixing desk was making scaled-down *son et lumière*. Out through another doorway, and into a small stone hallway, where a spiral staircase began.

And where Kurt spun at Cindy, his mouth in a snarl, his forefinger rigid. 'I don't know how you got in here, you bastard, but if you think you can—'

'Listen to me, Kurt.'

'If you think—'

'Of course, you *could* try to mesmerize me again,' Cindy brazenly sought out Kurt's eyes, 'or you could engage me in conversation, and we could talk at length. We could talk of the National Lottery and the Sherwin family of Banbury and the celebrated fitting up of the unfortunate Billy Spindler.'

Kurt's hand dropped to his side. 'Get out.'

'We could talk about the time you went whingeing to *Gary* about how the Welsh poof had done you out of a job then made a fool of you. Knowing how much Gary hates poofs, isn't it? Deviants and cross-dressers. All Welshmen, too, probably on principle.'

'You're fucking mad.'

'But what I would very much prefer to discuss is the location of the *real* seance. Where is it, Kurt? Where is Gary Seward?'

'Get out of my house.'

'As distinct from Mr Gary Seward's house?'

'This is *my house*.' Kurt seized Cindy's arms, beginning to shake him, thrusting him back against the stone wall.

'And where . . . is Grayle . . . Underhill?'

'I've never heard of a Grayle Und—'

'Before you hurt me, Kurt, let me make it . . . clear to you . . . that it will not happen. Miss Callard will not . . . be – you must believe me – will not be able to do what you require. Do you . . . understand me? When she refused it was because she could not . . .'

Kurt stopped shaking him.

'It may already be too late,' Cindy said. 'There was a shot, as you heard. From the cellars? Where are the cellars, Kurt? Don't fool about, boy, we have to stop this abomination.'

'There are no cellars. I don't know what you're talking about. And you're pushing me too far.'

'Oh Kurt, you've already gone too far, lovely. Further than you would have ever imagined before you entered dear Gary's social circle and began letting him do all those favours for you. And then—'

Kurt slapped him hard across the face with his left hand and then punched him savagely in the left breast with his right. Cindy went down on his knees. He did not stop talking.

'. . . those deaths. The poor pilot and the man who took on a blonde too big for him. Pure coincidence, of course. But what if there was a third, more appalling, more devastating? A beautiful, multiple death? Well . . . a piece of—'

Kurt slammed an elegant foot into Cindy's face. Cindy collapsed.

'. . . piece of cake for Gary and the boys from . . .' he found his face against a cold stone flag, blood oozing from his mouth '. . . Forcefield.' He coughed feebly, spat out a tooth. Heard footsteps, voices, people calling for him.

'But who should it be?' His words thickened by blood. 'Who should it be, Kurt? Must move now . . . while the story's hot . . . don't delay, don't miss the opportunity . . .'

'*Cindy? CINDY!*'

Hands. Many hands.

Cindy back on his knees. A blur of faces. Could not focus, could not think quite where he was.

'Who should it be?' he murmured. 'Who were those stupid people . . . with the fleet of BMWs? *They* deserve it, the crass . . . crass idiots.'

545

54

It wasn't long before Maiden became aware that whatever Seffi Callard usually did, she wasn't doing. Whatever customarily happened was not happening.

She would close her eyes, throw back her head, as though someone was pulling on the rope of her hair, draw in another slow breath. But when he looked at her again, the amber glow would be back in her eyes, wide open again, desperate.

Pleading. Saying, *Someone has to stop this.* Knowing that no-one could.

Maybe ten minutes passed. Gary Seward watched in silence from outside the handcuffed seance.

All he wanted was to see Clarence Judge again. In the end it was that simple: Gary Seward and Kurt Campbell wanted proof, for themselves, of a certain kind of life after death. Abblow's kind. The transference of the human essence to a parallel, godless existence where Victorian values survived the grave, where a life of crime would not rebound on you, where the spirit of Clarence Judge remained unsinged by the fires of hell.

The thought of it made Maiden scared and depressed. It too much resembled the colourless, ill-formed memories of his own death experience. And he was going back there very soon; death as the end of everything would be an infinitely more appealing prospect.

His eyes met Seffi's before she closed them again. He eased his hand over hers and their fingers enfolded, slippery with cold sweat and despair. When he closed his own eyes and tried to pray, what came to him was an image of the salmon-coloured dawn at High Knoll, layers of cloud interwoven with the distant Malvern Hills. Which was here. From the Knoll, this was where the dawn began. And none of them were going to see the next one, were they, not from anywhere?

He didn't know Seward was behind him until the barrel of the shotgun came down and broke three of his fingers.

The whisper was close to his left ear. 'Now, that ain't how we arranges our hands, is it, cock?'

Kurt Campbell must have been well away before they came – Maurice and Lorna and Harry Oakley. Well away before Cindy was able to pull together his thoughts and was struggling to say, *Find him . . . stop him. He's the only one who can tell us where . . .*

But it was far too late. This was Kurt's house. A thousand places to go, including the dreadful cellars.

Lorna Crane was trying to clean up Cindy's face with his own lavender-scented handkerchief. 'I'm all right,' he was telling her through bruised lips. 'I'm all right, lovely.'

'You want to bloody see yourself,' said Maurice.

'Maurice . . . listen to me, boy . . . you have to find the entrance to the cellars.'

Lorna muttering. 'God, I think he's lost a couple of teeth. Oh Christ, could his jaw be broken?'

'Do you *understand*?'

Maurice said, 'Because of that shot?'

'Find the entrance, but do not, on *any* account, go in. Fetch me at once. It may be a flight of steps, it may be a trapdoor. The most obvious area is the kitchens, but it could be anywhere . . . at the side of a fireplace, beneath a carpet, in a cupboard under stairs to the first floor . . . Look everywhere.'

'All of us?'

'Everyone. Go in groups. Fours and fives. Don't let anyone put you off.'

'The dungeons,' Mr Oakley said. 'Crole and Abblow's dungeons.'

'Do you know where they might be?' Cindy demanded, his whole face ablaze with pain.

Mr Oakley shook his head. 'Only that it was where they murdered my great-grandad. They've killed someone else now, haven't they?'

'Just find the entrance. Tell me. I shall be in the great hall.'

'I'll stay with you,' Lorna said.

'Thank you. And . . . pray, all of you. Pray to your several gods that we are not too late.'

But he thought they were.

'This is good,' Seward confided to Maiden. 'This is excellent, how that happened. I once saw Clarence do a geezer's hands. Some nonce. Not wiv a sawn-off, mind. Wiv a piece of pipe, but still . . .'

Seffi was staring down at the table. Their hands were separated. Maiden's fingers were turning black. The pain was dull and distant.

Across the table, Grayle was unnaturally still. Shock. Behind her, Clarence's grey suit hung limply

548

from its hanger. Maiden thought he could see smoke from the oil heaters funnelled from its collar. He thought he could see part of Ron Foxworth's white jaw, with teeth, on the table bearing the sepia photograph of Clarence Judge. The face became, for a moment, very clear, and it seemed to Maiden that the bulb had become much brighter.

Seward straightened up.

'Is he here? Is that him?'

At that moment Foxworth's body slid a few inches down in the armchair and the cuffs dragged painfully on Maiden's left hand, and the bulb was dark again, under its skin of dried blood.

Seffi Callard didn't react. Her eyes were closed again. The cellar smelled sweetly foul.

Seward hissed, 'You see him?'

Seffi gulped air through her mouth. There were tears on her face.

Grayle said, '*I* see him.'

Seward swung round, the sawn-off at his hip.

Grayle stayed motionless, opposite Maiden, her back straight, both hands on the table, one pulled slightly askew by the slippage of the corpse but she seemed no longer affected by its proximity.

'Hi, Clarence.' Grayle giggled.

Oh, no, Maiden thought. He watched the expressions – scepticism, suspicion, hope, yearning, hunger – chasing across Seward's face like a speeded-up film of storm clouds. This was the real, unpublic face: charmless, cheerless, flabby, the mouth turned down, the dyed hair sweated to the forehead. The bow tie was off, the shirt undone.

Seward said, 'You?'

Grayle was staring past him with a lopsided smile. 'You don't scare me, Clarence.'

Seward moved back against the wall, the shotgun pointed upwards. 'What's he look like? You tell me exactly what he looks like!'

'You do not freaking *scare* me!' Grayle screamed.

'What's he *look* like, bitch?'

'He, uh . . . he's just like . . . I . . . I don't know . . . He's not here, not like you and I are . . . Oh Jesus . . . He *is* here. Now he *is*. Now he's like . . . he's *really freaking here*. He's just . . . standing here. He's wearing a suit. And a white shirt. And like a thin, black tie. Like a funeral tie. Maybe . . .' Grayle let out a wild peal of laughter. 'Maybe he just went to his own funeral . . .'

Seward's breath was coming faster. 'You better not be fucking wiv me, lady. Go on. What else? His shoes. Describe his shoes.'

'I can't see his shoes. He like . . . he isn't too defined down there. It's like he goes into mist, and his . . . he's off the ground is what I'm saying. It's like he's maybe six inches off the ground. Jesus, he's . . . you know, he's awful. This is a dead man.'

'Ask him if he can see us.'

'Yeah . . .'

'*Ask him!*'

'I'm asking him! In my head. You can't just . . .'

'What's he say?'

'He isn't saying anything. He's just there, is all. All he is is *there*.'

'Then why can't *I* see him?'

''Cause you're an insensitive asshole, how the fuck should I know?'

'All right.' Seward was feverishly breaking and

snapping shut his shotgun. 'You said you can see him now, yeah? Clear?'

'I can see him very well.'

'So you tell me what he looks like. His face.'

'All right, he . . . he's got a thin face and this hooked kind of Roman nose. His hair is slicked back. It's that style that was fashionable for guys over here not all that long ago. Like shaven hard up both sides and real thick on top. Only you can tell this isn't one of those fashion cuts, this is how it's always been. His eyes are . . . pale, I guess. Like watery. And no colour . . . no colour that I can make out. His whole face has no colour. He's a dead man. Uh, he has this scar.'

As Grayle talked, Maiden was picturing his drawing. She was describing it. And because there'd been no published photograph of Clarence Judge since he was scarred in prison by the fish-slice bloke, this was where Grayle started walking the tightrope. Suppose the scar was nothing like the drawing?

'OK, the scar . . . Clarence, will you stop freaking looking at me like you wanna . . . ?'

'The *scar*,' Seward hissed.

'It . . . it's cutting across the side of his head from the left eye . . . the left eye as you look at him. It runs almost but not quite horizontally from the eye to the ear, like half of a pair of glasses.'

'Go on.'

'Well, that's it, it's a scar. Oh. Except, about three-quarters along, it kind of disappears under a fold of skin. Like, it's not a pretty scar, but this part is . . . it's like you would say it was stitched up by two different guys working from different ends and they didn't quite meet up. Plus, it looks kind of livid.'

'Christ,' Seward said.

'Maybe . . . I don't see that part too well, he never turns his head . . . maybe that's not part of the scar at all.'

'It's another scar,' Seward said, almost breathlessly, to Maiden. There was either a shadow or a big patch of sweat across his shirt. 'About two months before he died, he was moaning about the scar irritating him, pulling down his eye. Reckoned it was affecting his sight. He got mad with it. One night, he takes a kitchen knife, slices into it. Sews it up hisself, different. He could do fings like that and hardly feel it. How would *she* know about that, Bobby? She never knew Clarence. You bleedin' swear to me she never knew him?'

'She's American, Gary.'

'You think she's seeing him?'

'I don't know.'

'What do *you* see?'

'Nothing.'

'Tell him *I* wanna see him!' Seward roared. 'Tell him I need to fucking see his ugly face!'

'You don't get through to him, OK?' Grayle said testily. 'He does not respond. It's just like he's a dummy. A dead dummy. This is . . . He doesn't hear me. Jesus, did Campbell hypnotize him to just . . . be like something out the basement at Madame Tussaud's?'

Seward moved nearer the circle. He stopped.

'What did you say?'

'I . . . said . . . I . . . the basement at Madam . . .'

'*Before that.*'

Maiden said quickly, 'Ask him if he knows who killed him. Ask him if he knows who shot him from behind.'

Seward spun, crouching, with the shotgun out-

552

stretched. Maiden staring down the two black holes. *He's going to kill me anyway. It's got nothing to do with any of this. He's doing it for Riggs. Payback for Crewe. An arrangement.*

He said, 'Grayle, ask Clarence if he remembers who shot him and where it . . . ?'

'Hold it!' Grayle cried out. 'He . . .' She looked at Seward, her voice dropping to conversation level. 'You killed him, right, Gary? You did it in the apartment near the Rotunda in Cheltenham.'

Persephone Callard's eyes came open. She looked stunned.

'I'm seeing this quite clearly,' Grayle said firmly. 'Here's what happens. First, Kurt hypnotizes him and he plants this . . . a post-hypnotic suggestion that like . . . when Clarence hears the words, "The lines are open", he'll come back from wherever he is. Like, wher*ever* he is. And then, while he's still in trance, Gary just like . . . blows him away. From behind.'

'*What* . . . ?' Maiden said.

Sounding, he hoped, as though this was a big shock . . . that it was taking some getting his mind around. Like the same theory hadn't been forming in his head most of the night. Forming out of Grayle's idea that Kurt had hypnotized Seffi. Hardening up at the first sight of the Cheltenham furniture, here in the cellar where Crole and Abblow . . .

He said, 'This is what they did to John Hodge, isn't it? They killed him after ordering him under hypnosis to come back. To return to the place he loved most in all the world. So attached to it his family used to joke about him haunting it when he was dead.'

Seffi Callard said, 'The first experiment in hypnosis beyond death. The obvious conjunction of spiritualism

553

and mesmerism.' She gave out a cracked laugh. 'Only a Victorian English gentleman would see instructing the dead as the best way in.'

Maiden went on looking down those cold black metal corridors.

'You want to talk about this, Gary?'

The entrance hall, with its vaulted ceiling, its coats of arms and crossed pikes, its stags' heads on shields, its wrought-iron chandelier with the candles.

And many people. New Agers mingling with the councillors and tourism officials and the local aristocracy – these individuals bemused or offended and pursued by a harassed, perspiring Francine. No sign of Kurt, but there wouldn't be. No visible Forcefield uniforms. Occasionally, one of the dignitaries would glance at Cindy, half-recognizing him, but no-one asked about his swollen and bloodied face, his crooked bosom.

Then Maurice Gooch was there, quivering with agitation. 'Cindy, there's . . .'

'The cellar?' Cindy snapped. 'Did you find a way in?'

'No, but . . .'

'There has got to be an entrance!'

'We've been everywhere, man,' Maurice protested. 'We've been into every room, including two locked ones. We've ripped up carpets, we've moved dressers, we've levered up flagstones. Either there's no way in, or there's no cellar. Only, there is, according to my pendulum. It's got five rooms.'

'Did you ask Vera in the kitchen?'

'We've asked every bugger, Cindy. I'm sorry. But, listen . . .'

'They can't have blocked them off,' said Mr Oakley.

554

'A gun went off down there,' Cindy reminded him. 'We shall have to call the police. No option now.'

'And how are the police going to find their way in?' demanded Maurice. 'Take up t'bloody floor? But, aye, you'd better get 'em in, because of the body.'

Cindy stiffened.

'In the lavvy.'

'Where?'

'The toilet, just along there, through yon place wi' t'tables. A man. Just lying there by the urinals, wi' his . . . Like, he must've been having a piss when he were . . .'

'Shot,' said Mr Oakley. 'Shot in the head. Killed instantly, I reckon.'

'Not Kurt.'

'No.' Maurice shook his head. 'Older.'

Cindy thought drably of Bobby Maiden.

'Show me.'

'St Kurt,' Bobby said. 'Remember? All that stuff in Marcus's cuttings about Campbell giving his services free to help dying people, terminal patients?'

'Oh, Jesus, he was messing with their minds.' Grayle found she was staring at the blood-drenched, headless remains of Superintendent Ron Foxworth and it was just another sad, stinking piece of meat, a reminder of why she was vegetarian. What she was hearing about, this was still-active, insidious evil.

'Kurt was planting stuff on them before they died, wasn't he? Post-hypnotic suggestion. *When I call you, wherever you are, you'll come back to me.*' Bobby turned to Seward. 'Did it work, Gary?'

'Nah.' Seward leaned back in his chair, the shotgun on his knee. 'None of the sods came back. Kurt figured

555

it was all the morphine and stuff they was getting intravenously at the end. Plus the time lapse. It was often three, four weeks between the hypnosis and when they snuffed it.'

These bastards, Grayle thought. These unbelievable bastards.

'Crole and Abblow tried the same thing,' Bobby said. 'It was noticeable at the time how concerned they always were for the welfare of the local dying. Hovering around deathbeds. Unhealthy. Well, obviously, it didn't work for them either, and people were getting suspicious. Abblow presumably decided what they needed was someone fit and well who had no idea his card was marked.'

Grayle said, 'John Hodge.'

'And he come back,' said Seward. 'He did. Loads of people seen the bleeder.' He looked at Bobby. Grayle saw that he'd never looked at Foxworth's body; it didn't disgust him, it didn't offend him. Like guys around slaughterhalls their whole working lives would fail to register an extra carcass. 'Where'd you get this stuff, Bobby?'

'Bloke called Harry. Hodge was his great-grandad.'

'Yeah, we seen him with his posters. We invited him in for a drink. He wouldn't come.'

Smarter than us, Grayle thought wretchedly.

'He told you what they did with Hodge, Bobby?'

'Seems obvious what they did. Must've been obvious to Kurt Campbell from the beginning.'

'Not *quite* the beginning. Stories about this place, they been going round for years on the psychic circuits Kurt's plugged into. It was when we sent a surveyor round and he found these cellars, and a tin box with

Crole's notes, written in his own writing. Exciting, Bobby.'

'I wonder what the phrase was. The one that was intended to bring Hodge back. Like "The lines are open."'

'Gotta be more than a phrase,' Seward said. 'We don't know how they did it, but it must've been easier with Abblow being a medium. What *we* done, we played Clarence a tape of Callard's voice saying it.' He gave Seffi a sly glance. 'Kurt recorded it when you was together. So it had to be you, sweetheart, no substitutes.'

'This was just before you killed him?' Bobby said. 'Or did you have someone else do that?'

'Nah. I done him, like she said. Only fair. Only decent, poor old love.'

'What I thought,' Bobby said. 'How it seemed to me was that he must've been a bit of an embarrassment to you, Gary. Useful in the old days, long as it wasn't anything too complicated. But you were probably glad when he was put away for the rape. Times were changing. Old-style hardmen like Clarence – the ones you couldn't take to a party – were getting to be of limited value.'

'Hadn't got the GCSEs, Bobby.'

'And, like I say, by the time he came out, you'd done your book, and you were a public figure. The chat shows. The Rotary Club dinners. No way Clarence was going to fit into that circuit – not very smart, no sense of humour, no particular personality at all. A charmless bastard, on the whole.'

'You'll pay for that in a minute, Bobby. But, yeah.'

'All Clarence is good at is harming people, and

suddenly he's back on the streets and nobody to turn to for work but his old gaffer. Must've been a bit trying for you, Gary.'

'Nah. It was him hated it more than me. Fish out of water. Cops watching every move he makes. Memos about him computered to every nick in the land. He was too innocent for this hi-tech world, Bobby. Would've been back inside in no time at all.'

'And who knows who he'd have accidentally taken with him.'

'He wouldn't grass nobody, you know that. Nah, this was a sweet way to go. And if we coulda told him he was coming back, we would've.'

'The flat,' Bobby said. 'The one you later passed off as Barber's. Why did you kill Clarence there?'

'Well, we had all them flats, didn't we? Used for this and that. How it happened, Clarence's chest was bad when he come out, wiv all them years of bad snout. So he wants to give up the weed. I says, " 'Ere, I know just the geezer." We takes him up the flat, sits him down all comfy, then Kurt puts him under. A jewel of a subject. Like that!' Seward snapped his fingers.

'A faithful servant,' Bobby said. 'Foot soldier.'

'Yeah.'

Grayle was blown away by the bizarre glint of tears in Seward's hard eyes. No remorse – just nostalgia, sentiment, warm affection. If there was anything left down there in her shrunken gut she could've thrown up all over again.

'And you played him the tape,' Bobby said. '"The lines are open." Seffi's voice. And you told him that when he heard it, he would come back. And then . . .'

'One shot. Pffft! Clean as a whistle. I cried afterwards, it was so swift and clean. Moving, know wha' mean?'

'And then you packaged him up and loaded him in a van and drove him down to the Thames Valley, left him in a skip.'

'He'd've understood. A memorial service wouldn't've been appropriate, would it, seeing none of us reckoned much to the All bleedin' mighty? But we had a few beers down Clarence's old boozer in Saxton Gate, and that was very nice.' He smiled at the memory. 'A very pleasant night.'

He stood up. He went and stood with his back to the oak door.

'You never saw him, did you? You never saw a bleedin' thing, you bitch. You was pissing right up my leg.'

'You can believe what you want,' Grayle said.

'And that black slapper, she conned me too.'

'They don't realize all the trouble you went to,' Bobby said. 'I don't know how you tolerate it.'

Seward hefted the sawn-off, turned on Bobby.

'I warned you.'

'So you did, Gary,' Bobby said wearily. He put his head back, closed his eyes. 'So you did.'

Grayle thought, *I would rather go first than see or hear this.*

'Open your eyes, cock. I want you to see. I want you staring down the little black tunnels.'

'Piss off, Gary. Ron was right. You're just a toerag in a fantasy world.'

'What if I'm doing it now, Bobby? What if I'm aiming for just over your belt, so you die wiv your guts in your hands? What if I'm coming in close? What if I'm giving you the countdown. Three. Two . . .'

559

'Look!' Grayle screamed. 'Can't you see him? Can't you see Clarence? He's staring right at you, Gary! And you know the reason you can't see him?'

Seward breathed out roughly. 'You know I'm tired of you and your games. How about, if I turn around, and if I don't see Clarence, I do *you*? How you feel about that?'

'The . . . the reason you don't see him . . . is you'd just be looking at yourself. You and Kurt. What you made. That's not Clarence, it never was. All you'd see is what you made.'

'I turn round and if I don't see him, I blow you through the wall. Is that a deal, darlin'?'

Grayle said steadily, 'That's perfectly fine.'

Seward began slowly to turn.

Bobby threw himself at Seward, dragging the corpse and Grayle and Seffi Callard, pulled the whole damn table over but Seward moved easily away and stood with his back to the door and his shotgun at his hip, fully turned and cold and relaxed. In the dimness Grayle saw the fire from both barrels.

55

The spiritualists said that when you died, friends and relatives who'd gone before would be waiting for you, to welcome you, show you the way to wherever it was – the endless garden with birdsong and angelsong, fountains of sound.

Bobby Maiden arose from blood and looked up into whiteness and psychotic eyes.

It was not inappropriate that he should be met by the amiable cross-bred bull terrier called Malcolm. It was not unlikely that Malcolm had gone before, shot by one of the Forcefield men.

Moments passed.

The strip light zizzed and flickered.

He could not feel his hands.

He saw a face on the flagstones.

Spirit-voices chattered all around him. The room shimmered blue-white, in all its horror, like the deep-freeze in a meat-packing plant.

'Bobby?' A small voice.

'Grayle. Are you—?'

'Yeah. You?'

'Sure.'

At some point he became aware that the face on the flagstones was Gary Seward's. Maiden raised himself and peered over it.

In the back of Gary's skull was a bullet hole. The most beautiful bullet hole he'd ever seen. He kept looking at it and looking away and looking back. He wanted to frame the memory of it.

Malcolm sniffed at Gary's head and then turned away.

'Vera?' Grayle's voice again.

The figure in the doorway was big and still and black and white, except for . . .

'Vera!' Grayle shouted. 'Vera, hold on . . . !'

The woman looked once over the room and then turned away. She was all in black and white, except for the yellow rubber gloves. A black pistol, a revolver, pointing down from one of them.

Bobby Maiden said, in disbelief, 'Connie . . . ?'

As the woman quietly went out, Grayle said, 'Oh, Jesus, no . . .'

Cindy stumbled into the kitchen. It stretched away before him like an old-fashioned hospital ward.

He saw Vera before she saw him.

She was at the bottom end, near the fridges. She was tearing off her Victorian waitress's costume. When Cindy came in, she snatched up something wrapped in brown paper. Instinctively, Cindy didn't ask her if she'd heard the shot. He asked her how he might get into the cellars.

'Those outbuildings at the back?' Vera's voice had toughened, was like whipcord. 'The middle one, the stable. Third stall. Where the manger's been moved.'

'Thank you.' He turned, saw Maurice enter the kitchen.

'From what I gather,' Vera said, 'they needed to be able to get in and out from the grounds. That was those . . .'

'Crole and Abblow.'

'Yeah, them. Needed access separate from the house. You go down a bit careful, Cindy, but there won't be a problem. Don't worry about them security men, they're staying well out of it. Nobody to tell them otherwise. They ain't stupid.'

Cindy nodded. Beckoned Maurice.

'You never saw me,' Vera said.

'No.'

'Him neither.'

'Him neither. Count on it.'

Persephone Callard, liquid-eyed, was slowly shaking her head.

'Silly. Really, really silly, Bobby.'

The liquid in her eyes was blood. Her upper face was all blood, to beyond the hairline.

She laughed. 'I suppose that's my . . . TV career fucked.'

'Just don't move, Seffi,' Grayle said. 'Don't move a goddamn inch.'

Maiden and Seffi were still joined at the wrist. Maiden tried to reach for her hand. His fingers refused to respond.

Seffi smiled. 'He done for me, guv.' Em's voice, ironical.

No. Please, no. Please not again.

Grayle hauled on the horror behind her to try and

reach Seffi. 'I guess he fired when Vera shot him. Most of it went high. The table protected us, maybe. I guess Seffi must've . . .'

'I want to say . . .' Seffi spoke softly but firmly, her lip quivering just a little '. . . I want to explain why he . . . it . . . didn't come. Perhaps the one time it would've helped, there's the irony.'

'It did come,' Grayle said.

Maiden stared at her. 'I thought—'

'You thought I was faking. Well, some of it. Some of it was faked. Like, it didn't talk. It was a dead thing. I guess that's what you get, with hypnosis. Aw . . . Just forget it. I feel stupid now. I don't know what I saw.'

'Very good,' Seffi said. 'And there'll be a vacancy now, too.'

No!

'Listen, I want to tell you where I went, after the window . . .'

'It doesn't matter,' Maiden said. 'Just . . .'

'I took the Jeep and I parked it about . . . half a mile away. Then I tried to sleep for an hour or two. In the car. And then I walked up to that place . . . with the burial chamber.'

'High Knoll,' Grayle whispered.

'Yah. I took the cross from around my neck and I laid it on the stone, and I sat there and I waited for the dawn. Wasn't much of one, but I felt . . . I felt some strange things. I mean, it was . . . good. And I was able to . . . you know, pray and things like that, and I . . . I told . . . whoever . . . that I didn't want to see anything like . . . again.'

'Honey,' Grayle said, 'you must've been freezing.'

'Froze my ass.' Seffi smiled. 'Actually I didn't feel

564

cold at all. I feel . . . I suppose I feel rather colder now.'
She reached out. 'Just a bit. Hold my hand, Bobby?'

He tried. He couldn't.

Her hand lay still as stone between them.

'Thank you,' Seffi said. 'That feels so much better.'

Epilogue: Lines Closed

The hospital administrator at Elham General has tried to reason with her. Talked about staff shortages, about her pension.

Sister Andy Anderson told him to go boil his head.

Before she can think better of it, she drives home to the red-brick street by the derelict furniture warehouse, does the usual slalom between the old cars, about three per household, and rushes in to pack a case, leaving the front door open behind her.

When she comes down from the bedroom, there's this woman sitting bold as bloody brass on her sofa, under Bobby Maiden's gouache of the ruins at Castle Farm.

'Whit the *fock* . . . ?' Andy's accent is always made denser by shock.

The woman sits quite calmly, bag on knee. She's wearing a shapeless old fake-fur jacket. 'Message from Bobby, Sister Anderson. He says if you can make it to Castle Farm your healing skills would be most appreciated.'

Andy relaxes. 'Already on ma way, hen. I must be psychic.'

Earlier, from the hospital, Andy left a furious message on the answering machine at *The Vision*.

This followed the call she had in the middle of the night from Marcus Bacton, in another hospital. *Bastards have abandoned me, Anderson. I'm giving them precisely one hour and then I'm pulling this bastard monitor out of the bastard wall and calling for a bastard taxi.*

Andy suspected the Health Service had done all it would ever be permitted to do for Marcus Bacton.

She remembered what she'd said to Bobby Maiden when he told her she'd never leave Elham. *It'll happen. One day soon, I'll be just a memory here. A grating Glaswegian growl in the night. A stale smell of high-tar smoke in the lavvy.*

Happened sooner than she'd figured. Looked like only alternative medicine was going to get Marcus Bacton back on his feet.

'Don't I know you?' she inquires of the woman. 'Like from years ago? Were you no' once brought in from Feeny Park with . . . ?'

'That's right. Consuela. Connie.'

'Aye. So you would be Vic Clutton's . . .'

'That's right.'

'I'm so sorry, love.'

'Yeah.'

'Wis down tae Riggs,' Andy says. 'You do know that?' What the hell, she's away from here today; doesn't matter what she says now. 'And one day, they're gonnae—'

'Riggs is dead,' Connie tells her.

'Nae kidding,' Andy says slowly.

'He was shot. In a lavatory. At a big house in the Malverns.'

570

'Where'd you learn that?'

'In tomorrow's papers,' Connie says.

'I see.'

'What I reckon, somebody with a real grudge must've been tracking his movements for several days. Must've known somebody inside Forcefield Security. Learned he was due to attend this reception. And . . . you know . . . planned ahead.'

'That's bloody devious,' Andy says.

'Anyway, I just happened to be passing that way last night, and I run into Bobby, and I said I was coming back this morning, and he said would I tell you the score. He said you was . . . all right. But I knew that anyway. From Victor.'

'I'm honoured, hen.' From Consuela, Andy learns what she already knows about Marcus Bacton. Also that Bobby is going to need his hand bandaging regularly while he thinks – very hard this time – about leaving the police. And that Cindy Mars-Lewis is considering minor corrective cosmetic surgery.

'Wee Grayle?'

'The American girl's all right, the dog's all right. The police are looking for Kurt Campbell, the hypnotist. Oh. Yeah. Persephone Callard – you've heard of her? The psychic?'

'Aye, I have.'

Connie says without emotion, 'She won't be seeing any more spirits. She was in a shooting incident.'

'Oh.'

'She was blinded,' Connie says.

'Jesus God.'

'Madman with a shotgun.'

'Have they got him?'

'He's dead.'

571

'I see. Is all this gonnae mean a lot of explaining for Bobby?'

'I wouldn't know, sister.' Connie stands up. Her small handbag seems surprisingly heavy.

'Or for you?' Andy lifts an eyebrow.

'Well, Bobby . . .' Connie hesitates. 'Bobby thinks I'd be better off never having left town these past few days. Though, obviously I couldn't've spent them at home.'

'On account of it was too upsetting for you. Keep looking out the front window, seeing where it happened to Vic. I can understand that. It's probably why you'd've been better off staying with me.'

'That's what Bobby thought.'

Andy nods. Thinks about it.

'Well,' she says, 'it's been nice having you, hen.'

LOTTO BLAZE WAS CINDY STITCH-UP!

MIRROR EXCLUSIVE

by Gregory Cook

The Lotto inferno which wiped out a whole family may have been started in a bid to destroy top TV host Cindy Mars-Lewis.

The amazing allegation came last night from Cindy's former producer after police revealed that the fire in Banbury, Oxfordshire was arson.

Jo Shepherd, 28, said, 'I know it sounds incredible, but we've all known for some time that certain people had it in for Cindy.

'When two jackpot winners died in close succession, it's my belief that somebody saw their chance . . .

'I think the Sherwin family were the tragic victims of a secret vendetta that's gone way out of control.'

The BBC were thought to have fired Cindy after he was accused of jinxing jackpot winners with a series of cruel jibes.

BBC chiefs refused to support Jo Shepherd's theory last night. But a spokesman said, 'We do agree that this curse story has got completely out of hand, and we would very much like to talk to Mr Mars-Lewis.'

Cindy, however, was still in hiding last night . . .

THE COLD CALLING
By Will Kingdom

Life isn't easy for Detective Inspector Bobby Maiden. Death is even harder.

When Maiden is revived in hospital after dying in a hit and run incident, his memories are not the familiar ones of bright lights and angel voices, only of a cold, dark place he has no wish to revisit . . . ever.

But his experience means that Bobby Maiden may be the only person who can reach The Green Man, a serial murderer the police don't even know exists . . . a predator who returns to stone circles, burial mounds and ancient churches in the belief that he is defending Britain's sacred heritage.

Meanwhile, New Age journalist Grayle Underhill arrives from New York to search for her sister who's become obsessed with the arcane mysteries of the Stone Age.

The bloody trail leads to a remote village on the Welsh Border . . . and to people who know that *there are more crimes in heaven and earth* . . .

0 552 14584 X

A SELECTED LIST OF FINE NOVELS
AVAILABLE FROM CORGI BOOKS

14783 4	CRY OF THE PANTHER	Adam Armstrong	£5.99
14497 5	BLACKOUT	Campbell Armstrong	£5.99
14667 6	DEADLINE	Campbell Armstrong	£5.99
14646 3	PLAGUE OF ANGELS	Alan Blackwood	£5.99
14775 3	THE EXORCIST	William Peter Blatty	£5.99
14586 6	SHADOW DANCER	Tom Bradby	£5.99
14587 4	THE SLEEP OF THE DEAD	Tom Bradby	£5.99
14871 7	ANGELS & DEMONS	Dan Brown	£5.99
14919 5	DECEPTION POINT	Dan Brown	£5.99
14579 3	THE MIRACLE STRAIN	Michael Cordy	£5.99
14882 2	LUCIFER	Michael Cordy	£5.99
14738 9	THE SMOKE JUMPER	Nicholas Evans	£6.99
13991 2	ICON	Frederick Forsyth	£5.99
14526 2	STARING AT THE LIGHT	Frances Fyfield	£5.99
14602 1	SEA CHANGE	Robert Goddard	£5.99
14376 6	DETECTIVE	Arthur Hailey	£5.99
14623 4	THE RETURN	Andrea Hart	£5.99
14985 3	OUTSIDE THE RULES	Dylan James	£5.99
14584 X	THE COLD CALLING	Will Kingdom	£5.99
14717 6	GO	Simon Lewis	£5.99
14870 9	DANGEROUS DATA	Adam Lury & Simon Gibson	£6.99
14797 4	FIREWALL	Andy McNab	£6.99
14631 5	THE GUARDSHIP	James Nelson	£5.99
14666 2	HOLDING THE ZERO	Gerald Seymour	£5.99
14391 X	A SIMPLE PLAN	Scott Smith	£5.99
14565 1	TRINITY	Leon Uris	£6.99
14794 X	CRY OF THE CURLEW	Peter Watt	£6.99
14765 6	THE WITCH'S CRADLE	Gillian White	£5.99
14773 3	WINTER FROST	R.D. Wingfield	£6.99
14047 3	UNHOLY ALLIANCE	David Yellop	£5.99